DEMETRI

THE VOLKOV EMPIRE

CRYSTAL DANIELS

SANDY ALVAREZ

PROLOGUE

Demetri

De Burca. The name alone leaves a bad taste in my mouth. I've never dealt with this particular family personally, but I know they are the bottom feeders of organized crime in the United States. Make no mistake; Ronan and his men will die. That is a guarantee. If it weren't for the fact Jake deserves to kill the motherfucker himself, I would break every bone in Ronan's body before making him choke on his own blood for what he did to her — the woman I'm currently finding it hard to ignore.

Glory Keller

I keep trying to make sense of my behavior. I've learned from experience that women should be kept at arm's length. No relationships. This is how I've chosen to live my life.

I grow increasingly frustrated with myself and look away.

I run the most powerful crime family in Russia. My soul is tainted with the blood of others and scarred by acts of corruption from my own family — those I trusted. I don't believe in anyone these days — only a select few. So, why does this particular woman, whom I've never met before until today, have this dominant hold on me that I cannot explain? My eyes travel to the other side of the SUV once more, landing on Glory's battered face. Despite the bruises and swollen eye, she is stunning. My hands clench and rage forms in my gut, knowing some bastard's filthy hands have harmed her.

Why the fuck do I care? All these things should mean nothing to me. *She* is nothing to me, but I can't keep my attention off of her; something I've had a problem with from the moment I laid eyes on her.

My attraction to her is intense.

Beyond anything I have felt before.

I feel tension start to build at the base of my neck. My eyes drop to her full lips before drifting lower, taking in the fullness of her breasts.

Bringing my attention back to her face, I find Glory scowling at me. I also notice her rapid pulse beating in her neck just before her eyes cut away then quickly begins whispering to her friend sitting beside her.

Her strength intrigues me. For two years, this woman devoted her life to keeping her friend's daughter safe and out of the hands of evil. It takes guts to do that. It's a huge glimpse into the woman she is. Devotion to the people we care about and loyalty to them is a characteristic you don't find in many people these days. And in my opinion, because I'm jaded when it comes to women in general; finding a woman with the grit and integrity Glory has is rare.

It's also a huge fucking turn on.

Hours later, compelled with the need to make sure she is safe, I find myself back at The Kings clubhouse, in a darkened room, watching *her* as she sleeps. The only audible sounds are her soft breaths, and the sound of my heartbeat pulsing through my veins. If she knew the kind of man I am, who I can become, she wouldn't want me. And make no mistake, she wants me. Glory tries to hide her attraction for me with icy stares and her sassy mouth, but I see past all her bullshit. The pull between us is too strong to deny it — no matter how hard we try.

Glory

It's Saturday night, and I'm sitting at home in my pajamas. I have spent every weekend doing the same thing since moving into my new apartment. I missed the days when I was the carefree woman who grabbed life by the balls; the woman who worked hard during the week and played hard on the weekend. That woman was fun. She was fearless and lived each day to the fullest. I'm not her anymore, but I want to be. I don't want to be afraid to live my life. I don't want the past to determine my future. I also don't want to keep waiting around on *him*. My hopes that the only man to make me feel anything other than fear dwindled a long time ago. That he will come to the conclusion; he wants me too. Not that I blame him. I've only ever been a raging bitch toward him. There was a time when I thought he could see past my rough exterior to the real me. When I thought his heated gazes and lingering looks that made my insides fill with butterflies were a sign of his desire for me.

It turns out I was wrong. He never said as much, but he also never made a move. I feel foolish for thinking he could ever be into a woman like me. Pushing those thoughts away, I stand from the sofa and make my way into my bedroom. Enough is enough.

Tonight, I am going to be the old Glory. I'm going to put on the sexiest dress I own and go out to the new bar that just opened five blocks from my apartment.

Stepping into my closet, I sift through the clothes hanging in front of me. When I spot the dress I'm after, I snag the black scrap of material from the hanger and carry it with me into the bathroom. I strip out of my pajamas, toss them to the floor then slip the material on over my body. The dress is a black, satin, spaghetti strap number that ends five inches above my knees. The front has a low V-neck that shows the perfect amount of cleavage. Next, I apply a minimal amount of makeup, topping it off with red lipstick. Reaching up, I release my long auburn hair from its ponytail and let it fall into loose curls that hang down my back. I finish off by spritzing myself with my favorite perfume. Inspecting my reflection in the mirror, I decide I look damn hot. Striding out of the bathroom, I sit on the edge of the bed and slip my feet into a pair of black five-inch strappy heels.

With my clutch in hand, I step out of my apartment, lock the door, and toss my keys inside my bag. By the time I ride the elevator down to the lobby, my Uber is waiting for me out front. After sliding into the back seat, I tell the driver the name of the bar. It's only a few blocks from where I live; we arrive in just minutes. I step out of the car directly in front of the entrance to see a line has formed. Trying my luck, I stroll up to the big guy manning the door. He doesn't hesitate to let me pass. Tipping his chin, he opens the door for me. *Guess I picked the right dress.* Although having an ample size chest doesn't hurt either. My tits have gotten me into more bars and clubs than I can count and gotten me out of a speeding ticket or two. Yes, I'm that woman and make no fucking apologies.

The moment I step through the door, a sudden wave of panic threatens to take over, but I tamp it down. *You can do this Glory. You can enjoy a regular night out.* Scanning the dimly lit room, I spot the bar to my right and make my way in that direction. My first initial thoughts of the place are it's pretty chill. The music is not too loud, and the floor is not overly crowded. I also like the fact it's not your typical twenty-something scene, which surprises me with the bar being so close to the university.

When I take an empty seat at the bar, the female bartender gives the man three stools down a beer then makes her way toward me. "What can I get you?"

"I'll have a Gin and Tonic."

"Sure thing." The bartender steps away and goes about fixing my drink. When she returns, she sets the glass down in front of me. "Thanks." I place a twenty on the bar only for her to shake her head. "The gentleman over there said your drink is on him." She points toward the end of the bar to a man in a dark gray button-down shirt with the sleeves rolled up to his elbows, showing off a set of tan arms. Turning in my seat, I lift my glass to my lips and give the man at the end of the bar a look. Taking my gesture as an invitation, the stranger tosses a few bills down on the bar and makes his way in my direction. My nerves start to kick in once again as the man stalks closer to me. I've done this a dozen times; come to a bar, pick up a guy, and have it end up in one of two ways — his place or mine. There is a voice in the back of my head telling me this is a bad idea. But there is another voice telling me I need to move on from what happened in the past and get my life back. Not only do I need to move on from what happened to me, but I need to forget about *him.*

"Hello," a deep voice rumbles over my left shoulder. From the corner of my eye, I watch the man sidle up to the bar beside me.

He holds his hand out between the two of us. "I'm Eric."

"Glory." I place my hand in his. The spark I was hoping for when our skin touched isn't there. Eric is an attractive man, and precisely what I would go for in the past, but now, everything about him is wrong. His hair is the wrong color, his voice lacks an accent, his arms are missing ink, and his eyes are brown, not the unique combination of one green and one blue like a specific person I seem to be comparing him to. And even though the guy in front of me is all wrong and the voice in my head is screaming that what I am about to do is a huge mistake, I make it anyway.

"Want to get out of here, Glory?"

Setting my drink down, I swivel on my stool and stand. "Yes."

Eric and I take a cab back to his place on the other side of town. The moment we step into his townhouse, we're all over each other. His hands on my body feel all wrong. His kiss is all wrong, and the smell of his cologne is nauseating. By the time we stumble our way into his bedroom, panic sets in, and the whooshing sound in my ears becomes deafening. The reality of the situation I have put myself in smacks me dead in the face when Eric pulls the straps of my dress down, exposing my breasts. His palms graze my nipples, and it causes my body to shutter. But not in a good way. His touch has my brain catapulting me back to a place I desperately want to forget. My dress pooling to the floor has me choking back a sob as bile rises in my throat. "Stop," I plead, bringing my hands to Eric's chest, pushing him away.

He stumbles back and scrunches his forehead in confusion.

"What's wrong, baby?"

"I can't do this." I try to clear my head as I pick my dress up off the floor and quickly cover my body. Eric holds his hands out in front of himself in an attempt to mollify the situation that has taken an ugly turn.

"Alright." He's looking at me like he already regrets picking up the crazy chick in front of him. "Would you like me to take you home?"

I shake my head, unable to look the man in the face. Instead, I dart out of his bedroom with my shoes in hand. I'm on the verge of hyperventilating and in a full-on panic attack. I don't have it in me to care how humiliating this whole ordeal is.

I ignore Eric calling my name out behind me as I swing the front door open and make a mad dash down the steps of the stoop. My bare feet slap against the sidewalk as I walk in a hurry down the street. Keeping a steady pace, I glance over my shoulder to make sure Eric is not following me and relax when I see he hasn't. But what I do see is a black sedan driving at a snail's pace behind me. Wrapping my arms around my waist, I pick up speed while keeping an eye on the car. When I look back again, the car is still creeping along behind me. *What the hell?* I am officially creeped out. Thankfully, a cab turns the corner down the street and heads in my direction. Breathing a sigh of relief, I step to the curb and flag it down.

An hour later, I'm back home in my pajamas and have gone through half a bottle of wine. I sit on my sofa alone in the dark with my thoughts running rampant. I don't know who I have become. Will I ever be able to overcome what happened to me? Can I get back the person I once was? And most importantly, can I get over the one person I think has the power to help heal the pain that is slowly suffocating me?

1

DEMETRI

The dull throb radiating from my temples is starting to become a full-fledged migraine. Pushing the laptop to the side, I reach for my glass of whiskey only to find it empty.

"Would you like another, Mr. Volkov?" Victor goes to stand from his seat on the opposite side of the plane.

Raising my hand, I stop him. "No, my friend, I'll be in my room. I don't want to be disturbed until it's time to land."

"Yes, sir."

Walking toward the back end of the plane, I slide the door open. Motion sensors activate a dim light above the head of the queen-size bed in front of me, basking the space in a warm glow. We have a few more hours ahead of us before landing, so I'm taking advantage of the alone time I have before reaching my homeland. Shrugging off my suit jacket, I lay it across the back of the black, leather chair before loosening the tie around my neck, undoing it entirely and placing it on the table by the small window along with my cufflinks, then roll up my sleeves. Emptying my pockets, I toss my phone, wallet, and money clip alongside the rest of my things and toe off my shoes before stretching out on the bed.

I want nothing more than to be back in Polson, in the comfort of my home, but the call I received at 2:00 am this morning warranted a quick decision to make my presence known elsewhere. Rubbing my temples with my fingers, I try to release some of the tension in my head as I replay the call from one of my associates. Apparently, the Petrov family is trying to overstep their bounds and have been encroaching on turf that they have no business being in. My territory, to be precise. The Volkovs have been in control for over one hundred years; going all the way back to my great-grandfather who built our empire with respect, integrity, and a firm hand. One I once hoped to pass down to my youngest son Nikolai.

My other son, Logan, wasn't brought up in the mafia life, and even though he has all the ability to quickly adapt to my specific lifestyle due to being raised in the MC, I know it's not for him and would never ask him to give up the life he has made for himself. Logan is right where he belongs amongst his brothers and his family. Nikolai, however, has been raised and groomed since the day he was born to one day take over the family businesses. And up until the past few years, I thought that would never be an issue.

The Petrov family and ours have had a mutual long-standing, blood binding agreement that we each keep out of one another's way, and that includes staying out of the pockets of the people I deal with. Vadim, the son of Yerik, has partially taken over as head of their small empire since his father has fallen too ill to run things on his own merit and isn't expected to make it another couple of months. Needless to say, Vadim is a hot-headed, power hungry young man. It seems to me that someone might need a little reminder of who he is dealing with.

Closing my eyes, I let my thoughts drift elsewhere. To one

particular person. A woman to be exact. Glory Keller — a friend of my oldest son Logan's MC club, The Kings of Retribution. She is absolutely breathtaking, with dark auburn hair, icy green eyes, a body made for pleasure, and a mouth so full of sass I want to fill it full of my cock. There has been something about Glory ever since my eyes first fell upon her. I was in Polson, helping Logan and his club. The Kings' President Jake was trying to track down a man who had become a threat to his woman, Grace, and his club. Glory took a beating by the man who the club was trying to hunt down — all to protect her best friend, Grace. But her fire and her tenacious attitude kept her going. The fact that she had been through hell and pushed through it like it was nothing fascinated me. Glory unintentionally lit a spark I thought had been extinguished forever. Feelings I never thought I could feel for another woman started to flare up like wildfire and only grew stronger each time I got the chance to be near her. Obsession is not my thing. It's not who I am, but this woman has consumed me. I think about her night and day.

I keep tabs on her to satisfy my own irrational need to keep her safe. From the moment her eyes connected with mine, Glory had rewritten my future. I know it, and furthermore, she knows it. There is no denying the raw sexual pull we feel for one another. Oh, she fights it. Glory hides it with fire and venom, but she wants me just as much as I want her. Make no mistake; I will have her. She will be in my bed. I want nothing more than to leave my mark on her. My cock twitches with the mere thought of reddening her lusciously round ass. With those thoughts, I finally fall asleep.

I wake when I hear Victor call out my name. Cracking my eyes open, I notice him standing at the bedroom door. "Sir, we land in twenty minutes."

"Thank you, Victor." Sitting up, I swing my legs over the edge of the bed and run my hand through my hair. Standing, I gather my things and put myself back together before stepping into the main cabin and taking my seat.

"Sergei will be waiting on the tarmac as soon as we land to take you downtown," Victor tells me as he adjusts his black tie. Victor has been with me for many years. He is as loyal as they come, and I trust him with my life. My gaze shifts from the time on my watch to the airplane's window. It's mid-afternoon here in Russia.

"I'd like to go home first. I have some things in the study I need before we make a trip to the city."

"I'll let the staff know."

It doesn't take long to drive from the small airport to my estate. Having to return to Russia has me in an ill-tempered mood and Sergei not showing at the airport like he was advised has added to my irritation. My son Nikolai has expressed his dislike for Sergei, and I will be the first to admit my feelings are becoming much the same. Placing my annoyance with Sergei aside, I take in the familiar sights of my hometown as we drive away from the airport. This is the place I grew up; the only home I have ever known. However, deciding to run things from the States for the past few months was the best decision I made at the time. I needed to form a stronger relationship with my firstborn son Logan and watch him and Nikolai form the brotherly bond they deserve. The Volkov's have owned this land for several generations. The ground is flat and lush with green grass, and the horizon lined with a dense tree line. On the backside of the property to the east runs a river which divides my property from the small town nearby. Maybe this is why I love the town of Polson, Montana so much, because it reminds me of home.

The house comes into view once we crest the hill. When I say 'house,' I use that term loosely. Manor would be a more accurate description. Volkov Manor was built in 1928 by my great grandfather with almost sixty-thousand square feet of living space. It's extravagant, but it is my home, and I cherish it.

"Sir — sir."

Blinking away the fog of memories, I turn toward Victor as the car rolls to a stop and take in his expression as he tucks his phone inside his suit pocket.

"You have a visitor. *She*," he emphasizes, letting me know the 'she' in which he is referring to, "is in your study."

My blood starts to boil. "Who let her in?"

"Gordon," Victor informs. "He and Luca are keeping an eye on her." Gordon and Luca are two of my soldiers. I have warned my men not to allow my ex to come anywhere near my residence and they will be dealt with for disobeying my orders, although Sergei should be on top of things in my absence. I'll be talking to him as well. Not waiting for someone to open the door, I fling it open and make my way up through the side entrance of my home, shortening the distance between me and my study. She knows she isn't allowed on my property. "Where is Sergei?"

"At the office in the city waiting for you, sir," Victor informs just before my hand grasps the door handle, shoving it open.

I pause a moment. "Tell him I'll be late." The door slams against the wall as I step into the room. Sitting in my chair, behind my desk is none other than my ex-wife Ivanna. "Get the fuck out of my home and off my property," I growl.

Unfazed by my presence, she stands. "*Dorogoi*, you've been away for months, and this is how you greet me?" She lurks around the corner of the desk like a snake after its prey, stopping in front of me. The smell of her expensive, heavy perfume fills the air around me. Leaning in, she places her palms on my chest. "I miss us," she pouts.

I may be ruthless in many things I do in life, but hurting a woman is not one of them. Although Ivanna tests my ability to keep my anger in check, I calmly remove her hands from my body and walk around her taking my seat. "Leave, Ivanna. We have nothing to say to each other." I notice immediately the sting of my rejection written all over her face and the flirty demeanor she was exuding changes quickly.

"You smell like a cheap woman."

"The only woman I've been near recently is you." I raise a judgmental brow in her direction as I lean back in my desk chair. Ivanna saunters across my study and retrieves a cigarette from her clutch sitting on a small table near the minibar. I watch her light it and take her first drag.

Ignoring my demand for her to leave my home, she takes a seat in a brown leather chair behind her. I continue to stare at her as she crosses her legs. She is far from the type of woman I am attracted to. Ivanna is thin — too thin. I want something to hold on to. She's a tall woman with straight blonde hair, which is not her natural color, and her eyes are dark, like her soul.

Her eyes catch my inspection.

"You like what you see?" She runs a hand between her petite breasts. Again, not what I want in a woman.

"I don't have time for your games, Ivanna, so spit out the reason you have disobeyed my rules." I start to grow more impatient as the seconds tick by.

"Can we not be enemies anymore, Demetri? I want us to start fresh. Bury the past. I've grown tired of the distance you have put between my son and me."

"The things you have done — the destructive role you played a part in can never be undone." I grow angrier. "Distance and what little kindness I choose to show you because you are our son's mother is the only reason you are not buried in the past and rotting alongside my father in a shallow grave where you belong. And as far as Nikolai goes, he is a grown man and heir to my Empire. He makes his own choices, and he decided to cut you from his life, not me. Perhaps if you had been a loving, caring mother, instead of putting your own wants and needs ahead of his, he would see you differently, but lucky for him he sees you for who you truly are."

Quietly she sits and snubs her half-smoked cigarette out in the ashtray on the table and silence fills the room. Vivid memories of my first love start to play like a movie reel in my mind. Ivanna's family and my father stole everything from me back then. They schemed to take the life of the woman I loved and my precious son. I was going to leave all of this — my entire life behind for happiness, and they stole it from me. Ivanna weaseled into my life. She plotted and planned right along with my father and hers to keep me here, and they killed to do so. Her hands are covered and stained in the same blood as my fathers. I will never forgive her.

"Demetri—"

"ENOUGH!" I roar, cutting her off as I stand from my chair. Rage radiates in waves through my body. Her presence has thrown me back into a dark black hole. My study door opens; Victor takes two steps into the room and takes in my appearance. I'm on edge, and he knows it. He knows if he doesn't remove this bitch from my sight, I will kill her where she stands. Walking across the room, he grabs her by the arm and guides her to the door. Before the door closes, I inform him. "If she steps foot into my home again—" I leave my sentence hanging, but he more than understands.

"Yes, sir."

Needing to channel my rage, I head straight for my gym located in the opposite wing of the house where my bedroom suite is also located. After I have shed my suit for sweats, I hit the weights before moving on to the treadmill. Keeping myself fit is essential, but it also has become a way of maintaining self-control over the years. It helps me focus. I'm on my fifth mile running when Victor makes his presence known. Slowing down my speed, I finally come to a stop. Grabbing my towel, I wipe the sweat from my face and down half a bottle of water. "What is it, Victor?"

"There is an issue in the city that requires your presence, sir."

"I'm aware I am late for my own meeting. They can wait." I finish the rest of my water and start to head toward the shower.

"Yerik Petrov has just been found; shot dead in his hospital bed."

I pause. My grip on the towel in my hand tightens. *Fuck.* Yerik was the last thread keeping the peace between the two families. "We leave in thirty minutes. Make the call."

2

GLORY

"Miss Keller," the deep voice in front of my desk asks.

Peering up from the stack of papers I'm grading, I give Jackson Owens, the seventeen-year-old student in front of me, my attention and glance over at his two buddies gawking in the doorway of my classroom. Straightening my back, I reach up, slide my leopard-print, cat-eye reading glasses off my face, and give him a sharp, no-nonsense look. "What can I do for you, Jackson?"

Giving me a dimpled smirk, which I'm sure makes every girl at Macon High swoon, but has zero effect on me, he says, "I was wondering if you'd be willing to tutor me. I really think my performance would benefit from some one-on-one lessons."

Leaning back in my chair, I let out a huff of annoyance. *Cheesy innuendo. I swear these high school boys think they're so clever.* "What you need, Mr. Owens is a swift kick in the pants. Now, I suggest you and your friends run along before I'm tempted to do just that," I finish with a flick of my hand dismissing my student.

I don't particularly like teaching high school. When I applied for a position six months ago, the eleventh grade was all that was available. I began working at Macon Middle School straight out of college. Back then, I was teaching history to sixth graders. Now I teach eleventh-grade history at Macon High. For as long as I can remember, I wanted to be a teacher. In my opinion, middle school is the perfect age to teach. Also, I don't know how to act around little kids. They make me feel awkward. And don't get me started on teenagers. I have to ask Jesus every morning before work to give me the strength and patience I need for dealing with these kids. I mean, it's not like there is some unwritten rule about educators having to love children of all ages. I'm not saying I don't like all kids, because I adore my two Godchildren.

A few years ago, I dropped everything to help my best friend. Grace and I grew up together. She's more than my best friend; she's like a sister. So, when she made the brave choice to leave her abusive husband; I didn't hesitate to help. I spent over two years of my life moving around from one city to the next with Grace's daughter, Remi. Grace was terrified her shitty husband would one day find her, so Remi lived with me, and Grace would visit as often as she could.

We never lived more than a few hours from each other during that time. I had argued with my best friend at first, insisting we stay together, but Grace chose to keep her distance to protect her child. Things worked out for my best friend in the end. The last town she moved to, she met Jake Delane. Jake happens to be the President of a motorcycle club, The Kings of Retribution. Jake and his club along with Demetri Volkov put an end to Grace's sorry ass husband and his family. Now she is living her happily ever after with Jake in Polson, Montana, along with Remi and their new baby girl Ellie, just as she deserves.

Thinking about my best friend and her new family also has me thinking about him — *Demetri*. Demetri Volkov is the most arrogant, controlling asshole I've ever met. Never mind the fact I have to change my panties every time he's in my presence.

Dickhead.

I'll never forget the first time I met Demetri. It was a couple of years ago. I was still living in North Dakota, in the apartment Remi and I stayed in before she went back to live with Grace and Jake. I had taken my Basset Hound Bo out for a walk, and when I returned to my apartment Ronan De Burca, Grace's husband was standing in the middle of my living room along with a couple of his goons. A chill runs through my body, and I shudder at the memory of the punishment I received at the hands of Ronan De Burca.

I've never told anyone everything that happened to me in that apartment, not even my best friend. Grace already carries around a shit load of guilt for what happened; I don't want to add to it. I met Demetri the day I was discharged from the hospital after my attack. The tall, dark, silent, domineering man that trailed behind Grace and Jake when they walked into my hospital room. The man quietly stood off in the shadows, not saying a word. Grace told me the silent Russian was the father of one of Jake's men and a friend to the club. Demetri Volkov stands at six feet two inches tall, with dark brown hair mixed with a bit of gray. He's lean, with wide shoulders and a broad chest, which I'm sure leads down to some chiseled abs. Although I've never seen for myself, I can imagine. Even through his suits, I can tell Demetri keeps his body in shape. But his body is not his most spectacular attribute; it's his eyes. He has one green eye and one blue. *Holy shit, my mouth is watering.* "Get your overactive dirty thoughts under control, Glory," I mutter to myself. I am not about to let Demetri's sexiness rule my body's reaction. *Oh, who am I kidding? My panties are wet right now.*

Damn that Russian.

"Would you like me to walk you to your car, Glory?" Kevin asks from the doorway of my classroom effectively snapping me away from my wayward thoughts.

Kevin Learner teaches biology across the hall. He's asked me out a few times since I started working here. He's a sweet guy and not bad in the looks department, but he does nothing for me. Kevin is an average size man. I stand at five feet eleven inches, and that's without heels. Kevin is five feet ten inches at best. I have nothing against a shorter man, but let's face it, I'm a whole lot of woman. I need a man that can handle all of me. Plus, he's a bit persistent. In fact, it's borderline pushy, and that alone is a turnoff. When a man becomes pushy, it makes him look desperate. I'm not really the dating type anyway. Whenever I have an itch that needs to be scratched my battery-operated friend gets the job done just the way I need it to. I used to have no problem going out and finding a man to tend to my needs but those days are in the past. My only problem is that lately, my love oven is only interested in one particular warm body.

Standing from my desk, I smooth out the knee-length red pencil skirt that I paired with a long sleeve button down leopard print blouse, and black four-inch heels. My personal style is not like the other female teachers on staff, and I don't give two shits about the disapproving looks thrown my way when I walk the halls. I am who I am. My style is loud and at times sexy, but always appropriate when at work. Although my co-workers believe if my curves are on display, it's considered poor taste. *What the fuck ever.* I'll never understand why women feel threatened by one another. We should stand together and have each other's backs.

"Sure, I'll walk out with you." Just because I'm not interested in dating Kevin, doesn't mean we can't be friends.

When Kevin and I push past the double doors of the school's entrance, he makes a move to place his hand on my lower back, and I step away from his touch. It's also the moment I feel my skin prickle. I cut my gaze around the parking lot. Brushing off the feeling of being watched, I tip my head in Kevin's direction once I've reached my vehicle. "I'll see you Monday," I say then climb into my car. Kevin gives a slight look of annoyance at my rebuff before he turns and makes his way to his own vehicle. I guess I need to rethink trying to be his friend if he's going to act like an ass. I don't need that kind of drama. I've had enough over the past few years to last a lifetime.

After parking in the garage beneath my apartment building, I step into the elevator and make my way up to the tenth floor. I finally moved into my own place six months ago. Since my attack, I had bounced around from being in Polson with Grace and Remi to being here in Chicago with my parents. Grace came to me one day and asked me to move to Polson permanently. The offer was tempting because I desperately wanted to be near my best friend. But the truth is, as much as I wanted to be near Grace, I knew if I stayed in Polson, she would have become my crutch. I have been feeling confused and out of sorts now that I am no longer caring for Remi. I can't explain it. It's like I've lost a part of me. There was no way I would be placing that burden on my friend; not after she finally got her happy ending. So, instead, I came back home to Chicago and moved into my parents' house. It took me several months of feeling out of place and restless even with them that I decided what I needed was to get back to the life I had before. Only now that I am back to living on my own and teaching, I still feel off. Something is missing; only I don't know what.

With my keys in hand, I open the door to my apartment, and a smile takes over my face when Bo greets me. Setting my purse down on the table next to the door, I crouch down and give my boy a belly rub. "How's momma's little boy doing? Huh?" Giving his fat belly one last rub, I stand and pat my leg. "Come on, Bo. Let's get you something to eat." Once I've given Bo his dinner, I make my way through my living room and past the grand floor to ceiling window that overlooks the city. I love my apartment and pay a pretty penny in rent for it too. I love the finer things in life. I guess you could say I grew up privileged. I come from money, and my trust fund allows me to enjoy a particular lifestyle. But having money does not mean I don't work hard every day of my life. My parents did not raise me to be a spoiled brat. In fact, I had to work for my allowance growing up. They made me keep my room clean, wash the dishes every day after school, vacuum, clean the bathroom. You name it, I did it. I didn't receive my trust until I finished college. School was something else my mom and dad insisted I excel at.

Ambling to my bedroom and into my walk-in closet, I step out of my pumps and place them on the shoe rack. Once I've stripped out of my clothes, I walk into my bathroom and start the shower. When the steam of the hot water fills the room, I step inside the tiled stall and under the hot spray of water. Tilting my head back, I close my eyes and relish the feel of the water beating down on my body. In an instant, my thoughts drift to Demetri, and it causes a familiar ache between my legs. The very ache that as of late seems to be owned by Volkov. I hate how my body only responds to thoughts of him; the very man I have spent months and countless hours trying to forget.

Giving in to the urge, I run my palms up my hips, and along my ribs until I reach my heavy breasts. I cup my them, then let out a throaty moan as I tug on my nipples. The sensation causes my clit to throb with need. The moment my hand makes contact with my wet center, the sound of the doorbell ringing blares through my apartment. *Fuck.*

Turning the water off, I step out of the shower, grab the robe that's hanging on the back of the door and wrap it around my wet body. The bell goes off again, followed by a loud knock adding to my frustration. "Hold the fuck on! I'm coming!" I shout.

Flinging the door open, I square off with the twenty-something guy standing in front of me with his mouth gaped open. Probably due to the fact, my wet body has soaked through my robe, and my hard nipples are on display. Who the fuck cares? I'm not shy. I'm sure my tits are the best thing this dude has seen all week. "What!" I fume. When the pervert doesn't speak and continues to ogle my breasts, I snap my fingers in front of his face. "Yo, dipshit. Eyes up here," I say while gesturing to my face, knocking the guy out of his stupor.

"Sorry, ma'am. I have a delivery for a Miss Glory Keller," he says thrusting an abundant bouquet of Morning Glory flowers toward me. As soon as the flowers are in my arms, the guy continues to stand there and stare as if he's never seen breasts before. "You can go," I say dismissing him, before shutting the door in his face.

With my flowers in hand, I walk out onto my balcony and place the crate down on the patio table. Spotting the card sticking out of the arrangement, I pluck it out and open it. Although I already know what it says and who they are from. I get the same delivery every week since I moved into my apartment. And considering who he is and the connections he has, I don't have to ask how he knows where I live. My balcony is overflowing in Morning Glories. Each week a different color. Todays are blue. Opening the card, I read the same word I read every week.

Krasivaya.

"Nice fucking timing, asshole," I mutter out loud. That man is confusing. I have no idea what his intentions are when it comes to me. I'd like to say I have come a long way in recent months when it comes to moving on from my past, but I fear Demetri Volkov will always be my weakness.

3

DEMETRI

"Sergei, have all my associates arrived?"

"Yes, sir."

I straighten my tie as I climb out of the car with my cell phone pressed against my ear. "Good." Pressing end, I tuck the phone into the inside pocket of my blazer and step inside my office building located in the heart of the city right next to the waterway. Volkov Architecture is one of my family's legit businesses. It is also used to filter money. I debated selling the company after my father's passing, but Nikolai's passion for the place is what had me reconsider. Ever since Nikolai was a boy, he was interested in building things. It is that reason why I wasn't surprised he teamed up with Logan's club to start up a construction company. Nikolai has always been one to get his hands dirty and dive head first into something he feels is worthwhile. With his knowledge of architecture and his passion for creating beautiful structures, he is one of the reasons he and The Kings have such a successful company.

I was informed an hour ago about Yerik's death — his murder, but word tends to travel fast within our circle. By now, everyone will have heard of his demise and the way he met his maker. The problem is who in the hell would want to kill a man already on his deathbed? Despite the fact he didn't have enough energy to walk on his own; he still had a clear and present mind. He had all his wits about him. However, that also made him a sitting duck for many of his enemies. It's a known fact a couple of well-known wealthy businessmen tried to off him a few times in the past. Maybe they finally saw their opportunity. Still, why not wait for him to die? Yerik had his hands and money in many ventures, so there is no way of knowing just yet what or why.

My leather shoes clack against the black marble floor of the lobby as I make my way toward the elevator.

"Good evening, Mr. Volkov," the young receptionist greets me as I walk past her desk. She's a beautiful, petite brunette. As we pause for the elevator doors to open, I notice Victor's gaze locks on her.

I clear my throat. "You may go home for the day, Natalia." I watch the blush turn her cheeks a soft rosy hue and her eyes quickly shift to mine.

"Thank you, Mr. Volkov," she softly replies, just as we step into the elevator.

The ride to the top is swift. When the doors slide open, I find Sergei leaning over the desk of my personal assistant Anya, who has made it known to me in the past that she is profoundly uncomfortable with his advances.

"Sergei," I bark.

"Mr. Volkov." His eyes dart from me to Victor. "It's good to have you home."

"I believe we had a conversation a few months ago about your interest in Anya."

"Yes, my apologies, Mr. Volkov."

Standing directly in front of Anya's desk, I make myself clear for the last time on the matter. "It is not me you need to apologize to. I believe you owe Anya an apology." I level him with a hardened stare.

Turning his attention from me to Anya, he looks down and offers his apology. "Forgive me for my unwanted advances. It will not happen again." Anya says nothing, but nods then goes about her business.

Victor steps to the side, toward the boardroom to my right and opens the door. Inside are all the men I requested except for Vadim, the son of Yerik. Given the circumstances, I'm going to let it pass for the time being, but I will be making a trip to his home after this meeting is over. "Gentlemen, thank you for waiting, you'll find yourselves compensated for your time." I continue to stand at the head of the table. "So," I look around the table, "Yerik is dead. Shot in the head to be precise." The men in front of me give each other conspiring looks. "Initially, I called this meeting because it has come to my knowledge; one of you has gone behind my back." I don't out the deceiver just yet. "You see. I provide you with my services and my merchandise. However, recently, my goods have made their way into the hands of a known associate of the Petrovs." I start to prowl around the table. "I tag my merchandise. I keep records of all serial numbers. I had contact with Yerik Petrov himself after I was informed of this, where he stated he had no knowledge of the matter but would quickly investigate it for me. To our surprise, it was true." The man I do business with from South Russia stands. "Sit," I demand, clutching his shoulder, slamming him back into his leather chair.

"Mr. Volkov, I—"

"Save your breath, Mr. Gulin. I give no second chances. It seems very suspicious that mere hours after the news and investigation Yerik himself ends up dead." Muffled sounds from the other men whispering amongst themselves fill the room.

"I — I. I didn't kill Mr. Petrov," Gulin stammers.

"Victor, please escort Mr. Gulin out of my building." Victor snatches him by the arm. "We no longer have business with each other Mr. Gulin, and furthermore, you have no protection under the Volkov name as well."

Struggling against Victor's hold, Gulin says, "word will spread. People will think I had something to do with Petrov's murder. I didn't — I would never —," Sweat beads on his forehead and fear shines in his eyes. "The Petrov family will come after me, and I have done nothing."

"That is not my problem," I answer. With a jerk of my head, Victor walks him out of the boardroom. The meeting doesn't last much longer after that point. The day is starting to turn into night, and I still have one more visit on my schedule.

The Petrov estate is a thirty-minute drive from town. Already being made aware of my arrival, I'm greeted by Yerik's longtime bodyguard Andrei.

"Mr. Volkov. Vadim and Mrs. Petrov are waiting for you in the family room. Follow me."

With Victor at my side, we enter the Petrov family home and led into the room where Yerik's wife Elena is seated, and her son Vadim is sitting in a chair opposite of her with a bored look on his face as he smokes a cigar.

I take in her red-rimmed eyes as I stop in front of her.

"Mr. Volkov, thank you for coming," Mrs. Petrov extends her hand, which I grasp in mine.

"Sorry for the loss of your husband, Elena."

"Thank you. Won't you sit?"

"Sorry, I won't be staying but a moment. I wanted to offer my condolences and extend my services in any way I can. Our families have had mutual respect for one another for a very long time. If there is anything you need—" I offer.

"We need nothing from you, Volkov. Your presence isn't wanted here," Vadim sneers.

"Vadim." His mother closes her tired eyes. "Please show some respect."

He lets out a huff. "I don't answer to you." His eyes glance in his mother's direction before standing, then directs his attention toward me. "Or to a Volkov. I'm the head of this family now. People answer to me."

I step into his personal space. Vadim stands a few inches shorter than me and is the exact image of his father. Looks are all he gets from Yerik. Vadim has not one ounce of respect or honor. "I answer to no one."

"I have just lost my husband, I do not wish to start a war or lose my son tonight," Mrs. Petrov pleads. Finally, Vadim retreats to the opposite side of the room and pours a dark whiskey into a glass tumbler.

"After tonight, you are no longer welcome in my home," Vadim says with his back turned. Elena peers up, giving me a somber look.

"There is one thing I may ask of you?"

"Certainly."

"You fly to the States often. Misha doesn't wish to return home, not even for her father's funeral. I worry about her. She loved her papa. Could you see that she gets something?" Standing from the sofa, she retrieves an envelope from a table drawer. "Yerik wrote it just this morning—" She peers across the room. Turning my head, I eye Vadim who is watching intently. She hands it to me, and I tuck it inside my jacket. Their daughter had her reasons for leaving years ago. This life wasn't for her, and Yerik knew it. She lives in the States now with a loving family and a happy life.

"You have my word. I will hand it to her myself," I promise.

Pulling in a shuddered breath, she excuses herself and walks out of the room. I don't bother to look back. I take my leave as well with Victor at my side, and we climb into the car.

As the driver takes off, Victor says, "He's going to be a problem, sir."

"Yes. He is," I agree.

Ascending the steps to Misha Petrov's townhouse, I survey the nearly empty Chicago streets. At seven o'clock in the morning on a Saturday the city is quiet; almost somber. As if the energy here knows I come bearing bad news. When Misha's front door opens, and she appears in front of me with a red face and tears in her eyes, I know she has already heard of what had happened to her father.

"Demetri," she greets with a sad tone. "I've been expecting you. Thank you for coming."

Pulling Misha close to me, I kiss the top of her head. "I'm sorry about your father."

"Thank you. Won't you please come in. Do you have time for coffee?"

"Of course," I accept while stepping inside, and Misha shuts the door behind me. I follow her into the living room, and her husband Brooks greets me. Brooks and Misha met six years ago when she moved from Russia to Chicago. Yerik had been worried about sending his baby girl out into the world alone and hired Brooks to look after his only daughter. Brooks owns a security company here in the city. They have been married for almost four years and have two children. Alena is two, and Luka is three months.

"Mr. Volkov," Brooks addresses, offering his hand, and I accept.

"Good to see you, Brooks. I hope you are well."

A few minutes later, Misha returns with a tray of coffee and pastries. "How are the little ones?" I ask as she takes a seat next to her husband after handing me a cup. Even though the devastation of losing her father is written on her face, the mention of her children makes her smile. I'm thankful Misha has her husband and children to cling to during this time. She will need them.

"The children are wonderful."

The three of us sit a moment silently before I speak again. "Do you have any questions for me?"

Shaking her head, Misha places her coffee cup on the table in front of her. "No. I already know what happened to my father and who is responsible. I haven't been home to Russia since leaving and don't know how business has been as of late, but I do know Vadim, and I believe my brother is behind this."

I cut my eyes to Brooks, then back to Misha. "May I speak freely?"

"Of course. I keep nothing from my husband. He knows of my family and my past."

"Very well. I don't have proof, but I suspect Vadim is responsible for your father's death as well. Vadim has been persistent in taking over Yerik's role since he became sick. Your father knew the direction his son wanted to take the family business and was reluctant to hand over power. In the end, Vadim took it."

"Have you seen my brother?"

"Yes. I spoke with him face to face. If he is a smart man, he will heed my warning."

"He won't," Misha says vehemently.

"I know," I tell her. "Vadim will be dealt with in due time."

Nodding her head, Misha drops the subject. She is trusting me to avenge her father's death and handle the situation with her brother.

"Has Vadim tried reaching out to you recently? Do you feel he will be an issue for you? If so, I can have one of my men watch over your family."

"Thank you, Mr. Volkov, but that won't be necessary," Brooks cuts in. "I've already taken the proper measures to see to my family's safety."

Standing, I offer my hand to Brooks. "You'll call me if you need anything?"

Brooks nods. "Thanks, Mr. Volkov."

Turning my attention to Misha, I kiss both her cheeks. "I'll see myself out. Don't hesitate to reach out for anything."

Reaching into my suit jacket, I pull out the envelope Mrs. Petrov gave me. "Your mother wishes for you to have this." Taking the letter from my grasp, Misha takes notice of the handwriting on the front of the envelope and clutches it to her chest.

"Thanks for coming all the way to Chicago, Demetri. I know how much my father respected you. It would have meant a lot to him to come here to check on me."

Making my way outside, Victor opens the door to my car, and I slide into the back. Once he has taken his position in the driver's seat, he peers at me through the rearview mirror. "Where to sir?"

Without missing a beat, I give him the orders for my next destination. "Take me to her." Nodding, Victor pulls out into traffic. He doesn't have to ask who *she* is. He already knows. It's been a few months since I've seen Glory. I have decided we've been dancing around each other far too long. It's time to claim what's mine. What's been mine for two goddamn years. *She's going to be pissed when I show up unannounced.* I grin at the thought.

Parking along the curb in front of Glory's apartment, Victor climbs out and steps around to the passenger side. Just as he's opening my door, I spot her rounding the corner of the building at the end of the street carrying two grocery bags. I'm not at all surprised to see her up and out this early in the morning. If I know Glory, she's been up for hours. I also know she jogs every morning before the sun rises. Seemingly unaware of her surroundings as she stares at the pavement in front of her while she walks, it takes Glory several beats before she notices my presence. When she does, her steps falter.

With Victor flanking my left, I hold my stance. Glory and I

hold each other's stare. A brief look of uncertainty crosses her face; one that says she's tempted to flee. I shake my head, warning her not to. In true Glory fashion, she squares her shoulders and continues toward me.

"Well, hello, asshole," she sasses, coming to stand in front of me. "What brings you to Chicago? More importantly, why are you perched outside my apartment?"

Unfazed by her verbal tongue lashing, I chuckle. "I had business to handle, and now, I'm taking you to breakfast."

"Thanks, but no thanks. I have my breakfast here," she says, holding up her bags, "and my breakfast companion is waiting on me upstairs." Glory smiles smugly.

Giving Victor a signal, he strides over to Glory, taking the bags from her hands and places them in the trunk of the car. "I'm sure Bo can do without you for a bit," I say, putting my hand on the small of her back, ushering her into the backseat.

Once we're in the car, Glory huffs and glares at me. "You're so fucking bossy."

Leaning back in my seat, I level her with a heated gaze. "Keep talking to me with that filthy mouth of yours, *Krasivaya*; it only makes me harder." At my confession, I see Glory's eyes cut down toward my crotch and my apparent hard on causes her eyes to widen. Realizing she's ogling my dick, she snaps her head up and meets my gaze once again, and I grin. Giving me another nasty look, she rolls her eyes then turns to look out the window. Glory's problem is she wants me, but she doesn't want to.

Arriving at a bistro two blocks from Glory's apartment, one I know is her favorite since she eats breakfast here every Sunday, I place my palm on her hip, pull her into my side and guide her inside. When the host shows us to our table, I pull Glory's chair out and allow her to sit before I too take my seat.

"Hello, my name is Carol. Are you ready to order, or do you need a moment to look over the menu?" the waitress asks.

"That won't be necessary," I say. "The lady will have Duck Confit Hash with water and a Mimosa. I'll have Eggs Benedict and coffee."

"Very well. I'll be right back with your orders," our waitress chirps.

"I can order my own damn food, Demetri."

"I know you can, *Krasivaya*. Ordering for you is not me taking anything away from you. I'm taking care of what's mine. You order the same dish every Sunday, so I knew what you wanted. When you're with me, you'll always get what you want."

Sensing the sincerity of my comment, and not bothering to ask how I know so much about her, along with ignoring the fact I just called her mine, Glory decides to change the subject.

"I know you said you were in town on business, but why come see me? Why all of this?" she asks, gesturing around the restaurant. "I get that we have mutual friends, but we haven't seen each other in months. In the time we have known each other, your actions toward me have been all over the place. You're hot one minute then cold the next. Is it because of your past; because of your son Logan and the relationship you—?"

"My past is not up for discussion," I snap, cutting Glory off mid-sentence, but immediately regret my outburst when I take in the look of hurt on her face. Her pain is quickly replaced with anger as she stands abruptly, tosses her napkin to the table then storms out of the restaurant. "Fuck," I hiss getting to my feet. Throwing a few bills on the table, I go after her. By the time I exit the restaurant, she is already halfway down the sidewalk heading back in the direction of her apartment, and I take off after her. "Follow behind the car, Victor!" I call over my shoulder. Once I've caught up to Glory, I stay about three strides behind her.

"Stop fucking following me, dickhead!" she growls.

"No," I say evenly and continue to follow her into her

apartment building, onto the elevator, and down the hall to her front door.

Turning on her heels, a heaving, red-faced Glory jabs her finger into my chest. "I don't know why you showed up here today, and I don't know what kind of twisted, fucked-up mind games you're trying to play, but you can't—"

Before she gets a chance to finish her tirade, I grab hold of her wrist, push her back against the door, and pin her arm above her head. Taking my right hand, I grab a fist full of her long auburn hair and pull her head back — slightly exposing her neck. Glory's breath hitches, and I notice her hard nipples protruding through her top. Taking one step further into her personal space, I shove my knee between her legs, allowing my hard cock to brush against her heated center. Before Glory can utter another word, I crash my mouth down on hers.

4

GLORY

Demetri's hand fisted in my hair delivers equal parts pain as it does pleasure. I gasp at the sting to my scalp, which allows him to take advantage of my parted lips as he delves his tongue inside my mouth. The bite of pain Demetri rewards me with overrides my pissed off attitude and replaces it with hunger. Demetri being the cocky bastard he is, knows I crave the dominance and pain. Notably, by the way my body is ignoring the logical part of my brain that wants to fight this infuriating man. The man whose leg I am currently grinding myself against. My pussy is a traitor, and I'm not even ashamed. She does tend to have a mind of her own.

If someone had told me when I woke up this morning that I'd be dry humping Demetri Volkov in the hallway of my apartment today, I would have said they were out of their fucking mind. The only thing not shocking about this situation is that the Russian can kiss. Fuck he can kiss. I should have known the son of a bitch was going to deliver. His taste alone is intoxicating — Demetri tastes of mint with a hint of cigar. Now, usually, smoking is a deal breaker for me, but tasting it on Demetri is my new addiction. Like a junkie needing their next fix, I deepen the kiss. But the second I try to take control, Demetri snakes his hand up between our bodies and wraps his large hand around my neck, giving it a light squeeze. His actions are a warning that he's the one in control.

I'd be lying if I said I didn't like it because I do. Demetri seems to know exactly what I want; what I need without me having to speak. My whole adult life, I have wanted a man who wasn't afraid to take control. One who wasn't intimidated by the kind of woman I am. Let's face it. I'm a bitch. I'm loud and opinionated. I have no filter, and at times, I am difficult to put up with. The men I have bedded in the past, not one of them has been able to handle me in the way I need; the way I crave...until Demetri. And all without me having to say a single word. As much as I want to deny it, deep down, I knew it would be like this. I knew if this moment ever happened, it would be explosive. The problem is I know Demetri has the power to destroy me. I know he'd be able to give me what I have craved for so long but also has the ability to take it away. I'm not sure I'm willing to take that risk.

As if he knows where my mind is going, Demetri breaks our kiss. "That would never happen, *Krasivaya*." He says vehemently, his accent sounding stronger than it did minutes ago.

Still trying to catch my breath, I stay silent and give him a look that says I don't believe him. His gaze is unrelenting as his eyes bore into my soul, reading every single thought I possess. With his palm still wrapped around my neck, he gives it a slight squeeze. "From this moment on, everything changes. You. Are. Mine. So, get those thoughts out of that gorgeous head of yours. Trust me, *Krasivaya*."

"I don't know if I can," I admit finally finding my voice and I'm surprised at how strong it sounds considering his words scare me.

A throat clearing from behind Demetri brings us out of our fog. Demetri doesn't take his eyes off me as he answers the man standing over his shoulder. "Yes, Victor?"

"I have Miss Keller's bags."

Without saying a word, Demetri steps away from me taking his heat with him. I instantly feel a loss with his actions but do an excellent job at masking my feelings by keeping my face neutral as I turn my attention to Demetri's friend. Although I'm not sure what Victor's title is. All I know is wherever Demetri is; Victor is with him. "How are you today, Victor?" I greet him.

Victor gives me a curt nod. "Miss Keller."

I turn my attention back to Demetri and watch in shock as he pulls a set of keys from his pocket and proceeds to unlock the door to my apartment. My shock is replaced with anger. "You want to explain to me why the fuck you have a key to my apartment?" I fume getting directly in Demetri's face. Something in Demetri's demeanor snaps and a look I can't decipher crosses over his face as he shoves the door to my apartment open, grabs hold of my arm, ushering me inside.

"Victor, place Miss Keller's things inside then see yourself out," he says in a tone that causes a chill to run down my spine. I look over my shoulder to see Victor do as he is told while Demetri leads me through the living room and down the hall to my bedroom. Once we are inside my room, he slams the door shut. With my arm still in his grip, I'm spun around until my back is against the wall; though Demetri's hold on me is firm, he has yet to hurt me. But that hasn't stopped the erratic beat of my heart and the thought he might physically harm me to enter my brain.

Seeing my thoughts play out across my face, Demetri drops his hold on me and his nostrils flare. "I'd slit my own throat before I'd harm a hair on your head, Glory."

"Could have fucking fooled me," I mouth off. Why? Because I can't help myself, it seems.

"As much as I love that sassy mouth of yours, I will not stand for you to speak to me in front of one of my men the way you just did. I will not be disrespected. Do I make myself clear?"

I go to open my mouth to tell Demetri to go fuck himself but stop when he gives me a look that says I better think twice. Do I listen? "You have a key to my apartment; one I did not give you, and you think I don't have the right to rip you a new asshole?" I scoff. "You're talking to the wrong woman because that's not me."

Demetri's lip twitches at my statement. "Oh, I fully expect a tongue lashing, *Krasivaya*. But that shit happens in private." His face turns serious once again. "Had anyone else spoken to me that way, they would be paying the consequences."

I stand stock still for a moment while letting Demetri's words sink in. I may not know all there is to know about the man in front of me, but I know he is ruthless, and he speaks the truth. While I can see that ripping into Demetri in front of one of his men was wrong and his anger is justified, it also serves as a reminder just who Demetri Volkov is. I've had enough drama in my past to last a lifetime. The dust has finally settled in my life, and I don't need Demetri coming in here and turning things upside down. Not after it took me nearly a year to get back some normalcy.

Keeping my features impassive, I step away from Demetri and stroll in the direction of my bathroom. With my tone neutral, I peer over my shoulder to see Demetri's eyes trained on my every move, his jaw tight. "You can see yourself out." I step into the ensuite bathroom and close the door behind me. I don't bother demanding he leaves the key to my apartment. I'll call and have the locks changed first thing tomorrow.

Deciding a soak in the tub is what's needed to help me relax after my intense encounter with Demetri, I turn the hot water on and draw myself a bath. Once I've added some of my favorite lavender oil to the water, I turn, face my reflection in the mirror and start stripping out of my clothes. After I have tied my hair up, not wanting to get it wet, I step into the tub and ease my tension filled body into the hot water. I let out a deep sigh, close my eyes, and rest my head against the back of the tub as I sink further into bliss. I breathe in the smell of lavender and will all thoughts of that insufferable Russian to leave my head, but it's no use. No matter how hard I try, Demetri is there. He's embedded himself permanently into the forefront of my brain.

I don't know how much time has passed, but by the time I open my eyes, I note the water has turned cold. And when my stomach rumbles with hunger, I realize I still haven't eaten today. After stepping out of the tub and drying my body off, I make my way out of the bathroom and to my closet. Going for my usual weekend attire, I snag a pair of cut-off shorts from the shelf and a white t-shirt that reads *Freshly Squeezed* across the front. Once dressed, I make my way out of my room and down the hall to the living room. I come to an abrupt halt when I see Demetri sitting on my sofa, looking completely relaxed. I spot his suit jacket draped over the back of one of the dining room chairs and ignore the fact his holstered guns hang beside it. I cut my eyes away from the chair and back over to the man currently sitting on my sofa with his shirt sleeves rolled up to his elbows, allowing his tattoos to peek through. Demetri has his phone pressed to his ear as he speaks a hushed tone.

"*Seychas!*" he raises his voice and barks into the phone before he hangs up on whoever he was talking to.

"Is there a reason you're still here?" I ask once he's put his phone away.

"Come and eat," Demetri orders without turning around and ignores my question. When I don't do as I'm told, he looks over his shoulder. I watch as Demetri rakes his eyes up and down my body then stops when his heated gaze lands on my shirt. His lip twitches. "I had Victor go back to the restaurant for our order."

Deciding my hunger overrides my irritation at the moment, I stroll over to the sofa and take a seat in front of where Demetri has my food laid out. We eat together in silence for a few minutes before he speaks. "When I met my oldest son's mother Rose, I was already promised to another woman; an arrangement made by my father." I stop eating and face Demetri. When I don't interrupt, he continues. "As you already know, I have an estate in Polson, Montana. The Volkov's have been doing business in that part of the States for many years. The summer I met Rose was the first time my father had brought me along with him to Polson. I had been groomed since I was a boy to one day take over The Volkov Empire. I also knew from a young age that I was to marry whoever my father chose for me. In my world, there was no room for love. The Volkov reputation is built on power. To keep that power, my family merged with the Solov's to become stronger. My falling in love with Rose set off a chain of events that would forever alter my life. I pursued her knowing it was wrong and knowing my future was promised to another. We parted ways at the end of our summer together, and I returned home to Russia while leaving my heart behind in Polson. As the following months since returning home ticked by, I began fighting my father at every turn. I was being forced into a life I wasn't sure I wanted anymore. In the end, I fulfilled my family obligation and married Ivanna. We had our son Nikolai soon after."

"How did you find out about Logan?" I ask knowing he only recently discovered his oldest son Logan but have never asked the details. Not even from my best friend Grace, who is a part of Logan's family. All I know is Logan's mother is named Rose. She died in a car accident when Logan was a boy. Jake, who is the President of The Kings of Retribution MC is Logan's uncle. He took Logan in after his mom passed away and raised him in the MC back in Montana. Then Demetri showed up out of nowhere claiming to be Logan's father. I have always wanted to know Demetri's side of the story.

"When my father died, I discovered some documents in his office. Evidence that he had Rose killed and that I had a son. I also discovered my now ex-wife, and her father played a role in killing the woman I loved and kept my son from me. I found letters and photos from Rose in my father's safe. Rose would write to me every year on Logan's birthday and include a picture of him with the letter. Each letter was addressed to The Volkov estate in Polson. The staff there would then forward the letters to my father. I, of course, never saw a single one. I had already been planning on divorcing Ivanna. Finding out what she did was the final nail in the coffin. The fact she is Nikolai's mother is the only thing allowing her to breathe," Demetri states with conviction.

"So, you found you had a son, and that's when you sought him out?"

Demetri shakes his head. "It was nearly a year before I went to Logan. My father had just died, and I had divorced Ivanna. I spent months securing the structure of my businesses. I had to be sure there would be no blowback from Ivanna's father since I tossed her out on her ass and severed my ties to her family. Divorce is not something we do in my world. Severing ties can lead to dangerous consequences. But with my father gone, I became head of The Volkov family. Unfortunately for the Solov family, I give no fucks about whatever agreement they had with my father. Their binding became void the moment my father drew his last breath."

"So, your ex-wife knew all along about Logan?"

"Yes. She not only kept my son from me, but she kept Nikolai from his brother. That is the very reason Nikolai is estranged from his mother now. I can't say I blame him."

My heart aches for Demetri and for what he and his two sons have gone through. I now understand why he has kept himself closed off all this time. "What about your mother?"

"I don't remember much about my mother. I was very young when she died in a car accident." Demetri's features harden.

It suddenly dawns on me that his mother's death is eerily similar to how Logan's mother lost her life. "Just like Rose," I state.

"Yes. After Rose's death, I started suspecting that my father may have killed my mother as well."

Needing to steer the conversation in a slightly different direction, I ask, "While we are on the subject of you and your family; will you tell me what exactly it is you do?" Demetri's eyes snap in my direction at my question. I know The Volkovs are mafia, but curiosity has me wanting to know more. Oddly enough, knowing Demetri's life reeks of danger and violence doesn't scare me. Maybe it's because I've been around the MC life for a couple of years, or perhaps it's because I feel the safest when Demetri is nearby. And though his life goes against the law and is full of danger, I find myself more and more drawn to him with each second we spend together. My feelings for him outweighs everything else.

"My business is not up for discussion," is his curt reply.

I shrug my shoulders. "Fair enough. Friends don't need to know everything about each other." I stand and begin clearing the food from the coffee table. "I mean, Grace and I have been friends since we were kids, and she still doesn't know everything about me." I scrape the leftover food from the plates into the garbage and load the dishes into the dishwasher. I don't take offense to Demetri's rebuff of my last question. I have a hard timesharing details about my life and don't begrudge anyone else for doing the same. I'm pulled from my rambling when a firm hand clutches my bicep, and I'm flipped around, coming face to face with a pissed off Demetri.

I watch his nostrils flare as he grinds out, "What we are is a hell of a lot more than friends, and you damn well know it."

I suck in a deep breath and stare into his eyes. There is so much truth written on his face, but I don't know if I can allow myself to trust it yet. Demetri's actions sans run hot and cold. Most of the time, I can't make heads or tails of what his intentions are. "I can see you are still confused by what's happening here, so let me be clearer since you seem to have forgotten what I told you in the hall after you had your sassy tongue in my mouth. You. Are. Mine.

You were mine the moment I laid eyes on you for the first time in that hospital bed, and you've been mine every day since."

Demetri steps further into my space, and I can feel his rock-hard erection pressing against my hip. Being the hussy, I am, I lean into him and a moan escapes past my lips. I wish I could blame the dry spell I've been having for my actions, but the cold hard truth is, it's Demetri. Volkov has worked himself so far under my skin; I crave everything about him. I want his heat, his touch, his taste. I crave the way his eyes devour my every move, and most of all, I crave the power he has over me. I want nothing more than to let go and submit to the man in front of me, knowing he is the only one that I can be myself around; he's the only man I have ever wanted to give myself to completely. "Tell me what you need, *Krasivaya*," Demetri rasps his accent becoming stronger as his fingers work the button of my shorts. "Say it," he demands. "Tell me what you want, and I'll give it to you."

"You," I breathe giving in. "I need you."

"Good girl," Demetri growls into my ear the same moment his hand slips past the band of my shorts finding my slick center. The second his finger slides through my wet slit my entire body shudders.

5

DEMETRI

I begin working Glory's swollen clit. Her lips part as she moans, causing my cock to strain against my trousers. Letting go of her arm, I cup her breast in the palm of my hand and run the pad of my thumb across her erect nipple. She bites her bottom lip, trying to suppress her reaction to my touch. "Don't hold back. Let me hear your desire, *Krasivaya*." Dipping my head, I kiss the shallow of her neck, caressing her skin with my tongue, tasting of her flesh as I take her nipple between my thumb and forefinger and squeeze.

"Demetri," she whispers my name as her fingers tangle in my hair, and her hips jerk forward. "Please," Glory begs.

I sink two fingers into her heated center. "Please what, *Krasivaya*?" I ask her. Glory's hand drops between our bodies, and she rubs her palm up the length of my cock.

"Fuck me," she says, locking her eyes with mine.

I smirk and begin working her clit once more. "No," I say, taking control of her pleasure, which is far more important than my own. Her eyes flare with anger. She isn't used to not getting what she wants. She will soon realize how I like things. "You are mine." I sink my fingers into her once more, then press my palm against her clit. "I want nothing more than to fuck you right now, but before that can happen," I roll her nipple between my fingers once more. "You have to surrender yourself to me completely. I won't give you all of me until I have all of you." I bring my mouth to hover over hers, feeling the heat of her breaths against my lips.

"You'll be waiting forever." Glory pants as I increase my speed, bringing her closer to climax.

"I'm willing to wait." I search her eyes as she lets my words sink in. "Come for me, *Krasivaya*," I command and watch her gorgeous face as she comes undone. Her walls tighten and flex around my fingers as she moans and rides out her orgasm.

I pull my hand from her shorts. She watches as I place my fingers in my mouth, tasting her, and lick them clean. My cock twitches with need, but I ignore it. "Perfect," I growl, her taste exploding across my tongue.

Almost immediately, Glory's demeanor changes. "I don't think I can do this," she says, turning her face away, refusing to look at me. "You and I will never work. I mean, the orgasm was nice and all, but it doesn't change the fact that I can't be what you want." She eases herself away from me and walks across the room, stopping in front of the double doors leading out to the apartment balcony. Glory crosses her arms as if to hug herself and stares outside, with the sunlight on her face. She closes her eyes.

"What is it you think I'm looking for?" I ask her.

"You want complete control of me. I'm not that woman. I can't give you all of me, Demetri. I won't be controlled." I carefully gauge the expression on her face, and it doesn't match the words coming from her mouth. "So, tell me, Demetri. How is it you know so much about me and what I do every day, where I go, what I like to eat. Do you have cameras watching my every move?" she asks, never looking back at me, keeping her face passive.

Reaching around her body, I unlock the French doors in front of her, turn the knobs and push them open. "Step outside with me," I tell her, and she does. Holding onto the railing, Glory gazes out at the city in front of us. Pulling my phone from my pocket, I dial Sasha.

"Sir," he answers.

"Step out onto the balcony," I order him; ending the call, I slip my phone back into my pocket. A few seconds later, Sasha steps out onto the terrace neighboring Glory's apartment. "*Krasivaya*, I'd like you to meet Sasha. He is one of my trusted men. He has been watching over you — protecting what is mine for the last few months," I admit and watch her face morph into anger.

"My neighbor is your spy?" her voice hints at her rage. "That explains a whole hell of a lot."

With a nod, Sasha disappears back into his apartment.

"You know what? I don't need this shit in my life. I don't need you or your dominating ways. I'm not going to obey you. I won't be some kind of sex slave you keep on a leash. And I won't have you spying on my life. You can call your guard dog off as well." Glory storms back into the apartment, and I follow her inside. "You can see yourself out." She stomps across the living room, heading toward her bedroom.

"You are confusing what I want." I choose my words carefully and try to explain to her some of who I am. "Sexually, yes, I want you to give yourself to me. Completely. It's something I want. I crave it. My hunger for you to hand over all control is strong, *Krasivaya*, but I will not demand it, nor will I take it from you. That is something you have to submit to on your own free will." I sigh. Running my hand through my hair, I cross the living room and come to stand behind her just as she places her hand on the knob to her bedroom door. "Outside the bedroom, I won't demand complete compliance, but I do expect a certain level of respect, just as we discussed earlier." Gently wrapping my arms around her waist, I show Glory I can and will be gentle with her. That I'm not the monster she may think I am. "Most of all, I need your trust."

Her head shakes. "I want to, but trust is not something I have much of these days. I understand in some ways why you have one of your men watch over me, but I don't like it. Sometimes things are taken from you, and you can never get them back. Like my privacy, which you have so clearly invaded." Silent tears roll down Glory's cheeks, and she turns away from me once more. This moment feels like so much more than her being mad at my actions right now. Something has broken her spirit in some way, and that does not sit well with me.

Turning her to face me, I ask. "If I am the sole cause of the state you are in, I am truly sorry. I never meant to upset you like this." I run my knuckles across her cheek, wiping the tears from her face.

"It's not just you." She drops her eyes.

"What more is troubling you? Tell me what sorrow has such a hold on your soul, *Krasivaya*. Show me what is broken so that I might put the pieces back together."

She laughs. "I'm a hopeless cause. Can't you see that? There are some things we can't fix. Shattered souls are one of them." She says the words like they are the truth.

I do not give up so easily. Grabbing her hand in mine; I place her palm on my chest. "You feel that?" Glory rolls her eyes, but nods. I then put her other hand over her heart. "You feel it?" Her heart pounds against her palm. Her eyes lift to mine, and she nods, as more tears spill from her beautiful eyes. "You are alive. You are a strong woman. Whatever happened — whatever you have been through did not defeat you because you are still here. If you cannot do it on your own, I will help you." Lifting my hand, I cup her cheek. "I am asking you once more; trust me."

Searching her eyes, I wait for her to process her thoughts. After a few shuddered breaths, Glory pulls away and makes her way to the kitchen, grabs a couple of wine glasses from the cabinet, and a bottle of red wine from the small wine rack sitting on the countertop. Walking back into the living room, she lowers herself to the sofa, sets the glasses on the coffee table in front of her and pops the cork on the bottle. "I need a drink. Care to join me?" She pours the wine, filling each glass halfway. She looks up at me. "You look like a whiskey man, but this is all I have to offer. Take it or leave it." Taking a seat beside her, I pick up my offered glass, give it a few swirls then take a sip. Sitting back, I watch as Glory downs her wine, then refills her glass. She does this one more time as I wait.

"Most people think I'm nothing but a slut." Her eyes cut to mine. Her shoulders shrug. "I enjoy men, with no strings attached. If that gives me the title then, well..." She sighs. "I just don't see the point of involving feelings. If we both have an itch to scratch, then what harm will come of it? Not that I was always like this." Glory sips her wine. "I used to want to fall in love. The Prince Charming on a white horse fantasy, just like many other women have. But I've been used too many times by men. Eventually, the fairytale dream became lackluster. The men all lost their shine. So, I started using them before they could use me. They got what they were after, and so did I. No relationships. No commitments. No one to answer to." Her eyes land on mine again. "Just sex."

I feel my jaw tick. "I don't want just sex."

"I know." She sits back on the sofa and tucks her legs. "I don't want what you want — a relationship, that is. I'm not capable of giving myself to one man. Men can't be trusted. All they do is take and take until you have nothing left to give. They beat you. They rape you. They leave you for dead. I have nothing left to give to you or any other man. Nothing." The look on my woman's face tells me she is shocked at her admission. Glory covers her mouth as she starts to tremble.

A fire rages inside of me. I want to rise off the sofa and tear down the walls, but I keep my anger contained, for Glory's sake.

My grip tightens around the base of the wine glass, and I have to place it on the coffee table in front of us before it shatters in my hand. Doing my best to keep a soft tone, I ask one question. "Who raped you, *Krasivaya*? Who dares put their hands on you? Tell me this so that I can make him suffer. The pain I will inflict on him will make him wish the devil himself would take him, because I am far worse." My nostrils flare as my breathing increases.

A manic laugh escapes her. "You're too late. He's already dead."

"Name, Glory." Lifting her head, Glory looks at me, and her shoulders sag.

"Ronan De Burca."

I've never had to rein in my temper and keep myself under such control in my life, but I close my eyes for a brief moment and collect myself once more. He beat the hell out of her when he was looking for Grace and his daughter. Beat her so bad she had to be hospitalized, but not once did she mention sexual assault. "I won't ask you to relive those moments if you don't wish to tell me all the details," I assure her.

She wrings her hands together. "I didn't know what else to do. He had already beaten me by that point. I had no more fight left in me to fend him off."

Gently tugging on her wrist, I pull Glory onto my lap and hold her there for a moment. "Who else knows?"

She buries her face into my chest. "No one."

"Jesus," I sigh. She's been keeping this to herself all this time. Holding her in my arms, I stand. Crossing the room, I carry her to her bedroom and lay her down on her bed.

"Demetri, I can't have sex with you."

I settle in behind her and pull her body as close to mine as I can get. "No sex. I want to hold you — protect you. That is all."

6

GLORY

I wake the next morning to the sound of my alarm blaring. Cracking my eyes open, I reach over to the table beside the bed and tap the screen of my phone, cutting it off. I don't have to turn over to know I am alone. I felt Demetri's absence the moment my eyes opened. When I sit up on the edge of the bed, I stretch out my sore muscles and rub my eyes with the palms of my hands. They feel swollen and scratchy. I surprised myself yesterday when I made my confession about Ronan to Demetri. My rape was something I had planned on taking to the grave. I told myself over and over again, the only way to move on from the ordeal was to forget about it and pretend it never happened. But once the words left my mouth yesterday, I felt as though a weight was lifted off my shoulders. I realize not talking about it is one of the things that kept me from moving on ultimately with my life; a reason I never quite felt settled. My rape has been a constant dark cloud hanging over my head. Closing my eyes, I can't help being transported back to when I was at the mercy of Ronan De Burca and powerless to stop him.

Grabbing a fist full of my hair, Ronan pulls my battered body from the floor of my kitchen. "You were always getting in between my wife and me, sticking your nose where it didn't belong," Ronan sneers into my ear his tone, causing my skin to crawl. "I told my wife you were a whore and a bad influence. Now, look what's happened. She's shacked up with some piece of shit biker. It looks like my wife picked up some of your slutty behavior, Glory." Ronan slams my body down against the kitchen table, all while pinning my arms behind my back in a vise-like grip. Seconds later, I hear the clinking sound of his belt just before my jeans are yanked down to my knees. Realizing what his intentions are I begin to fight against his hold, only when I do, Ronan pulls my head back by the hair on my head and slams it back down on the table. I feel an intense pain explode through my scalp as flickers of white light dances all around me. "There is only one way to teach a whore a lesson. By the time I'm through with you, Glory, you'll think twice about sticking your nose in my business where it doesn't belong."

A cold, wet nose nudging my bare leg brings me out of the past. I look down at Bo, who is sitting at my feet. Reaching down, I rub the top of his head. "Good morning, Bo. How's my boy today?" Bo leans his head into my palm, eating up the attention. When I stand from the bed, a piece of paper lying on the pillow where Demetri slept last night catches my eye. Walking over to the opposite side of the bed, I snag the paper from the pillow. I take in Demetri's handwriting and smile.

Good morning, Krasivaya.

I have business to attend to, but I will pick you up from school later. Sasha will be driving you this morning. He will be waiting outside your door at 7:00 am sharp.

Demetri.

PS. I had Sasha take Bo out for his morning walk.

I don't bother questioning why Sasha will be taking me to work today. I find myself letting go of the anger I felt yesterday when Demetri told me about my secret bodyguard. I have to give Demetri credit; when I let my bitch flag fly, he took it like a champ.

Two points for Volkov. I should be freaked out. The man has had someone following me, but I realized Demetri just wants to protect me. How can I be mad at that? Besides, it's not a hardship having someone haul my ass around.

On the way to the bathroom, I drop the note on the top of my dresser. When I step into the bathroom, I take in my reflection in the mirror. Though my eyes are a bit swollen, I don't look as bad as I was anticipating. Turning the faucet on, I go about washing my face and brushing my teeth. Deciding to leave my hair down today, I plug in my curling iron and let it heat as I go about applying my makeup. Thirty minutes later, my smoky eye shadow has concealed the redness around my eyes, making my green irises pop, I've applied my signature red lipstick, and my hair is styled in loose curls that hang down my back. Strolling out of the bathroom and into my closet, I choose my high waisted hunter-green slacks and pair them with a cream-colored blouse and my nude heels.

Patting my leg, I have Bo follow me out of the bedroom and down the hall to the kitchen where I take his food from the cabinet and feed him. I watch as he scarfs it down eagerly before he takes his chunky butt over to his pillow in front of the living room window. He's lazy and will sleep all day. Peering down at my watch, I see I have just enough time to spare before work to stop for coffee and a bagel at the coffee shop two blocks from the school. With my purse in hand, I make my way to the door. When I swing it open, I'm greeted by Sasha's large frame; waiting for me just as Demetri said he would. I pause at my door a moment and take in the man who has been looking after me for months. Sasha is at least six feet tall, has inky black hair and eyes the color of chocolate.

"Miss Keller," he greets with a slight nod, his accent strong.

"I guess I'm with you this morning," I say as I turn, lock my door, and toss my keys into my purse.

"Yes, ma'am. I will be escorting you to work."

"Please don't call me ma'am; I'm Miss Keller to my students. You can call me Glory. Besides, you've been following my ass for months, no reason to be so formal."

"I'm sorry, but I have been instructed to address you as ma'am or Miss Keller."

"Fuck me," I mutter, rolling my eyes. "You should tell your boss to lighten up," I say as I make my way toward the elevator with Sasha following close behind.

"If I wish to keep my tongue, I will do as Mr. Volkov instructs," he says, his face serious.

"Demetri wouldn't do that, would he?" I ask unbelieving.

Sasha gives me a look that says he is deadly serious, and I snap my mouth shut.

"Alright, Miss Keller it is."

I look Sasha up and down. "I'm sure the ladies would be disappointed if something happened to your tongue."

Sasha curses under his breath. I think I shouldn't have said that, but Demetri knows by now I have no filter. I can't help the shit that comes out of my mouth. When Sasha steps onto the elevator behind me, I shrug my shoulders, and he shakes his head.

When we step out of my apartment building and onto the sidewalk, I breathe in the warm fresh air. Today is the last day of school and summer is approaching. With school ending, I wonder what I'll do with my time off. My mind drifts to Demetri, and I find myself hoping it is spent with him. Maybe I should fly out to Polson and see Grace and my Godchildren. Shaking those thoughts away, I take in the sleek black car parked on the street in front of me. Sasha steps up to the back passenger door and opens it. Once I climb inside, I watch as he rounds the hood of the car. I don't miss the way his eyes scan everywhere and his alertness as he takes in our surroundings.

"Can we stop at the coffee shop a couple of blocks down from the school?" I ask Sasha after he climbs into the car. "I'm in desperate need..." My words get cut short when he passes me a white bag and a foam cup with the coffee shop logo on the side. I take the offered coffee and peek inside the bag to find a bagel and cream cheese. There is even a little pack of honey. "Do you also know what brand of tampons I use?" I ask jokingly.

"I can pick some up for you and drop them by your apartment later," Sasha answers in a perfectly calm tone.

"Jesus Christ. I was only kidding. I'll get my own damn tampons for crying out loud."

Sasha shrugs then proceeds to put the car in drive and pull out into traffic. Thirty minutes later, I'm settling in behind my desk at school as my students begin to trickle in. "Alright, kids. Come on and take your seat. The sooner we start, the quicker we can get out of here!" I holler over their murmured chatter. Taking the stack of test papers from my desk, I hand them to each student sitting in the first desk at the front of each row. "Take one and pass the rest back. You all have one hour to complete your final exam."

An hour and a half later, the classroom is empty, and I have just finished clearing out my desk drawers. Just as I drop the stapler into the box sitting on top of my desk, I hear a knock on the door. Peaking over my shoulder, I see Mr. Learner striding toward me.

"How was your last day, Glory?" he asks.

Without giving him a second glance, I continue with my task of packing up my supplies. "Oh, you know. Same as any other day." I don't ask him how his day was, hoping he will leave. The man has gotten on my last nerve.

"Have you signed up to teach summer school?" Kevin continues.

"Nope," is my reply.

Without warning, I feel a hand on my hip and Kevin's voice too close for comfort as he comes to stand directly behind me. "Now that school has ended, how about I take you out? I know you were worried about starting anything because we worked together, but now there is no reason we can't see each other."

Turning around to face Kevin, I give him an annoyed look. "I haven't accepted your invitation to go out because I am not interested. It's not because we work together."

Kevin takes one step closer into my personal space as if he didn't get the fact that I have rejected his advance yet again. "Look, Glory..." Kevin goes to speak, but this time he's cut off when out of nowhere a red-faced Demetri wraps his large hand around the scruff of Kevin's neck. I have never seen the pure animalistic look he is currently sporting; the veins on his forehead look like they are about to burst.

"I should cut your hands off for touching what's mine," Demetri snarls, shoving Kevin against the whiteboard behind my desk.

"Hey. Take it easy man. We were talking," Kevin says, unable to hide the tremor in his voice. Because not only does Demetri tower over him, he also looks seconds away from committing murder.

Kevin cuts his gaze to me; his eyes pleading for help.

"Do you know this guy, Glory?" I raise a brow at Kevin's question. One would think I'd be scared as to what Demetri might do, but I'm kind of curious to see how this plays out. With lightning quick movement, Demetri pulls his gun from the inside of his suit coat and presses it against my colleague's head. "Glory is not your concern. The only thing you need to know is she belongs to me. That means you don't look at her and you sure as fuck don't touch her. She does not exist to you," Demetri says his tone calm, yet something evil lies behind it. I cut my eyes to the door of the classroom to see Sasha standing guard with a bored look on his face.

"Alright, man! I'm sorry. Glory doesn't exist. I won't bother her again." Kevin pleads with Demetri to let him go.

Demetri holds his weapon against Kevin's temple a few

seconds longer before he releases the hold on his neck, steps back and holsters his gun. Kevin doesn't hesitate to make a quick retreat out of the room. Demetri then turns his attention to me. He stares at me, waiting for my reaction.

I cock my head to the side and smile. "That was a bit extreme, don't you think?"

"No," Demetri says, his face void of any expression.

Rolling my eyes, I turn, grab my purse, sling it over my shoulder and heft the box off my desk. By the time I turn back around to face Demetri, Sasha is by my side taking the box from my hands. He tips his head toward Demetri. "I'll be waiting in the car."

Demetri doesn't take his eyes off me as Sasha exits the room, leaving the two of us alone. "Come, *Krasivaya*. We have a plane to catch." Placing his hand on the small of my back Demetri, and I make our way out of the classroom.

"What do you mean a plane to catch? I wasn't aware I was going anywhere."

"We are going to Polson for the weekend."

"Really?!"

"Yes. I know you haven't seen Grace in months and your godchildren are due for a visit."

I smile at the thought of seeing Remi and Ellie Kate. We stop next to the car where Sasha is waiting for us, and I turn to Demetri. "This trip is exactly what I need. Thank you, Demetri."

Roughly an hour later we are in the air aboard Demetri's private plane. We stopped by my apartment long enough for me to pack, change into a pair of jeans and call my mom to come by sometime this evening to pick up Bo. Peering around the inside of the plane, I fidget in my seat. Demetri hasn't spoken five words to me since we took off and instead of sitting beside me, he has chosen the seat furthest away. Yesterday he couldn't keep his hands off me, but today he is different. I feel sick to my stomach with the realization that my confession about Ronan might have Demetri seeing me differently. It would explain why he is no longer eager to put his hands on me.

"You're thinking too hard over there. What's got that look on your face?" Demetri asks as he sips the brown liquid in his glass.

"Nothing. I'm just anxious to see my friend is all," I lie.

Demetri's eyes bore into mine as if he knows I'm bullshitting him. Thankfully, he doesn't call me out, especially since Victor and Sasha are sitting within earshot. With time to kill, I pull my laptop and file folder from my backpack and decide to finish grading final exams and getting the grades logged into the parent-student portal.

Before I know it, we have landed in Polson, and I am exiting the plane with Demetri. There is a black SUV waiting for us on the tarmac. Victor climbs into the driver's seat the same moment Sasha opens the back hatch and deposits mine and Demetri's luggage inside. Just as I go to open the back passenger door, Demetri blocks my move, flips me around to face him and presses his body against mine, catching me off guard, and I gasp. "What—" I go to say, but I'm cut off when Demetri brings his face an inch from mine.

"I want nothing more than to put my hands all over your body. And that's what I would have done on that plane had I not separated myself from you. But the first time I have you ride my cock; it won't be on my plane or with an audience. It will be in my bed, where I can spend the entire night worshipping your body and fucking your tight pussy so raw, you'll be feeling me for days."

"Holy shit," I breathe. "You sure know how to woo a girl. I'm going to hold you to that." I wink. "Especially the part where I'll be feeling you for days."

"What the hell am I going to do with you, *Krasivaya*?" Demetri says with a grin as he opens the door to the SUV, and I slide in.

"Exactly what you just promised."

The drive from the airport to The Kings clubhouse takes twenty minutes. The closer we get, the more excited I become. I opted not to tell Grace we were coming and decided to surprise her instead. It's already dark by the time we pull up to the gated compound. Demetri pulls his phone from his pocket and fires off a text. Seconds later, the gate slides open, and Victor drives through. The parking lot is full, the lights around the back of the property are on, and I hear music. The whole family must be here. The second Victor shifts the truck into park, I fling the door open and jump out of my seat. Demetri chuckles as he keeps in stride behind me. When the two of us round the corner of the clubhouse, I see our family and friends milling around the yard. Music is playing, a fire is burning, and laughter fills the air. Out of nowhere, I hear a loud squeal. I watch as my best friend Grace untangles herself from her husband Jake's lap and dashes across the yard in my direction. I break away from Demetri to meet her halfway. Once we are within arm's length of each other, we pull each other in for a hug. I didn't realize how much I missed my friend until this moment.

"I can't believe you didn't tell me you were coming," Grace cries.

"You know I like to make an entrance," I tease.

Grace cuts her eyes over my shoulder to Demetri, who is standing across the yard with Logan. "Demetri brought you?" "He did," I admit picking at the imaginary lint on my shirt.

"And?" she hedges.

"And what?" I fake innocence but fail when I sneak a glance in Demetri's direction to see him not bothering to hide the fact he's staring at me.

"It's about time, Glory," Grace says with a huge smile and tears in her eyes. I don't get a chance to answer her when suddenly a small body comes barreling into me.

"Aunt Glory!" Remi, Grace's daughter, screeches, wrapping her arms around me.

God, I miss this kid. "Oh, my God! Look at you. You've gotten so tall. I swear you've grown five inches since I last saw you," I gush.

"And where is the little one?"

"She fell asleep an hour ago. I put her down inside," Grace tells me.

"Damn. I guess I'll have to wait until tomorrow to get my Elle Kate love then."

Grace chuckles. "How about we grab a drink and sit with the girls? I know they are on pins and needles right now."

I look over Grace's shoulder, and sure enough, all the women dart their eyes back and forth between Demetri and me. No doubt wanting details.

"Alright. Let's go put them out of their misery."

As we walk across the yard, Grace nudges me. "I'm so happy you came."

I smile. "Me too."

7

DEMETRI

Watching Glory's face light up the moment she saw her best friend helps smolder the fire burning in my gut. Having the knowledge that Ronan De Burca, a man who is now dead, had his hands on her, putting her through the worst kind of hell has not exactly been sitting well with me. But my anger is nothing compared to what Glory went through and what she has continued to go through for too long.

"Demetri," Jake greets me as Glory and Grace take off across the yard. I watch as the other women embrace Glory. "It's good to see you." He shakes my hand.

"It's nice to be back in Polson," I tell him.

Jake studies me for a beat. "From the look on your face, I take it you've claimed your woman." He smirks.

"Something like that," I admit. "I brought us a bottle of whiskey. I would like it if you could join me for a drink later after I've seen my sons and grandchildren," I mention to Jake just as I catch sight of Logan and Nikolai.

"You got it. I'll catch up with you later." Jake raises his bottle of beer at me, then strolls back to his lawn chair.

Crossing the yard, I greet my sons, who are deep in conversation. "Logan. Nikolai."

"Dad," Logan answers. "Good to see ya." His glance lands on Glory and the other women, who are all smiles and talking amongst themselves. "Thought you wouldn't be back for another couple of weeks." Before I can answer him, I hear my grandchildren's excited laughter as they call out. "*Deda!*" Turning around, I watch as Breanna toddles toward me, along with Bella, who is making her way over with my grandson on her hip. Little Jake has his arms stretched out in front of him, eager for me to take him from his mother before they even reach me.

"*Deda!*" Breanna reaches me first, so I pick her up off the ground, and she wraps her arms around my neck. When Bella reaches me, Jake is climbing his mother like a tree to get out of her arms. Taking him from her, I now hold both my grandchildren.

"I think maybe they missed you just a little," Bella laughs.

I love my family. My sons are everything to me, but my grandchildren have brought more joy to my life than I ever could have imagined. Hearing them call me *Deda*, and watching their tiny faces light up when they see me can make a lousy day fade away. Giving them a final squeeze, I set Breanna on the ground and hand Jake back to his mother. "Have you been good for your mother and father?" I regard both children, holding a stern look on my face. My grandchildren look at each other and smile before looking up at me.

"You spoil them too much." Logan chuckles at Breanna and Jake's excitement.

"It is my job to spoil my grandchildren. Besides, it doesn't take much to make them happy." From one pocket I pull out a small toy car and hand it to Jake. His face lights up with joy.

"What do you say, Jake?" Bella asks.

Jake lets out a string of baby babble. His eyes look so much like mine and his father's when he glances back at me, and I smile.

Turning my attention to my granddaughter, I take her gift from my other pocket. Glory helped me pick this one out. It is a small, beaded heart bracelet. Kneeling, I place it on Breanna's tiny wrist.

"Mommy, look it." Breanna beams up at her mother.

"What do you say to *Deda*?" Bella prompts her daughter, and Breanna throws herself into my legs.

"I love you, *Deda*."

My heart melts as I kiss the top of her head. "*Ya lyublyu tebya.*" Standing, I watch as Breanna ambles her way back across the yard to join the other kids playing on the swing set. Bella reaches up, pulls Logan's head toward hers and kisses him. "I'm going to rejoin the girls." Then she turns to me. "We missed you." She gives me a warm smile, and I return one of my own before she takes her leave.

"I see you brought Glory with you," my youngest son, Nikolai, mentions as he comes to stand beside me. I raise my brow but say nothing in return. "I'm happy for you, Father," he adds.

"I second that." Logan raises his beer, agreeing with his brother.

As the evening is winding down, a few of us men find our way inside gathered around one of the tables as we pass the whiskey bottle around.

"So, how did things go back home?" Nikolai inquires as he lifts his glass filled with amber whiskey to his lips. My face must show my thoughts, as my mind shifts to the death of Yerik, then straight to his underhanded son Vadim. Nikolai leans forward in his chair and places his glass down on the table. "Trouble?" At his question, Jake, and Logan train their eyes on me. I look at each of them. They are my family. Jake is my friend, so I do not hesitate to speak freely.

"Yerik is dead." I look at Nikolai, and he nods.

"He's been ill for a while. We knew his time was nearing its end."

"He was murdered," I state, and Nikolai's body becomes rigid.

"Who?" he asks as the other men hang on our conversation. Before I further explain the details, I decide to fill Logan and Jake in on who we are speaking of. I glance around the table, directing my conversation to those sitting with me. "Yerik Petrov was the patriarch of the Petrov family. My family and his have had a mutual respect. An understanding of power amongst the two empires. Him being murdered, on his deathbed, has had a ripple effect within the hierarchy of our two families." I look to Nikolai once more. "His only son, Vadim, challenged my authority the other day when I stopped by the Petrov estate to pay my respects to Yerik's widow. He was none too pleased by my presence, and all but made his intentions clear that he does not wish to hold up the alliance our families have held for many years now." I let all the information I've handed so far sink in. The expression on Nikolai's face tells me he understands the caution we need to have moving forward.

"This guy, Vadim," Jake inquires. "You gettin' the feeling he's about to start a shit storm?"

I nod. "Vadim hated his father. He hated the alliance between the families." Reaching for the whiskey bottle, I pour myself another drink. "Elena asked that I check on Misha. She is Yerik's daughter who lives in the States, Chicago to be exact."

"And how are Misha and her family?" Nikolai asks.

"Doing well for herself and being happy." I pause to take a sip of whiskey. "She believes it was Vadim who killed their father. If not himself then he had someone do it for him."

"Killed by his son? You have to have a lot of hate to kill your own flesh and blood," Logan quips.

Nikolai shakes his head. "Vadim is a spineless weasel. He does not have the guts to get his pretty manicured hands dirty. I can agree with Misha that her brother is to be suspected of the crime, but like the coward he is, he hides behind someone else as he watches his father die."

We sit silently for a moment drinking our liquor before Jake tells me, "You know the club has your back if you need us. You've done a lot for my men, and I'm happy to repay the favor anytime." I raise my glass and accept his offer before downing what's left of my drink.

"It's getting late. I say we find our women and go home for the night." Logan downs his final shot then stands.

"I'll crash here for the night," Nikolai announces, then makes his way upstairs to his room here at the clubhouse.

Joining Logan and Jake, we walk outside finding the women gathered around the fire, several holding sleeping children in their arms as the older kids roast marshmallows over the open flames. Glory catches my stare, whispers to her best friend, Grace then stands. After saying her goodbyes to the others, she saunters in my direction. She stops in front of me. "You drunk, *Krasivaya*?" I smirk when she wobbles a bit.

"Nope," she smiles. "Just a little buzzed."

"Victor should be here. I'm taking you home with me tonight." Her eyes trail my body. The heat in her stare causes my cock to twitch.

Glory licks her lips. "Maybe you'll get lucky tonight." Her fingers trail down the front of my shirt. My phone rings interrupting us. Pulling it from my pocket, I answer.

"Yes?"

"Sir, I'm out front," Victor informs me.

Taking Glory's hand in mine, I thread my fingers with hers; then I turn to Logan and Jake, who have been watching us. "Son, Jake. We have enjoyed ourselves. I will see you again soon." I shake Jake's hand, then direct my next words to Logan. "Bring the family over for brunch soon?"

"You got it," Logan agrees, and I nod.

With Glory's hand in mine, I lead her around the building to the front of the clubhouse where we find Victor waiting beside the car. Opening the door, I wait for her to climb in and slide across the backseat before jumping in myself. The ride to my estate is quiet, but the air is thick with sexual tension pouring off both Glory and me.

Once Victor pulls the car to a stop at the front of my home, he peers in the rearview mirror. "Do you need anything else for the night, Sir?"

"No, Victor. I will see you in the morning."

"Thank you, Sir." He waits as I climb out, and escort Glory from the car to the front door before driving around back to the small guest house he has to himself. Once inside, Glory follows me up the stairs.

"I'll show you to your room, which has an ensuite. I had the housekeeper prepare everything before we arrived. If something is not to your liking, please let me know, and I will make changes."

Glory comes to a stop. "My room?" she asks.

"As much as I want you in my bed, I won't presume that is where you want to be until the words leave your mouth." I turn to continue down the hallway.

"I want to be in your bed, Demetri." Her words halt my movement just as my fingers grip the knob to open her bedroom door.

Turning, I face her. "Make certain this is what you want." I take two steps toward her, coming face to face with the woman who has captured my heart. "You will not use me, Glory. I will not use you. This will not be just sex," I warn her.

"I'm willing to try."

Those were the only words I needed to hear. Pressing her back against the wall, I bring my mouth down on hers, kissing her as if my life depends on it. Gripping her ass, I lift her off the floor, her sandals falling from her feet as she wraps her legs around me.

Glory grinds down on me. I growl feeling the heat from her center. Keeping my hold on her, I step away from the wall and walk us further down the hall. Throwing the door open, we enter the master bedroom.

"Fuck, where did you learn to kiss like that?" Glory rasps as I lay her down on my king size bed that sits directly in front of the large floor to ceiling window overlooking my property. Reaching up, Glory tries undoing the buttons on my dress shirt, but I stop her.

"No." I pin her hand above her head, then place her other hand beside it. "Keep them there." I watch her bite her lower lip. I can tell she wants to talk back with some sassy retort on the tip of her tongue, but she remains quiet as she watches my every move. Leaning down, I slowly start peeling articles of clothing off her body. Her shirt is the first to go, followed by her jeans, leaving her in nothing but her bra and panties. "Fuck. There are no words to describe just how breathtaking you are," I admit as I take her in. Glory's body is a dream. Full and curvy. Her tits alone could bring grown men to their knees. What's even sexier is Glory embraces her curves. She is confident and loves her body. That in itself is a turn-on.

"What are you waiting for?" She wiggles her hips from side to side.

"I'm taking my time with you, *Krasivaya*." I undo the front clasp of her black lace bra, freeing her perfectly sized breasts. Eager, I dip my head, taking one of her taut nipples into my mouth.

"Oh, God." Glory's chest rises from the mattress, pressing her body further into mine. Her fingers thread through my hair. Her nails drag along my scalp. I bite down on her erect nipple, drawing a gasp from her mouth.

"Harder," she moans.

Taking hold of her other breast, I give it a firm squeeze. "These tits are perfect." I take her other nipple into my mouth, giving it equal attention before slowly working my way down her trim body. My lips kiss, and my teeth nip at her soft flesh along the way until I reach the small triangle of material that covers what I know is going to be the sweetest pussy I'll ever have the pleasure of tasting. She moans as I press my tongue against the lacey barrier letting my hot breath tease her swollen clit. Her hips levitate off the bed as her hand's fist my hair, pulling me closer, pressing my mouth down on her eager pussy.

I inhale her scent, and my need to taste her overtakes me. With one swift movement, I rip the scrap of cloth from her body, and run my tongue through her center, tasting my woman for the first time. An animalistic growl reverberates through my chest as I claim what is mine. Slipping my hands beneath her body, I cup her firm ass in my palms, keeping her hips lifted for me to feast on her. "This is mine now." I Dip my head again, sucking on her bundle of nerves.

"Demetri!" She cries out my name as I pleasure her.

"Tell me you are mine, Glory," I demand.

"God, yes. I am yours. My body is yours." Her hands fist the comforter.

Without warning, I stop what I am doing and stand.

"Demetri, please don't stop now," she begs, then reaches down and touches herself, her eyes never leaving mine. I let her stroke herself a few times, more for my pleasure than hers. My cock throbs as I take her in.

"Enough," I order, my voice stern enough to cause her to pause and glare up at me as I stand over her. She groans in protest but does as she is told.

"I was so close," she breathes.

"When you come, it will be on my cock."

Stalking around the bed, I strip my clothes from my body.

Glory's eyes travel straight to my heavy cock the moment I set it free. She licks her lips.

"Can I taste you?" she asks, rubbing her thighs together seeking relief.

Stepping to the foot of the bed, I wrap my hands around her ankles, pull her body down toward the end of the bed, flip her onto her stomach, and bring my hand down across her firm ass cheek. Glory sucks in a sharp breath, and my cock grows harder at the sight of my mark on her skin. She doesn't protest, so I do it again. This time enticing a pleasurable moan to escape her mouth as I watch her ass turn red.

"Again?"

"Demetri, please," Glory begs, and I bring my hand down again.

"Tell me what you need, *Krasivaya.*" I run my palm over my mark.

Glory looks over her shoulder, and her eyes lock on mine. "I need you to fuck me."

Flipping her back over, I kneel on the bed and hover above her body. Gripping her knees, I push them open as far as they will go, baring her glistening pussy. "Keep them open. Do not move," I order as I begin fisting my cock at the sight in front of me. Glory's pupils dilate and her body trembles with need as she watches me run my palm up and down the length of my cock and licks her lips at the sight of pre-cum leaking from the tip. Angling down, I tease her swollen clit, rubbing her bundle of nerves with the head of my cock. "Perfect," I rasp as I glide the head through her wet slit.

"It would be perfect if you'd get on with it," Glory grits her teeth as she rocks her hips upward, eager for me to be inside her.

Halting my movements, I snap my attention away from Glory's pussy to her eyes. "I could just fill that sassy mouth with my cock until I come down your throat. Then once you have taken every drop I give you, I'll deny your hungry pussy until you've learned your lesson." If looks could kill, I'd be dead with the glare Glory is currently sending my way, but she chooses to remain quiet. I grin.

"Good girl."

As a reward, I give in to her needs and my desire to please her by lining up at her center and slowly sinking into her tight heat. "Fuck," I growl at how perfect she feels wrapped around my cock. Glory shows her restraint by keeping herself open just as I instructed before. She bites her bottom lip and closes her eyes on a moan. "Look at me," I bark. Her eyes snap open, and her pupils dilate. "Keep those gorgeous eyes on me while I fuck you." Lifting one leg to rest over my shoulder, I open her up more and begin to move. My strokes are slow at first, letting her body adjust to my size before they become hard and powerful. I watch as her tits jiggle with each thrust I deliver. Glory's lips part as her body syncs with the rhythm of mine. Leaning down my lips hover a mere inch above hers. "You feel that; feel us?"

"I feel it," she admits, her breaths coming out in pants.

Glory's grip on my shoulders tightens, and her nails dig into my skin, causing a twinge of pain, which only entices me to fuck her harder. I roll my hips, grinding down on her, creating extra friction against her clit. "I'm close, Demetri," she warns. The moment the words leave her mouth, I pull out, causing a strangled cry to leave her mouth. "Demetri, please."

Ignoring her plea, I flip Glory over onto her stomach once again. I then tug on her hips and bring her to her hands and knees. I don't waste a single second before I drive my cock back into her drenched pussy. Her cries vibrate off the bedroom walls as I bury myself balls deep the same time, I bring my palm down on her already reddened ass. Taking a fist full of Glory's red locks in my hand, I tug her head back. "Grab hold of the headboard, and don't let go." Doing as I say, Glory reaches in front of her and wraps her fingers around the iron bars of the headboard. The second she has her grip, I keep one hand fisted in her hair and bring the other around to her neck. The moment I squeeze it, I feel her pulse throbbing against my grip and her pussy spasms around my dick. *Fuck, my woman likes that.* With the moonlight shining through the large window in front of us, my eyes lock on Glory's reflection. Without losing our connection, I drill into her without abandon. I know she's close when her pussy flutters around my cock. I continue to deliver long hard strokes as sweat drips down my back, and the only sounds heard is my harsh breathing, Glory's moans, and the sound of flesh meeting flesh. Seconds later, I feel my own orgasm ready to explode, and I growl.

"Come, *Krasivaya.*"

8

GLORY

There is no greater feeling in the world than having Demetri inside me. My eyes are locked on his reflection in the window in front of us, and I don't dare break the connection. I'm hypnotized. My core clenches with each powerful thrust. I feel my desire start to run down the inside of my thighs as his thick, rigid cock delivers equal parts pain as it does pleasure. My marked ass is on fire, and each time his pelvis slams against my ass, it only heightens my need to come. I knew being with Demetri would be like this. It's one of the reasons I have fought our connection for so long. I was always too afraid to have someone give me what I need, only to have it ripped away. That, and a part of me feared I would never be able to find pleasure in a man's touch again. I think deep down I knew Demetri would be the one to heal me. Without having to say a word, he gives me what I need. He is in tune with my body.

When Demetri's dominant hand wraps around my neck and squeezes, a jolt of electricity soars through my body and my center flutters. My orgasm is close. Demetri must feel it too. Using the fisted grip, he has on my hair; he pulls my head back and growls into my ear. "Come, *Krasivaya*."

My body does as he commands, and I come. I scream out Demetri's name as white flashes of light dance behind my eyelids. The moment my orgasm crashes through my body and my pussy clamps down on his cock, it triggers his release. Through the reflection in the window, I watch as the beast behind me grabs both sides of my hips, plants himself deep inside me, throws his head back and lets out a roar. I feel the head of his cock swell inside me, as he fills me with his warm release.

Seconds later, Demetri pulls his cock from my pussy, and I collapse to the bed; my body boneless and spent. The last thing I remember is Demetri kissing my bare shoulder before my eyes grow heavy and sleep takes me.

I don't know how much time has passed when I crack my eyes open and stretch out my sore muscles. Hearing a deep voice, I look over my shoulder to see Demetri standing next to the bed, peering out the window into the dark sky with his phone to his ear. Rolling over, I place my palm under my cheek and take in the naked man standing in front of me. Earlier this evening, I was completely overtaken by my lust-filled haze that I didn't take the time to admire all that is Demetri Volkov. The first thing my eyes zero in on is his long thick cock hanging heavy between his legs. My eyes then travel up to his well-defined abs. For a man in his late forties, Demetri is in better shape than most men in their twenties. Roaming away from his abs, I trace the array of tattoos that cover his chest and arms. I've only ever seen Demetri in suits. I had seen his ink peeking out from his shirt collar before but had no idea the extent of his ink. His tattoos are beautiful. By the time my eyes make their trek up to his face, Demetri's lip is tilted up into a smirk. He's caught me ogling, but I could care less. He says something in Russian to the person he's on the phone with then hangs up. "What time is it?" I ask.

"Just a little past two in the morning," he tells me.

"You don't sleep much, do you?"

Tossing his phone to the table, Demetri slides into the bed next to me. "I sleep enough." Resting his back against the headboard, he pulls my body into his, and I rest my head on his chest. I breathe in his scent and allow the rhythmic beat of his heart to relax me.

The two of us are quiet for a few minutes before I blurt out something that has been weighing on me. "I tried to sleep with a man six months ago. Right after I moved out of my parents' house and into my apartment." Demetri's whole body tenses beneath me but continue. "I wanted to move on from what happened. I thought I was ready. I went out to a bar, started chatting with a man and when he invited me back to his place, I said yes." Even though I can sense Demetri's anger, I keep talking. "The entire cab ride back to his house, I knew I was making a huge mistake, but I ignored the little voice inside my head telling me to go home. The second we stepped into his townhouse, we began kissing, but the moment he started to take my clothes off, I froze. I completely freaked out." Breaking away from Demetri, I sit up and look at him. His eyes are hard, and his jaw is clenched. I knew my confession would set him off. "I couldn't do it, Demetri. I didn't go through with it. The memories of my nightmare came flooding back, and I freaked out. I ended up running out of his house without any explanation." Demetri's features soften at my confession.

Letting the sheet fall away from my body, exposing my breasts, I crawl onto Demetri's lap, straddling his thighs. "Last night, with you, I had no fear, Demetri. There were no bad memories — no demons haunting me. I realized the reason I couldn't go through with it was that he wasn't you," I confess. Demetri's gaze turns heated and the grip he has on my hips tightens. "I only ever want it to be you who touches me from now on. I don't think I could stand another man's touch, Demetri," I choke out, letting my emotions get the better of me.

"You're right," he says, moving his hands from my hips up to frame my face and kisses me gently on the lips. "I'm the only man allowed to touch you. There will be no others; just me. And I'll kill any man who so much as thinks about putting their hands on you. It was all I could do not to order Sasha to go into that fucker's house and put a bullet in him."

His confession stuns me. "What are you talking about?"

"I knew the moment you left the bar with that man."

"Sasha?" I have a question. In fact, thinking back to that night, it all makes sense. "The car that was following me. That was Sasha, wasn't it?"

Demetri nods. "Yes. He was the one who followed you. Sasha was also the one who called the cab that picked you up. As much as I wanted to kill the man you left the bar with, seeing you get home safe was more important. That and I had not claimed you yet. My anger was misplaced."

Demetri kisses me again, this time it's not gentle. I feel his cock harden beneath my bare sex, and I start to grind down on his length, coating it with my arousal. I gasp, and he growls into my mouth when the head of his dick makes contact with my clit. In a blink of an eye, Demetri has me on my back, and enters me in one fluid motion, burying himself inside me, knocking the breath from my lungs. Holding himself still, he looks down at me, his gaze burning into mine. "Only me," he grinds out, thrusting his pelvis against my clit, and I groan.

"Yes. Only you, Demetri." This time, his movements are slow and lazy.

Before he took me, Demetri claimed me, but this time is different. This time he makes love to me; showing me what we both already knew. We fit together perfectly. That he is the only man who can make me feel good; make me feel safe, and that I am his. I know there is no going back. There is no way I can deny what we are to each other. There will be no more fighting the pull we have. I have given myself to Demetri Volkov. For the first time in a long time; I feel complete.

9

DEMETRI

The sun rays filtering across the bedroom dance across the surface of Glory's skin as she lays sleeping. After a couple of hours of sleep, and many thoughts on my mind, I slide my body from beneath hers. Sitting in the leather chair, a few feet from the bed, I take in her sated body as she lies stretched out on her stomach, with one of her legs intertwined in the sheets. My feelings for her are far more profound than I thought. Needing Glory was never a question I knew right away. I wanted more than sex with her. I knew once we both gave into our desires it would be explosive, but what I wasn't ready to encounter was the fact I never thought I'd love another woman, yet here I am thinking those words and feeling it as I look at her, while she lightly snores in her sleep.

Glory has gone and proven all I thought wasn't possible wrong.

She is a game changer.

She is mine.

My phone rings, bringing me out of my thoughts, and I decide not to answer and close us off from the outside world for a little longer. The ringing stops then starts back again. Not wanting to disturb my woman as she rests, I snatch the phone from the bedside table, swipe the screen, and lift the phone to my ear.

"Speak," I bark.

"Sir, we have a situation," Luca says, then silence.

Huffing a breath of frustration, I command, "spit it out."

"Two containers of inventory were broken into last night, and one of our men is dead. His body was found inside the container. Shot in the back of the head." Luca's words sink in, and my blood begins to boil. Glory stirs, and the sheet covering her luscious ass slips, revealing her backside and causing my cock to throb with need once more. Pushing my desire aside, I stand. Facing the window in front of me, I stare out at the sky.

"I want answers."

"Yes, sir." The phone call ends.

I regret having to leave the States so soon, but I must return to Russia. Incidents like this are happening more often, and this time, one of my men has been killed.

A slim pair of arms wrap around my waist, and Glory's warm breath skirts across my skin as she presses her lips against the back of my neck. "You're tense. I could fix that," she teases, her tone sensual.

Closing my eyes, I suppress the urge to press her body against the windowpane and fuck her until we are drunk on each other. I bring her hand up and softly kiss her palm. "I need to fly back home today."

Glory presses her cheek against my back between my shoulder blades and sighs. "When will you be back?" is the only question she asks. Not why or for how long, and that makes me think.

Perhaps she would be willing to come with me.

Before I give it much more thought, I ask, "Come with me?"

She laughs softly. "To Russia?" Hinting that she is not taking my invite seriously.

Tugging on Glory's arm, I bring her to stand in front of me. My eyes drop, drinking in the perfection before me before I bring my focus back to her beautiful face. I cup her cheeks in the palms of my hands. "When I leave today, I would like for you to be by my side." I search her eyes. "Say you will come with me."

Glory processes my words. I need for her to understand what it is I do. Who I am, and it is far better to show her my life outside of Montana — away from my life here in the States. As much as I want her in my life for good, I want to be as transparent as I can about my family and what lies below the surface of what she has seen so far. Glory deserves to choose whether she can handle the truth. She deserves to have the right to walk away if she wants.

"Okay. I'll go." She blinks up at me, her eyes falling to my lips before pressing hers to mine, giving me a passion-filled kiss. When we break away, her lips are swollen, and her breaths are heavy.

"Thank you."

"What can I say?" Glory throws her arms around my neck; her fingertips play with the short hairs at the base of my scalp. "I'm in a good mood today." Her eyes twinkle, and her lips lift in a smile.

Fuck, I would give anything always to be the reason she smiles like she is now.

"Go start a shower. I'll join you just as soon as I make arrangements for our departure." Glory steps around me. Turning, I watch her saunter across the bedroom. Once she has disappeared into the bathroom, I retrieve my phone, calling Victor.

"Sir."

"Have the plane fueled and ready. We leave for Russia soon." I go to hang up the phone, but as a thought enters my mind, I speak again. "Glory will be accompanying me on this trip. I want to take her to dinner. Call Nadia. Tell her to have a selection of gowns prepared for my woman to choose from."

"Reservations at The Tavern?"

"Yes."

"I'll make the calls."

"Thank you, Victor."

A couple of hours later, Glory is packed, and the car is pulling onto the tarmac where my private plane is ready to go. Victor climbs out and hands the keys to another man, who will take care of parking the vehicle, then retrieves the luggage from the trunk. Opening the door, I climb out. Reaching out, Glory takes hold of my hand and slides across the leather seat. My eyes land on her red high heels, before traveling up her long slim legs as she steps out. After closing the car door, I rest my hand on the small of her back and guide her toward the aircraft.

We climb the steps and enter the main cabin. "You dodged this question before, but what exactly is it that you do to afford all of this luxury you live in?" She runs her fingertips along the Italian leather seat. Sitting her handbag on the floor, she takes her seat.

Victor and Sasha enter the cabin. "I'll inform the pilot we are ready." Victor says before the two of them enter the cockpit, then close the door behind them, leaving Glory and I alone.

Before taking my place next to Glory, I reach down, pull the seatbelt across her lap, and lock the buckle. Her brow is raised when my eyes lift to her face; her look causes me to smirk.

"I'm a grown woman, Demetri. I'm quite capable of doing things for myself." She sasses, and I tighten her restraint a bit more, causing her to suck in a sharp breath.

"Keeping what's mine safe, *Krasivaya*." I kiss her forehead, then lower myself into my seat and ready myself for takeoff.

Moments later the plane taxis down the runway and we are lifting into the sky. Once in flight, and we can safely move about, I stand and make my way to the other end of the cabin to the minibar. "Would you like something to drink?" Grabbing my liquor of choice, I pour the amber liquid into a glass tumbler. "This early?" Glory questions me.

"Flying makes me tense," I admit.

"You wouldn't happen to have anything for a mimosa, would you?" she asks.

I put the top back on the glass decanter, placing the whiskey back on the shelf, and grab a bottle of chilled wine from the small wine cooler, then look inside the mini fridge, finding orange juice. With her wine glass in one hand and my whiskey in the other, I cross the space between us.

"Thank you." Glory takes the glass I hand her, and I sit in my chair.

"We have fresh pastries and fruit over there as well if you are hungry," I tell her.

"This is good for now." She takes a sip.

We sit in silence for a few moments before I speak. "You asked me earlier what it is I do to make my money." I take a drink, savoring the oak flavor as the warmth travels down my throat.

"It's none of my business. I was only thinking aloud." Glory tries to brush off her curiosity.

"I make money buying real estates; commercial real estate to be exact. My architects polish the building up; creating works of art, then sell the multimillion-dollar skyrises and properties to wealthy businessmen and women; keeping a stake in most of them. I also deal in international trade." Glory sips her wine, and I wait for her reply.

"You've done well for yourself. What kind of international trade are you involved with?" She crosses her legs, which causes the hem of the wrap dress she is wearing to rise, exposing more of her thigh.

"Weapons." I don't bother lying. Why should I? I am not going to hide who I am from her. She needs to see how things operate in my world. I need to know whether or not she can handle being with a Volkov. Glory doesn't bat an eye. Not one look of concern or judgment crosses her face.

"Guns?" she asks, and I nod.

"Amongst other artillery." I bring my glass to my lips once more, keeping my eyes trained on hers, still gauging her reaction.

"Okay. So, you're a real estate mogul and a weapons dealer." She shrugs.

"My life is much different in Russia, and I need you to understand and be prepared for that once we land. I run an empire, *Krasivaya*. The Volkov's are a powerful family. I don't want to hide anything from you." I sit my now empty glass down on the table beside me. "You also need to know this about me. Men fear me, and for a good reason. I've killed." Glory's eyes widen, but not with fear. More like my confession confirming what she may have already concluded for herself about me. "In my world, I'm referred to as the Taker of Souls."

With a calm demeanor, Glory finishes her mimosa, then sits her glass to the side. "I've always known there was more to you than what is on the surface, Demetri. You exude power. My instincts told me from the first time I saw you that you were a dangerous man." Glory slides to the edge of her seat then sinks to the floor; positioning herself on her knees in front of me. I stare down at her as she continues to speak. "I see who you are."

"And what do you see?" I run my fingers through her silky hair.

Her palms run up and down my thighs. "Someone who cares for his family." Her fingertips graze the outline of my cock. "A good man." Glory pulls the leather belt strap through the loop of my slacks and unfastens my belt buckle. Popping the waist button loose, she slides my zipper down and pulls my cock free. Her eyes lock on mine as she strokes my length a few times before taking just the tip of my hard cock in her mouth. I watch her as she takes more than half of my length into her mouth, her teeth lightly grazing my flesh as her mouth slides up my shaft. She does this for several minutes, each time her tongue brushing against the sweet spot just beneath the head of my cock and making my toes curl.

Grabbing a fist full of her hair, I watch my woman suck my cock until she makes me come undone, then finishes by swallowing my release down her throat. Giving it one last lick, she allows my cock to pop free from the warmth of her mouth.

Glory gently tucks me away, putting my attire back as if nothing ever happened, then rises on her knees, and hovers her lips a breath away from mine. "I'm yours, Demetri. Nothing will ever change that." A primal growl escapes me, and I capture her mouth with mine.

"You were made for me," I tell her between breaths as I kiss her.

A throat clearing grabs our attention. Breaking our connection, I look up to see Victor standing just outside the cockpit door. "Sir."

"Victor."

"You have a phone call."

"It can wait." I look back at my woman, her lips pouty and red.

"Yes, sir." Victor takes his leave, closing the cockpit door behind him.

I run my fingers through Glory's hair once more. "You are so bossy," Glory states.

"And it makes you wet," I remark, watching her eyes darken and her thighs clench.

"And you like my sass," she throws back at me, making me chuckle. God, she is perfect in every way. A man like me does not deserve a woman like her, but I don't give a damn. I am staking my claim on her. It's in this moment as she smiles at me, I know without a shadow of a doubt what I feel for this woman is stronger than love. What I feel for her cannot be defined. I would give Glory my last breath and not have any regret doing so; as long as I knew she would continue giving her light to the world.

"Come." I stand, bringing her with me. "It will be a long flight. Let's rest for a while." Instead of guiding her to the room located at the back of the plane, I settle us down on the sofa on the other side of the cabin, then tuck her into my side.

By the time we near landing in my country, the two of us are rested, relaxed, and hungry. "I can't believe I'm in Russia. This is insane." Glory stares out the window as we pass over the city below us, the closer we get to our destination.

"That is where my office is located." I point out the window of the plane as the city disappears amongst the clouds rolling in.

"I can't wait to see the sights. I bet it's beautiful."

"Yes. It is beautiful," I tell her.

"Do you live in the city? I've always preferred the hustle and bustle of city life vs small-town living." She looks from the window to me as I roll the sleeves of my dress shirt up to my elbows, exposing my colorful array of tattoos. "No offense to Montana or our friends and family who live there."

"Though I do have a place in the city, my family estate is located in the countryside. We should be flying over it at any moment. It is equally as beautiful."

"Holy shit." Glory continues to stare out the window. "Look at this place." I step behind her, and peer through the window and take in my home.

"Welcome to my family home." I kiss the side of her neck.

Her head whips around, shock on her face. "That castle down there is yours? You grew up in that?"

I nod. "I did. Everything — all the land you can see until it reaches the small river belongs to my family," I confirm.

"Do you have horses?" Glory's face lights up, and I smile.

"You like to ride, *Krasivaya*?"

"I haven't in a long time." She settles back against the sofa.

"Then, while we are here, I will show you the property on horseback." The pilot announces we are making our descent to land, so Glory and I secure ourselves where we are sitting and wait to land.

A car is waiting for us at my private landing field when we exit the plane then we drive ten miles to my family estate. With her hand resting on my thigh, I watch as Glory takes in her surroundings as we ride. "In many ways, it looks like Montana." I nod, agreeing with her, but she doesn't notice. She is too busy taking it all in as we travel down the long road leading to my estate.

When the car rolls to a stop, I open the door, climb out, and wait for my woman to join me. Without speaking, I take her by the hand and lead her inside. The moment we enter the foyer, one of my men, Luca, appears in the doorway leading to my office.

"Sir, there is a situation."

By the tone in his voice and look on his face, this is something I shouldn't ignore. I turn, facing Glory. "I need to take care of a little business before dinner. Victor will show you to my suite. You'll find everything you need to freshen up. In the closet, you will also find a selection of evening gowns." I brush the hair from her face. "I'm taking you to the city," I inform her.

"Are you trying to show me off?" She presses her body against mine.

"Take your time getting ready." I rub her arm as I lean in to kiss her lips. Standing to the side, Victor waits for Glory to join him. I wait until she is up the stairs and no longer in sight before stepping into my office. "What is it that requires my attention?"

"We have one of the men we believe was involved with the disappearance of the merchandise the other day."

"And where is he now?" Opening the humidor sitting on top of my desk, I retrieve a cigar.

"Holding cell down at the shipyard," Luca informs me as I snip the tip of the cigar off, then strike a lighter as I bring it to my lips and take a toke.

"As you can see, I have company. Let the men know I want to speak with this trash myself. He's not to be touched until then."

Walking over to the window, I stare at the river in the distance as the sun starts to disappear. "Keep me informed."

"Yes, sir," Luca declares before walking out of the room.

"May I speak freely?" I turn when I hear Victor speak. He may work for me, but Victor is a friend and a loyal man. His speaking freely, with honesty is something I've come to allow within reason.

"What's on your mind, Victor?"

"Do you think it was smart bringing her here?" he asks.

"Glory needs to know who I am, my friend. She needs to see it."

"You have many enemies in Russia."

I take another toke from the cigar. The white smoke billows around my head as I exhale. He's right. Many men wish me dead, but none of them dare try to harm my family, and Glory is my family. "We need to be vigilant, Victor." I snub my cigar out in the ashtray. "I want all the men to be alert and extra security detail on my woman at all times. She doesn't step one foot outside alone. Understood?"

"Yes, sir." Victor's demeanor shifts from a friend to a professional.

"Have a drink with me, Victor, before I freshen up for dinner." I clasp his shoulder on my way to the liquor bar behind him. Pouring us a drink, I carry my glass across the room where I sit in silence. Lifting the glass to my lips, I take a sip and think about the situation at hand. Someone has stolen from me and killed one of my men. *Does this theft have any connections to my ex-associate Gulin, and his side dealings with the Petrovs'.* I stare at the amber fluid in my glass before pushing my thoughts to the side. My thoughts shift to Glory. Keeping her safe while we are here in my homeland is my main concern. I won't let any harm come to her; anyone who tries will meet an early death.

A short while later, I'm dressed in a black tailored suit, with a blood-red rose in my hand. I wait at the bottom of the winding staircase for my woman to join me. I stop breathing the moment

Glory ascends the stairs, her curves hugged in all the right places by a crimson red gown with a plunging neckline. Once again, I can't take my eyes off her.

"I take it by the lack of words you like what you see?" Glory twirls.

"You are stunning, *Krasivaya.*" I run the rose petals across her cheek, down the soft curve of her neck, then drag the rose between her breasts. Glory glances at several of my men standing in the room.

"What's with the extra muscle?"

"I take your safety very seriously. They'll be our escorts tonight."

With a gleam in her eyes, my woman places her palm on my chest as she leans in, bringing her lips near my ear. The smell of her perfume fills my senses. "I have a secret," she whispers; her warm breath grazing my skin causes my cock to stir.

"Tell me," I demand, pulling her body flush with mine, not giving a damn that my men are watching our exchange.

She licks at my earlobe. "I'm not wearing anything underneath this dress." Glory teases me, and my fingers flex against the small of her back. The little vixen knows the thought of her pussy being bare will consume my thoughts. Looking around the room, I notice my men's eyes dropping to the floor, acting as if they didn't hear Glory's dirty secret.

"I'm going to redden that sweet ass of yours later," I warn her. She looks at me, her eyes filled with lust. "Promise?"

10

GLORY

As I walk into the restaurant with Demetri's hand resting firmly on the small of my back, I choose to ignore the attention we gain from several of the patrons followed by murmured voices and accusing stares. These people know who Demetri is and it's me they are curious about. Two seconds after stepping through the doors, we're greeted by a middle-aged man wearing a dark gray suit. Adjusting his cufflinks, he steps up to us. "Mr. Volkov, Miss Keller, it's a pleasure to have you dine with us tonight," he greets in a deep Russian accent offering Demetri his hand.

"Thank you, Maksim. I trust my usual table is ready?"

"Of course, Sir, but I would like to inform you the Solov's are in the house tonight." I notice Demetri's body lock up at the mention of the name, but his face remains impassive. Without saying a word, he gives Victor and Sasha a look. Both men nod and make their way to the bar while Demetri and I follow Maksim as he leads us to our table. "Your waiter will be right with you," Maksim says as we take our seats.

Once we are left alone, I ask, "is everything okay? You got pretty tense back there."

"Everything is fine. Maksim informed me that my ex-wife and her family are dining here tonight."

"Should we leave?"

Demetri lifts a brow. "This is my city, Glory. I bow down to no one."

A moment later, we are interrupted by the waiter. He offers me a polite smile before he begins speaking to Demetri in Russian. I don't bother looking over the menu since it's in a different language and allow Demetri to order for me. "*Spasibo.*" Demetri thanks the waiter, handing the menu back to him. He then proceeds to pick up the bottle of wine sitting on the table and pours the red liquid into the empty glasses sitting in front of us. Picking it up, I bring the glass to my lips to take my first sip when a man steps up to mine and Demetri's table. The guy is not very tall standing at maybe five foot seven inches. He has broad shoulders and a round belly. He has thinning gray hair and looks to be in his late sixties. His cold dark eyes don't waiver from Demetri. Not once does he acknowledge my presence. Out of the corner of my eye, I spot Victor and Sasha stand from the bar and appear at Demetri's side in a flash. I remain rooted in my seat while studying the man who has so brazenly interrupted mine and Demetri's date. And given Sasha and Victor's demeanor, I'd say the guy's company is not welcome.

"I'd like a word with you, Volkov," the man spits his demand.

Taking a sip of his wine, then giving him a bored look, Demetri replies. "As you can see, Artem, I am in the middle of having dinner. So, if you will excuse us." The man addressed as Artem clenches his fist at his sides and his face turns red. He doesn't like the fact that he was dismissed.

"Have you forgotten who you're talking to Volkov?" Artem spits, and Demetri's eyes that were on me pan toward Artem. A dark look crosses over his face; one I haven't seen before.

"I know exactly who the hell I am speaking to. It is you who needs reminding." At Demetri's harsh warning, both Sasha and Victor have drawn their weapons and are holding them down at their sides. Artem takes notice of the threat then cuts his eyes over his shoulder toward the entrance of the restaurant. I follow his line of sight to see another one of Demetri's men, Luca. It's then I also notice the owner looking on with worry but making no move to interrupt. Knowing the odds are not in his favor, Artem gives Demetri one last menacing look before walking away.

"What was that about?" I hedge the same moment our waiter returns, placing our meal in front of us. I politely thank him then take in the food Demetri has chosen for me. I don't know what it is, but it smells delicious.

"It's Borscht," Demetri tells me.

Picking up my spoon, I bring the first bite of the ruby colored soup to my mouth. *Oh my God, that's good.*

"I take it you like?" Demetri grins when a moan escapes my mouth on the second bite. Swallowing it down, I wipe my lips with a napkin. "Yes. Very good. Thank you." Satisfied with my response, Demetri goes on to answer the question I asked a minute ago. "Artem is my former father-in-law."

"Ah," I nod while glancing around the dining room. Knowing his ex-wife is here is driving me nuts. The nosy bitch in me wants to size her up. I'd be lying if I said I wasn't curious about the woman Demetri was once married to. The way Demetri has described her she sounds like a real peach. When I bring my attention back to Demetri, he has a knowing look on his face. "Their table is on the other side of the restaurant."

"Whose?" I feign innocence, and he shakes his head.

"Whatever," I roll my eyes. "Can you blame me for wanting to get a glimpse at your ex? As a woman, I can't help myself. We're curious creatures by nature. We are talking about the woman you were married to. I have this overwhelming need to size her up and see all the ways you traded up."

"You have no shame, do you *Krasivaya*?" Demetri chuckles.

"Hell no. I'm just saying what most women and even men think but don't have the balls to admit. Don't sit there and act like if my ex was sitting in the same room, you wouldn't be thinking or doing the same as me."

"Excuse me, Sir," Victor interrupts. "You have a call."

"I told you no interruptions, Victor."

"It's urgent, boss," Victor insists.

Placing my napkin on the table, I stand. "It's okay, Demetri. I need to use the ladies' room anyway. Take your call."

Demetri stands and signals for Sasha, who swiftly makes his way toward us. "Glory needs to use the ladies' room."

Plucking my clutch from the table, I make my way to the restroom with Sasha trailing behind. As we pass the bar and step into the adjacent dining room, the hairs on the back of my neck stand on end, and I get the uneasy feeling of having someone's eyes on me. Cutting my eyes around the room, my gaze connects with the cold black orbs of Artem as he tracks my every move. Noticing the gained attention, Sasha moves directly to my left, blocking Artem's view of me. I give him a small nod with a look of gratitude because Artem gives me the chills. I briefly wonder where Ivanna is. The only woman I notice at his table is definitely too old to be her, so I'm assuming the lady must be Artem's wife.

Pushing those thoughts away, I continue to the bathroom.

"I'll wait here for you, Miss Keller," Sasha informs.

Walking into the bathroom, I go about taking care of business. When I step out of the stall, I'm met by a blonde woman in a black dress, standing in front of the mirror, applying lip gloss. After washing my hands, I take the tube of red lipstick from my clutch and begin applying it to my lips. The whole time tension hangs in the air between the blonde woman and me.

A second later, she is the first to speak. "Are you enjoying your dinner with my husband?" she asks, not taking her accusing eyes off my reflection in the mirror. It suddenly occurs to me; this is Ivanna. My movement doesn't falter as I lift a brow and continue with my task as I take in the very woman I have been curious about for too long. Ivanna is my complete opposite in every way. She has her blonde hair pulled back in a tight bun at the nape of her neck, while my long auburn hair hangs in curls down my back. The woman in front of me has the body of an adolescent, and I have an abundance of curves. Curves that are on full display with the dress I am wearing. With one last swipe to my bottom lip, I place the top back on the lipstick tube and put it back in my clutch. Smiling at Ivanna in the mirror, I don't bother correcting her use of the term husband.

"I'm having a wonderful time with Demetri. Thank you for asking."

"I wouldn't get too comfortable being on Demetri's arm if I were you. He'll come to his senses soon enough, and I'll be back at his side, just as things should be."

"Keep telling yourself that lady." I shake my head.

Ivanna cackles at my last statement; the noise is like nails on a chalkboard. *Jesus Christ. Demetri was a saint to have been married to this woman.*

"Stupid American woman. You have no clue the way mine and Demetri's world works. Do you think you're the first whore my husband has kept? You think this is his first indiscretion while we have been married?"

Lifting my hand, I cut Ivanna off. "You can save your breath for someone who wants to listen to your bullshit. First of all, you and Demetri are no longer married, so what we are doing is not cheating. Besides, I don't blame any man who has the misfortune of being married to you and keeps a woman on the side. Jesus Christ, your voice alone will drive anyone to drink. Second, your little name-calling and intimidation tactics won't work on me, honey." Ivanna's eyes flash at my bold statement. If the woman was looking for a weakling, she's barking up the wrong tree.

Before either of us can say another word, the bathroom door bursts open, and Sasha takes in the scene with a concerned look on his face. His eyes land on me first. He looks me over making sure I'm okay before he turns his attention to Ivanna. His features change from one of concern to one of cold indifference. "Miss Keller, are you ready?"

"Yup. I'm finished here." Without giving Ivanna a second thought, I turn and walk out of the bathroom. Instead of being led back to the table, Sasha ushers me outside where Demetri and Victor are waiting for us next to the car.

"I'm sorry, but dinner has to be cut short," Demetri informs me, and I give him a sweet smile, but when he glances over my shoulder at Sasha, his jaw clenches. I know the look on Sasha's face is a telling one. "What happened?"

"I found Ivanna in the bathroom with Miss Keller," Sasha says, and Demetri's eye snaps from Sasha to me then back to Sasha. I'm about to jump in and explain to Demetri I'm fine and Ivanna accosting me was not Sasha's fault when Demetri opens the back door to the car.

"Get in."

I narrow my eyes, but ultimately decide I'm not in the mood to argue and I slide into the backseat. Once the door shuts, I watch as Demetri and Sasha exchange words. When they've finished, Demetri climbs in beside me the same moment Victor and Sasha climb into the front. Victor pulls the car out into traffic while Demetri retrieves his phone from the inside of his suit jacket. Tapping the screen, he brings the phone to his ear. I listen to him as he speaks in a clipped tone to someone in Russian then hangs up. I let out a heavy sigh. "It's not Sasha's fault your ex stopped me. She was already in the bathroom when I got there. He didn't know."

"It is not your job to defend Sasha, Glory," Demetri says in a bitter tone. "It is, however, his job to protect you. Had he done his job right; he would have checked the bathroom before you went in." Demetri levels me with a hard look. "Sasha fucked up, and he knows it."

Knowing this is one argument I'm not going to win; I drop the subject.

11

DEMETRI

After several moments lost in thought, my attention lands on Glory who out of character sits in silence, carefully observing my demeanor. Keeping my eyes trained on hers, she sighs, then finally speaks. "Talk to me, Demetri. I can hardly believe this tense atmosphere is all due to your ex and our little run-in." The mention of Ivanna causes my jaw to clench. The incident should never have happened in the first place, but Glory's observation is correct; my ex at the moment is far from being the reason we had to leave dinner so abruptly.

Glory reaches out; her fingertips caress; lightly massaging the nape of my neck. Her touch temporarily relaxes the tension in my body, and my shoulders sag.

"Though my ex and her disrespect have left a bad taste in my mouth, it is not the reason for cutting our evening short," I begin. "A package was delivered moments before your unpleasant encounter with Ivanna." A vision of the items contained in the black box distracts my train of thought for a moment. Inside laid a single red rose; next to it, a picture of Glory, and a small note that read *we know your weakness*. My face heats with anger. Victor was right to question Glory's presence in Russia. Someone has made it clear they are out for blood. My blood, and The Volkov Empire.

The only way to ensure my woman's safety is to send her home. "I'm sending you home," I inform her.

Her eyes widen. "What?" She drops her hand to her lap. "We just got here. Look, Ivanna is harmless, I can assure you. She's merely trying to intimidate me, but her efforts don't faze me, Demetri. I hardly think a woman scorned warrants my quick departure." Folding her arms under her breasts, Glory becomes irritated. "Sending me away sends her a clear message that she succeeded in what she was trying to accomplish." Glory lifts her chin. "Ivanna doesn't scare me. I can and will hold my own against a jealous woman who wants nothing more than to sink her claws into my man."

Despite the circumstances, I smirk. "Your man?" I lift a brow.

She rolls her eyes. "Give me the truth, Demetri." Glory softens her tone.

"Something has happened that requires my full attention." I try being vague, but my words only cause Glory to become irritated.

She huffs in frustration. "I see. So, just like that, I've become a distraction?"

"No," I bark, a little harsher than intended. Hurt flickers in Glory's eyes before she quickly hides behind a mask of anger. I softened my tone. "Baby, you are not a distraction." Glory chooses not to respond. Instead, turning her face from me, she stares out the window. Opting not to make the already tense situation worse, I give her the space she needs.

Instead of turning toward home, the car takes a sharp turn in the opposite direction we came, taking an alternative route to ensure we are not followed.

"What happened back there?" Glory breaks her silence. "Give me something, Demetri. Is this about the package you mentioned?"

"It is," I confirm.

The car slowly rolls to a stop. Outside, a few yards away, several of my armed men wait as instructed at the gates to The Volkov estate. The partition separating us from the driver rolls down. Victor speaks from the front seat. "Sir, the plane is ready to depart," he informs me as he drives us down the driveway.

"Thank you, Victor. Give us a moment."

"Yes, Sir." The privacy window closes, and I turn, fully facing Glory. "I'm sorry we don't have much time. I can't tell you much, but I will give you this; in the package I received was a threat."

Her forehead creases in confusion. "That's all you are going to give me?" She waits for me to elaborate, but I don't offer any more information. "What happened to being transparent. Wanting to tell me everything. Share who you are with me?" She uses my words against me, and it stings.

"I'm sorry, *Krasivaya*. For now, all you need to know is that you are not safe here."

Glory shakes her head. "None of this is making any sense right now. We just got here."

"I have just as many enemies as allies, Glory. Those enemies are always watching, looking for weaknesses in my empire and my defense. Someone has made it clear they know you mean something to me and would use you to get to me." I let my words sink in.

Her shoulders sag. "Fine," she says her voice filled with sadness. I sense she wants to say more but holds back.

"Once you've changed into something more comfortable, Sasha, along with a couple more of my men will be accompanying you on your flight." Glory huffs.

"*Krasivaya*," I take her hand. "Understand that I'm doing this to protect you. If something were to happen—" I let my words stop there. The thought alone causes my stomach to knot.

"I get it. I don't like it, but I get it."

With her hand still in mine, I lead her from the car and walk her inside. "I need to make another call." Pulling her into me, I kiss her lips. "Take your time." Without speaking, Glory gives me a weak smile. Holding onto my bicep, she slips her heels off before making her way up the stairs.

The instant Glory is out of sight, I pull my phone from the inside pocket of my suit and place a call to Jake.

"What's happenin', brother?"

"I need a favor," I reply. "I'm getting ready to put Glory on a plan to Polson."

"You have my attention." Jake's tone lets me know he senses something isn't right.

"A clear intent to harm her was made tonight by an unknown source. She isn't safe."

"And Chicago?" Jake asks, fishing for more intel.

"She wouldn't be safe in Chicago either. Someone knows who she is, which we can assume they possibly know where she lives as well. She's safer surrounded by you and your men, and with the comfort of her best friend."

Silence hangs between us briefly before Jake asks his next question; one I knew he would get around to asking soon enough.

"You claimin' her?" I can hear the smile in his tone.

"I claimed her the moment I laid eyes on her two years ago," I confess to a man I consider to be a friend.

He chuckles. "About damn time."

"I have some business to take care of," I tell Jake. "I'll be in touch. One of my bodyguards, Sasha, along with two other men, are going with Glory. I hope you can provide them with a place to stay?"

"You got it."

"Thank you," I tell him just as Glory reappears.

"Anytime, brother." Jake hangs up.

"I know this makes me sound like one of those clingy bitches, but will you be returning to Chicago after you sort out your business here?" Glory stops in front of me.

She is not going to like the next words I have to say. "I won't be joining you in Chicago." Her face falls. "I'm sending you to stay with Grace in Polson."

Her hand flies in the air between us. "Hold up. Polson?"

"Yes. I've already called and talked with Jake. He and the rest of The Kings are expecting you." Sasha walks down the stairs and out the front door with Glory's suitcase in his hand. "Ready?"

"Do I have a choice in the matter?"

"No," I tell her.

"Then why even ask? You're doing a bang-up job making all my decisions for me." Glory storms out the door into the chill of the night.

Victor steps beside me. "She is a feisty woman."

"That she is."

Fifteen minutes later, we are at the tarmac. We sit unmoving as the car idles in place. Seeming to have calmed down since leaving the house, Glory lifts her hand, cupping my cheek. "You think this threat is serious enough for you to send me to Montana; surrounded by a bunch of sexy bikers?" I sense my woman is trying to get a rise out of me.

"Everyone knows you are mine, *Krasivaya*." I bring her palm to my lips, kissing it. "Let's go."

Opening the door, we exit the car. I tug on Glory's arm as we stop at the steps that lead up to the plane and pull her close.

"Trust me?"

"I do."

"Good." I kiss her long and hard, leaving both of us breathless by the time we break our connection. "I'll be back for you."

"You'd better." Glory gives my lips one last kiss before walking up the steps and into the plane. Sasha is the last to board. Stepping back, I wait by the car, watching the plane taxi down the runway. I don't move until they disappear amongst the gray clouds in the night sky.

"Any word?" I ask Victor who stands beside the car, smoking a cigarette.

"Nothing."

"Take me to the shipyard." I pull the car door open.

Victor flicks what's left of his cigarette to the ground, snubbing it out with the toe of his shoe. "You think this guy may know something?"

"We'll find out soon enough. Let's go," I order.

Loose gravel crunches beneath the tires as we enter the furthest end of the shipping yard, just near the river, stopping a few yards in front of three cargo containers. Climbing out of the car, I walk toward the middle container where one of my men is standing. With a nod, he opens the heavy door.

An amber glow is cast inside of the nine by forty-foot cube from a small bulb hanging from the roof. Seated in a chair up against the wall, his hands, and feet bound together is the man accused of stealing from me. Per my request, he hasn't been touched. His eyes are trained on me as I drag a chair across the floor. Spinning it around, I straddle the seat. Reaching into the pocket of my suit, I pull out a pack of cigarettes, shake one from the package, then offer our guest one. Sweat beads on his forehead and slides down the sides of his face as he shakes his head. Victor leans in, striking a lighter. I take a few tokes until the end of the cigarette burns a bright red. Propping my arms on the back of the chair, I take a long drag. "Who's your boss?" I ask him as smoke plumes between us.

"Fuck you." He spits at my feet. "You will kill me anyway, so I'm not telling you shit."

I continue to smoke my cigarette. "True. I will kill you." I snub my cigarette out on the back of his bound hand, causing him to flinch in pain.

"Then do it already, motherfucker."

Standing, I remove my jacket, laying it across the seat of the chair, then begin to roll up my shirt sleeves. One thing that separates me from other Bratva is that I like to get my hands dirty. Lead by example. My men don't respect me for my title alone. My men respect me because I don't hide behind them; I stand with them. They shed blood in the Volkov name because I fight beside them in war. "String him up," I order.

Dragging him a few feet, they cut the tape wrapped around his wrist. Lifting his arms above his head, they shackle him to the chains hanging from a pulley welded to the ceiling. Unbinding his feet, they spread his legs, binding his ankles to the floor. Pulling on the winch lever, fastened to the other end of the chain, Victor hoists the man until the shackles on his ankles become taut.

I circle the man. "Do what you want. I won't break," he spews. His face twists in pain as Victor pulls the handle down on the wench, stretching the guy's limbs to the point of dislocation.

"We're just getting started." Walking beside a table, I pick up a pair of pliers. With a brief look, one of my other men rips the shirt from the man's torso, exposing his flesh. "I see you've done some time?" I take in his various prison tattoos. Using the pliers, I grasp some flesh on his chest. "Who do you work for?"

"Go to hell," he growls, and I rip a piece of his skin from his body, and he cries out in pain. "Someone stole from me." I pace back and forth in front of him. "Someone is trying to get their filthy hands in my business." I stop directly in front of him. "You know anything about that?" I repeat the process with the pliers.

"Ahh! Fuck you!" he screams through clenched teeth.

Each time I ask him the same question I receive the same fuck you cry of agony. Tossing the pliers onto the table, I pick up a battery pack. Lifting the drill from the table as well, I snap the powerpack on. The sound of the drill head spinning as I press the trigger causes the man to thrash his body back and forth as he hangs, suspended in the air. I walk up to him. "Give me answers, and I'll make your death swift," I warn him as I press the tip of the drill bit against his knee cap.

"I don't know shit." Spit flies from his mouth, and blood from one of his wounds drips onto my dress shoe.

"This will probably hurt." I give him no time to react. Pressing the trigger, I drive the drill straight into his kneecap, watching as the long spiral rod exits through the backside. He writhes in pain as I put the drill in reverse. I then move to his other knee.

His face pales. "Wait — wait — wait," he pleads. "I don't know the guy's name — I swear. We never met in person. He left payment for my services at a drop point, along with an address to deliver the goods." He mutters the address to a storage facility on the other side of town, and Luca takes the information down. "That's all I know, man. I work for no one." His face twists in pain.

"Please. I beg you to give me a second chance."

All thieves ask for a second chance when death waits for them. His plea means nothing to me. "Kill him." Without pause, Victor pulls his weapon, places the barrel against the back of the man's head, and pulls the trigger.

12

GLORY

Sasha and I landed back in Polson fifteen minutes ago. Demetri and Victor stayed behind in Russia, but Demetri assured me he wouldn't be gone long. I knew him sending me away had something to do with the phone call he received at dinner. I'm surprised when I pressed for information he was pretty forthcoming. Now, we are currently driving through town and have just passed Grace's bakery, The Cookie Jar. We also drive past the turnoff to Demetri's house. Looking over at Sasha, I ask, "where are we going? You missed our turn."

Not taking his eyes off the road, Sasha answers my question. "I have been instructed to take you straight to The Kings' compound."

"Oh. I forgot," is my reply. Demetri wanting me to stay at the clubhouse means whatever threat he received is serious. Twisting in the passenger seat, I regard Sasha. "Will you be staying at the clubhouse too?"

He nods. "I stay where you stay."

"Hmm," I hum. "And what about the other two men who came with us. Are they staying at the clubhouse too?"

"Yes," Sasha answers but says nothing else.

"You're not much of a conversationalist, are you?" All I get is a grunt in reply.

As we turn onto the dirt road that leads to the clubhouse, I peer down at my watch and note it's near lunchtime. The clubhouse will be buzzing with activity by now. When I called Grace last night from the plane, she told me Jake had already informed her I was on my way back to Montana. As Sasha pulls the car through the gate of the compound, I take in my best friend who is standing just outside the door with my Goddaughter Ellie Kate on her hip. My heart warms at the huge smile directed toward me.

Jumping out of the car, I return a smile of my own while holding out my arms. Ellie Kate squeals as she catapults herself from her mother's arms into mine. "How's my sweet girl doing?" I coo, nuzzling her close and breathing in the smell of her baby shampoo. "Where's Remi?" I ask.

"She had a sleepover at a friend's house last night. She'll be home in a few hours," Grace informs me. It's also then the door to the clubhouse opens, and Jake steps out.

"How ya doin', sweetheart?"

"I'm doing okay, Jake."

Jake smiles then turns his attention to my bodyguard, who is standing to my left.

Sasha offers a hand. "Mr. Delane."

Jake accepts his offered hand and gives him a chin lift. "You can call me Jake." Jerking his head toward the door, Jake says, "Let's head inside. I want to speak to you in my office." Scrunching my forehead, I look to Grace. She merely shrugs her shoulders as I pass Ellie back to her and follow Jake to his office with Sasha trailing behind.

The three of us step into his office. Jake settles in behind his desk as I take a seat in front of him, while Sasha stands back by the door. Reaching into the pocket of his cut, Jake pulls out a cigarette, lights it then tosses the lighter to the desk before he speaks. "As you know by now, you'll be staying here at the clubhouse until Demetri arrives."

"Did he tell you details?" I ask.

Jake takes a drag from his cigarette. "He did."

I sigh. "I assume you're not going to tell me what he told you? You know, so we can compare notes," I ask. Even though Demetri told me the gist of what is going on, I have a feeling there is more.

"It's not my place, Glory. The only thing I can tell you is Demetri called me asking for a favor; for the club to keep you safe."

"Am I on lockdown?"

Jake shakes his head. "You're not on lockdown, but if you leave the compound, you are to take Sasha and one of my guys with you."

"Okay," I agree.

Jake squints his eyes and levels me with an accusing look.

"Okay?"

I raise my brow and shrug. "Yeah, Jake, okay. I won't go anywhere without Sasha or one of the guys."

Jake continues to eye me skeptically. "That's it? You're not going to fight me on this or run your mouth?" he smirks.

"If I had a set of balls, this is where I'd tell you to stop busting them. I'm not always a pain in the ass," I scoff, rolling my eyes. Even Sasha has a hard time holding back a snicker at my comment, and I snap my head in his direction. He schools his features rather quickly when I glare at him. Sasha is a bit uptight. I didn't think he had it in him to even smile. "I'm not always difficult," I jest. Jake tips his head back and lets out a roar of laughter.

"Not difficult?" He shakes his head. "I believe difficult is your middle name, Glory. It looks like Demetri was finally able to tame you."

"Ha, ha. Very funny. For the record, I can't be tamed, but a good dicking will mellow me out." A choking noise comes from behind me, but Jake is unfazed by my inappropriate confession. He's used to my mouth by now. "Are we done here? Grace mentioned something about margaritas and tacos when we talked last night, and I'm ready to throw down after the last forty-eight hours I've had."

Jake grins. "Yeah, sweetheart. We're done. The girls are waitin' for ya out back." Just as I am about to exit his office, Jake calls out.

"Glory?"

I look over my shoulder. "Yeah?"

"I didn't get a chance to tell ya the other night, but we've missed havin' your crazy ass here; Grace, especially."

My expression softens. "I miss being here too." I look down at my feet for a moment, then back up. "I just might have to do something about that."

Before going back to see the girls, I head upstairs to the room I usually stay in when I visit. As expected, I open the door to see my suitcase and purse sitting on the bed. Walking over to the bed, I rummage through my bag until I find my cell. Tapping the screen, I place a call to Demetri. I talked to him a few hours ago, but I can't help wanting to hear his voice again.

"Glory." He answers on the second ring.

"Hi," is all I say as I sit on the edge of the bed.

"What's wrong, *Krasivaya*?"

"Nothing. We just made it to the clubhouse, and I wanted to hear your voice is all. You must be busy though, so I'll let you go."

"I'm never too busy for you, Glory. Even if it's for you to hear my voice."

I close my eyes and let out a deep breath. "Okay."

"Everything will be fine, baby. I'll call you tonight before you go to bed. Try and have some fun with the girls. I'm sure they already have something planned."

"They do." I chuckle. "I'll talk to you tonight."

"Tonight, *Krasivaya*," Demetri promises, and we hang up. I don't want to be the clingy girlfriend who's always looking for reassurance, but with Demetri, I find not doing so is difficult. It took us forever to get to this place. I think for Demetri, part of it was because of the world he lives in. I think he's kept me at arm's length because he didn't want to put me in harm's way. Now with everything that has happened over the last twenty-four hours, I fear he will change his mind about wanting to be with me. That he is afraid his world will somehow bring me harm. The way he sent me away so abruptly has put me on edge. It's making me think Demetri is having doubts; that I am not strong enough to be at his side. Those are the only two scenarios I can come up with. I hope Demetri will let me prove I can be the woman he needs; the kind of woman who is strong enough to handle whatever life throws our way. He and I have wasted too much time, and I am willing to fight for us if he is willing to do the same. I have never entirely given myself to a man the way I have Demetri. He was somehow able to break through my walls, and it allowed me to bare my soul to him. I have made it through some of the most horrific experiences life can throw at me, but Demetri letting me go is one I know I won't survive.

Shaking those thoughts away, I scold myself. "Demetri wouldn't give up on you, Glory. He is not having second thoughts." Saying those words out loud makes me realize how crazy I sound. Demetri Volkov is not the kind of man who gives up what he wants, and I know he wants me. I have to stop letting my insecurities get the better of me. Standing from the bed, I go to toss my phone back in my purse when it rings. Demetri's name flashes across the screen. *I wonder what's up. We just spoke a few minutes ago.* "Hello," I answer.

"You have nothing to worry about, *Krasivaya*."

Seven words. All it takes is for me to hear those seven words from Demetri's mouth, to put my mind and my heart at ease. I take a shuttered breath and try to control the crack in my voice but fail. "How do you do that, Demetri? How did you know what I needed to hear?"

"You already know the answer to that question, Glory. Now, let me hear you say it."

Allowing my vulnerability to show through is no easy task. Closing my eyes, I take a deep breath. "I'm your woman, and you'll always give me what I need."

"Good girl," Demetri's smooth voice rumbles through the phone. "Now go have fun with your friends, and I'll call you tonight." Demetri and I end our call a second time only this time I feel lighter. Doing what he said, I go see my girls.

Standing at the back patio door, I stare through the glass at my best friend who is sitting on a lounge chair laughing at something Bella said. Seeing Grace full of happiness and living her best life fills my heart with so much joy. The woman in front of me doesn't look like the same woman from two years ago. Two years ago, Grace was someone who was broken down and lost. I thank God every day for bringing Jake and The Kings into her life. And with The Kings came Demetri. A shiver runs down my spine, and I smile at the memory of the first time I met him after my attack; more specifically the memory of how he used to come into my room here at the clubhouse and watch me sleep after I was released from the hospital. Some might say what he did was creepy given we didn't know each other, but for some reason, I found his presence comforting. For two years, Demetri has been my protector. He is the reason I feel safe.

"Hey, you," Grace says, sliding the door open, bringing me back to the present. "What took you so long? There's a margarita with your name on it just sitting here."

I wave my hand as I step outside. "You know how your man is. He had to lay down the rules."

"He's just looking out for you." Grace's voice softens.

I pull my friend in for a hug. "I know he is. I'm trying to make light of the situation is all."

"Yeah, I know." Grace pokes me in the ribs. "Always a pain in the ass."

"I do try," I affirm, causing Grace and the rest of the women to giggle. Picking up a glass filled with frozen margarita off the table in front of me, I take a sip and moan. "I see you all left Bella in charge of the alcohol," I say smacking my lips. "Girl, you know how to do it right." I take a seat in a chair next to Grace and peer around my circle of friends. Grace, Bella, Alba, Mila, Emerson, and Sofia. "I sure do miss you bitches."

They all smile. "We miss you too, Glory," Bella replies.

Over the next several hours, the seven of us consume a copious amount of alcohol along with the tacos Bella made. Day has quickly turned into night, but us ladies are no closer to winding down. Jake came out thirty minutes ago to start a fire but quickly retreated back inside when our conversation turned to sex and the mention of Quinn's cock piercing. He muttered something about not needing to hear about his brother's dick and how us women are worse than men before he high tailed his butt into the clubhouse. It's true. Us women are worse than men when talking about sex.

"Okay, Glory. It's time to give us all the juicy details," Emerson jumps in. "You were very vague the last time you were here."

"Um, I can do without the details," Bella fake shutters. "Demetri is my father-in-law, so it's kind of weird."

"Well, you'll just have to plug your ears, because the rest of us want to know." This is coming from Mila. "I've heard it's the silent men who are all dominating and wild in bed." Mila turns to Alba and waggles her eyebrows. "Am I right, Alba?" Alba blushes with embarrassment and tries to hide her face. Alba is the soft-spoken, shy one of the bunch and married to Gabriel.

Taking a sip of my drink, I cock my head to the side and try to come up with the best words to describe Demetri. "Demetri is..." I pause. "He's intense."

"Intense?" Grace scoffs. "That's all we're going to get. He's intense?"

"And perfect. Demetri is perfect for me in every way. He is caring yet dominating. He pushes me out of my comfort zone because he knows that's what I need. He forces me to bare myself to him and show all the ugly hiding behind the facade. He loves me unconditionally and comforts me even when I didn't know he was doing it. And most of all, he makes me feel safe. With Demetri, I can be myself. With him, there is no hiding. With him, I am free. *That* is the kind of man Demetri is."

By the time I finished my spiel, I have six sets of eyes staring at me. Grace is the first to speak. "Do you feel like you can't be yourself with us; with me?" Her voice sounds hurt.

I set my glass down on the table and turn to my best friend. "I wanted to," I tell her honestly. "I wanted to come to you so many times in the past couple of years and tell you the truth, but I couldn't. You're finally happy. You have the life you deserve, Grace. I knew that if I told you the truth, you would have blamed yourself." I shake my head. "If anyone in this world deserves to be happy, it's you. There is no way I was going to take that away. Not after the hell you endured." I try to choke back my tears but fail.

Grace lets her tears fall as she looks at me with confusion.

"What truth, Glory? What have you been keeping from me?"

It's in this moment I know, I can no longer keep my secret. The secret I have only shared with Demetri — the nightmare that has haunted my dreams for two years. "Ronan," I choke out through my tears.

"Ronan, what? What happened, Glory?"

"The day he found me. The day he came looking for you and found me." I take a deep breath as I try to muster the courage to say these next words. "He didn't just beat me."

"Glory, no," Grace cries and covers her mouth with her hand.

"Ronan raped me, Grace." Collective gasps come from the other women, but I keep my focus on Grace.

"Oh, God. What have I done?" Grace covers her face with her hands and begins to rock back and forth in her chair. She is doing what I knew she would; she is blaming herself.

I'm about to go to her when Grace springs from her seat and drops to her knees in front of me. "I understand now. I understand why you didn't want to stay here. If you had stayed, then looking at me would be a constant reminder of what he did to you. I'm sorry, Glory," she sobs. "I'm sorry I made you sacrifice so much for me. If it hadn't been for me, that monster would have never put his hands on you."

I slide out of my chair and to the ground in front of the woman who has been like a sister to me for more years than I can count and take her hands in mine. "I helped you and Remi because I love you and I know you would have done the same for me. Ronan raping me was not your fault. It's not my fault either. I was wrong for keeping something like that from you, but I don't regret doing it. I meant it when I said you didn't deserve to carry the burden of my rape, Grace. Me telling you now is not for you, it's for me. Demetri has taught me it is time for me to stop hiding. It is time to show my truth. And he was right. For the first time in two years, I feel lighter. I feel like a weight has been lifted. I no longer feel chained down by what Ronan did to me." I pause for a second to allow my words to sink in before I speak again. "I don't want your guilt. I only want my best friend. I want your support and to know I no longer have to be afraid to confide in you."

"Always. I want you to always come to me, Glory. For anything," Grace sniffles. "No more secrets. Promise me, no matter how bad; you won't keep anything like that from me again."

"I promise, Grace. No more secrets."

By the time Grace and I are done holding each other, and our tears have dried, I look over my shoulder, remembering we have an audience. The girls have kept quiet through the whole exchange, aside from the soft sound of their sorrow. When I glance behind me, I notice mine and Grace's breakthrough has drawn the attention of their men. Standing in the yard is Jake, Logan, Reid, Gabriel, Quinn, and Sam. Judging by the looks on their faces, I know if Ronan were still alive today, these men would bring an abundance of torture down on that monster. As I sit here on the cold, damp ground with my best friend, I surprisingly don't feel any shame or embarrassment. These people, after all, are my family. There is no pity in their eyes as they look at me — only love, support, and loyalty.

13

DEMETRI

The longer I stare at the computer screen, the more the numbers blur together. Rubbing my tired eyes, I blink a few times, focusing on the numbers at the bottom of the page. Those two container thefts cost me over two million dollars and some rather pissed off associates who had already paid half the cost upfront during negotiations.

Pushing myself away from my desk, I stand. "Where the fuck is Sergei?"

"Haven't heard from him since last night," Victor states standing as well; looking just as tired as I do. Pulling his phone from the inside of his pocket, he makes a call.

Twisting the top off a pill bottle, I pop the migraine medicine in my mouth, then wash it down with the rest of my coffee. I haven't slept since those few hours in bed, with Glory tucked into my side, and I'm still wearing the suit I wore the night before; the same suit stained with another man's blood. For now, all we have is a location, given to us by a desperate man in his final moments before Victor put a bullet in his head.

Tucking his phone away, Victor informs me, "he's not

answering his phone." Victor follows me as I exit my office. "He's probably fucking around with Samara down at the strip club," he mentions.

I rub my temples to ease the pressure building in my head. Dealing with Sergei and his bullshit is not on my radar at the moment. Saying nothing, I decide to head upstairs and shower and deal with Sergei later. "I'm not to be disturbed for a couple of hours. Get Veno to take over for you and get some rest."

Victor nods and walks in the direction of the other men that have gathered in the foyer as I continue walking up the stairs. Once in my room, I close the door, shutting the world out for a few moments. Stripping from my day-old suit, I discard the articles of clothing in the hamper, then stride into the bathroom and start the shower.

I stare at my reflection in the mirror. Closing my eyes, I think about Glory. So much so, I can still smell the light scent of her perfume hanging in the air. Fuck she was much more than beautiful wearing that red dress. She surprised me yet again last night. Part of me expected more of a fight when I informed her, she would have to leave, and she wouldn't be returning to her apartment in Chicago. Instead, despite her sass, Glory listened and took in everything I was telling her.

Once steam fills the room, I step into the stall. The moment the hot water hits my skin, tension leaves my muscles, and my body relaxes. The past couple of years mostly spent in Polson without a doubt have been the best years of my life. Creating a bond with Logan, his wife Bella, and those grandchildren of mine have brought me so much joy. I've even become closer with Nikolai as he navigates and finds his path in life. But I also realize it's left my empire vulnerable in the process. My absence has created chaos amongst those who wish to harm me. Greed drives them. They want the control I have, and it encourages people to make a decision that will cost them their lives. And the only way to show people my empire is not for the taking is with action. No excuses. No second chances.

Sometime later, and somewhat recharged from the long shower I took, I make my way downstairs. The smell of Borscht fills the air, causing my empty stomach to growl. Following the scent into the kitchen, I find Victor sitting at the prep table, eating. Mrs. Ivanov, who has been with the family since before Nikolai was born, is pulling freshly baked bread from the oven. She sits it on the stovetop.

"Smells good, Marta."

"I'll get you a bowl," she tells me as I sit on a stool opposite Victor. Marta places the bowl in front of me along with silverware. "Migraine again?" she questions as she waits for me to taste like she always does. I lift a bite to my mouth.

"Good as always, Marta. And to answer your question; yes, another migraine."

She scoffs at me as a mother would do to her child. "You should take better care of yourself, Mr. Volkov."

"Yes, I should."

"How is Nikolai? I haven't seen him in so long." The warmth in her eyes for my son shows. Marta is the closest thing to a grandmother Nikolai has ever had. She helped raise Nikolai and gave him the love his mother never did. For that, I will always be grateful to her, and she will always have a place in my family.

"Nikolai is doing well."

"Does he have a sweetheart yet?" Marta continues to ask questions, and I chuckle at her persistence to know more.

"I believe he has a soft spot for a young woman." I continue to eat my meal.

"That is good news. Nikolai's happiness makes me happy, as well." Marta turns back, toward the stove and stirs the simmering pot cooking on the stovetop.

Receiving a call, Victor excuses himself from the table and

steps out of the kitchen as I'm finishing my meal. He's not gone long before reappearing, with a laptop in his grasp.

"Sir."

The tone in his voice has me looking in his direction.

"The men are sending surveillance footage captured early this morning," he tells me. I then look at Marta.

"Say no more." She throws her hands up. "I'll leave you men to your business." Wiping her hands down the front of her apron, Marta exits the room.

Opening his computer, Victor clicks on the email, and the video file sent starts to play. As we watch footage of a small storage facility, in the location given to us last night, a silver car with tinted windows rolls into the frame. The car sits there for several minutes until another vehicle pulls in behind it. Three men step out of the silver car, none of which I recognize.

"Do you know them from anywhere?" I ask Victor as our eyes stay fixed on the screen.

"No."

The door to the other vehicle swings open and I watch a booted foot appear, planting itself on the gravel ground. I'd know those snakeskin boots anywhere.

"Fuck." Victor shakes his head as the rest of Sergei's body emerges from the shadows of the driver's seat.

I feel the cords in my necks tighten as a fiery rage builds inside of me as I watch a man I have known and put my trust in betray me. Sergei shakes the hands of each man, then walks to the storage building they've parked in front of. Removing a padlock, he lifts open the door. I continue to stay silent as one of the men takes a crowbar and opens one of the wooden boxes, then pulls out a gun. There is only one way Sergei could have gotten his hands on massive amounts of inventory. He stole it. From me. "Do we know where he is now?" I question as I bottle my anger.

"Luca is out looking for him now."

Snatching the clear vase from the table sitting in the center of the table, I hurled it across the room, watching it shatter against the brick wall. "Bring him in," I growl. I pause, controlling the urge to destroy everything around me. I let out a heavy breath. "Victor."

"Sir," he answers after quietly standing by while I lost my temper.

"Call Ruslan. I want him and his men out on the streets. I want them to do whatever it takes to find answers. I'm through playing these childish games of cat and mouse."

Forty minutes later, I'm pouring myself a drink, when Sergei walks into my office. "You wanted to see me, boss?"

"Have a seat." I lift the tumbler in my hand, "Drink?" I offer.

He laughs nervously, and his eyes dart around the room. "Uh, yeah, sure," he answers, and I give Victor the whiskey I poured, and he hands it to Sergei.

I pour another for myself. Crossing the room, I sit in the chair across from Sergei. The room falls silent, and the atmosphere in the room changes. "Tell me, Sergei. Have I not been good to you all these years?"

I notice the slight tremble of his hand. "Yes, Boss." His voice breaks a little when he answers.

"You've proven overtime I could trust you. I put you in charge of my companies whenever I'm away from home. Correct?"

Beads of sweat form above his brow, and he goes to stand.

"What are you getting—"

His words are cut short when Victor clamps his hand down on Sergei's shoulder, forcing him back into his seat. "Mr. Volkov asked you a question."

Sergei swallows hard; his eyes fixed on me. "Yes."

Sitting my whiskey down, I lift my gun off the table and rest it on my lap. Leaning back in my chair, I drink in the fear written on his face for a moment before lifting my weapon and pulling the trigger. The bullet shatters Sergei's left knee. His screams of pain echo off the walls. "I have given you so much over the years, and you betray my faith in you by stealing from me." Blood from his wound soaks his pant leg and begins to pool around his shoe slowly. I stand, and his watery eyes stay on my every move.

"I didn't. I swear!" Sergei screeches. His lie earns him a blow to the side of his head with the butt of my gun.

"More lies!" I bellow. "Tell me, Sergei. Where does one get millions of dollars worth of artillery to sell to low life street thugs?" Sergei starts to open his fat trap once more, but I warn him. "Lying will only make this worse for you." I allow a few seconds for him to confess his sins. "You disappoint me," I tell him. Crossing the room, I set my gun down and snag a cigar from the box sitting on top of my desk. Picking up the cutter, I walk toward Sergei. "Do you know anything about the package delivered to the restaurant last night?" I ask, knowing he was made aware of the incident.

"Your new pussy means nothing to me," Sergei spews, spittle flies from his mouth. Turning, I pick up my gun and put a bullet in his other leg for his loose lips and disrespect toward my woman.

Sergei roars through the pain.

"Fuck! I told you, it wasn't me who sent the package last night."

Cutting the cigar, I place it in my mouth. Grabbing Sergei's right hand, I slide his ring finger into the cigar cutter. He struggles to pull away. "You wear expensive things. Things my money has afforded you, and yet you feel as if you have nothing." Pressing down, the blade slices through his finger. I sit the cutter on the table beside him and wipe the blood on my hands off on the sleeve of his suit.

Cradling his hand, Sergei grinds his teeth. "You don't deserve what you have. The money or power." He laughs hysterically. "I don't fear you as these other poor bastards do. So yeah, I confess. I did it. I stole from you." He continues to laugh as the blood bubbles from his missing appendage, and the blood seeping from both legs gathers in more substantial quantities on the floor beneath him.

His words strike a nerve, and I snap. In the blink of an eye, I grab hold of his face and force the cold hard barrel of my gun in his mouth, and Sergei's eyes widen. "You feel that motherfucker?" I shove the barrel further down his throat until he starts to choke on it. "That's fear." I waste no more of my time on him and pull the fucking trigger.

After my adrenaline subsides, I pull the barrel out of his mouth and lay the gun on the table. Victor stands a few feet away, waiting for my orders as I stride across the room. Picking up my lighter, I light the cigar still hanging from my lips. "Someone get this shit cleaned up."

14

GLORY

I'm sitting outside in a lounge chair curled up with a blanket sipping on a steaming cup of coffee while watching the sun come up over the mountain top in the distance. The stillness of the early morning allows me to be alone with my thoughts as I reflect on last night. I hadn't planned on telling Grace about Ronan, but it felt freeing to purge my secret. The rest of the night was spent engaging in meaningless conversation for which I was grateful. The guys joined us women around the fire, and I began to realize how much I had missed my family. Something akin to regret began making its way to the surface from where I had buried it two years ago, causing a twinge of pain to weigh heavily on my chest. I initially told myself leaving Polson was because I didn't want to be dependent on my best friend. I told myself my demons were my own and not anyone else's burden to bear. I now see how wrong I was.

"What ya doing up this early, darlin'?" a deep voice echoes from behind me, and I startle. When I whip my head around, I'm met by Quinn.

. . .

"Not much," I smile. "Just enjoying the view while I drink my coffee. What about you? What has you up this early?"

"I got up with Lydia so Emerson could sleep," he informs, taking a seat across from me and lights a cigarette, then gestures to his right.

Turning in my seat, I look through the sliding glass door that leads to the kitchen and spot Quinn's daughter sitting in a highchair at the table eating, and sitting beside her is Sasha. I take in his stiff posture, and the look of discomfort on his face as Lydia tries offering him a bite from her tiny spoon, and chuckle. I can tell he's not around children often. When I turn my attention back to Quinn, he's taking in the same scene with a massive smile on his face. "How's fatherhood treating you, Quinn?"

"Best fuckin' thing in the world," he boasts. "I'm trying to convince Emerson to give me another one."

"And how's that working out?"

"I think I've about worn her down." He grins.

"Yeah, keep dreaming, babe," Emerson's sleep filled voice says as she steps outside with a mug of steaming liquid in her hand. Reaching out, Quinn snags his wife around her waist and pulls her down onto his lap. I watch as Quinn whispers into Emerson's ear, making her giggle. Witnessing their public display of affection makes me miss Demetri that much more. Demetri called last night just as promised and hung on the phone with me until I could no longer hold my eyes open. I told him about last night's events, and he expressed how proud he was of me. We ended the call with him telling me he was wrapping up business there in Russia and would be home sometime tomorrow.

"So, what time do you ladies plan on heading out today?" Quinn asks, glancing from me to Emerson. The girls and I made plans to hit up a few shops for some retail therapy. Quinn will be tagging along with Sasha today to help keep a watch on us.

I peer down at my watch noting it's already 8:00 am and I've been sitting out here since 5:00 am. "In a couple of hours. I'm going to grab a shower and eat breakfast. Is Lisa here? I've been dreaming about her French toast."

"She is," Emerson confirms. "She was already in the kitchen cooking when I walked out here." Quinn quickly ushers Emerson off his lap. She scoffs as he stands. "Really, Quinn? Must you always think with your stomach?" Emerson rolls her eyes.

Quinn pulls Emerson close. "I'm always either hungry or horny, babe. If you see me without a boner, make me a sandwich." He smirks, then gives her a hot as hell kiss, before walking away.

Sure enough, when I look through the sliding glass door, I see Lisa bustling around in the kitchen. Standing from my chair, I follow behind Quinn and Emerson as we make our way inside. "Glory!" Lisa calls out for me. Her face breaks out in a warm smile as she wipes her hands on a towel. "Come here, child." Lisa holds her arms open, and I step into her embrace. Lisa is the mother hen of the club. She spends her days looking after everyone.

"It's good to see you, Mrs. Lisa."

"Oh, you too, Glory. We've missed you around here." She takes a step back. "You hungry?"

"I'm hungry." Quinn butts in before I get a chance to speak.

Emerson pinches his side. "She wasn't talking to you."

Lisa waves her hand and rolls her eyes. "Your plate is in the microwave, sweetheart."

Quinn gives us a look as to say *See I'm special* as he breezes past us, heading straight for his food.

Lisa turns her attention back to me. "Now tell me what you want for breakfast."

I smile. "I'd kill for some French toast. If it's not too much trouble."

"No trouble at all. Sit. I'll have some whipped up in no time."

Taking the oatmeal covered toddler from the highchair,

Emerson props her daughter on her hip. "I'm going to get her cleaned up."

When Emerson leaves, I take a seat next to Sasha, who at the moment, is shoveling eggs and bacon into his mouth. "I see you're finding out pretty quickly that being my babysitter comes with perks. Not only do you get the pleasure of my company, but you get your meals made by the best cook in the world."

"You got that right," Quinn adds around a mouthful of food.

Later that afternoon I'm shopping with Grace and Bella at a boutique in town. Alba was unable to make it because her son came down with a fever overnight, and both Emerson and Mila had to work. Grace is sifting through the clothing rack next to me when she asks, "When is Demetri going to be here?"

I look up from the denim skirt in my hand. "I spoke to him last night. He said he'd come home sometime tomorrow. Possibly in the morning."

"How were things in Russia? What was it like? I can imagine how beautiful it is."

"What little I saw was beautiful. Demetri's house is beyond comprehension. He did take me to dinner. I also had the pleasure of meeting his ex-wife." At my last statement, both Grace and Bella freeze.

"Holy shit." Bella's eyes widen as she abandons the blouse she is holding by tossing it to the top of the rack. "What was she, devil-like?" The question coming from Bella. "I don't know a whole lot about the bitch, but from what Logan has told me the woman is horrible. What she did to Demetri..." Bella shakes her head.

"Oh, she's a bitch of epic proportions. Ivanna cornered me in the ladies' room at the restaurant Demetri took me to. It turns out she and her family were having dinner there. Anyway, she had the nerve to ask me if I was having a good time with her husband."

"You're kidding?" Grace gasps.

"Nope. But you know me; I wasn't playing into the twat's

games. I told her I was having a lovely time. She went on to give me a lame underhanded threat and spew some bullshit about Demetri going back to her."

"Uhg. I hate women like that." Bella scrunches her face in disgust. "She's delusional to believe Demetri will go back to her. I mean her son won't even speak to her." The three of us are quiet for a minute, and I can't help thinking of Nikolai. Finally, Grace is the one to change the subject. "Your mom called the other day."

"Yeah?"

"Yeah, and I might have accidentally mentioned Demetri."

When I eye my best friend, she's wearing a guilty expression on her face.

"What do you mean you 'accidentally' mentioned Demetri?"

"Well, I commented on how you showed up for a surprise visit before flying to Russia with your boyfriend. Your mom was under the impression you were still here in Polson with me. How was I supposed to know you hadn't told her?" Grace cries, throwing her hands up in the air with exasperation.

Bella cuts in, "Uh, why is your mom knowing about Demetri a big deal?"

Grace is the one to answer her question. "Because Glory has only ever had two boyfriends in her life."

"What?" Bella gives us a look of disbelief.

"Yup. One in high school and one in college. Her mom has been waiting for the day a man knocks Glory on her ass." Grace grins.

"Yeah, and I bet she started talking about wedding invitations by the time you ended the call," I retort. By the expression on Grace's face, I'm right.

"I'll bet my left tit my mother is hunting down Demetri's phone number so she can unleash her crazy on him."

At my backhanded comment, Grace ducks her head and avoids all eye contact with me. I point an accusing finger and narrow my gaze at her. "What did you do?" When she doesn't speak, I press. "Grace!"

"It was an accident!" she cries, and Bella laughs.

"Before I knew what was happening, she had wrangled Demetri's cell number and his home address from me."

"Oh, God. I need a drink," I declare closing my eyes and bringing my palm to my forehead.

Fifteen minutes later, after my declaration of needing booze, we walk into Charley's. Charley's is Polson's only bar. The guy who owns it is also a friend to the club. "Well, look who we have here. How are you ladies doing this evening?" Charley greets us from behind the bar.

"Hi Charley," we say in unison as Quinn and Sasha file in behind us.

"Think you can fire up the grill for us, brother?" Quinn asks Charley.

"Of course. Why don't you all go have a seat, and I'll bring ya some beers."

Us women grab one of the booths on the back wall while Quinn and Sasha opt to sit at the bar. Grace slides into the booth first, and I take a seat beside her while Bella sits across from us. A moment later, a waitress greets us. "Hi, ladies. What can I get for you?" she asks in a soft tone.

The three of us order a burger, and fries then thank our waitress as she makes a quiet retreat. I study her as she walks away and note how drawn into herself she is. I find myself wondering what her story is.

"That's Kinsley." Grace answers my silent question. "Charley hired her a couple of years ago. I don't know much about her because she keeps to herself and she never engages us in conversation when we come in. Emerson says she has a little boy, though. She's treated him a few times at the clinic."

"Hmm," I nod, and hum in response as Kinsley makes her way back behind the bar.

"I need to go to the ladies' room before our food gets here." I slide out of the booth. "I'll be right back." As I walk past the bar, I catch Sasha's attention and gesture toward the bathroom. He gives me a nod. When I turn the corner that leads to the hallway where the restroom is, I notice the back door at the end of the hall marked *EXIT* is slightly ajar. Not thinking anything of it, I continue to the bathroom to take care of business. Once I have finished, I step back out into the hall to find Kinsley wrestling two large bags of trash through the back door. "Hey. Let me help you with that," I offer as I approach her.

"You don't have to do that. I got it."

Ignoring her, I take one of the bags from her hand. "Don't be silly. I want to help." I smile. "My name is Glory."

"Thanks, Glory. I'm Kinsley."

Striding up to the dumpster, we toss the bags inside. Just as the two of us turn to make our way back inside a scream erupts from Kinsley's mouth startling me. But before I can react, I'm shoved up against the wall of the building. My head bounces off the brick, and I feel a trickle of blood start to seep down the side of my face. It's also then I feel the hard plain of someone's body against my back and a hand fisted in my hair. "Volkov needs to be taught a lesson. And what better way than through his whore." When the stranger's rancid breath dances across my face, I panic, and I'm suddenly thrust back to a dark place. I struggle against his hold, and the feel of his erection digging into my backside causes bile to rise in my throat.

"No," I choke out as the grip on my hair tightens. *Not again. This can't be happening again.*

Without warning, I hear the recognizable blast of a gun being fired and a second later, the weight on my back is gone. It takes everything I have in me to open my eyes. And when I do, Sasha's large frame fills my vision as he stands beside me. On shaky legs, I turn and brace my back against the wall to keep from falling. It's then I notice the man lying at my feet with a hole in his head. My eyes go from the dead man to Sasha and then to my left where Quinn is standing over the body of a second man holding a gun at his side. Kinsley is just standing stock still with a blank look on her face and tears running down her cheeks. Quinn and Sasha don't waste time as they quickly usher Kinsley and me back inside and away from the gruesome scene in front of us. Quinn pulls his phone from the pocket of his cut and puts it to his ear. "Prez, we need ya down at Charley's. We'll be needing a cleanup too." Quinn listens to whatever Jake says on the other end then cuts his eyes to me. "She's okay," he conveys. Only I don't feel okay. I feel like I'm spinning on an axis. My breathing picks up, and before I know it, I'm fighting to catch my next breath.

Sasha steps up to my side and places his hand on my arm. "Slow your breathing, Glory," he urges. "Look at me." Doing as I'm told; I look into Sasha's deep blue eyes. "In and out. Slow like me." He demonstrates taking breaths, and I mimic what he's doing.

Before too long, the dizziness fades, and my breathing evens out.

"If I had known all it would take for you to call me Glory was to start hyperventilating, I would have done it sooner, Sasha." Even in the worst of the situation, I can't seem to control my mouth. Sasha looks at me like he usually does; like I'm crazy then shakes his head. Shrugging, I lean against the wall in the dark hallway, tip my head back, and take two more slow cleansing breaths. It's then I remember what the man said. "He said Volkov needed to learn a lesson." My voice shakes as I repeat the words whispered in my ear.

"What did you say?" Sasha asks, his accent sounding more pronounced.

Tearing my gaze away from the ceiling and settling it on

Sasha's face, I repeat myself. "The man. He said Volkov needs to be taught a lesson and what better way than through his whore. Also, he had a Russian accent."

I watch as several emotions cross my bodyguard's face — one of them being rage. I have witnessed the loyalty Demetri's men have for him, and in a short amount of time, the man in front of me has shown the same devotion to me. Pulling his phone from his pocket, Sasha places a call. Seconds later, he is speaking to whoever is on the other line. My guess would be Demetri. The call lasts less than a minute before he hangs up. "I'm taking you back to the compound." I nod and walk alongside Sasha out to the bar where I spot Grace and Bella pacing the length of the floor. When Grace sees me, she gasps.

"Glory. Oh, my God. Are you okay?"

Not in the mood to talk about what just happened, I nod. "Yeah. But I need to get out of here." Understanding, Grace doesn't ask questions as she and Bella trail behind Sasha and me outside to his car where he holds the door open, allowing the three of us to climb in. The ride to the clubhouse is silent, for which I am grateful. All I want to do is escape to my room and process my thoughts in private. By the time we pull through the gates at The Kings' compound, the sun has set. A cool breeze prickles the skin on my arms as I step out of the car.

When we walk inside the clubhouse, no one says a word as we make our way upstairs. I feel the weight of my best friends stare at my back. She's desperate for me to talk but knows not to push. Together we walk into my bedroom where I plop down onto the bed. Grace flicks on the lamp next to the bed, then disappears into the bathroom. I listen to the sound of the faucet running before she returns, holding a washcloth. Without a word, Grace lightly swipes the warm damp rag across the side of my face, wiping the blood away. "It's stopped bleeding. There is a small cut. I'm going to clean it with antiseptic and put a band-aid on it."

Once Grace has finished fussing over me, I give her a crooked grin. "Thanks."

"Do you want to talk about it, Glory?"

I shake my head. "I'm good Grace. I think I'm going to lay down a bit. But I promise, if I need to talk, I'll come find you." I was telling her the truth. What happened at Charley's has me shook up but as bad as it sounds, I was mostly grateful. Grateful Sasha and Quinn had been there. I don't have one ounce of remorse for the two lives that had been taken. Reaching out, I take Grace's hand in mine, and I give her a reassuring smile. Returning a smile of her own, she nods. Just as Grace walks out of the room, Sasha appears in the doorway. He doesn't say anything, but I know he wants to.

"Have you talked to Demetri?" Sasha nods. "I have. He's on his way." My shoulders sag in relief at the news.

"I'll be across the hall if you need me." Sasha turns on his heel, and I call out, stopping his retreat.

"Sasha."

"Yes?"

"Thank you for what you did. I don't know what I would have done if you hadn't shown up when you did."

Sasha stays silent, but his expression softens as he inclines his head just before closing the door.

Too exhausted to even change into my pajamas, I stand and strip out of my clothes, opting to sleep in just a tee and panties, then turn off the lamp sitting on the bedside table. Sliding into bed, I sigh as the crisp, cool sheets settle on top of my skin. The moment my head touches the pillow, sleep takes me.

"Tell me where my wife and daughter are?" Ronan roars as he slaps me across my face.

"Fuck you, asshole," I sneer as blood drips from my mouth. "I'm not telling you shit."

"You always did have a filthy mouth, Glory. Perhaps with the proper

training, we could fix that." Ronan's words are laced with a cruel taunt. I know what Ronan means by 'training.' I know the beatings and the hell he put Grace through for years. I add fuel to the fire when I open my mouth again.

"You're pathetic, Ronan. Sad really. Do you think beating a woman makes you a man? Well, it doesn't. It makes you a coward. A real man doesn't need to hit a woman to get her respect. Only spineless little weasels such as yourself do."

"You stupid fucking, cunt!" Ronan's face turns red at his outburst, and I know what's coming. I knew opening my mouth would be my end, but I'd never bow down to a man like Ronan De Burca. I won't give him the satisfaction. Rearing back with a closed fist this time, Ronan punches me in the jaw, a force so powerful it sends me and the chair I'm sitting in crashing to the floor, and my head bounces off the kitchen floor. There is no time to recover when there is a second blow to my ribs, Ronan begins to reign down blow after blow. To my face, my stomach. His fists are everywhere. My advances to fend him off are becoming sluggish, and my entire body screams in pain. My head is on fire, and my vision becomes blurry. The next thing I know I'm being pulled from the floor by my hair. Ronan slams me down face first onto the kitchen table.

My eyes fly open, and I sit up in bed gasping for my next breath. My heartbeat is erratic, and my body drenched in sweat. I blink my eyes in rapid succession, trying to clear the fog from my brain. For a moment, I forget where I am. Then it all comes rushing back. The attack at Charley's must have been what triggered the dream. I haven't had a nightmare in months, but each time I do, it's the same. Each time they feel so real. It's like I can still feel his filthy hands on my body. I can feel the weight of his body as he took what was not his to take. I can smell his cologne and the stench of his breath. Suddenly, I can't stand the feel of my skin. In a frenzy, I kick the sheets away from my body as a sob escapes my mouth, and I stumble out of bed. Rushing into the ensuite bathroom, I flip the light on. My trembling legs carry me over to the bathtub where I tear the shower curtain back, and my hands shake as I fumble with turning on the hot water. I am near hysterics as my vision starts to blur and uncontrollable tears stream down my face. Once I get the hot water on to full blast, I strip out of my panties and climb into the tub. The scolding water stings as it rains down on top of me, turning my pale skin red, but I feel no pain. I want his smell gone. I want to erase the memory of his brutal touch. I don't know how many times I run the washcloth over my body or how long I have been in here, but I feel like it's not long enough. Like no matter how raw I rub my skin, it will never be enough to erase the vile things done to me.

15

DEMETRI

We've finally landed on Montana soil; back where I feel most at home. Dealing with Sergei's unfortunate but necessary death proved to be the only way to make my message heard. Word spreads quickly in the world of organized crime, and his death and the death of the men associated with his betrayal served as a potent reminder in my community that I stand resolute. The Volkov Empire is strong, and it is not for the taking. I will spill the blood of those who dare fuck with what is mine.

Stepping off the plane, I inhale a breath of crisp air.

"I'll retrieve the car," Victor says, slinging his black duffle bag over his shoulder.

'I'll walk with you," I tell him, needing to stretch and move my legs after the long flight. Shoving my hands into my pockets, we stroll through the small airport before entering the parking garage. Victor pulls the keys to the SUV from his pockets, unlocking the doors. Instead of sitting in the back, I climb into the driver's seat. "Keys." I hold out my hand, and Victor tosses them. I glance down at my wrist to look at the time. It's early morning — around 2:20 am. Putting the key into the ignition, I tell Victor, "Get in touch with Jake's guy, Grey, and let him know he can expect us in thirty minutes." Leaving the garage, I head toward The Kings' clubhouse with one person on my mind. Glory.

Driving helps to clear my head. I need to declutter all the bullshit from the last two days floating around in my head. All I keep thinking about is the phone call I received from Sasha hours ago.

"Is she okay?" I demand as I storm out of the kitchen heading back to my office.

"Miss Keller is doing fine, Mr. Volkov," he assures me, and I let out a heavy sigh. "But there was an incident. That is why I am calling."

"What the fuck happened?"

"Her and the ladies were enjoying themselves down at a local bar here in town called Charley's." He begins to fill me in, and I recall having drinks at Charley's a time or two with Logan. "A couple of men approached her while she was helping a young waitress. One of the men roughed her up a bit by shoving her against a brick wall."

Knowing Glory is safe, puts my mind at ease. However, as much as I'm worried about her physical condition, I'm just as concerned with her mental state. I continue to replay the call.

"The men?" My fist clenches at my side at the thought of a man putting his hands on my woman. "Dead," Sasha states.

"Where is she now?"

"We're on our way to The Kings' clubhouse," he confirms.

"Good. I don't want her leaving the clubhouse until I get there. I'll be on a flight back to Polson in a couple of hours."

"There is one more thing, boss," Sasha quickly adds.

"Speak."

"Glory said one of the men had a thick accent. She said it sounded like ours."

"Russian?"

"Yes, sir."

"Spit it out, Sasha," I growl.

"He said Volkov needed to learn a lesson."

The hairs on my neck stand on end, and my blood runs cold — first the box, now this. My grip on the steering wheel tightens the more I process everything.

"Don't let her out of your sight. Understand?"

"You have my word."

"I want more than your word, Sasha."

"I'll protect her with my life, Mr. Volkov." "You better." Swiping the screen, I end the call.

I should have been there to protect her myself. I sent her home, thousands of miles away in the hopes of keeping her safe, and this happens. Filled with rage, I press the gas pedal to the floor, increasing our speed. "Fuck!" I roar at the top of my lungs, so hard my throat stings as Victor sits in the passenger seat, unfazed by my outburst.

Making a conscious effort, I regain my self-control. I channel it and focus on what I know. She's with Jake and his men. I keep telling myself this repeatedly. She's safe, and those thoughts alone are keeping me sane at the moment.

Thirty minutes later, we roll through the gates of the clubhouse. Jet lag setting in, Victor and I enter the quiet building, and up the stairs. No words pass between us as I stop just outside the bedroom Glory occupies and Victor continues down the hall to the room he will be resting in. Grasping the handle, I quietly open the door, trying not to wake my woman. The first thing my eyes land on is an empty bed, then a dim light coming from the bathroom along with the sound of running water catches my attention.

Closing the bedroom door, I start removing my clothes to join Glory in the shower. The state I find her in after pulling back the shower curtain pushes my thoughts of pleasure aside. "Glory. Baby?" I stare down at her naked body, as she sits under the scorching water, scrubbing at her skin with so much force her flesh is raw. Glory's head jerks up, her tear swollen eyes locking on mine.

"I smell him." She continues to scrub. "I can still feel his hands — his body on mine." Sobs continue to wreck her body.

Stepping into the shower, I lift her to her feet and pull her body into mine. Wrapping her in my arms, I hold her. "You're safe, baby. I've got you."

Once Glory has calmed down, and her body relaxes against mine, I reach behind her and retrieve the body soap from the caddy hanging from the showerhead. "Turn around, *Krasivaya*." I squeeze the floral soap into the palm of my hand then place it back in the holder. Without questioning my intentions, Glory spins, her lush ass brushing against the head of my cock. Pushing aside my selfish wants, I rub my palms together, working up a good lather before placing my hands on her shoulders. With light pressure, I massage Glory's shoulders, then work my palms down her back until her shoulders sag and the rest of the tension releases from her tight muscles. My hands travel the natural dip in the small of her back, then over the globes of her backside. Glory shifts, pressing her ass against my front. My cock heavy with need pulses from the contact. "Face me, baby," I order, and she complies. Glory's breaths become heavy. I watch her bite her lower lip, as her eyes follow my every move while I take care of her. The look of complete trust and submission in her gaze pleases me. Pooling more soap in my palm, I begin to wash her front, running my palms between the valley of her breasts, lightly grazing her taut nipples as I continue my path down her flat stomach. Kneeling, I bring her left foot to rest on my thigh. Starting at her ankle, I lather her skin, massaging her slim calf, working myself up to her thigh. Glory closes her eyes when my fingertips lightly graze her bare pussy as I wash her inner thigh. Repeating the process, I do the same with her other leg.

Glory's eyes flicker to mine, and she runs her fingers through my hair. "Make me forget, Demetri. I only ever want to remember what your touch feels like," she begs.

Continuing to kneel, I grip Glory's hips, pulling her forward. I swipe my tongue through her center and across her swollen clit. Her head falls back beneath the stream of warm water; her lips part, and she moans. My palms skim up her legs, one hand gripping her ass. Bringing my other hand between her thighs, I slowly sink two fingers inside her heat, at the same moment, I suck her clit into my mouth, and feast on her sweet pussy until she comes undone crying out my name.

"Demetri," she pants, as she rides out her orgasm.

Nowhere close to being done, I stand, and back her up against the shower wall. "Tell me what I want to hear." Lifting her leg over my hip, I line the head of my cock up with her center. The heat from her pussy makes me growl as I slowly sink my length into her.

"I'm yours," Glory tells me, and I slowly begin to move.

"Repeat it," I demand.

"I'm yours, Demetri. Every broken piece of me is yours," she groans as I make love to her.

"Wrong." I lock eyes with her. "You own me, *Krasivaya*," I confess, staring into her fiery green eyes. I thought I was lucky to have loved once, but as I look at Glory, I realize I've been given a second chance, and I'm not letting go this time.

Glory's eyes pool with unshed tears. "Kiss me," she demands, and my mouth crashes down on hers. I kiss her like it's the first and last time my lips will ever touch hers again. Communicating with touch, I tell her how much she means to me. How much I love all her jagged, beautifully broken pieces. Because in the end, we are all flawed creatures looking for someone to love our imperfections just as much if not more than those parts of us that are less messy. Glory's walls flutter and her pussy clamps down around my cock. I swallow her moans as her orgasm triggers my release. Waves of emotions wash over me as I stay connected to my woman as we both come down from our highs.

Finally breaking our connection, I rest my forehead against hers. Tears roll down Glory's cheeks, and I swipe them away with the pads of my thumbs. "I'm sorry you came home to this." Glory dips her chin, casting her eyes down.

I lift her chin, bringing her eyes back to mine. "Coming home to you is the only thing that matters, baby. I told you I would take care of you." With the water barely warm, I reach over and turn off the shower. Snagging one of the towels sitting on the shelf above the toilet I dry Glory, then wrap it around her body before grabbing a towel for myself. After we step out of the shower, I continue to care for my woman, as I retrieve the hairbrush sitting on the counter and run it through her damp hair. I then gather her hair, twist it into a loose braid, and secure it with an elastic band that was sitting next to the brush. Glory smiles at me in the mirror.

"What?"

"Mafia crime lord Demetri Volkov just braided my hair." She can't stop smiling at me.

Acting like it is nothing, I explain. "My granddaughter insisted I learn to braid her hair one day." I try to keep my face neutral, but Glory's amusement causes me to crack a small smile.

Glory turns and faces me. My hands move to her hips. "Made you?" Her palms rest on my bare chest.

"Don't let her tiny size fool you. She is very persuasive and has a way of getting whatever she wants."

"You mean she has you wrapped around her little finger," Glory teases. "I think it's sweet," she adds, tracing the tattoos on my arm.

Glory pulls her towel loose and allows it to fall to the floor. She then reaches between us and rids me of mine.

"You have me wrapped around your finger, *Krasivaya*." I let a more carefree side of myself I haven't seen in a very long time surface. Grabbing her ass, I scoop her off the floor and carry her out of the bathroom. Glory tosses her head back and laughs. I laugh with her as I throw her naked body on to the bed.

"You should do that more often," Glory tells me.

"Do what?" Spreading her legs, I settle between her thighs and hover my mouth above her pussy, my warm breath causes her skin to prickle.

"Laugh and smile." I circle her swollen clit with the tip of my tongue as her fingers thread through my hair. "You're insatiable," she hums.

"Only because you're mine," I confess.

Hours later, feeling rested for the first time in days, Glory and I finally make our way downstairs — the smell of bacon cooking in the kitchen lingers in the air. Spotting Logan and Jake sitting at the bar, both nursing a cup of coffee, I snag Glory around the waist, stopping her. "I need to talk to the guys. Why don't you go ahead and get yourself some breakfast," I press my lips to hers.

Striding across the room, I stop beside Jake. "Jake." I extend my hand, and he shakes it.

"How's it goin', brother?"

I look around the room, finding most of Jake's brothers are hanging out. "Looks like most everyone is here." I look at my son, Logan, and ask, "Where's Nikolai?" Before he can answer, the clubhouse door opens, and Nikolai walks in.

"It's good to see you." He walks up to me, and I notice his irritation.

"What's bothering you, son?"

"Nothing I can't take care of." He gives a vague answer.

Knowing I won't get more out of him until he is ready, I let it be. "Well," Jake stands, clasping his hand on my shoulder. "Let's get this shit show started, shall we?" Walking toward the other end of the room, he bellows, "Church!" And all his brothers stand following suit.

"Dad." Logan walks beside me.

"Son. How are Bella and my grandchildren?" We stop just outside the door where church is held.

"They're good."

"And your brother? He seems to be wound a little tight this morning," I mention.

"Not sure. He's been like this for a few weeks now. I'm guessing it has to do with a certain brunette." Logan smirks, and Nikolai's moodiness starts to make sense.

Once everyone has filled the room and taken their seats, including Victor, who was the last to enter, Jake slams the gavel on the surface of the table. "Alright, listen up. As you all know, we had ourselves an incident that took place out at Charley's." Jake looks at me. "Neither one of those fuckers had any identification on them, so we put the word out trying to identify who they are. Unfortunately, none of our contacts or people in town knew anything about them, and believe me, in this town people notice new faces hanging around."

"I contacted Lex and asked him for a favor. I sent him images of the guys from the security feed at Charley's. If he gets any hits on the FBI database, he'll email the results."

"These men threatened Demetri's woman. A threat none of us are taking lightly." Jake peers around the room. "With that said, I'm givin' the floor to our brother." Jake jerks his head toward me.

Leaning back, I let the words whispered in my woman's ear play on a loop in my head. Whoever is behind both threats wants to do more than hurt Glory. They want to hurt me. It's personal. "As most of you already know, a threat was made against Glory, and those details were shared with you. Because of that, and now with what happened here in Polson, I have to assume, both threats are related, yet we have no leads."

"Well, I sure as hell was hoping for more answers than what we have. Now, all we've got are a bunch of dead men and zero leads on who's fuckin' with my family," Logan quips.

"Unfortunately, my son is right." Standing, I stride to the corner of the room where a fresh pot of coffee sits and pour myself a cup. "My soldiers found nothing. No fingerprints left on the package. Surveillance video from the restaurant shows nothing but a young delivery boy arriving shortly after we did. The boy took off down the street. Nobody has seen the young man since. It was Victor who felt something was not right and opened the box." My anger builds thinking about the events.

"Where was Sergei during all of this?" Nikolai asks.

My hand tightens around the mug in my hand, his betrayal still fresh. I glance across the table at Nikolai. "Sergei is dead."

His face is indifferent as he asks. "How?"

"I killed him." Nikolai's eyes flick to the other side of the room where Victor sits, his arms folded across his chest. He gives my son a confirming nod.

"Why?" Nikolai asks.

"He stole from me. Over two million dollars to be exact."

Logan leans back in his chair. "Do you think he was behind these threats against Glory?"

"No. None of those leads back to him or the men he was selling my inventory to. Sergei simply became blinded by his own greed. In the end, it cost him his life," I tell him.

"We'll keep our ears to the ground. In the meantime, I want everyone here to keep their eyes open. Report to Demetri or me if you hear or see anything." Jake slams the gavel. Jake and I hang back as the rest of the men file out of the room. From where I'm standing, I catch sight of Glory sitting at the bar with Grace, the two of them laughing.

"She's a strong woman," Jake states.

"Yes," I agree with him as I continue to stare at my woman. Her head turns, and her eyes connect with mine.

"You plan on hangin' around for a spell?" Jake asks as Glory slides from her seat and walks in my direction, her eyes never leaving mine.

"I plan on taking my woman home," I reply, and Jake chuckles.

"Prez!" Sam yells from across the room, as he stands just outside the opened clubhouse door. His thumb points over his shoulder. "There's an older couple with a Basset Hound at the gate claiming to be Glory's parents."

16

GLORY

"Oh, shit," are the words that come from Grace's mouth, followed by a giggle. It takes me a moment to comprehend what Sam just announced.

"Glory!" My mother's voice calls out, and I inwardly cringe.

"Jesus take the wheel." Closing my eyes, I tip my head back and mentally prepare myself for what is about to go down. I love my mom; I adore her. But she is too damn nosey. Growing up, I had always wished for a brother or a sister — someone to take my mother's focus off me. Unfortunately, my parents couldn't have any more kids, so my mom had no other children to unleash her crazy on. "Mom, Dad, what are you two doing here?" I ask, making my way toward them. My mother is sporting the biggest smile as if she's not causing the most awkward scene, whereas my father grins and shrugs, going with the flow.

"Well, I figured you must be missing Bo something terrible, so I brought him for a visit." My mom chirps as if the words that came out of her mouth are not the most ridiculous thing we've heard. I cut my eyes to the sofa where my dog has made himself at home.

"Don't let your mom fool ya, baby girl. She's here to check out your new suiter."

"Charles!" Mom elbows my dad.

"My new suiter? Really?" I say, rubbing my temples. "This is not happening," I mutter.

Stepping away from mom, my dad holds out his arms and gives me a warm smile. "Come here, baby girl."

Being the daddy's girl that I am, I roll my eyes when he gives me a knowing wink and step into his embrace. I wrap my arms around his middle; breathing in the familiar scent of Old Spice when I rest my cheek against his chest. "It's good to see you, Dad."

His body shakes as he chuckles. "You're lying, but I figured I would tag along and act as a buffer."

I laugh. "Now who's lying? You tagged along for the show." I pull back and look into a set of eyes that match my own and see them dancing with mirth. "You're getting a kick out of this, aren't you?"

"You bet your ass I am." My dad kisses me, his stubble scratching my cheek. "Best go on and rip the band-aid off."

I look over at my mother to see her waiting expectantly for my manners to kick in and introduce her to the man standing behind me. Only I don't have to because Demetri beats me to it. I feel his heat as he steps behind me and places a possessive hand at the small of my back. He greets my father first by extending his hand. "Mr. Keller, I'm Demetri Volkov. It's nice to meet you." Out of the corner of my eye, I watch as my mother clasps her hands together and swoons at the sound of Demetri's voice. I hear Grace cackle behind me and know my best friend is getting a kick out of my apparent discomfort.

"It's good to meet you, Demetri." My dad shakes his hand.

Demetri then turns his attention to the woman standing to his left and gives her the biggest grin. "Karen."

Wait. Karen? Why the hell is he on a first-name basis with a woman he's never met?

"Demetri," My mom gushes, pulling him in for a hug. "You're just as handsome as you sound on the phone."

I narrow my eyes. "What are you going on about? Have you two been calling each other?"

My mother turns to me. "Your boyfriend and I had a lovely conversation the other day."

"Oh, Jesus Christ. Do you not understand boundaries, Mom?"

"What? It's not like you were going to tell me about him anytime soon. I had a sneaky suspicion you were up to something when you called me to pick Bo up at your apartment. A mother always knows when her child is keeping secrets. That's why I called Grace. I knew I could get what I needed out of her."

"Hey!" Grace gripes.

My mom waves her hand. "Child, please. The two of you were never any good at getting your stories straight. Besides, you're not very good at lying, Grace." My best friend crosses her arms over her chest with a pout, and it's my turn to snicker.

Jake cuts in, "How about we take this gathering outside? We can fire up the grill and have some grub while everyone gets to know each other."

"That sounds like a wonderful idea, Jake," my mother boasts.

"Doesn't it, Glory?"

"I'd rather have a root canal," I mutter under my breath and Demetri squeezes my waist telling me to behave. "Yeah, Mom. Sounds fun."

My mom's face lights up as she turns to my dad. "Charles, will you go to the car and get the brown suitcase; I brought my photo albums. I promised Demetri I'd show him Glory's baby pictures."

"Sure thing, sweetheart." Dad turns on his heel and disappears through the door behind him, and I groan. "Mom. Can we not do that now."

. . .

"What? You don't mind? Do you, Demetri?"

"Not at all, Mrs. Keller. I have been looking forward to it." Demetri offers my mom his arm, and she links her arm in the crook of his elbow. As they stroll past me, my mom looks over her shoulder at me.

"This will teach you not to keep secrets, won't it," she says in a low tone and a look in her eyes that means she's enjoying every second of embarrassing me. She knows exactly what she's doing.

As all the guys follow my mom and Demetri outside, I turn to Grace. "This is all your fault. Just remember payback is a bitch."

"Me?" Grace mocks innocently.

"Yes, you. You and your big mouth did this. Now come on." I grab her arm and tug her behind me. "Don't think you're getting off scot free. If I know Karen Keller as well as I think I do, I'd say she has pictures of you too. Like the one from the time you got that terrible perm and tried to dye your hair blonde using peroxide."

"She wouldn't dare," Grace gasps the same moment we hear Quinn's boisterous voice call out. "Holy shit! Is that Grace?"

Hours later, the afternoon turns into evening as the sun starts to disappear behind the mountains. Food and drinks are flowing, and the children are running around the yard playing. Watching my mom over by the swing set gushing over Grace and Jake's little girl, I feel a twinge of guilt, knowing I will never give her grandchildren. "What's on your mind, baby girl?" my dad asks, taking the vacant seat next to me.

"Nothing much." I lie.

When my dad doesn't say anything, I tip my head in his direction. His look says he's calling bullshit. I sigh and point across the yard. "When I see how happy mom is with Grace's children, it makes me feel guilty for not giving her grandkids." I shake my head. "I've never told you this, but I don't want to have children. Not that I don't like them, because I do. I just don't have the desire to have any of my own." After my confession, I keep my gaze forward, afraid to look at my dad. Afraid I'll see the look of disappointment on his face.

"Look at me, baby girl." When I look at my father, it's not disappointment on his face but understanding. "Your mom and I only want you to be happy, Glory. We had already figured kids were not in the cards for you. Not that we hadn't hoped, but it was your happiness that mattered the most." He squeezes my hand.

"Are you happy, baby girl? With this man?"

"Yeah, dad. Demetri makes me the happiest I have ever been."

Dad pats my hand. "That's good."

We're both quiet for a minute before he speaks again. "Looks like your mom will make out just fine in the grandchild department."

I look in the direction dad's eyes are trained to see my mom has abandoned the swing set and is now sitting on a chair in front of the fire with Demetri's granddaughter, who happens to be Bella and Logan's daughter sleeping in her arms. Her eyes cut across the yard to find mine, and she gives me a warm smile. The kind of smile only a mom can provide. The one that says everything will be just fine. With my feelings getting the better of me, I need a breather. "I'm going to get another beer. You want one?" I ask my dad.

He shakes his head. "I'm good, baby girl. I am going to get me one of those burgers Jake is cooking though."

We stand at the same time, and my father pulls me in for a hug, and I kiss his cheek. "Thanks for the talk, Dad."

When I walk up to the cooler to retrieve a drink, I hear Jake call out to Logan. "I need ya to go get more ice."

Logan lifts his chin. "No problem, Prez."

Remembering that I needed to pick up a few things from the store, I offer to go. "I'll go."

"Are you sure?" Jake asks.

"Yeah. I need to grab a few things anyway."

"I'll come with you," Demetri says motioning to Sasha who quickly joins us. "Boss?"

I cut in before Demetri opens his mouth. "You should stay here with Logan and Nikolai. You haven't seen much of them lately. I won't be long, and Sasha can take me." I can tell Demetri is reluctant, so I push further. "I'll be quick." Giving in, he nods then steals my mouth with a kiss.

Making my way around the side of the clubhouse to the front, I follow Sasha to the car. He opens the door for me, and I settle into the back seat. It's about a fifteen-minute ride to the store, where Sasha trudges along with me as I wander through the aisles in search of shampoo and conditioner. As I'm browsing through the selection, the tiny hairs on the back of my neck stand on end and I get a sudden uneasy feeling I'm being watched. I look to my left and then to my right, seeing no one. The only person on the aisle beside Sasha and me is an older man and a young woman with a little girl sitting in front of their shopping cart. When I turn my attention to Sasha, his body is rigid, his eyes focused and he's on high alert. He too looks up and down the aisle. "Is everything okay?"

"You have what you need?" he asks, not answering my question.

"Yeah. We can go." I don't have everything I came for, but the feeling I'm having along with Sasha's behavior has me wanting to get the hell out of here and back to the clubhouse. I bypass the long checkout line and opt for the self-check instead. The whole time I'm scanning my items, I continue glancing over my shoulder. Sasha notices my nervous behavior.

"Everything is going to be okay."

"So, you feel it too?" I ask as I swipe my card, paying for my purchase. Sasha doesn't speak, but his nod confirms he has a bad feeling as well. "We should call Demetri," I suggest as we walk swiftly across the parking lot to the car. Once I'm settled in, Sasha climbs into the front seat, starts the car and pulls out of the store parking lot. Next, he retrieves his cell phone, swipes the screen, then places it to his ear. A second later, he begins speaking in a hushed tone, presumably to Demetri. While Sasha is on the phone, I twist around and look out the back window of the car to see if anyone has followed us. That is when I see a large black SUV coming at us at an alarming speed. "Sasha," my voice quivers.

"I see them, Glory. Demetri is on his way." The words barely leave Sasha's mouth when, suddenly, there is a loud, ear-piercing explosion. Time slows to a crawl as the world around me becomes deathly silent. It's almost as if everything is happening in slow motion. I open my mouth to scream for Sasha; only I can't hear my own voice. When Sasha struggles to control the car, he calls out to me in return. I see his mouth moving, but I don't hear his words. Out of nowhere a large force slams into the car from behind and my body is thrown forward against the driver and passenger seats. The force of the impact is powerful, and I watch Sasha's head bounce off the steering wheel. The car loses control, hitting the guardrail. The moment of impact is when the silence is interrupted by the unmistakable sound of screeching tires and crunching metal. The next thing I know my body becomes weightless before it's slammed against the seat in front of me once more, before being slung against the passenger door. My head bounces off the metal frame of the door as glass explodes into tiny, jagged shards all around me and I'm thrust into darkness.

Blinking my eyes open, I try to clear the fog from my head, but it's no use. My vision is blurry, and my head is pounding. *Where am I?* As I fight off the darkness that is hell-bent on trying to claim me, the events that led me to my current state come rushing back to me — being at the clubhouse with friends and family. Me and Sasha at the store. An SUV was chasing us just before the crash. I let out an involuntary groan as I try lifting my hand to my face and struggle to move my body. Turning my head, I look to my left, and I am not at all prepared for what I see. A cry escapes my mouth at the sight in front of me. It's Sasha. He has blood coming from his head and his mouth. He hangs upside down, still strapped in his seatbelt. His arm dangles over his head and is twisted at an odd angle, leaving no doubt it's broken. "Sasha," I call out to him, but he doesn't stir. *Oh, God. He looks dead.* "Sasha," I try again. Still no response.

Out of nowhere, my senses pick up on a strong odor. The distinct smell of gasoline. Fearing the worst, I conjure all the strength I have and roll to my side. I push up to my forearms while ignoring the pain radiating through my body. The sound of screeching tires, followed by a car door slamming shut causes me to sigh in relief. Help has come. Demetri and the guys are here. But when I hear the voices of several men speaking in Russian, my hope turns to dread. That's not Demetri. Quickly I try to scramble around the twisted metal and broken glass to find a way to escape, but the thought of leaving Sasha pains me. I can't do it. A second option comes to mind. *Sasha's gun!* I know Sasha carries. I need to find his weapon. It's our only chance.

Army crawling my way toward the front of the car, I whisper, "Sasha." He doesn't stir, and the amount of blood coming from his body gives me little hope. Reaching up, I tug on his suit jacket. I cry in relief at the sight of his gun strapped in his shoulder holster.

Flicking the snap on the strap, I pull the weapon from the holster. I've never fired a gun before, and the weight of the metal feels foreign in my hand. But hanging around The Kings, I know enough about guns to do what is necessary. *Check the safety and aim.* Those are the only two things that matter right now.

With the car upside down and smashed all to hell, I watch

three men walk around the car as they look for a way to get to me. I know it's me they want. The warning at Charley's said so. These men wish to harm Demetri and to get to him; they want to use me. My eyes follow the black boots crunching on the gravel. Even though my heart is about to beat out of my chest, I keep the gun trained on the man standing at the back-passenger window. Without hesitation, I fire the gun, hitting him in the leg. The man bellows and spits out a string of words I don't understand. A second man runs in the direction of the car, and just as I am about to fire a second shot, two hands wrap around my ankles from behind, and I'm roughly yanked backward. The sudden movement causes me to flinch and lose my grip on the gun. I scream as loud as I can in hopes someone will hear me as I am drug across broken glass and out of the back window. The moment my body clears the car, I start kicking and hitting at the man trying to restrain me. "Get the hell off me, motherfucker!" I ball my fist and land a blow to the asshole's nose. He, in return, backhands me across my face. The slap knocks me off kilter long enough for my assailant to flip me over and zip-tie my hands behind my back.

Once I'm restrained a second man joins his friend and the two of them haul me up by my tied hands and drag me away from the wreckage toward a black SUV. When I look over my shoulder at the car, I see smoke and fire coming from the rear. "No!" I cry thrashing against my capture. The smoke emerging from the car becomes more intense. My struggle to break free is fruitless. I helplessly watch as flames engulf the car before I'm tossed into the backseat of the SUV. My last thoughts as the door slams in my face is of Sasha. I pray Demetri gets to him in time.

17

DEMETRI

Out of nowhere, a sick feeling comes over me. At the same moment, my phone rings. Pulling it out of my pocket, I swipe the screen. "What's wrong?" I bark.

"Mr. Volkov, we're being followed," Sasha says, his voice hinting at the urgency of the situation. My pulse quickens, and my heart beats heavy against my chest. "Who?" I flick my eyes to Victor, who is standing nearby.

"I don't know. A black SUV. Darkened windows. No way of knowing who is driving."

"I'm on the way." Tires squealing and Glory screaming is the final sounds to come through the phone before the call abruptly ends. I look up from the phone I have gripped tight in my hand to find all the men eyeing me. "They're being pursued by a black SUV." I start moving across the yard.

"Where?" Jake asks.

"They had just left the store."

"Jake, is everything okay?" Grace calls out as we rush past her and the kids. "Jake!" Grace's voice rises.

"Lock it down," Jake orders his men, as I break out into a sprint, heading for the front of the clubhouse, where my vehicle is parked, with Victor at my side.

Chaos erupts within the clubhouse. "Go. My brothers and I will catch up with you once we have the women and children safe." Logan tells me, holding my grandson in his arms.

"Demetri." Glory's father rushes toward me. "What the hell is going on?"

"Mr. Keller, Glory is in trouble. You and your wife stay here with the others. I'm going to get her." As I turn to leave, his hand shoots out, grabbing me by the arm.

"If something happens to my daughter, Mr. Volkov—" He leaves his sentence hanging, but the tone in his voice and the hardened look on his face lets me know his words are a warning.

"I'll bring her home. You have my word."

His eyes cut to his wife who is standing off to the side, her hand covering her mouth as tears roll down her cheeks. "You better." He warns his voice stern before letting go of my bicep. Walking up to his wife, he pulls her into his arms and comforts her.

Nikolai jogs up as I jerk the car door open. "Gather all my men. I want them to tear this town apart looking for those sons of bitches." I bark my orders to Nikolai. Racing to his ride, he throws his leg over his motorcycle. Gravel hits the front of the car as Nikolai takes off ahead of us.

Not far behind, Victor and I peel out of the compound parking lot. I punch the dashboard several times as we barrel down the highway toward downtown. "Fuck. Fuck. Fuck," I yell angry with myself for letting her leave my sight.

Rounding a bend in the road, we notice an orange glow contrast against the darkening sky accompanied by thick grey smoke. The world appears to slow down around me. My heart stops beating, and my breath gets caught in my throat. Instantly I recognized the overturned and mangled car on the side of the road up ahead. *Glory*. A couple of police cruisers block the short bridge we need to cross to get to the other side.

"Boss?" Victor's voice catches as he slows the car to a stop. The look on his face as he stares forward guts me, but Glory is my single concern now. Without hesitation, I fling the car door open and take off toward the accident scene as fast as my feet can carry me; the scene already riddled with first responders.

"Sir, you can't –" an officer calls out to me as I rush past him. Ignoring his warning, I storm toward the scene. Tire marks scar the road and shards of broken glass crunch beneath my feet the closer I get. As soon as I round the firetruck, I take in the firefighters unrolling water hoses to put out the blaze. With no thought to my safety, I run toward the fire.

"Stop!" Someone grabs me by the forearm and pulls me backward.

"If you value your life, you'll remove your hand," I warn the young man whose grip loosens. "What the fuck are you thinking?" the firefighter questions.

"My woman was in there." I point toward the hot blaze as water dousing the flames.

His expression changes. "Sir, we only pulled one body from the wreckage. Paramedics are tending to him now." *Sasha.*

"Sir — sir." The firefighter gains my attention. "Are you certain there were two occupants in this vehicle?"

"Yes. My employee Sasha Fedorov and Glory Keller," I confirm. The firefighter waves over an officer standing a few yards away then relays the information to him. The officer immediately acts, calling for a broader search radius looking for a possible second accident victim. The use of his word victim causes waves of emotions to hit me.

Looking beyond the flashing lights, I spot paramedics tending to someone laid out on the pavement. Pushing past the small crowd forming on the roadside, I take in the battered and bloodied form of Sasha. I rush to his side. "Sasha," I take him in.

One of the paramedics looks up. "Are you family?"

"Yes!" Victor yells from behind me, and I look over my shoulder. "He is my brother." Victor's voice rises above the noise surrounding us. I look back at Sasha laying on the ground. He looks bad. My stomach turns. I need answers, and the only person who can give them to me seems to be knocking on death's door.

"Lost his pulse." The EMT standing on the other side of the gurney yells sending him and his partner into lifesaving mode.

Victor drops to his knees, taking his brother's hand in his. "Fight, Sasha," he tells his brother. "Fight."

"How far out is medevac?" The paramedic questions as he begins chest compressions and the EMT bags, Sasha, giving him breaths of air.

He pauses and looks down at his watch. "Five minutes." He then addresses Victor. "Sir, please step back." Victor reluctantly releases his brother. He schools his emotions as they try to save Sasha. "We've got him back. Get him on the stretcher." The paramedics announce as the helicopter touches down in the middle of the highway several yards away. As they secure Sasha to the gurney, one medic turns facing Victor and me.

"They have room for one more!" he yells over the noise, and Victor turns to me, waiting.

"Go," I tell him.

Once Victor turns his back, following the medics, I process what I do know as I take in the scene around me. The distant rumble of motorcycles draws my attention, and I head toward Jake and his men, who have been stopped by the police.

"Glory?" Jake asks, sitting on the back of his bike.

"She's not here," I speak loud enough for all of them to hear. Jake's eyes follow the helicopter as it lifts in the air. "Sasha was the only victim on the scene. Victor is with him," I clarify.

Looking over his shoulder, Jake signals to his brothers sitting on their bikes behind him. "Search the roads for any possible leads that would give us direction to where Glory could be." Following orders, they make their way down the shoulder of the road, pass the ambulance and firetruck.

Dread causes my stomach muscles to harden, but I steel myself, masking my emotions. Glory is nowhere to be found, which can only mean one thing.

She was taken.

18

GLORY

I'm sitting in the back of the SUV I was tossed into moments ago; with the man who I shot in the leg staring daggers at me. I don't let his murderous glare intimidate me and give him a *fuck you* look of my own. The man is breathing heavily and sweating like a pig, clearly in pain. I get a sense of satisfaction, knowing I caused his current state of discomfort. I only wish I'd been able to aim higher. Him not breathing would have been a better outcome. "You're going to pay for what you did you fucking bitch," the man sneers in a thick accent when I refuse to cower to the threat he's throwing my way.

I smirk. "It's too bad I missed my mark. But that's okay because when Demetri comes for me, he won't. He's going to kill every one of you."

The second those words leave my mouth, the asshole loses the pissy expression he was sporting and replaces it with a different one — fear. He visibly swallows when he speaks again. Only his question is not directed toward me; it's now on the man driving.

"What is she talking about? I wasn't told this was about Volkov." The next thing I know, all three men begin talking back and forth in Russian. It doesn't take long for the discussion to turn heated. The dickhead in the front passenger seat had no idea he was coming after Demetri. The guy then points to me. "You are his? You belong to Volkov?"

"Yes." My reply causes the man's eyes to widen. Then without warning the guy driving pulls his gun, aims it at the man in the passenger seat beside him and pulls the trigger: blood and shattered glass sprays all over the front passenger side of the vehicle. I scream as sheer panic washes over me. The SUV pulls over to the side of the road, and the man sitting on the backseat beside me jumps out. He strides up the front of the truck, opens the door, and drags the dead guy out. His body lands on the paved road with a thud. With my flight mode kicking in, I take advantage of the open door. Even though my hands are tied behind my back, I manage to slide across the seat rather quickly. Only I am not fast enough. Just as one foot touches the ground, the goon who was disposing of the dead man blocks my exit.

Not giving up too easy, I lay back on the seat and start kicking. My foot makes contact with the guy's nose causing blood to start running down his face. He's momentarily thrown off-kilter by the impact as he stumbles backward, leaving me enough room to jump out of the SUV. I ignore the sting to my scalp as the driver rips a few strands of my hair out as he tries halting my movements by grabbing a fist full of it. "Fuck! Get her!" he hollers out behind me as I take off down the road. Running while having your hands bound behind your back is no easy task.

Unfortunately, I don't get far before I am tackled to the asphalt from behind. The impact is so brutal; two things happen simultaneously. All the air is knocked from my lungs, followed by a pop in my shoulder. I take a deep breath and try breaking free again, but the excruciating pain radiating from my left shoulder and down my arm stops my struggle. "You son of a motherfucking whore!" I spit with tears running down my face. I'm pretty sure my shoulder is dislocated. Not if, but when my man comes for me, I'm going to make sure this motherfucker behind me suffers. I have no fight left in me with the pain coursing through my body. And when the asshole hauls me off the ground, he does so by my left arm. The burning pain is so intense I become nauseous. It's all I can do to swallow back the vomit that threatens to escape my mouth. I briefly consider letting loose and allowing the contents of my stomach to wreak havoc on the asshole dragging me back to the SUV, but decide I am in no condition to test his limits at the moment.

Once we are back on the road, I try to keep my focus on where we are going and not on the pain. Beads of sweat drip down my face as I rest my head against the window. It's dark now, and when we make a familiar turn down a winding road, I lift my head. I am surprised we are not leaving Polson. Instead, the SUV comes to a stop alongside the boat dock on the lake. The moment we park, the door is ripped open by a large man in black dress pants and a white button-down shirt. The sleeves are rolled up to his elbows, and every inch of his exposed skin is covered with tattoos. "Out," he orders.

Careful not to jar my shoulder, I gingerly climb out of the SUV. With a gun in his hand, the man motions for me to follow him. I do so without protest and with the other two guys following behind. I take in my surroundings as we walk down the dock. I've only been to the lake once before with Grace, and the girls. Demetri has two boats out here that he lets the club and women use whenever they want. We walk past six boats before we come upon one of Demetri's. I know it's his by the name Volkov on the stern end. I'm confused as to why they brought me to Demetri's boat. I know he has nothing to do with what is happening, so whoever is behind my kidnapping either has a big set of balls or is very stupid. I'm going to go with my second assumption.

When I step onto the boat, I'm led to the cabin. I count six men, including the two who brought me here and the heavily tattooed man who goes and takes his place next to a guy sitting on the sofa with a tumbler in his hand. His posture is relaxed as though he hasn't a care in the world and as if he hasn't just started a war. Gauging from his seated position, the man is around five feet eleven inches tall. He has a slim build, black hair, and soulless eyes. If I had to guess his age, I'd say mid-thirties. His eyes rake over my body with bored interest. "Sit, Miss Keller." Nudging me from behind, the man who drove me here jerks his head toward the chair to my right.

"My name is Vadim Petrov." The man in front of me introduces himself. He looks at me expectedly as if that name is supposed to mean something to me.

"Okay," I say with a bored tone. My dismissive reply seems to get a rise out of Vadim. I can tell by the flare in his gaze and the way he's grinding his teeth. His reaction is an indicator he carries a level of arrogance.

"Don't be too hard on her darling," a familiar voice fills the room. Slithering into the cabin like the snake she is, is Demetri's ex-wife, Ivanna. Ivanna is wearing a white pantsuit, and her blonde hair is tied back in a ponytail at the base of her neck. She takes a seat next to Vadim and curls her body around his. I want nothing more than to wipe the smirk off her face. She and her family were burned by the Volkov's, and now she's involved with whoever this Vadim asshole is. Suddenly, the puzzle pieces are starting to come together. Without Demetri, Ivanna's family has nothing. They lost their power. Now, Ivanna and Vadim want that power back. Only I can't figure out how Vadim plays into all this.

"What's that look you have?" Ivanna's eyes narrow.

"Oh, I'm just putting two and two together. You see, I get what you're doing here. You are a deceiving, conniving, cunt who spent your days being a shitty wife and a terrible mother. Then when Demetri drops your ass, you and your family realize you aren't shit. And by some miracle, you were able to find some clueless asshat to sink your fangs into." I nod toward Vadim. "Exhibit A; the clueless asshat." I watch as Ivanna's face turns red with rage.

Leaping from the sofa, she comes at me. Unable to block her, she slaps me across my face. "How dare you talk to me like that." Ivanna raises her hand to come at me again only this time I'm not having that shit. Lifting my leg, I bring my foot to her stomach and kick. My action causes her to lose her balance as she stumbles backward. Lucky for her, Vadim catches her before she falls on her ass.

"See what I mean? Pathetic. You can't even kick my ass with my hands tied behind my back," I goad.

Ivanna lunges for me again. "Bitch!"

I go to stand only to be stopped by someone tugging me back down on the chair the same moment Vadim puts his arm out in front of Ivanna. "Enough!" he orders. "Keep a hold on her, Andrei," Vadim tells the man who stopped my forward momentum. When I look over my shoulder to see who has their hands on me, I notice it's the large tattooed guy. She-devil purses her lips, clearly not keen on taking orders from Vadim but does so anyway.

"Len, stay here with Miss Keller. I need everyone else up top." Vadim looks to one of his men standing off in the corner of the room, and he nods. The other five men, along with Ivanna, follow Vadim out of the cabin. Once the room clears, I keep my gaze on Len, the guy who is watching me. Luckily, he doesn't try anything, nor does he speak to me. Being the excellent lackey he is, he keeps to himself. I don't know how much time passes with me sitting down here, but the only thing I can concentrate on is the pain in my shoulder.

My fingers have long gone numb, and the zip ties are dug so tight into my wrist, my constant wiggling has caused them to rub raw. And if I'm not mistaken, that's blood I feel trickling down my palms. Also, with my adrenalin starting to wear off, I'm feeling the effects of the crash. I don't have to feel my head to know I have a knot on it because whenever I attempt to find a comfortable position on the sofa and lean my head back, I feel how tender it is. Between my body being knocked around by the accident and being tackled to the ground then Ivanna bitch slapping me, there's no telling what my face looks like. If I had to guess, it isn't pretty. Even with a dislocated shoulder, I've endured worse — these assholes need to bring a lot more to the party if they want to break me. Although, I don't think hurting me is what Vadim wants. What he wants is Demetri, and I'm his pawn. Ivanna, on the other hand, most definitely wants to hurt me. The bitch is lucky I'm tied up.

Hearing the clicking sound of heels against the wooden steps, Ivanna enters the cabin. She speaks in Russian to Len who is still standing in the corner. Len looks to me then back to Ivanna. He nods and strides across the small cabin, leaving Ivanna and me alone. I keep my eyes on her as she saunters over to the bar, picks up a slim stainless-steel case, opens it, and retrieves a cigarette. Ivanna doesn't say a word as she climbs up on the barstool, crosses her legs and lights it. Blowing out a plume of smoke, she rests her elbow on her knee. Ivanna takes her time looking me up and down, and I roll my eyes. All I can do is wait and see what idiotic thing is about to come out of her mouth. A second later she doesn't disappoint. "I don't know what my husband sees in you."

"Don't you mean ex-husband?"

Ivanna flicks her cigarette ashes on the floor, and I cock my head to the side. Now I am the one doing the appraising. I do the same thing she did to me moments ago. When my eyes land on her chest, I smirk. Ivanna is a B cup, and that's being generous. I flick my gaze from her body then look down at my double D's. "I can think of two things Demetri sees in me."

Don't get me wrong; Ivanna is a beautiful woman. I also think women of all shapes and sizes are beautiful. I just like getting a rise out of her. Because even though she's gorgeous, she's ugly on the inside. "Let me ask you something, Ivanna. Do you care about Nikolai? Do you care about how coming after Demetri affects him and his life?" I notice a flicker of something cross Ivanna's face, but she quickly masks it.

"You do not understand how my world works."

I shake my head. "Is that your answer to everything? Your son should be your world. I may not have children of my own, but I have people in my life that I would go to the ends of the earth for." I look Ivanna dead in the eyes. "It's not too late, Ivanna. You can still make things right. You don't have to do this. You don't have to go along with whatever Vadim has planned."

Ivanna studies me for a long moment. When I think I have gotten through to her, she proves me wrong. Her lips turn up in a vindictive smile. "You think this was Vadim's idea? Oh, he thinks he's the one running the show, but I'm the one who went to him and planted the seed. He's too young and power-hungry for his own good. All men are alike. They think they hold all the cards. In reality, it's us women. We just let them think otherwise." Hopping off her stool, Ivanna stands, drops her cigarette to the floor and stubs it out with the toe of her high heel.

"You're pathetic," I say, not trying to hold back my disgust. "You and Vadim are idiots if you think you're going to get away with what you're doing."

"I'll get what I came for. Make no mistake. As long as Demetri does as he's told; everyone will walk away, still breathing."

This woman is delusional. "Do you honestly believe the words coming out of your mouth right now? You were right when you said Vadim is young and power-hungry. I'm telling you those two things are a dangerous combination. You're stupid to think no one will get hurt."

Ivanna goes to say something but is interrupted by a deep voice. "Vadim is asking for you."

I look to my left to see Andrei. Ivanna doesn't spare me another glance before she walks away leaving me alone with him. I take in the man as he prowls toward me. Andrei is at least six feet four inches tall. He has dark brown hair buzzed close to his scalp on both sides, but the top is left long; long enough it hangs over one side of his face. Andrei also has eyes so dark they look black, and every inch of exposed skin is covered with tattoos, including his neck. My heart rate picks up with every step he takes in my direction. It's scary as hell the way his eyes are fixated on me. *Oh, shit. Did Vadim send him down here to hurt me?*

"What are you doing?" My voice shakes when Andrei drops to one knee in front of me. He doesn't answer. Instead, his big hands touch my injured shoulder. Shocked and confused by his actions, I flinch. His touch causes me to wince in pain. Andrei's voice is deep when he finally speaks. "I'm not going to hurt you."

"Then, what are you doing?"

"I'm inspecting your shoulder. I noticed earlier it was injured."

I look wide-eyed at Andrei as I gauge whether or not I can trust him. After all, He is one of Vadim's men.

"I'm not going to hurt you," he tells me a second time as if he can read my thoughts. I nod and allow him to continue. For such a big man, Andrei is surprisingly gentle when he touches my shoulder.

"It's dislocated," he confirms what I already suspected. "I can't reset it without untying you and untying you would raise suspicion."

"Well, unless you have the proper drugs to knock me out, I wouldn't want you doing anything," I retort. "Why do you care anyway? I'm pretty sure Vadim didn't send you down here to tend to my wounds."

"You're right; he didn't." Andrei stands and pulls his cell phone from his pocket, swipes his finger across the screen and places it to his ear. "Volkov."

19

DEMETRI

"Volkov."

I recognize his voice the moment he speaks my name. *Andrei.* He was Yerik's right hand man for many years. "Speak," I bark, my patience worn thin, and my time better spent trying to find Glory.

"I'm with your woman," Andrei says in a low tone, almost a whisper.

"If she has been harmed in any way—" I clench my hand at my side.

"She's alive."

I don't give him time to elaborate further. The fact he has my woman is enough for me to lose my shit. "I'm going to find you, motherfucker. When I do, I'm going to kill you," I threaten.

"That is unfortunate, and I hope it does not come to that. I respect you, Volkov. It is out of that respect, and the respect for my late boss Mr. Petrov that I am reaching out to you now. Vadim is a loose cannon and is making a mockery of his family name. I wish to have no part in what he is doing." *Vadim.* I should have known. He has been a nuisance to his family for years. The little weasel was always undermining his father and despised anything to do with the Volkov name. Andrei's betrayal comes with massive consequences. When you enter a family, you take a vow of silence; never speak to what you have seen or done. Petrov's soldier turning on him puts a mark on his head. In my world, it costs someone their life. Knowing this, I don't take his confession lightly. There is a short pause before he continues. "You'll find your woman at the harbor on your boat," Andrei informs me just before the line goes dead.

I briefly close my eyes, trying to rein in my rage. When I open them, several faces are staring back at me. An army of men waiting to make their next move; all ready to fight alongside me to get back my woman. Their willingness to kill for the family holds a lot of respect. There is not one man in my presence that I have not done the same for. "Vadim has her," I declare. Nikolai's face hardens. He understands what this means. A war between the Petrov and Volkov families can only end with one of us dead. "That was one of Petrov's men, Andrei." My information surprises Nikolai. "He has Glory on my boat," I inform the men before me.

"The ball's in your court." Jake steps forward. "How do you see this playing out?"

I look at Jake. "Vadim doesn't like to get his hands dirty. My boat is docked near the furthest end of the marina. His presence not only here but on my property lets me know he wants me to find him. We should assume he has an army of men protecting him."

"He's drawing us in?" Jake realizes, and his face darkens. "This fucker has no idea who he is dealin' with."

"How's your supply of weapons?" I question Jake.

"Ready for war, brother." He grins.

"Good. I want to send a few men out on the roads." I look around the room, finding my two sons standing beside one another as Logan loads his rifle. "Nikolai, I'd like you to join them. You know better than anyone what Petrov's men look like. Scope out the area between here and the Marina. They could be anywhere." Nikolai nods at my order. Jake chimes in as he slides a fully loaded magazine into his pistol.

"Gabriel, ride out with Nikolai, and take Blake with you."

More than thirty minutes have passed since finding out Vadim has Glory. The more time passes, the more I think about the what-ifs. Has he put his filthy hands on my woman? Is she still alive? Then I look across the room at Logan and think about my grandchildren along with the rest of the families confined to their rooms in the clubhouse several yards away. The Kings are no strangers to violence and retaliation. They've had their fair share of danger brought to their doorsteps, but this time, my enemies have put the ones I love in harm's way.

"Dad." Logan jerks his head, ushering me to follow him. Crossing the room, he opens a cabinet and pulls down a black lockbox. "I was waiting to give this to you, but now it seems like the perfect time." He sits the box on the table in front of us. Logan lifts the lid. Inside lays a Judge revolver. I pull my weapon from its holster and place it on the table. I grab the double-action single barrel revolver from its box. Logan slides a box of bullets across the table. "Appropriate, don't you think?" Logan smirks. I look at the word *Judge* etched on the side of the barrel. "We'll get her back." Logan states before walking away.

I then load six rounds into the cylinders. Six bullets I plan to take Vadim's life with. I plan on being his Judge, Jury, and fucking Executioner. Hearing the heavy metal door open a few feet away, I look over my shoulder to see Nikolai walking in with Gabriel and Blake right behind him.

"Found a body on the side of the road about six miles from the accident site." Blakes words catch everyone's attention. "I haven't seen his face around here before. But he had a tattoo on the left side of his neck of a scorpion."

"Petrov," I state. All his men wear the mark.

"We found nothing else between here and the marina. My guess is Vadim's army is small, and they've camped out closer to Glory's location," Gabriel informs us.

Ready for war, I look at the men in the room — my family. "This shit ends. Tonight," I declare and walk out of the small metal building and climb into my car. Nikolai quickly joins me.

A few minutes later, silence resonates — the calm before the storm. The only sound heard is the beating of my own heart and the rumble of six Harleys following close behind. The closer we get to the marina, the colder my blood turns. Adrenaline kicks in as we roll to a slow stop on the east side of the lake, opposite of where my boat is docked. Through the window, I watch as Jake and his men pull off the road. Nikolai, myself, and my men step out of the car. From here we go in on foot. Taking a moment, I eye each one of my friends. Most of them have been in my shoes. They have risked it all for the love of a woman. That alone makes any man a force to be reckoned with. All men ready their weapons — all waiting for my final words before the battle. I keep it simple.

"Kill them all." I grip the revolver in my hand.

Making our way through the entrance, Jake throws his fist in the air, halting our movements. Looking over his shoulder, he signals, pointing out three men walking the dock about thirty yards ahead. With fluid movements, as if the weapon is an extension of themselves, I watch Logan, Reid, and Quinn raise their rifles and aim. Simultaneously, they pull their triggers. Like domino pieces, the three men fall. Surging forward, we stride past the dead men, blood pooling beneath their bodies as we step over them.

Shots ring out. Bullets hitting boats nearby send us running for shelter. Bullets fly past us as we stay hunched behind several boats. As soon as the spray of gunfire ceases, we act. Jake quickly puts a bullet through the chest of one man before ducking behind another boat. Pushing forward, I catch another fucker aiming at

Gabriel, but before he gets a shot off, Gabriel puts a bullet between his eyes. In the distance, I see my boat, then notice it starts to drift away from the pier slowly. I take off running. Bullets whiz by, but I keep going. It is not until I near the end of the dock that I realize Nikolai is right behind me.

"Jump!" he yells, and I push harder, propelling myself off the dock.

My feet hit the deck; hard, causing my body to slam into the lower deck door, and land on my back, causing me to lose my grip on my weapon. As I reach for it, a single bullet whizzes past my head. Craning my neck, I look above me. A short bald motherfucker standing on the flying bridge has me locked in his sights. From the rear of the boat, a shot rings out, and the man above me falls over the side into the water below. When I look back, I spot his killer, Nikolai. Suddenly, a broad guy, with a boxer's build, rushes Nikolai. Grabbing my son's wrist, the man tries to disarm him, violently slamming his body against the railing. Looking around, I spot my weapon. Getting to my feet, I aim for the back of the large man's head. Before I pull the trigger, Nikolai's gun discharges, causing the son of a bitch to lose his footing, sending both him and Nikolai over the railing. I rush to the end of the boat, with my heart in my throat.

With one hand gripping the rail, Nikolai pulls himself back onto the boat. The other guy is nowhere to be seen. Blood soaks the front of Nikolai's shirt. He looks down, his hand touching his chest. "It's not mine," he verifies. "I lost my gun." He looks down into the water below.

"Stay close," I tell him knowing he is now unarmed. Turning my attention to the cockpit, I climb the stairs and peer through the glass, finding no one inside. I glance over my shoulder, shaking my head at Nikolai, letting him know, then point to the bow of the boat. Quietly, we make our way around the side.

"Show yourself. I know you're here, Volkov." The cold, detached voice of Vadim stops me in my tracks, causing Nikolai to slam into my back. "I've got a sweet looking redhead standing beside me." His words cut short the moment I hear my feisty woman's voice.

"Fucking touch, me again you prick, and I'll rip your dick off then shove it down your throat."

With the revolver held at my side, I appear from the shadows, Nikolai steps out with me.

"Mom?" Nikolai mutters under his breath, as my eyes land on Ivanna, who stands beside Vadim, and my woman near the railing. Vadim is holding a knife to Glory's throat with one hand and a gun pressed against her ribcage with the other. "Nice of you to join us," Vadim sneers, his lips upturned in a sinister smile. In the shadows a few feet from where Vadim stands, I notice Andrei. We make eye contact before my attention shifts back to Glory. Her eyes soften for a moment as I look at her. *I'm sorry,* she mouths then Vadim jerks her body closer to his, and she continues to struggle with her hands bound behind her back. *Now is not the time for her sass.* I give her a look, hoping she stops fighting, which she does. My eyes flicker back and forth between Ivanna and Vadim. Like the coward he is, he places Glory in front of himself, using her as a shield. "Ivanna," I say her name with disdain.

"Demetri." Her eyes cut to Nikolai. "Son."

"You lost the right to call me your son a long time ago." Nikolai grinds his teeth as he speaks. The sting of his words causes Ivanna to cast her eyes away, but only for a moment.

"This isn't a Goddamn family reunion." Vadim spits, digging the blade into Glory's flesh, causing her to wince in pain. "I don't know how you got tipped off to my whereabouts, but nevertheless, the outcome is still the same. You are here," Vadim spews.

"What was your endgame, Vadim? Did you think this poorly orchestrated attempt to overthrow me would succeed? Look around you." I raise my arms. "All your men are dead." I aim my weapon at him, waiting for just one good shot. Then look at my ex-wife. "And you," I glare.

"I've moved on to better things. Once you are out of the picture, we will merge the Petrov and Solov families; becoming the most powerful crime family in Russia." Ivanna folds her thin arms across her chest.

"Pathetic." Glory mutters, and Vadim applies more pressure against her neck. A drop of blood slides across the silver surface of the blade, and I lurch forward. Suddenly, Vadim points his gun at Nikolai.

"You take another step, and I'll not only slash her throat, but I'll put a bullet in your son's head." I freeze. "Come to think of it." Vadim cocks his head. "I think you should watch him die first." Turning his head, Vadim orders Andrei. "Don't just stand there. Kill him."

"Wait!" Ivanna turns and faces Vadim. "That was not part of the plan."

"Fuck the plan. I can't have any Volkov standing in my way." Vadim's grip tightens on his gun. His man standing to my right makes a slight move. The large man holsters the weapon he was holding and bows his head.

"It was I who called Volkov," Andrei confesses.

Vadim sneers. His eyes become wild with rage as he shuffles backward, pulling Glory with him. "You'll not live to see another sunrise," he warns Andrei.

Andrei lifts his head. "This is no longer my fight. I am and will always remain loyal to the family, but I will not play a part in the destruction of the empire your father built." Turning his back on his boss, Andrei walks toward the end of the boat.

"Looks like I have to take matters into my own hands." Vadim cocks his gun.

"He's my son!" Ivanna pleads. "Vadim. Please." Vadim pulls the trigger and Ivanna steps in the line of fire. The bullet meant for Nikolai rips through her chest, sending her body backward.

"Stupid woman!" Vadim yells as I step in front of my son, who kneels at his mother's side. Vadim points his gun at me, both of us at a standoff.

Nikolai doesn't speak as he looks upon his mother. She palms his cheek. "I'm sorry, Nikolai." Ivanna coughs, as blood flows from her mouth and seeps from the wound in her chest.

The boat veers to the left, and I realize Andrei must be operating the wheel, taking us back toward the marina. "You're all out of options here, Vadim." I take a step closer in his direction. "Let her go." He looks from side to side, clearly seeing he has nowhere to run.

"Okay, Volkov." The tone of his voice changes from determination to that of a man who has nothing left to lose. "I'll let her go." I see it before it happens. As soon as he pushes Glory, I take the shot. Pulling the trigger, I empty my revolver into his chest as I watch my woman fall over the edge of the railing.

20

GLORY

Everything happens in slow motion. From the moment I heard the first gunshot until now. Every single one of Vadim's men are dead. The man knows it's over for him. I had a gut-churning feeling something horrible was about to happen. Vadim is a man with nothing to lose. He has only one card left to play, and that's me. I know the exact moment it's all over. I see it in the way Demetri's eyes widen and the look of horror that dances across his face. With his gun raised, Demetri fires off several shots the same moment Vadim shoves me, and I'm sent free-falling backward over the side of the boat.

A scream escapes my lungs just before I hit the water below. My body becomes encased in wet darkness. I struggle against the ties bound around my wrists, knowing it's no use. I kick my feet and muster all the strength I have to fight my way to the surface, but my attempts to save myself get me nowhere. My lungs begin to burn from lack of oxygen, and the uncomfortable pressure in my ears lets me know I'm sinking deeper and deeper. My hope is fading, and I can't hold on much longer. The little bit of breath I'm holding escapes my mouth in bubbles the same moment I feel an arm wrap around my waist. *Thank you, Jesus.* Just as I don't think I can hold my breath any longer, my head breaks through the surface of the water, and I suck in a much-needed breath of air. Demetri's voice in my ear is the first thing I hear, and nothing has ever sounded sweeter. "I have you, *Krasivaya.*"

A sob escapes my mouth. "Demetri."

His warm lips press against my temple, kissing me. "Relax, baby. I got you."

It doesn't take long before Demetri's boat is in sight. It stops a few yards away from us, and the engine cuts off as Demetri begins to wade toward the back end with his arm still firmly around me. Once we reach the stern, Nikolai and Andrei are there waiting for us. "Give me something to cut her loose," Demetri says, and Andrei pulls a small knife from his pocket and hands it to him. Without being told what to do, Nikolai lays down on his stomach, reaches over the side of the boat and supports my head above the water as Demetri quickly cuts the zip tie binding my wrists. The moment my hands break free, a cold burning sensation radiates up my arms.

"Wrap your arm around Nikolai, baby. We're going to get you on the boat," Demetri tells me, then addresses his son. "Be careful of her shoulder, son. On three, I want you to pull her up. Andrei, you take Glory's legs."

I wrap my arm around Nikolai's neck as he braces his arm across my back, the same time Andrei grabs hold of both my legs. As calculated as they are, there is no way of helping me without jarring my injured shoulder. Together they carefully haul me out of the water, and I cry out in pain.

"Let's move," Demetri orders as soon as he pulls himself from the lake. Andrei dips his head and makes his way toward the front of the boat. A minute later we're headed back to the dock. The ride there is silent. Demetri sits on the floor and pulls me onto his lap while Nikolai is bent down on one knee next to us. His face is void of emotions, but behind that mask, I see pain. Nikolai's mother was killed tonight, saving his life. He has carried mixed feelings and resentment toward his mother for so long, but I don't doubt somewhere deep down, he loved her. As much as I despised the woman, I will forever be grateful for her actions. In the end, above all else, Ivanna chose her son. Suddenly, my thoughts shift to Sasha and dread settles in my stomach. "Demetri. What happened to Sasha?"

He strokes my cheek. "He was airlifted to the hospital. He was in bad shape when we found him, but alive. Victor is with him."

"I want to see him."

"Let's get you taken care of first, *Krasivaya*. I assure you Sasha is in good hands as long as he has his brother with him."

I pause, giving Demetri a confused look. "Brother? Sasha has a brother here? In Montana?"

"Yes. Victor is Sasha's brother. He will make sure Sasha is cared for."

By the time we make it to the dock, Jake and the rest of The Kings are there waiting on us. With me in his arms, Demetri steps off the boat. Nikolai and Andrei follow behind. "I need to get Glory to the hospital," he tells Jake.

"Alright, brother. Take Logan with you. My men and I will get this shit cleaned up. Grace will meet ya at the hospital with Emerson, along with Glory's mom and dad. Emerson knows the staff there. With her help, Glory will be a top priority."

"Thanks, Jake," Demetri nods.

When we arrive at the hospital, Logan pulls the SUV up to the ER entrance. As Jake promised, Emerson is waiting for us. And standing beside her is a doctor and a nurse. Demetri climbs out of the backseat of the SUV with me still in his arms. The doctor and the nurse rush over to us with a gurney. "Sir." The doctor addresses Demetri, who has yet to put me down. "Miss Keller will be in good hands. You have my word. But I can't assess her unless you let her go."

Placing my palm against the back of Demetri's head, I thread my fingers through his damp hair. "Demetri, I'm kind of in pain here, and I'd like not to be. So, why don't you put me down so these people can fix me up? When they're done, you can hold me as long as you want," I say trying to make light of the situation. It works, because Demetri gives me a soft look, then he lays me down on the gurney and addresses the doctor.

"I'll be coming with her."

"That's not really how we..." the doctor goes to say but stops short when Demetri gives him a sharp look. As Nikolai, Logan, and Andrei step closer, making their presence known the doctor changes his tune. "No problem, Sir."

"Grace and your parents are on their way," Emerson tells me just before I'm wheeled away to an exam room. Once there, Demetri steps back and allows the doctor and nurse to do their job; although, I can tell his presence is making the doctor a bit nervous.

"Can you tell me what happened, Miss Keller?" the doctor asks as the nurse cuts my shirt from my body then covers me with a hospital gown.

"Boating accident," Demetri answers the question for me.

The doctor goes about examining my shoulder. "Your shoulder is dislocated. I'm going to order an x-ray before I reset it. I want to make sure you don't have any further damage. You have some swelling around the joint. I'll also give you a mild sedative before I reset it. Once set, you'll be required to wear a sling for at least three weeks." Next, the doctor moves on to my wrists. They're in terrible shape, and there's no hiding the fact they were bound. My skin is raw and torn in some spots causing them to bleed. "And how did you obtain the injuries to your wrist?"

Demetri cuts in again. "None of your concern. Your only job is to treat Miss Keller so I can take her home."

I cut my eyes at Demetri and glare. "Demetri."

"Glory," he counters as his eyes bore into me, and I sigh.

"I'm sorry, Miss Keller, but as a doctor, I must ask; do you feel safe leaving with your friend?" he nods toward Demetri who lets out an audible growl and takes a step in my direction. Demetri's advance falters when a voice calls out.

"My daughter is alive because of that man," my father suddenly appears, with my mother and Logan. He juts his chin toward Demetri. "So how about you stop with the twenty questions and tend to my little girl, because right now that's your only Goddamn job, Doc."

My father's words shock me. My dad is the most easy-going and even-tempered man I know. It warms my heart to see the way he is going to bat for my man right now. I can see he's having the same effect on Demetri. Once my dad has finished giving the doctor an ass-chewing, he and Demetri share a silent look of respect.

When my father turns his attention to me, I smile. "Hi, Dad."

"Hi, baby girl." Dad strides toward me with my mom and Grace trailing behind him. The nurse steps out of the way or more like she is knocked out of the way when my mom steps up to the bed and starts fussing over me.

"Oh, my sweet girl. I was so worried." She kisses my forehead.

"Come on, Karen. Let's go wait outside so she can get fixed up."

My mom gives me one last kiss before she reluctantly lets my dad pull her away. As they are about to exit the room, Demetri steps up to my father. "Mr. Keller, I'd like to invite you and your wife to stay at my home. I'm sure you both would like to be with your daughter during this time."

My mom bobs her head up and down as she silently cries.

"Thank you so much, Demetri We'd like very much to accept your invitation."

Demetri and my father shake hands. "I'll alert the staff. Someone will be there to greet you when you arrive. Your daughter and I won't be far behind."

"If Grace doesn't mind catching a ride with Emerson, I can take Glory's parents back to the clubhouse for their things, then take them to your place, Dad," Logan cuts in.

"I'd appreciate that, Son."

When my parents walk out of the room behind Logan, I turn to the doctor. "Alright, Doc, let's get the show on the road so I can go home."

Thirty minutes later, I've had an x-ray, and I'm now back in the exam room where a nurse preps my shoulder with iodine. "Miss Keller." The doctor snaps on a pair of gloves and steps forward. "I'm going to inject the shoulder joint with twenty cc of one percent lidocaine; it will numb your shoulder. Then we're going to reduce it with external rotation." When I look at the huge-ass needle coming toward me, I begin to feel nauseous. I'm not good with needles. Never have been. Thankfully, Demetri senses my distress. Pulling up a chair, he takes a seat on the opposite side of the bed and takes my hand in his. Looking into Demetri's eyes, I pour all my focus on him and not the needle currently being inserted into my shoulder. "Alright, Miss Keller; you're going to feel a pinch. I want you to take a deep breath, then blow it out." I do as the doctor instructs while not taking my eyes off Demetri. The lazy circles he's rubbing on the inside of my palm soothes me.

"All done," the doctor announces. "Let's give that a minute to kick in."

Closing my eyes, I take a deep breath. I'm ready to get this over with and go home. The room goes silent as we wait for the lidocaine to do its job. Demetri continues to hold my hand. His touch relaxes me to the point of drowsiness. Just as I'm about to drift off to sleep, the doctor touching my shoulder brings me back. "How about we get this show on the road so you can go home and rest." He gives me a warm smile. Demetri glares. It's obvious he's not a fan.

It takes less than fifteen minutes for the doctor to reset my shoulder and put it in a sling. The nurse helped me into a scrub top since she had to cut the shirt I was wearing off me. Lastly, my wrists are bandaged up, and the doctor gives me a prescription for some ointment for my wrists and pain medicine for my shoulder. Just as the doctor hands Demetri the piece of paper with my prescription written on it, Grace and Emerson walk into the room. Grace immediately rushes to my side and gently puts her arm around me. Her tears mirror my own. "I was so scared. I came close to losing you again, Glory."

"You're never going to lose me, Grace."

My best friend and I hold each other for a minute before we are interrupted by Andrei stepping into the room. "Are you ready, Mr. Volkov?" he asks Demetri. It's also then I let out an audible yawn. I'm completely exhausted. All I want to do is go home, get some sleep, then wake up in Demetri's arms because being with him is what makes me feel safe.

"Yes, Andrei, we are ready." Demetri turns to Grace. "Why don't you come to my house around noon tomorrow. You can check on Glory then. For now, I want to take her home so she can rest."

Grace smiles. "Thank you, Demetri. And yes, I'll come by tomorrow. I'll bring Glory's things from the clubhouse too."

Demetri nods, strides up to me and scoops me into his arms. A nurse walks into the room, pushing a wheelchair. She goes to open her mouth, but when she takes in the look on Demetri's face, she thinks better of it. I lay my head against his chest, close my eyes, breathe in his scent, and shut out the world around me.

Later that night, we are back at Demetri's house where I'm

tucked into his bed. He has yet to leave my side. It's like he fears something will happen to me or I'll disappear if he turns his back for one second. He even carried me into the shower with him. I stood there while he washed my hair and body with such tenderness. Not once in the time it took him to wash my hair and lather my body did he take his eyes off mine: every touch and every stroke of his hands was done with love. There was nothing sexual or erotic about the moment. It was merely a man taking care of his woman. It was by far the most monumental moment of my life. Demetri Volkov saved me; literally and figuratively.

Letting out a heavy sigh, I snuggle into the crook of Demetri's arm, careful not to jostle my shoulder. "I want to thank you for what you did back at the hospital with my parents and for inviting them to come to stay here."

"What have I told you about thanking me for taking care of you and giving you what you need, Glory?"

I smile. "That you are my man, and you'll always give me what I need."

"Always, *Krasivaya*." Demetri kisses the top of my head. "I am a father, Glory. I knew your mom and dad would want to be close to you after what happened.

"Speaking of, shouldn't you be with Nikolai right now?" I ask.

"I want nothing more than to be with my son, but he is not here."

Lifting my head, I peer up at Demetri to see an anguished look cross his face. "What?"

"He took off almost as soon as we arrived home." Demetri shakes his head. "I know my son. He will come to me when he is ready."

The two of us are silent for a moment before I ask my next question. "How are you doing, Demetri? With what happened to Ivanna?"

"I am sorry my son lost his mother, but I am grateful she chose Nikolai's life over hers." He sighs. "Honestly, I am shocked by Ivanna's actions. I think that is what Nikolai is having a hard time with as well. He and his mother were never close. She was always cold and indifferent toward him when he was growing up, and now, he is struggling to make heads or tails of the events that have taken place."

I look at Demetri. "I'm sorry for yours and Nikolai's loss."

Demetri cups my cheek and kisses my lips. When he pulls back, I decide now is as good a time as any to broach a topic I have been avoiding. "Do you want more kids, Demetri?"

Demetri looks a little taken aback by my question, and I hold my breath while waiting for his reply. "Are children something you want?" he asks.

I shake my head. "No. I don't want children," I confess. "It's not that I don't love them, because I do. I love the hell out of my godchildren, and you know I adore Logan and Bella's kids. It's just that I have no desire to have any of my own."

"I'm forty-nine, Glory. I have two grown sons and two grandchildren. I am content with that part of my life. But you are only thirty-six. If you change your mind tomorrow and decide you want children, then I would give you children. I will spend my life making you happy because what brings you joy, brings me joy." Demetri kisses me again, and I realize I was stressing over nothing.

"What time is it?" I yawn.

Demetri looks down at his watch. "It's almost two in the morning."

"We both better get some sleep. My mom is an early riser. She'll be up at the ass crack of dawn making breakfast."

Demetri chuckles. "She does know I have staff that will take care of breakfast, doesn't she?"

"She knows. But don't be surprised if you wake up to find she's taken it upon herself to give them the day off. You might end up regretting your invitation."

"I want nothing more than for your parents to feel at home here, Glory. They are very much a part of your life and who you are. Your family is my family, *Krasivaya*." Tilting my head, I smile. "You sure about that?" "Positive." Demetri kisses me.

EPILOGUE

Demetri

"*Deda! Deda! Deda!*" My granddaughter squeals as she totters across the lawn as fast as her little legs will carry her. Scooping Breanna into my arms, I hold her to my chest as she squishes my cheeks together. "*Deda,*" she giggles.

I kiss the top of Brea's head. "Have you been a good little girl?"

Breanna bobs her head up and down. "I good, *Deda.*"

Setting her back on her feet, I squat down to eye level with Breanna. "Would you like to see what *Deda* brought for you?" My granddaughter squeals once again and jumps up and down. Holding a small box in front of Breanna, I remove the top to reveal a Russian Nesting Doll set. I watch her eyes light up as she takes in the array of colors. Without missing a beat, she plops down on the grass and pays close attention to me as I show her how to separate the dolls.

"You know you don't have to bring the kids a gift every time you visit, Dad," Logan says as he strides up to me.

"It's my duty as their grandfather to spoil them, son."

Logan shakes his head, but I don't miss his grin. We go

through the same ritual each time I return from being gone. "Come sit and have a drink with us." Logan tips his head toward the other end of the yard where the rest of the men are sitting around the fire; with them are their wives. My eyes zero in on one woman in particular — my woman. I've been in Russia for the past week. After the incident with Vadim, I stayed with Glory for a few days, but unable to hold off handling my affairs with the Petrov family and with Ivanna's father, I reluctantly had to leave her side. Being apart from her the past seven days have been torture, but I slept well knowing the club was watching out for her. Even though Glory was safe from any immediate danger, and knowing The Kings were well equipped to take care of her, I still opted for Andrei to stay behind in Polson.

Andrei turning against Vadim was like signing his own death sentence. However, his sacrifice did not go unnoticed, so I offered him my protection in return. He now works for me, and I dare anyone to question it. As for the Petrov family, Yerik's widow and daughter are the sole heirs to the empire now that both he and his son, Vadim are dead. Both are wanting no part of the world of organized crime, so Elena, under my guidance and protection, has secretly been dissolving all her late husband's business ties.

Sasha is back in Russia and on the mend. Aside from losing his heartbeat for a moment, Sasha suffered third-degree burns over thirty percent of the left side of his body, a broken arm, and collarbone, along with a concussion from the accident. Victor is with him and will remain with his brother until he heals from his injuries.

With my eyes trained on the woman who owns my heart, I set out across the yard toward her. Anticipating my approach, Glory stands from her chair with her beautiful green eyes locked on mine. A warm summer breeze kicks up and causes her fiery red locks to dance across the face I love so much. Glory is still recovering from the car accident, and her arm is still in a sling, but at this moment with the late afternoon sun shining down on her, she has never looked more stunning. "*Krasivaya*." I barely get the words out of my mouth when Glory throws herself in my arms. I catch her by wrapping my arms around her waist as she grips the back of my neck with her one free hand.

"I missed—" I cut her words off with my mouth on hers. A round of catcalls from behind us breaks up our reunion. I chuckle, but Glory is not amused by the banter being dished out by the guys. She shows her annoyance by flipping the bird over her shoulder.

Night has fallen as I sit by the fire with a beer in my hand, Glory on my lap and my family surrounding me. The children have long gone to bed, and conversation is flowing. "Did Nikolai say when he was coming back?" Logan asks.

I shake my head. "He didn't say, and I didn't press," I sigh. Logan and I share a look. Nikolai accompanied me to Russia and has decided to stay behind for a spell.

"So, what's next for you two?" this coming from Quinn. "When are you going to get hitched?"

Glory looks to me and our family and smiles. "Demetri and I have all the time in the world to get married. So maybe one day. For now, I can say that I am content, and I have never been happier than I am now." She regards our group. "Since when have I been one to play by the rules, anyway?"

"Never," Grace scoffs playfully, earning her a wink from Glory.

"I don't need a ring or a piece of paper to tell me we belong together. I love Demetri, and he loves me." Glory leans down and kisses me before turning her attention back to everyone. "I've decided to move in with Demetri. I'm moving back to Polson. I've already put my apartment on the market, and I sent my resume to the school here." When Glory says her next statement, she looks at Grace than to each one of the faces surrounding us. "It's time I come home."

There is a chorus of, "hell yeah" from the guys and and, "about time" from Glory's best friend.

"You know, Logan, if your dad does marry Glory, she'll be your new mommy," Quinn jokes.

I shake my head at his statement, and Glory rolls her eyes.

"Fuckin' Quinn," Jake mutters.

The same time Logan slaps him on the back of his head.

"Dipshit."

Jake's face grows from amused to more serious, then stands from his seat. "I think I can speak for all my brothers and the entire family when I say we are fuckin' thrilled the two of you finally pulled your heads out of your asses and found your way to each other." He holds his beer bottle up. "To Demetri and Glory."

"To Demetri and Glory," our family says in unison.

I look around at the people in my life who matter the most and know I'm where I belong. My eyes settle on the face of the woman sitting on my lap. *Damn, how did I get so fucking lucky?* Threading my fingers through Glory's silky red hair, I lower her head, bringing her lips close to mine. "Welcome home, *Krasivaya*."

Now, the part about the turtle. Is just that, a part of the story. A when, where, and why story that involves finding and rescuing a turtle.

On an average summer day, that turned into a turning point in my life. That led me to make a lot of positive changes.

The story is mainly about my first encounter with my Spirit Guides.

And how my life was forever changed after that blessed day. In this short story, I will be telling you about my experience with them. How our communications began, and how we interacted with each other in them.

You will be hearing about some of the conversations that I had with them. Most of it was on a very serious level.

With some of it being a little humorous at times. Which I certainly enjoyed experiencing. At last, now I know the answer to the question of whether God has a sense of humor. I thought it to be interesting to find a sense of humor in the Spirit Realms. My discovery of all of this took place when I was in the process of getting to know my Spirit Guides.

In this story, I will be telling you many things about myself. Some of it involves my upbringing and the things that I was taught. You will see what kind of life I was living. And you will know what my views were on life, up until the encounter.   You will be hearing about how I was programmed by my parents in their raising of me. And how

I was made to believe that life was a certain way. And that there is no other.

I am mentioning the programming to you now. Because it is another very important part of the story. How the programming that I received. Like so many other people in the world. Being taught through the passing down from one generation to the next. This is one of the main reasons why my Spirit Guides ministered these truths unto me.

Now, before you start reading the story, I would like you to get to know me a little bit. My name is Robert Jon Tengelitsch. I was born in Elkhart, Indiana, to my beloved parents, Beverly Ann Williams and Robert Lawrence Tengelitsch. My mother's side of the family was English, and my father's side, the Tengelitsch, came from Germany and were of Hungarian descent. My dad was also a little Irish from my grandma T's side of the family.

Both sides of my family came from less than the middle class and were immigrants who arrived here only 2 and 3 generations ago. We had more than some other people, but not much.

All of my life, I watched how my parents struggled to survive. From an early age into my adulthood. I knew nothing about a life of prosperity.

This is important because a life lived in poverty is extremely relevant to the story that I will tell.

I wrote this story with the intention that you will find it more than just entertaining. I even hope that you enjoy its content to a degree that you find it insightful. And even educational. More than mere entertainment.

I truly want to believe that you might come away with a different point of view on life. And that the content of this story had something to do with it.

I am also hoping that you find me the author to be an interesting person. Interesting enough that you might follow me and my writings about my journey, and all that I discover on the way.

And with that being said, shall we begin?

Chapter 1

It was only by chance.

It was a hot summer day in mid-July, on the state line of southwest Michigan and Northern Indiana. And I had just left the house, I was heading to Simonton Lake, where I wanted to do some running around, and a little shopping. At least that's what I was telling myself that day. I was only killing time out of my boredom. To be honest with you, I hadn't much going on in my life at that time.

After hearing me just tell you, that was the reason I was driving. It was because I was bored. I think it's safe to assume that you can see, that it was merely by chance. That I was traveling down this extremely hot road, at this particular time of the day.

It was a 90 plus degree day, and it was around 12 noon. And the sun was pretty much directly overhead. It was definitely the hottest time of the day.

And for you to have an idea of what it is like on this road. I would like for you to picture this in your mind. There are very few trees, so as you can imagine there is not much for shade. Especially not at this time of the day, or any time for that matter, until the evening. So shelter from the sun is not likely to be found. If you were walking or caught stranded. Possibly with vehicle difficulties or something. Like I have had happen to me, more than once in my life.

Chapter 2

My childhood

And I would know all too well about this. You see, I grew up here. And I spent a lot of time walking down this road. I have lived here ever since I was 5 years old.

And I was walking it long before it was paved over like it is today. I spent so much of my life on this road, with my friends, and my pony Dolly. That I feel as if, it is literally a part of me.

So you can understand more about where I lived. It was on a road that travels north and south that crosses the state line. I lived ⅛ mile to the south of the state line on county Road 15 in Elkhart Indiana. I lived on a small farm. I had a brown and white pinto pony, whose name was Dolly. We had three dogs, and some chickens.

We always had a few cats as well. I lived there all of my childhood years and into my adult ones. All the way up to writing this book. Out of 50 years, I only lived away from the farm for 15 of them.

And those years were broken up because. I had some hardships and had to come back home to get myself together a few times.

Living near the state line of Michigan, with it being so close. Made my life different from most of the other kids in my school. Because you see,   with me being on the state line. Many of my friends were from Michigan. They lived in Cassopolis Michigan, and if they didn't go to the Cassopolis schools. Then they went to the White Pigeon, or Constantine schools which are other school districts in Cass County.

You can say that I am a little of both states. I claim one as the state of my birth. And the other I claim is because I grew up spending so much of my time there.

If I wasn't on the Indiana side, I was in the beautiful state of Michigan. And believe you me, when I tell you that I love the state of pure Michigan.

I mean it wholeheartedly!!

Chapter 3

Finding Toby

So here I am driving along on this terribly hot paved road. Listening to a favorite on the radio. It was the Blue Oyster Cult Band, don't fear the reaper. And I had it turned all the way up, as loud as the radio and speakers would go. For some reason that summer, that song was being played a lot. And I enjoyed it every time I heard it. For it brought back memories of my dad and I.

When I was listening to the radio, and thinking about my dear ol pops. I couldn't help but notice how ungodly hot it was. And to top things off, my car's air conditioning didn't work. I was wondering how much it was going to cost, to fix my air conditioner. When I noticed my hands were glistening in the sun's rays, from all the sweat that was covering them.

And not just there, I was sweating everywhere on my body. It was like I was in a car sauna, and it was sucking the water out of every pour on my body.

Have you ever got straight into your car on a hot day. Without opening the doors, and windows for a few minutes first? Before you just hop in it and drive off, hoping that the car would cool down quickly? Well, that's exactly what I did. And my car was not cooling down like I had hoped it too.

" Damn it's hot."

I said while sweating my bajeebies off.

Driving with the windows down, reminiscencing the good old days with my pops. When I looked down at the speedometer. I blurted out, "dam."

When I noticed that I was going slightly over the speed limit. I was doing a little over 40, and 35 mph is what is posted on the road sign. But most people drive between 40 and 50 on this road all the time. That's probably why, I have been seeing more police driving down it.

I couldn't help it, but to second guess myself right then, when I reached for the seat belt. Oh good it's on, I thought. I don't want, and surely don't need, any tickets. Did I tell you that I am a Pisces with an extremely creative mind? Well, I am just that. And with that creative mind, I was picturing in my head a police officer. Beside my car sweating his bum off, while waiting for me to find my registration and insurance paperwork. I laughed under my breath like it was my little joke on a police officer.

That's when I first caught a glimpse of it, up ahead on the roadway.

My first thought was, what is it? Is it trash, maybe a beer bottle I thought. I didn't want to run anything over, let alone something that will cause me to have a flat tire. I remember talking to myself, saying out loud something like.

" Hell no ! "

Not today I ain't. I am not changing no tire on the side of this road.

As I was having this conversation with myself, about flat tires. I noticed that the air that was coming through my windows. Was like a dragon's breath. Hot, and dry with the stench of asphalt. And there was also a hint of somebody burning something off in the distance. I started to look around for the plume of smoke.

But I quickly put my attention back to the roadway. Remembering that I've been watching for the mysterious object on the road. And it's just about time to slow down. I can see it getting closer, I was about to go around it. When I began to see that it was not a beer bottle. That I had previously assumed it might be. It looks to be a round-shaped piece of trash, was my very next thought.

Maybe a ball cap? After I got closer to the object, I ruled out it being a ball cap. Because it was obviously too small to be that. You know it's absolutely amazing, how many things can go through your mind in only a second or two.

To my surprise, I came upon the object a little bit faster than I had expected. And when my eyes had become fixed on it. It was already too late.

At that time all I could do. Is blurt out another cuss word. When I safely stopped my car 10 or 15 feet past the object. " SMH " I was shaking my head, questioning myself. About what I thought I had just seen.

I looked in my rearview mirror before putting my car into reverse. And when I was backing up, I realized that I hadn't even looked behind, me when I slammed on the brakes.

I said there ain't no way that I just passed a painted turtle, there just isn't any way possible.

After backing up to where I could open up my car door. To take me a closer look at what I think is a turtle. I then opened up my car door and mumbled some words out of my mouth.

"How in the fudge did you get here little buddy?"

At the same time, I was thinking. Oh my god, I can't believe this. I reached down to pick the little guy up, he had not been run over. I gave out a sigh of relief, with a sincere feeling of gratitude.

Just so you know, I love all animals. And I do not like to see any of them get hurt. Especially to lose their life on the road from an automobile. As I was holding him and wiping his face off with my fingers, I looked into his shiny little eyes. He looked scared. His little turtle face appeared to be sad when at the same time he was looking scared.

That's when I told him, you're gonna be ok. I got you now, bud. Right then I felt this connection between us. And I thought I had seen him smile, so I immediately smiled back. Even though I wasn't sure if he did because he was badly covered in dirt and dust. That's when I reached back into my car, to grab my water bottle.

I dumped some water on him and then started to wipe the dirt and dust off.

I was being very careful when I was wiping him, just in case he was hurt. And when he was cleaned up a little better.

I began to look him over more closely, examining him thoroughly. And when I felt that he had no injuries. At least not any that I could see.

I stood there for a minute, trying to get a grip on the moment. I was standing there, in my thoughts with my eyes looking in every direction. For what, I don't know. I began to notice that there wasn't any wildlife to be present. Not a bird anywhere that I could see. Maybe it's the heat I thought. It just looked so barren, and lifeless where I found this turtle.

There off in the distance across the cornfield. That plume of smoke I was looking for a minute ago, there it is.

I immediately turned and looked down the road to see if any cars were coming. And when I did You could see the heat waves over the road. I turned again, to look the other direction. To see the same heat waves of energy, as far as I could see.

Still, no cars coming, that is good and unusual. I look down at this turtle that I was holding in my hands. He wasn't any bigger than one of my fists he was so tiny. I told him, you got blessed today bud. That's when I gently put him on the floorboard of my car. My first idea was, to put him on my soft car seat. A little luxury would be a nice part of this rescue mission. I was about to place him on the seat when I stopped and said. Nope,

Don't do that! You just got done slamming on your brakes a minute ago.

I laughed at myself and agreed with the floorboard
idea. Lol!

Chapter 4
Getting personal

A him? I don't know for sure. But I did kinda connect with him like he was a masculine turtle. I was relating to this turtle, because my own life was similar. At that time I was feeling like I was in a place where I did not belong. Like this turtle, the both of us were in some messed up hopeless situation. A long way from where we would rather be.

If you know what I mean?

Well needless to say I had a change of plans, the turtle gets first priority now. I wasn't really doing anything anyhow. Remember?

I was only killing time.

"Lol"

I was puzzled at how this turtle got here. So I began to take a closer look at the side of the road.

I remembered that the ditch was known, for having a little bit of water in it this time of the year.

It's important to know what the landscape in this scene looked like. So I want you to try and picture this. Tall grass on both sides of the road. Some of the grass is from last year. It is light tan in color, and some of it is still standing. The rest of it has been blown down.

And is now lying in big clumps here, and there. And pretty much everywhere.

Now picture the tall light tan grass, with new grass growing throughout it.

This makes it easy to see, the dark green of the new growth.

As it fights its way towards the sun.

Struggling to get through all the dead grass.

Making itself, so ever obvious with the dark green colors of new growth. With a background, of an endless sea of tan grasses, blowing in the summer breeze.

All of this grass is making the landscape appear flat, and level to the untrained eye. Giving you the impression that there is no ditch there.

But o'l boy, let me tell you. You better believe that there is one. That is for sure. I have seen many trucks stuck in this ditch. Because the drivers thought they would pull off the side of the road, and park.

Sorry, Charlie. It's anywhere from a two and a half, to a three-foot deep drop-off. The depth of this ditch might vary on different parts of the road. But one thing is the same.

That is this ditch starts as soon as you leave the edge of the road.

When I took a closer look, I could see that the ditch was dry. I then noticed something that I had not previously seen before. A big steel tube, a covert to help the farmers.

With the water that runs off the fields in the wet season. It looked as though it also assisted with the water from the roads when it needed a place to run off too.

I could see all the erosion, that was left behind from the heavy rains. From the looks of it, there must have been a lot of rainwater, and snowmelt from last year. It was all funneled into a place where the farmer's field was at its lowest elevation. It was easy to see that it was once a big pool of water.

Seeing this I tried to remember if I had ever noticed it before. Nevertheless, it was bone dry and all Cracked up, from the merciless summer sun. That's when it hit me. It makes perfect sense now. This is why, this turtle was trying to find a new home.

Chapter 5

Finding a new home

Well, I guess I'm that guy. Is what I said to myself, as I spun around on the heel of my foot. I was suddenly filled with joy. And I had this strange feeling of a purpose to fulfill.

" I got you now bud."

I had to find this guy a new home!

I'm on a mission with a purpose now!

I am gonna save this little turtle's life and become its hero. This will also give me an opportunity to become a conservationist for a day.

Whoo hoo!!

A chance to express my love for wildlife.

If you know me, then you know how much I love animals. And it would be no secret to you that I love turtles. So this was a little more, than being just a good Samaritan. It was indeed a privilege for me. To have my hands involved in the rescuing of a little turtle, who is in such dire straights….

Finding a home was an easy choice to be made.

In fact, it almost felt destined. If you remember right, I was heading to Simonton Lake. Which is in fact, a lake. But it is often referred to as a place where you are going to, when you have no plans or intentions, to be near the lake.

If you were not from here, and you heard someone say. I'm going to Simonton Lake. You might assume that they were going swimming or boating. But that is not always the case here. For your information, It's also a community with the conveniences of Hotels, and gas stations.

More motels, a Dollar store. A Martin's grocery store, and some restaurants. All of this is conveniently located right next to the 80/90, Indiana Toll Road. In the RV capital of the world, Elkhart Indiana. We are the largest producer, of Recreational Vehicles, in the world.

If you were not already aware of it. And you're wondering if your RV was made here? I would have to tell you, yup. It was more than likely built. In Elkhart County, Indiana.

The lake

I was picturing the lake and beginning to imagine, the life this little turtle was about to experience. When I turned my focus back to driving. I was coming up on the road, that heads straight to the public boat launch. I am no more than half a mile away now, only a few minutes of a drive left. Before I put this little turtle in the lake.

As I made my turn onto Lk.Shore dr. I couldn't help but replay in my mind what just happened. I was at home just 10 minutes ago, when I got the idea to drive to the store. What if I was still at home right now? This poor little turtle would still be on that hot road. Being slowly baked in the sun.

If I hadn't left, I wouldn't have found this little guy.

" Turtle."

If I hadn't been so bored, with nothing to do.

I wouldn't have found him.

I kept thinking about this, and how it was all just by chance. That I was at that place, at that specific time. The same time as the turtle.

Right then I was telling myself, I need to get some goals. To keep myself in a productive state of mind.

" I think I'm going crazy here"

I had to chuckle at this. I mean that's funny in itself. "Right?"

There is always something to do in life. I believe that most of us as adults, have heard this said before.

That's when I caught myself, I was smiling. I was looking in the rearview mirror when I noticed that I had a big smirk on my face. It must have been because I was on a mission with a purpose. And I'm feeling happy, I'm not even sure why I'm feeling so happy.

Of course, I am happy to be able to help this unfortunate little turtle.

Right then, deep in my heart, I couldn't help but think how lucky this guy was. Seriously, all of this is because I had nothing going on today.

Chapter 6

The Voice

It was then when I was in deep conscious thought. That a voice appeared, and this is what it said… …   .. .. … …

" A weary traveler you are, far from your home. Lost and lonely confused with what you do not know".

Okay hold up, this thing just got crazy as hell.

I mean I just picked this turtle up from out of the middle of a road. And now I am hearing a voice in my head. Speaking to me like, some kind of mystical elder.

The voice was soft, yet powerful. Divine in itself, giving off an angelic presence in its essence.

I hit my brakes while simultaneously looking in the mirror.

Oh god, I did it again.

Thinking back only a few minutes ago when I found him.

At the same time, I was saying at the top of my lungs.

I will let this turtle out, right mother loven now!

I don't remember if I screamed it, or not. But I said.

" Oh My God" !!!

What in the fudge happening here?

I am literally in shock now!

Nothing like this has ever happened to me before. Not In the 47 years that I have been alive.

I looked in my mirrors, I looked at both sides of me. As if I was looking for someone. Not the Voice, no, I was seeing if anyone was watching me.

The look on my face had to of been, one of pure bewilderment.

All of a sudden, I become conscious of it all.

I had a visual picture of everything that had just happened. It was like in a slow-motion picture. Where time stood still. What a strange feeling, I thought.

This picture in my mind was so full of detail. It had feelings, smells, and sounds. The vision went all the way back, to when I woke up this morning. I saw myself making a second pot of coffee. I was bringing my cup up to my nose, and I was smelling it with its hazelnut aroma. I then fed the animals. And started walking back, and forth through the house.

Omg, I didn't even remember doing that. This is the part that really blew my mind, and threw me completely off balance. I just saw my whole morning flash through my mind, in detail. I have seen myself unconsciously pacing back and forth in my living room.

Unbelievable how all of this was revealed to me, in the blink of an eye. Leaving me with this unsettling feeling of, uncertainty.

What is going on here? This voice, who is it? It's not the one in my head, I know that one really good.

And yes, I do talk to myself, just so you know. And when I do, I will hear a voice in my head. I am more than comfortable, with talking to myself.

"Lol"

I even answer back out loud. And this has gotten me into some weird situations. Sometimes when someone does hear me, and they weren't supposed to. I will say something to them like.

Yeah, no worries here.

I'm just having a little meeting with my advisors.

Then I will say. To the 3rd party, that no one can see.

" Leave a message, I'll get back to you later."

Then with my most apologetic expression. I will look this person who overheard me, right in the eyes. And say, I am very sorry. What was that, that you were saying? I usually get some sort of strange look from the person. That is involved when this happens.

Different voice

I can tell this voice is different than mine.

Well, this is what I was telling myself anyway.

I am always talking to myself in this way. And my voice doesn't feel like this. This voice doesn't even feel like it's mine. And this is the craziest part, I can feel this voice. Strangely enough, it's as if it is familiar to me. Almost like, I know it from somewhere.

This caught me off guard and even gave me the ebeejeebees. But yet at the same time, it was comforting to me In a strange way. It was such a weird feeling. And as I was giving this some more thought. I couldn't help but question myself.

Was I trying to ignore this Voice?

Yes, I was!

I was trying to resist listening to this voice who had just made contact with me.

I had to give out a little laugh at that thought.

How in the heck am I gonna do that?

And why would I want to?

Maybe I was supposed to hear what the Voice had to say.

All I know is that, at the time. It was making me feel uncomfortable. And even though I didn't like how it was making me feel. I somehow knew that I was supposed to be hearing whatever it was. That is being told to me.

You know, like when your grandmother is telling you something.

That you don't care to hear at the time, but you listen to it anyway. Because you can feel your grandmother's love in her voice. And it's probably some good advice, that you should listen to anyhow.

" Yup "

It was kinda like that.

I mean just like that!   Even still lingering around like grandma's words used to. This event reminded me of leaving g-mas house, where I so often heard grandma saying. " Bobby Jon, remember what I said." But the only words I am hearing now, are from the riddle. That the Voice said.

" Riddle"

A weary traveler you are, far from your home. Lost and lonely, confused with what you don't know. So far from the way you want to go.

What is this?

Is it a riddle, or rhyme?

What's the meaning of these words?

I don't even know why I'm still thinking about this. The Voice is gone! And it can stay gone, as far as I am concerned.

I'm just saying, the Voice that I am usually talking to in my head. At least It makes some sense, out of the words it uses.

Still, I can not help but wonder. Who is this voice?

Could it be because I miss my Pops? Is that it?

It's plain as day to me what my dad would have said If he was with me today. We would be doing this very same thing, putting this turtle first. Before we went about doing whatever it was, that we were doing.

That is why I have to consider that.

I was just thinking about my dear old dad. Only moments before.

Could that be it?

I keep thinking this same thought, over, and over again.

" Stop Bob! "

I said in my frustration.

The daddy ghost theory was shot out almost immediately. Believe me, it was my first idea. After all, I was just reminiscing about my dear old dad. When all of this was happening…

The voices…???

I can see the lake straight ahead. There is a truck, with its boat and trailer, in front of me.

" WoW," I said, that's a really nice flippen boat. I wonder how much it cost? I'm just wondering, it ain't like I will ever be able to afford one. Hey, I can dream, can't I ?

Making sure that I kept a safe distance between the boat trailer, and me. With myself being a respectful person who always tries to be courteous to other lake lovers. I started slowing down to give the boaters their right away. I thought I saw some passengers, but it was hard to tell. With the boat and a giant innertube in the way.

I know that he, or she, will be positioning the boat trailer. Where it can be easily backed straight down the boat launch and into the water

After slowing down to put some space in between us. I was now back several car spaces from this boat that I was still envying. And in between envying the boat and my driving. I was considering, where I was going to park.

When the Voice appeared again.

Saying … ..

" Take this turtle, and set it free,

in the place that it is meant to be.

For this turtle, is worlds away from its home. Much like you are!! Who is lost, and looking in this endless sea? For your own possibilities. That is being stolen from you, in this reality. That you are choosing to be !!! "

Okay, this situation, just got mind-blowing.

Even for me.

The voice is back, but it is not alone.

I heard three voices this time.

I am, sure of it.

I heard three different tones in their voices when they were telling me that rhyme.

This whole thing has been bazaar. From the finding of this turtle, where there isn't any water. To the strange vision that I had in my head. Replaying my morning activities in such a vivid recollection. And then these voices, come on here. This is enough to creep anyone out. These voices are not like anything I have ever experienced before.

I had to question myself, are these of a Divine origin?

Angelic maybe?

This is what I was thinking when the voice asked me.

" Are you confused, Bobby?"

" YES! "

" I AM! "

I said out loud with some attitude. I could feel myself starting to get a little uncomfortable here. And I don't like anything, or anyone's messing with my comfort zone. But strangely enough, I started laughing at the same time. Laughing at what, my own self? With a voice in my head that seems to be in more control of the conversation than I am.

At this moment in time, I have begun to analyze my situation. And I am now questioning myself if I had smoked or drank anything to have possibly caused me to hallucinate.

No! I was not hallucinating, not from the heat or anything else. This voice is from a Divine origin, I'm not saying it was God or an Angel. But it is of something far greater than I have experienced before.

" I Am Listening "

Saying, yes of course agreeing.

Then asking, What do you want me to do?

And this is what I heard: " Take your brother this turtle you call it, and free it in the lake. " I can't remember if I replied out loud or in my head, but I said yes, sir.

I was already thinking this in my mind. The decision was made in a millisecond.

Voice;

Now, imagine what kind of life your brother, this turtle, will have now.

!!! Omg !!!

That's when it hit me, I was not just saving the turtle. I mean, I could have put him in a fish tank and given him a name and promised to take care of him and protect him. I mean, that's way better than death, right? Or I could have put him in the small pond down the road from me. That we all swam in as kids. The pond was only 1 mile down the road. But no, I was putting him into a beautiful spring-fed lake that is 302 acres in size. Profound my thoughts were. A million miles an hr they went searching the possibilities this turtle could have. And that I was going to be the one to make this possible. I smiled as I pondered on the thought of. . ..

I   mean isn't this what I have been praying for? Dreaming of for myself?

I was in deep thought and was subconsciously driving when the Voice said, you are here. " I know, "

I said with my sarcasm. Is there any place you want me to park?

Oh, no!

I know I did not just speak sarcastically to this Devine Voice. That I think is in my head. But faster than I could think that. I was instructed to park next to the boat ramp out of the way of the boat that I was following. When I agreed to these instructions.

I was already thinking to myself, that I wouldn't have blocked the boats from accessing the ramp anyhow.

The Voice:

Park close to the water's edge, where the people are playing with the children. With no words needing to be said. I knew they were supposed to witness an act of conservation being done. To quite possibly inspire more of the same.

They looked at me strange and with concern as I parked and got out of my car. Picture this, me a bald-headed white man with no shoes or shirt on and tattoos everywhere.

Anything could be assumed at that point with children being involved. I could see their faces and I noticed the man become aware that I was looking for something in the back seat area. Good Lord! , I think I am scaring these people. I'm only 15 feet away from them digging around in the back of my car. Turtle where in the hell are you? And there he was, at last I found him, he was under the seat. It only took 30 seconds but it felt like 2 minutes. The look on that dad's face when I came up with a turtle in my hand, was a look of relief and joy. Look he said to the children, look at the turtle.

I quickly smiled and said yeah, I found him on Stateline Road. The dad's eyebrows went up with a look of surprise like he knew that would be a strange place to find a painted turtle, but that is as far as that went.

Everyone looked at the turtle without touching him for a few seconds and said. "You gonna put it in the lake?"

Yuper, you bet I am was my reply. Are you guys ready, here we go. To myself, I was thinking that this would be the magical moment where I release this turtle into a whole new world.

No wait a whole new Universe of unimaginable adventures. A life with so much to offer. This turtle

hasn't ever seen anything like this. I mean look, I'm staring at a school of minnows around my ankles and that is just for starters.   There are Lilly pads everywhere, and over there look some ducks and geese. And just then I heard a bullfrog croaking. And over there a red wing black bird on a cattail singing his song.   There was so much life all around us.   I paused, it looked like they all came to watch.

An enchanting moment it was.

As I began to lower this little turtle down to the water I thought, wait! I don't even know your name, and how could I?

Lol, to myself I thought, Omgoodness it's not like I was talking to this turtle, or was I?

Toby I said out loud, it's Toby that's what your name will be. Somehow I felt like I already knew that Toby is what his name is.

Anyhow I smiled great big and said. Here you go Toby welcome to your new LIFE!!!

That Is what I said out loud on a count of the mom and Dad being right there making my ego act all shy.

But in my mind, I was thinking this. Toby little guy, you are gonna love it here.

Let me tell you. Yup, you will meet a bunch of new friends to do all kinds of cool and fun things like climbing up on logs and soaking up the sun for fun bud. All this went through my mind while these few words were spoken and as I was bending over to gently put him in the lake.

I was thinking I hope he is ok. Because I didn't know how long he had been out of the water when I had found him. In the few minutes that he was in my hands, he had been hiding in his shell.

All we could do was try so I slowly lowered him into the water, still holding onto him with these hands of love.

With an Oh so gentle touch of love, as if I am already attached to him.

As I was lowering Toby into the lake I noticed how warm the water was when it touched my hands. I said, Oh looky there. There are minnows all around him. Right then he pokes his head out, now his feet and legs O my, he's wanting to swim. The children are watching with excitement the dad and mom are smiling. I let him go and he started swimming away like he knew where he was going. Suddenly, I am filled with joy that I have not known since I don't know when.

As I stand there in ALL, Dad says lookie there and pointed with a finger. It looks like he's saying thank you. And to my surprise, Toby the turtle had swum out only about ten feet from us and resurfaced. I felt like Toby was looking right into my eyes.

Yes, it was as though Toby was grateful, and he was thanking me for what I did for him. I was so filled with joy my eyes were beginning to fill with water. Omg, don't cry over a turtle. Especially one that I just met, no wait I mean just found. Holding back these tears of joy I said to Toby. Go, go start that new life. And as soon as I spoke those words he went under and swam away into the deep turquoise blue water never to be seen by me again.

Chapter 7

Saying Goodbye

I said well, it looks like he is a happy turtle now. And the mission is accomplished !!!

Everyone was smiling great big as he swam off into the beautiful turquoise, blue, and green water of Simonton Lake.

Right then, the dad and I looked at each other, both with eyes of envy. And when our eyes locked for this short, but intense moment, it was as if I could hear his thoughts. He was thinking about how this turtle's, life just got unimaginably blessed.

I smiled great big at the dad and gave him a wink, letting him know I felt the same way.

I politely said goodbye to the family, assuming that they were one. I never heard mom or dad, but I couldn't help noticing that the children looked just like the adults.

We were all still standing in the water up to our knees while saying our goodbyes. When we were done, I slowly turned towards the shore, touching the water with both of my hands. The water was very warm today. Of course, it would be that's because the water is always shallow where they launch the boats.

Surly the warm water is why Toby was so quick to swim off into the deep unknowns of the lake.

I then stepped back out of the lake and started walking the eight or ten steps it took to get back to my car. The sand and gravel was a little bit too hot for my bare feet.

I was still holding back my watery eyes when it hit me, and a few of my tears began to slowly run down my cheek. All of a sudden, I was overwhelmed with this feeling of peace. No, it was even more than that. I have never felt this way before. I had something happening inside of me. It was like an explosion of emotions. All at once, I was feeling loved, I felt joy, and happiness with a hint of sorrow and fear.

I felt as if everything was going to be okay. That's when a serene feeling of peace and knowing came over me. I felt like I was right where I was supposed to be. I felt safe and secure. But at the same time, I was feeling fear and a little bit of uncertainty.

Uncertain about what?

Is this uncertainty the fear that I am feeling? Am I scared of what I don't know? And why would I be scared of something that is not even a something yet?

I was in some really deep thought, trying to analyze everything that had just happened. I was intently wanting to know why I was having these mixed emotions. This can't be normal, I thought. It is easy to be confused with all of the feelings that I am experiencing all at once.

Chapter 8

Confused Conversations

While I was in those deep thoughts, the Voice returned, this time with a question.

"How do you feel, Bobby?"

I was instantly surprised and put into shock, like a deer caught in the headlights.

"Whoa, hold up, wait a minute here. What did you just say? Seriously, I thought you left with Toby."

The Voice;

"You mean Toby-I-Am-Ziy-Nor-ic-Ki?"

My reply was "Huh, that's his name?"

"Yes", replied the Voice.

"Toby works just fine for me. And what does a turtle need that big of a name for anyhow?"

"And how are you gonna ask me, how I am feeling when you are the one who is making me feel this way?"

Honestly, I don't know how I am feeling. I haven't ever experienced anything like this.

"I am in some shock here, I can tell you that much. And that you are beginning to make me feel like I am going crazy!!" "Do you want to explain to me what is going on here? .. .. . Please!!" I asked the 'Voice.

"If it is an answer that you seek, then you must ask me a question," the Voice replied.

"Riddles? More riddles? Are you kidding me?" I said, exasperated.

"I'm already riddled with confusion, and I just told you I was in shock from all of this.

Honestly, you're starting to freak me out a little—with all this weird crap."

Voice:

"What is this that you are calling this?"

Me:

"What did you say?" I asked, with some attitude.

I could feel that I was beginning to get upset. I was even getting a little angry at this point.

This is a normal reaction for me when I am frustrated by something that I do not understand… … Ugg!!

Voice:

"No riddle, it's a simple question, Bobby."

"How are you feeling?"

How am I feeling? Is he really asking me this?

Me:

"Confused, I am definitely feeling some confusion here."

Voice:

"Which part is most confusing?"

Ok, time out here! Stop talking for a minute, and let me think.

Now I am in my car, and I am opening the door. I just want to sit down for a minute.   So I have a seat behind the driver's wheel. As soon as I sat down, I leaned back and let out a sigh of relief. For what, I really don't know, but it did feel good, as I dramatically let it out.

I then looked in the mirror to see if the family was still there. I think I was checking to see if what happened did, in fact, really happen. Oh yeah, it happened for sure. I can see the children playing in the lake. They were splashing each other and laughing at Dad because Dad was getting wet where he didn't want to.

Lol

Ok, it's time to go. I make sure it's clear by looking in all four directions. I can see the children, and they are safe. As I put the vehicle into drive and start to pull away. (SMH) I'm shaking my head and debating on driving at this time. I am considering maybe I should park over there underneath those big oak trees for a few minutes where it is shady..

There are two spots open to choose from that I can park in. I like the one underneath the biggest oak tree, there's a bit more shade in that one.

As I was pulling my car into position to park, I was listening to the gravel that was crunching beneath the tires. That's when I heard the Voice again, saying.

"That would be a great idea, Bob."

Me:

"What did you say? I thought I asked you to be quiet!"

I can't believe this. It's gotta be this heat. This has gone too far. I am definitely pulling over and parking for a few minutes. I have got to get my head together here before I drive any further.

Chapter 9

The Parking Lot

I pulled into the parking spot nice and slow and put my car into park. Then I turned the radio on and leaned the seat back a little. That's when I told myself.

" Relax, Bob."

"Yeah, that's it, close your eyes and take some slow, deep breaths."

While I was breathing, I was also trying to relate this experience to something from my past. Was it something I ate? Like mushrooms or some kind of hallucinogen? I laughed out loud, quite literally, because I did not eat any mushrooms, and I am not hallucinating. But it is pretty freaking hot. Remember me mentioning that the air was like a dragon's breath? Well, I don't actually know what a dragon's breath feels like. But I do know what a heater vent feels like. And this air, when the breeze does blow, feels really close in comparison to that.

"OK, focus on your breathing, Bob, just breathe nice and slowly. That's good, now let's take another deep breath. There we go, good job Bob, now let's do that ten more times. And then we'll see how you're feeling, bud."

After my little self-pep talk and ten deep breaths later, I tell myself, "Looky there, all better now. See, you just needed to get out of the sun for a few minutes, that's all."

Now, what was I doing before all this fiasco with the turtle started?

Oh yeah, I was going to the store to do some shopping. Feeling glad that it was all over now, I let out a sigh of relief as if I was overwhelmed by all this turtle-rescuing stuff. I said to myself, "No problem. All better now."

Nope, because right then, the Voice asks,

"Are you trying to figure out what just happened?"

Me:

"Omg! Are you still here?"

Verbally saying it out loud. In my frustration, I got back out of the car without even meaning to, slamming the door a little bit too hard. It made a loud noise, and a couple of boaters turned their heads and looked in my direction. I accidentally slammed the door because of this frustration that has come over me all of a sudden.

Then I started walking away from my car as if I was leaving the Voice in it. What was I supposed to do? I'm literally freaking out here. And now, I am standing in the middle of the parking lot. Right then, I began to look around, and that's when I noticed that there were more than just those two boaters who were looking in my direction. It was more like ten or more people staring at me.

Now, picture this, here I am just now noticing that the boat launch is packed full of trucks and trailers, and there are people everywhere. I mean everywhere! And some are beginning to stare at me. Staring at this bald-headed guy with the tattoos who is now slamming car doors on this beautiful summer's day.

It was an uncomfortable feeling to have all these people staring at me. Oh my goodness, even that couple down by the lake has taken notice, seeing that I haven't left yet. And now, they're staring at me, standing in the middle of the parking lot, looking confused. They probably heard me slamming the car door, too. Now my ego is in shock, and I'm freaking out on the inside. I had like a hundred things running through my mind all at once.

At this point, I don't even know if anyone has seen me talking to myself. Or even if I had been talking to myself. How much of this is in my head, and how much have I said? And now look at me, I'm questioning myself. Have I been talking out loud? Or am I just freaking out here over nothing?

Chapter 10

Parking Lot Paranoia and Celestial Giggles

Oh, I'm definitely freaking out over something here, that's for sure. And adding some paranoia to the situation. I feel like all these people are staring right at me. I'm the only person standing here in the middle of this parking lot. It must be a sight to see, especially if I look anything like the way I am feeling.

What an awkward feeling this was, and I didn't want to stand here for too long. But still, I'm looking for a way to cover up for this buffoonery.

As I turned towards the car, something caught my eye on the ground. So, I looked down at it to see that it was a smashed aluminum can. That's it! A piece of trash, that's why I'm in the middle of the parking lot. I bent down real slow and all to make it as televised as I possibly could.

When I picked it up, I held it out in front of me. Making sure that people could see that I was picking up a piece of litter. I took my time standing there for a moment longer, turning my head so as to be obviously looking for the closest trash can. Oh, would you looky there?

Is that a trash can that I see? One right over there, by my car. How wonderful, things are starting to look up. I'm not so embarrassed since I just managed to cover up that incident in the parking lot. That was a relief, and I did it with some more good Samaritan stuff to add to the turtle-rescuing adventure that I am on.

Right then, I began walking toward my car and the trash can. I was saying to myself, Boy, oh boy... for as crazy as all this is, you sure are doing a pretty good job of keeping it all together here, bud. Before I could answer my own thoughts, I was interrupted with a question from you know who, asking me, " Are you ok?"

Me:

"No", I replied

Then, whispering, I said, "Be quiet until I'm back in the car, damit! You got me out here looking like a damn fool."

Voice:

"I do?"

Me:

" Yes, you do!"

That's when I heard someone giggle a little, and then I thought I heard a chuckle, and then more giggles.

"Hey, what is this?" I had to call it out because I felt like I was the center of a joke or something. Not that I was feeling bad, I felt some love in it. A gentle, joking sense of humor. But with a little love, too. While still picking on my ego enough to get on a nerve. And from not just one voice this time. But two, and possibly even three voices now.

Almost back to my car, just a few more steps.

As I was reaching for the door handle, I grunted Ugg! Because of the aluminum, it was still in my hand. I turn and look at the trash can, it's right there. I can toss it in from here, so I try shooting it like a basketball.

" Ugg". Again I miss the whole damn trash can. I didn't even hit the side of the damn thing.

" Now what?"

 Starting to laugh at myself under my breath, I then quietly say to myself. "Can you believe this crap? I mean like seriously, can you believe this?" And I was sincerely asking myself a legit question.

Anyhow, like I was saying, this is a hard one to believe, and for a good reason. I don't care who you are. If you were having a day like mine, you too would be feeling a bit lost. I mean, just look at all of the things that have happened to me since this morning.

It is confusing to have this kind of mind-bending, mind-blowing stuff taking place in your head. Especially this early in the day, and in this short amount of time span. On a day as hot as today, it would make the devil sigh. That's why what happened next seemed like the only thing a guy like me could do.

I just started laughing.

Not loud, I kept it down, of course. I was already feeling embarrassed from all the eyes that were previously on me. Honestly, there's not really any other thing that a sane person could do. Right? But to start laughing, like I did.

It was like I had no choice in the matter. Anyhow, it just kinda involuntarily came out of me. And, on top of that, strangely enough, it even sounded a little bit like I was enjoying the laughter. But not for long, it wasn't that funny. The joke did have me scratching my head, wondering why. Why am I laughing at a joke that is on me?

After I stopped laughing at myself, it got quiet. I could still hear boat motors puttering around on the lake. But that wasn't the quiet that I was referring to. No, I was talking about the quiet that was now in my head. For what seems like the first time in forever. I start to take a few deep breaths, being careful to focus only on the breath. I don't dare think of the Voice again, thinking, if I ignore the Voice, it might go away. Here I am, sitting here hoping that it will just go away back to wherever it came from.

Breathing in and out. I paused for a few seconds, holding my breath, as I was listening. I did not hear anything until I started breathing again. Listening to myself breathe in and out. Still trying not to think of anything but my breathing is when I thought I heard something that sounded like another one of those damn giggles.

"Huh?"

What was that? Nothing, no sounds, nothing but my breathing. But now I'm having this weird feeling, though. Like one of those awkward silences, when there are two people in a small room and they're being shy towards each other.

Now all of a sudden I started to feel a little bit nervous from out of reflex. I reached for the car's ignition, turning it on. The radio comes on, but there is no sound. Oh yeah, I remember that I turned the volume down when I found the turtle. No problem, I was only after the clock to see what time it was anyhow.

Chapter 11`

The Question

Eleven twenty, in the am! That can't be possible. There just isn't any way that could be the time. Wait a minute! Let's think about this a little bit. Let me see, it was around Eleven o'clock when I left the house. And if you figure in the ten minutes of drive time plus the five minutes it took to stop and pick up the turtle. That makes fifteen minutes in total so far. Then there was the talking with the family when we were releasing him. Yup, that sounds about right, it all adds up to about twenty minutes or so. It all adds up, and it makes perfect sense. So I'm just gonna have to accept that it was the longest twenty minutes of my life.

It just seems like it has been a couple of hours, that's all I am saying. It was as if time stood still, and life didn't.

Whoa, that was deep. It even gave me some goosebumps on my arm. Just to make sure that I wasn't dreaming. I did myself a reality check. I pulled a hair out of one of the goosebumps. Ouch! Yup, I'm here and it's not a dream. That's my arm hair, and that looks like the root of it.

Face it, Bob, you got distracted by all of this excitement. And let's not forget that your brain is a little overheated. You simply lost track of time, bro. It's as simple as that. And that works just fine for me as I sit here in my car beneath these mighty Oak trees, enjoying the shade that they are providing me.

As I took a closer look at the tree, I noticed something. The two trees were actually just one great big one that put a big smile on my face, and I started admiring this big beautiful tree a little more when I began to feel an overwhelming sensation of being grateful. Not so much for the shade of the trees, this was different. This had a deep inner-standing feeling of gratitude. It even felt kinda separate from me. But yet, it was still me. Almost like it was someone else's feelings of gratitude.

Feeling all of these emotions, and all of them at the same time, was intense, that's for sure, and then to have it feeling foreign to me, like it belonged to someone else. That was too much for me to handle.

The voices in my head, and some goosebumps, that I can handle, but these feelings of unconditional love and this intense feeling of gratitude are making me begin to question myself. Am I having an out-of-body experience? I mean, an inner body experience. None of that makes any sense to me, only adding to the confusion. I can't tell which feelings are mine anymore, and that is way beyond anything that I have ever imagined.

Sitting here in my silence, listening to my breathing, I am wondering what to think next. You know, it's getting pretty bad when you have to share control of your thoughts with someone else. And I no sooner thought that. I mean, at that exact same moment, when I heard the Voice again, this time in a soft soothing tone.

"The turtle represents you, Bobby, and you represent us."

I did not speak, not even in my mind.

All of my attention was hanging on these few words as I tried to grasp hold of them. I kept getting hung up on the part where I was the turtle, but when I finally did have an idea, I asked the Voice a question.

"How is it that I represent you in all of this?"

The tone changed again, this time I felt a slight sense of sarcasm in it, with a humorous reply.

"Aren't you a bit more curious, Bob, to be asking how the turtle is in representation of you?"

I said, "Yes, I am now that you mentioned it. How does the turtle represent me?"

It was silent again while I was thinking about the question, and this time I had an eerie feeling that my thoughts were being listened to. With a strange feeling that the Voices were also being courteous to me, like they were giving me time to think for a minute. So I did think. I was thinking that there are multiple Voices in my head now. Not just one, but two of them, and maybe even more of them than that, with the possibility that they are listening to my every thought as I am thinking them.

That was it! I couldn't take it anymore. I said it's all your fault. I started accusing them by saying.

"You guys are not helping me here. You said you came to help. But you are only making me go crazy here!"

I look at the clock on the car radio, and it says eleven twenty-five. Right then, I tried to change the subject by pointing out that only twenty minutes ago, I was perfectly fine sitting at home. Yeah, I may have been lazy, but at least I was thinking normal thoughts. Look at me now. I try to be a good Samaritan and save a turtle from a horrible outcome, and now I'm feeling lost in my own mind. I'm hearing voices in my head, and I'm beginning to feel like I'm going a little crazy here. Next thing you know, it's gonna be off to the loony bin for me all because of that God bless it, turtle.

Wait a minute, wait a minute!

Can we hold up for a minute? This is getting way too intense, guys. Did I just say that? Yup, I sure did. I can't believe I'm talking to these voices like I'm the 3rd party in this conversation. Seriously, please, someone tell me what is going on here. No reply, only silence.

"Now you guys don't want to talk to me, is that it? Hey, you, I said !!"

"I want some answers, and I want them now!"

I was upset now, I said it with a stern voice this time. And I didn't even wait before I asked another question.

"Did God send you? Please tell me that you were sent here by God to help me! And you better not say I'm having some mental problems."

The softer of the three voices gently said, " No."

Me:

" No, no to what?"

"No, Bobby, you are not having any mental issues."

I said, "Ok, that's good, that's comforting to know. Now, how about it?"

Voice:

"How about what?"

Me:

"Did God send you here to talk to me?"

Voice:

" Yes, you could say that."

Me:

"Okay, how are you gonna help then?"

Now I'm starting to calm down a little, I mean I am not freaking out as much as I was.

That's when I started to remember that I was just jamming out to that song, 'Don't Fear the Reaper', and now these voices are telling me that they were sent by God. Right then, I hear a giggle and another chuckle.

Me:

"What's so funny about that? And would you please stop listening to my thoughts? For God's sake, can a guy have a little privacy in his own head?"

Some more laughing before their reply.

" Bobby, we did not tell you that God sent us here to talk to you."

I simply agreed and said you could say that.

Me:

"That's great, more of your riddles! I can't take this anymore, honestly. Please, can I get a straight answer? I mean, look here, guys, I have been playing along with you. And whatever it is you're trying to do to me, I'm not playing anymore, I've had enough of this share raid."

Inside I was laughing my ass off because it wasn't like I was in any kind of control here.

And then I hear…

Chapter 12

The Turtle, the Test, and the Truth

The Voice continued.

Voice:

"Bobby, why did you relate so strongly with this turtle that you found?"

I really wanted to point out that I'm the one asking the questions here. But I didn't, instead I intuitively became curious about the question that I was being asked. It only took about a second before I replied.

Me:

"It's because I feel like I don't belong here, I feel like I am stuck in a place that I need to leave. And like this turtle who was in a dire situation, I, too, am in a place where I am dying a slow and miserable death. Trapped in a barren wasteland, far, far away from where I belong."

That's when it hit me. Right that very moment, I experienced what could only be described as experiencing stillness. It was as if I was separated from the world for a minute. All alone in my mind, but connected to the Universe. Millions of pictures flew by in my mind like a film projector running wild. Some of it was my memories, and the rest of it was of things that were not familiar to me. I was in a bazaar state of mind, feeling connected to something much bigger than I had ever imagined. At the same time, I am feeling pretty small in my own existence.

In my new awareness, I felt significantly like I am a part of God's creation, even though I feel like a really small part. I was beginning to feel like I am the turtle here, dumb as to what is going on here. Believe me, I am trying my best to grasp hold of what is happening here.

As I was thinking about how I was in comparison with Toby, a super bright light entered my mind for what felt like a minute or two. All I could see was the light. It was so very bright, it was blue and white, and it had a feeling attached to it. Like the light was something solid. A bright, transparent light that was energy. I felt a sense of peace and knowing that I'm going to be just fine.

"That is it, isn't it? This has all been a test for me. All of it! Starting with the nudge you gave me at home to leave, to the feeling of going to the store, it was definitely you. Because I didn't even want to go anywhere. I was gonna stay right where I was and do nothing. But you were insisting on it. Somehow, without even speaking to me. You somehow gave me the nudge from inside. Somehow, you put the idea into my head. And you knew I would find that turtle, and you wanted to see how I would react when I saw it. If I would be compassionate and stop, or if I would just drive on by, leaving that turtle on the road to die."

If this is a test, I was given the role of a God figure to this turtle.

And I became this turtle's Almighty Savior, blessing this turtle with much more than just saving its life. No, I put this little turtle in a big beautiful lake and gave him a chance of a lifetime, and now, when it comes to you and me. It has gotta mean that my role is being switched around. To you being my savior now, that must mean you are here to save me. Is that it?

Right then, I started to feel a little dazed and confused. I felt like I used a lot of energy while I was doing all of that mental work. I think I got a brain strain.

A strange sense of knowing came over me. Now I had this strange feeling of communicating with the voice through telepathy. I couldn't remember if I replied verbally, or if I thought of the words and they felt like I was saying them. This was so mind-blowing and amazing to me, but it was very confusing too.

I began to pay close attention to how I was responding to our conversations, especially how I was communicating back to them. That's when the voice that calls me Bob said.

"Not quite, Bob."

Me:

"Not quite what?"

Me:

"I was thinking that you guys are here to take me away to a better place. A Paradise for me to live in because of my good deeds. Please tell me that you are."

Voice:

"No Bob, we are not taking you anywhere, not in your physical body!"

Me:

"Then what in the hell is this all about?"

I definitely spoke verbally this time, and as soon as the last word left my lips, a soft warm feeling hit me, and then the other Voice began to speak saying something that I couldn't make out. I was overwhelmed with this feeling of pure love. The most intense feeling of love yet. It just surrounded my whole being. It's like it was inside of me again and also all around me at the same time. That's about as close as it comes to me describing it.

I could literally feel an energy all around me almost caressing my skin. It was everywhere. It is even inside of me now and this is getting a little bit scary. But all I could feel was love, and now I can feel this love energy inside and out of me.

It was the most beautiful feeling of bliss leaving you in a feeling of euphoria. It was the most soothing and peaceful place imaginable. I must be experiencing nirvana, as I sit here paralyzed in this blissful sensational feeling of peace and security. I was lost in my thoughts until the voice started to speak again.

Voice:

"Bobby you are not a turtle. You are a special human being, you are so much more than you currently know and understand."

Me:

"Then please, help me to understand."

This time, both of the Voices spoke in perfect harmony.

Voice:

"That's what we are here for Bobby. To help you. To help you see that you are so much more than you currently think. We want you to know that you are a divine piece of creation."

Me:

"Yes, of course, I am a part of creation! But would you please tell me something that I don't already know like why are you calling me divine?"

Chapter 13

The Dream

Voice:

"You are divine because you are a part of the Divine that you are calling your God. You are a fractal of the Source of Creation. A miniature version of the whole that you come from."

Me:

"If you mean I am made in the image of my God, then that is a yes, for it is even written in my Bible. But, it doesn't make anyone divine. I've seen people who go to church be and are the most ungodly people alive. So, if I'm a fractal and I'm made in his image. How does that make me divine?"

Voice:

"Free will."

Me:

"What do you mean by free will?"

Voice:

"You are a piece of the divine. In your free will, you are choosing not to live in truth with love. Here, I will give you another example. Is your son still your son, if he chooses to live differently than you?"

Me:

"Well, okay. If you're gonna put it that way. Then I am divine. I'm just not living like the old, man does. Ha, ha, I've been telling people for years. That I'm a work in progress, just like it says in my Bible."

Voice:

"Do want to ask another question?"

Me:

"The dream I had, what does it mean?"

Voice:

"What dream are you referring to?"

Me:

"The one I had the other night? Wait a minute, how would you know about that dream? I just met you.

Voice:

" Laughing."

Me:

"What you Laughing at?"

Voice:

"Because you said that we just met."

Me:

"And what's so funny about that?"

Voice:

"I have known you many lifetimes. It is just that you can not remember them. At least not right now, at least not while you are in this lower vibration."

"Why don't you tell me about your dream Bobby And I will try to help you understand it."

Me:

"Okay well, let me see. I remember standing in front of a glass wall, but I didn't know that it was one yet. In my dream, I was standing in the life that I have always known. This one, I was even wearing the clothes that I am presently wearing. And the side that I was on in my dream. It looked dimmer in the lighting, and it had a depressing feeling to it."

"It was the very same life that I am stuck in today. And on the other side was an entirely different life. But it was mine too, and in it, I could see the life that I have always dreamed of having. On the other side in the life of my dreams, I could see a different version of myself. And in my dream, I was looking right at myself on the other side of the glass barrier. And over there I looked happy, and I appeared to be successful, and even prosperous.

After seeing everything on the other side, I got so excited that I tried stepping into it. But I couldn't, so I started banging on the glass. When it didn't break, I began banging on it harder, and harder. I even started kicking it. I used all of the strength that I had. But nothing was working to get through the glass wall. I kept trying my hardest to get to the other side. But it would not break. As I stood there exhausted from my desperate attempts to break through the glass. I realized that I was trapped. Trapped on this side of my dream. Where I am now for some God-forsaking reason."

Voice:

"The glass represents the invisible barrier that your self-doubt has created".

Me:

"What do you mean? How did I create a glass wall between me and my dreams."

Voice:

"She softly asked, Bobby what was on the other side of the wall where your dreams are at?"

Me:

"You want to know what things were over there?"

Voice:

"Yes."

Me:

"Omgoodness let's see, there was a big beautiful two-story house. It is up off of the ground on these huge pillars for legs. The home is near the ocean, and it's off the ground to prevent water damage from storm surges. The pillars make the house look like it has three stories to it. It had a grand look to it like a rustic beach log cabin. And it was built on the side of a cliff that was overlooking the beachfront. The ocean was in the sight of my house. It had a long driveway with buildings staggered on both sides of it. I could see some classic cars with a couple of trucks parked in one of them.

Yes, classic cars with some hot rods mixed in the collection. In another building there was a huge collection of motorcycles, so many that I wouldn't ever be able to ride them all. And the horse barn was right behind this building. Built tight to the side of the mountain like the house. That is where I was at. I was in the barn tending to my horses in the dream. There were animals everywhere, dogs were running around barking, and playing in the yard. There were cats in the barn near me and the horses. I even saw a cat in the pen with peacocks and chickens.

It was a paradise that I could only dream of. It must have been worth a couple of millions of dollars. And that is something that is just not possible for this guy. "

Voice:

"She asked, what do you mean Bobby?"

Me:

"Repeating her question back to her. What do you mean? With a sarcastic tone. Then saying to her, exactly what I said. I could never afford that kind of life."

Voice:

"When did you make that decision Bobby?"

Me:

"What? I'm not sure."

Right then, without saying anything to me this time. She somehow showed me my life, and I saw the many regrets that I have.

Like a job that I passed up one time because of my lack of confidence. Only to have someone else get it. This was devastating to me because later on down the road, I found out that I was more qualified and better for the job than the guy who got it. The sad part was that this guy was now my boss. When I should have been his.

She showed me a lot of my memories, all with regrets of missed opportunities. But this one was for sure the one, that was my biggest regret. I don't think I ever really got over it. I could remember saying to myself. *See Bob, you are always gonna be working for the man.* I didn't even look at a manager position after that experience. I was done and decided it was not for me. I pictured myself as a worker bee or a worker ant.

All of these memories flooded my mind, in a blink of an eye.

I immediately became upset, when I saw all of these missed opportunities of mine. This angered my ego, and that made me feel compelled to send my anger back to her, '*the voice.*'

I have to laugh about this as I'm writing this story. I mean honestly, how am I gonna telepathically send a vision back to this benevolent being in the defense of my ego?

If I could, or couldn't. It did not matter; my ego was definitely offended. And that made me wanna point some things out in my defense.

That's when I said,

"What are you doing? Why did you show me these regrets? Are you saying that this is all my fault? Are you trying to point out the part where it looks like I started to give up when I missed out on the job promotion, is that it?"

Voice:

"You asked me about your dream Bobby. I am only trying to bring into your awareness, that it is your limiting beliefs. Of you not being worthy of such a life. That has become this barrier that is keeping you from achieving your dreams."

Me:

"Are you saying that I can achieve my dreams? That the glass barrier is only because I lack confidence in myself. That my lack of confidence is because I don't feel worthy of an abundant lifestyle? And that's why it is only a dream to me. That I have already made my mind up on these things? That I have given up on my dreams? And why is it? Is it because someone told me that this is not something that I could ever attain for myself? My mindset is limiting me. That's it, isn't it? This is the part you are referring to when you asked me. When did you make that decision Bobby?

Chapter 14

Excuses

Let's stop right there for a second. I think it would be a good idea if we talked about communicating with only the conscious for a minute.

I just want to say that this conscious communication stuff is kinda tricky. For example, everything that I just told you about my regrets in chapter thirteen. Was all done with us only using my mind. But I swear it sounded and felt so real. So real, that it was real!

The voices did not need a body to feel like they were presently there. And the Voice, how in the hell did it telepathically send me all of my memories with emotional feelings attached to them in only a blink of an eye??

In our communication with only conscious. It was like we were already aware of what we were talking about instantly. Before even needing to attempt to communicate it.

Before I said something back to her in consciousness. It's like I could feel that she already knew what I was going to say before I said it. And yes I know all of this sounds crazy. It seems like you have to experience it before you can truly believe it. It is pretty crazy sounding. But still in the midst of all this unbelievable crazy stuff that I was experiencing. I knew it was all real. From deep down in my soul I knew that everything that just happened really did happen. It is as real as you and me, and this book that you are reading. It was so real that it left me feeling really small, and insignificant at that moment.

In my opinion, all this was way out of my league. Kinda like a fiction story to me, full of unbelievable things. Much like this story probably is for you.

Smiles!

Now back to that question, she asked me. When did I make this decision that I could never achieve my dreams of being wealthy?

In my defense, I replied with an excuse. Saying, come on now, honestly, please. I came from a poor family with no education or money. No one is successful in my family. I myself did not get an education that would provide me with a job to make that kind of money. And seriously, a two-million-dollar pad with all the extras.

Please!

I dropped out of school at the age of sixteen, in fact, I did it on my birthday. I specifically went to school that day. Just to walk into my principal's office, and say, Mr. Krazyack I quit! For your information, (FYI) I had about three months of Saturday school detentions that I did not have any intention of attending… Lol…

Suddenly I realized that all of these thoughts came so quickly that I didn't even know if I communicated them to her, or them, or not at all. Confusing isn't it?

This is very confusing I thought. I'm feeling mixed up in

my own mind. I wanted to ask, did you hear me? But I didn't, I continued on now with what seemed to me like my own defense of the current life that I have. Saying it in a way that was as if I was asking her for some pity on my behalf.

That was when my ego was quick to add its two cents to my thoughts, in its own sarcastic way. Saying, look at you asking an Angel for pity, for being a quitter. Ok, this is really messing with my mind now. My ego isn't showing me any empathy for one. And I am a little confused in this three-way conversation. So, who just joined the conversation? Is it my Higher Self who is pointing this out to me?

Or is this my hurt ego? Confusing this was for me, at the time. I noticed that I was getting a little agitated now. And with my ego being hurt, I replied back in a defensive tone. If there is such a thing in telepathic communications.

I said In my defense, when I was younger, I was stronger without a disability.

And I was able to make good money with my hands. I was too busy trying to survive. I was trying to live a happy life. I gave no thought to my future. I had no extra money it seemed, so I did not invest in anything.

No, I did not save my money wisely. I only used it to live on and survive. And I made sure that I spent it carelessly on things that made me feel good at that time. This Is what I was trying to say, or thinking, or maybe both.

Honestly, I'm not exactly sure at this point with my being in a state of confusion, like I was in.

It's like Sometimes my lips were moving when I was communicating and sometimes they were not. And for you the reader of my story. You are probably thinking something like what do mean you can't tell? If you are talking out loud or if you are only speaking telepathically.

And that's a good question.

 It's just that everything was happening so fast and my concentration was all scattered about trying to piece everything together. Leaving me in a state of reflection about this communication with telepathy.

Chapter 15

Telepathy

Oh my God, did I just communicate all of that with only my thoughts? Yes, I did!

What was so strange about communicating telepathically was that it was so effortless. And here I was making it difficult by trying to speak it in my mind like it was coming out of my mouth. I know this sounds silly. But I would think it and then I would try to say it again. But without speaking it from my mouth… Confusing, huh?

I definitely felt like I was trying too hard when it came to communicating telepathically with my Guides.

What I meant to say, is that when I was ready to communicate my thoughts. It was as if it was already done. Once I thought about it it was instantly communicated.

It was so easy that I couldn't seem to grasp ahold of the idea. I only had to think about my reply in order to communicate my thoughts. Confusing it was to me because nothing can be that easy.

Imagine only having to think about it once and then believing that it was received by your Guides. This sure isn't like an email, or a text message you can look at. And there are no eyes to look into making sure that you have their attention. There wasn't anything physical for me to connect to. This is probably why it felt so uncomfortable for me at first.

Experiencing an extraterrestrial form of communicating.

In my opinion, this would have been difficult for anybody to experience for the first time. So of course it was for me, it wasn't like anything that I had ever experienced before.

How is this possible? Is this even for real? I had a hundred things running through my mind. In what seemed like a quantum fast speed. I just had a conversation with a spirit Guide, and my higher self.

My ego added in its defense that it was not to be blamed for my current living situation in life. That until now I didn't even know I was feeling ashamed of. I thought I was living comfortably enough with no shame in the choices that I had made.

And while I was struggling to understand what exactly was happening. She visited me in my confusion to comfort me. I could feel that her energy was sincere and compassionate. It reminded me of my mom when she would comfort me.

I literally felt that her love for me was genuine.

I could feel that her intentions were only to help.

And that in some way, or another, they were here to help me.

I must say that in the midst of all this chaos in my head. There is also a peaceful feeling that everything is going to be okay. I feel like my higher self is here to help me understand the things that I'm having trouble with. I almost feel that my higher self is here from some other place in time. Possibly even the future.

I probably should have already told you this.

A lot of the words I am using in my writing were not part of my vocabulary at the time. I knew nothing about spirit guides or anything about my higher self. And I especially didn't know anything about my ego. I had no clue how the ego has its part in all of our decision-making. Or how the ego is so strongly opinionated in our thoughts. It's like I was discovering that there are three of me. My higher self, my ego, and me all rolled up in one.

And who is this higher self? Who is referred to as being me but at the same time is a separate version of me.? Who could also be from a future timeline or from completely different realities hopping dimensions and traveling across spaces to places in time to help poor me in this reality.

And this higher self, it seems is still directly connected to the source with this version of me retaining the knowledge from all of my past lives. Who has returned here now in order to help me.

Wow!!

Now that is some really deep stuff to try and imagine. Did I really come from the future to help this version of myself in this timeline now to evolve into who my higher wants to become? When I was asking myself about that and who these other Voices are. The Voice softly says.

Voice:

"Bobby, your higher self is always with you and you can always connect to your higher self in consciousness. Your higher self is often depicted as the angel on your shoulder. Who is instructing you to make wise choices? In your religious teachings. You have a God who has Angels who are watching over you. And then you have an adversary who is named the devil who is out to get you.

This devil is who your ego plays the part of, and it seems is always on your other shoulder whispering in your other ear to make poor choices. And the other voices that you have been hearing today, are other benevolent, beings who are here with me to help guide you through your ascension process."

Me:

"This is incredible. You mean to tell me that I am both my God and my devil. And I am the man in the middle listening to my higher self who is representing God in my thinking. And who is also the one that is giving me good advice? And in my other ear, I hear the devil who is my own ego. Who oftentimes wants me to be angry at everything. Sometimes even with vengeful intentions being whispered into my thinking."

"I am like a walking heaven and hell all rolled up in one. This is incredible, and at the same time, it's absolutely mind-blowing. I have the opportunity to take the stairway to heaven or the highway to hell and it's all right inside of me. This was the most profound thing I have ever heard. Are you telling me that the devil didn't make me do it?"

Me:

Saying it like I meant it, but with a slight touch of sarcasm.

"Okay, you've done it, you have my full attention now."

It was as if all of my skepticism just vanished. And I felt as though I could trust her now. I have to admit that this was a lot to handle. And, it was all pretty freaking crazy. So crazy that it was beginning to make me feel like I was going crazy.

At first, this seemed to be too much for me to handle with it changing everything that I know. And I was beginning to feel unsure in my thoughts about some of it, even a little bit scared questioning myself if I should be listening to these voices. And, at the very same time acknowledging that I am feeling safe.

The emotions that I was feeling were of love and compassion. They gave me a sense of security. These feelings were very real and they had a Divine Angelic presence about them. One that I hadn't ever felt anything like before.

I was feeling emotionally safe which was leading me to believe that all of this must be of a Divine origin and even though I was having these mixed-up feelings of fear and uncertainty, I was still feeling perfectly fine and safe as I could be.

Let me tell you, I have been in some really spooky places. That would literally put the fear of hell into you, giving you chills all up and down your spine. I remember a graveyard where I felt like I was being watched by something that wasn't a person, and it made the hair on my neck stand up. Believe me, I left that place in a big hurry. I remember that I had to keep looking over my shoulder to see if I was being followed. That was the scariest graveyard I had ever been to.

Then there was that time in the Haunted house that was at least 150 years old.

When I went into the basement it felt like there was something cold, and angry giving off this evil presence from inside of that basement. That place scared the living daylight out of me. And when I was walking up the steps from the basement, every hair on my body was standing up in a way that was scaring me. I felt like somebody was right behind me. As I went up the steps, I started taking each step faster and faster until I got to the top when I quickly closed the door.

So. this weird kind of stuff is not all totally new to me. On rare occasions, a time or two I have experienced a supernatural spiritual encounter of the sort. But of course, they were nothing like this one. There weren't ever any voices or any kind of communication going on in them. For that matter, the only thing that I experienced in those encounters was the feeling of being in the presence of a strange energy.

Chapter 16

The Turtle's Tomb

This encounter is the first of its kind for me. The biggest difference in comparison is that someone or someone's are trying to communicate with me telepathically, and that definitely sets this one apart from all of my other experiences with energies that were unknown to me. Some being spooky in nature and might even be called a ghostly encounter.

Honestly, when I look back at life and remember all of my previous experiences, they just add to how bizarre this one is beginning to make me feel. This one is almost like I am in a Stephen King sci-fi novel. And I am the writer of a story about a person. Who is totally unaware that it is me that I am writing about.

In this story, the main character believes that he knows which reality he is in. But, in reality, he is in a completely different one from the one that he believes he's in.

In this reality, he is unaware of being in it. He is writing about his experiences and all the things that he wants to experience not knowing that he is creating this new reality that he wants to be in by literally writing it into existence.

Well if that's the case, then I wish to live an abundant life where I am wealthy and prosperous, and I get to travel the world meeting new people and learning new things sharing nothing but ♡ love along the way…

But, that does not look like the case here because I am not in a movie or a book. Nope, I'm sitting in my car in an extremely hot parking lot communicating with voices in my mind who might as well be extraterrestrials to me for as far as I know. And, if I am communicating with extraterrestrials, then It is not like anything that I had ever imagined it to be like.

For one, I'm not scared or feeling inferior to a superior being. Not like I have always thought it would be like. And if you ask me like I already have, I would tell you that all of this is checking out to be pretty f*ac*t☆al real enough to lead me to believe that I am having a spiritual encounter involving extraterrestrial entities from some other place who are here to help me to ascend, elevating my life to a higher consciousness.

That's when I said,

"Ok, guys! Now, what? I am all ears, and you have my full attention! Now, that you have me all conscious and stuff."

That's when I began to connect the dots and see that it is me who is limiting my life from becoming more, by accepting my life as it is, like a hand of cards that I've been dealt. I had already made up my mind that my life was an unfortunate one making it impossible for my dreams to get started, let alone being able to come true. With this poor me syndrome telling myself this is my life, I have to accept it for what it is and tough it out until the end.

Me:

Saying out loud to myself.

"No, I do not have to !! Not anymore."

I said with a tone that implied a sense of confidence.

I suddenly felt empowered, it was like everything instantaneously became so clear to me. I am not sure when it happened, but it is obvious that somewhere along the line in my life I gave up on my future. And, if I had dreams then I gave up on them too giving in to a life of poverty and accepting a life of lower standards.

When did I give up? And this turtle Toby, why did I find the turtle today?

Is this turtle Toby here to tell me something?

Omg! It is Toby. It's the turtle and his struggle to survive.

Toby, he never gave up.

As I began to ponder on this. My thoughts were gently interrupted by a suggestion, from my guide saying.

Voice:

"Bobby. I want you to close your eyes. I will show you the struggle that this turtle had to go through to make it to a place where it had a chance to continue living."

I closed my eyes as I was agreeing with saying okay, while suddenly becoming aware that I had become trusting with the voice. Right then with my eyes closed it was like someone had turned the movie on. I could see him now, and there he was in a drying-up mud puddle. The stream that once flowed there is all dried up. I could see where the stream had been a part of the pool of water that Toby called his home. But is now gone, leaving only this dried up, cracked up. Mud pud of a puddle.

In this vision that was given to me, I could see him in this terrible situation. The detail in this vision was graphic and was in full color with sound and the smell of mud. It was a really earthy smell. Then suddenly, I could feel his fear, he was scared. I could see that he had already buried himself deep in the mud when there was still a pool of water. He had buried himself because the water was disappearing. As it was evaporating becoming less and less water, it was getting too hot for him and he couldn't stay out of the water or he would dry up.

He kept digging deeper and deeper into the mud trying to get further away from the heat until he couldn't go any further. The ground has become too hard for his little flippers to dig. There is nothing he can do but stay hidden from the scorching heat of the sun and the rising temperature of the water.

He is scared now, I can feel his fear and this vision is so vivid and real to me. I think I am breathing harder myself while having this vision. This vision of Toby was so incredibly real, that for a brief moment it felt like I was Toby. Could it be that Toby's thoughts are mine for this brief moment? Can I feel him in this dire situation? It was like Toby himself knew that this was it. This was going to be his tomb. All he could do now was wait for whatever his fate would be. His instincts told him to slow his heart rate down.

I could feel him begin to go into a deep sleep. He was slowing his heart rate down using less oxygen in his blood. He was going into a hibernation state of some sort. He was conserving all that he had holding on to his last minute. The vision didn't have a sense of time to it who knows how long he was in the mud. I felt like it had been for some time though. Strangely enough, it felt like he had been buried for a week.

All of a sudden, I am having this feeling of anxiety. I can feel it, the top of his shell, it was beginning to feel the heat. His sleep was disturbed, and the mud was becoming uncomfortable. Now he is panicking, and I can feel his fear again.

Now what?

What can he do? He has already done all that this little turtle can possibly do! Or has he now? He could feel the mud on top of him, and it was feeling different to him. It was beginning to dry up and it was becoming difficult to move. Where he was able to squirm and move a little bit, was now becoming impossible.

It felt like a weight on top of him. I could feel a sense of panic, he was feeling trapped now. He is beginning to panic even more. He starts to squirm harder and starts trying to dig. He is not trying to dig down this time, no he is digging and pushing upwards with all of his might. It is difficult now the mud is thicker, and has even begun to harden. He is pushing up with all of his might, but still, it's too heavy. It's the surface, that has now dried up and begun to seal Toby in his tomb made of mud.

In my vision, suddenly it appeared like I was in it. I even wanted to dig him out with my hands. But, I could not Intervene, I couldn't do anything but watch. I did try to yell at Toby though, saying come on bud you can do it. You are almost out bud don't give up now. Toby, opened his eyes to see if he had broken free of the mud. I could see through his eyes for a second when he opened them. It was scratchy, and you could feel the pressure of the mud against his eyes. He couldn't see anything but the darkness of the Earth.

He starts to use his head now, moving it from side to side, digging with all 4 paws. I could feel him putting his last bit of strength into his efforts trying his hardest to dig himself out. It is all that he has left to give, he is trying his hardest to survive.

That's when it happened, the most beautiful thing imaginable. Through a crack in the mud that had hardened on the surface a little bit of sunlight touched Toby's little turtle nose. Hurray, he made it to the surface. Suddenly everything changed in my, and Toby's energy. Our emotions changed from hopelessness and desperate feelings of despair to excitement now, giving Toby this newfound strength, a burst of energy that I would call adrenaline that energized Toby who only a moment ago was an exhausted, and tired little turtle.

Now, there through the cracks in the dried mud. Toby's little head pops out and looks around, but he doesn't move anymore though. It looks like he is taking a break and I feel him breathing. I can feel Toby, his heart beating fast. He is exhausted but he is relieved. There is a feeling of joy in Toby since he has saved himself.

The Sun is hot. And it's beating on his face. He takes another breath in and when he is letting it out. A cloud appears from out of nowhere, covering the sun up and bringing some God-blessed shade on Toby's head.

It felt like a few seconds went by. Ok, it looks like he is ready now, and oh boy is he. His strength is back and he wants out of this hot mud right now!

Here comes his front right leg, and it digging hard trying to pull the rest of his body out of the thick hot mud. His back legs are pushing with everything he has got. His struggle is hard but he is not giving up. He is almost free of the mud and that's when the other front leg comes out. Hurray again, this time the celebration is because he is now over halfway out of this gooey hot mud bath of a death trap.

He stretches his neck out as far as he can trying to use it for some leverage. While using his front legs with his paws claws slipping in mud. It's slippery, he can't get any traction. He continues his digging into the mud trying to pull his back legs out. He is beginning to get some traction now. A little bit more and he's got it, there's one. He has a back leg out. Hurray, then the other one comes out, Toby is free, he is free of the sticky slippery mud trap.

He's out, but it's hot, it's too hot! So, he just takes off in a hurry scurrying over to the edge of the mud puddle where the grass begins. Unaware of where he is going, he just starts crawling through the tall grass as if anything is better than where he just came from.

There was a feeling of relief that was so intense, that I honestly felt like they were my own. It was difficult to tell if these were only mine, or if it was the both of us that I was feeling for. I'm just saying that the intensity of this vision was as real as if it was my own life that I am describing.

And now Toby has a new challenge. For he has never seen grass like this before, and it's in his way. He doesn't know where he is going, but the grass is definitely in his way. And his Schell is getting caught up, snagged on the thick wild grasses. The grass is over two feet tall to him, they are like a bunch of trees growing too close together to crawl through.

But Toby pushes as hard as he can and is able to knock some of them over enough that he can crawl over them and then he pushes the others to the side. But, some are too thick and he gets stopped. This happens again and again but Toby keeps going because now Toby is feeling a sense of urgency as if he has to get somewhere important and he must get there right now.

Toby has managed to get through the tall thick grass, and now the grass has become much shorter. Yes of course it is, it has been mowed by the county. What a relief, finally Toby gets a break from his tiring trial of life or death.

Oh, my goodness! Toby has done it, he has crawled all the way out from that muddy mess of the drainage ditch that he almost died in. He managed to crawl all the way through a jungle of tall grass, and up a small hill that must have seemed like a mountain to him. Toby has reached the top of the ditch. He spreads the grass open with his front legs like he is parting some hair trying to have a look. What did Toby see, nothing but blue sky and the edge of an asphalt road. He stops with one of his front paws on the pavement. Toby took a breath and looked both ways down the road like he was checking to make sure it was clear. The roads clear so he doesn't stop there.

Oh no, he climbs onto the pavement crawling to the middle of the road where he stops in a small piece of shade cast by an old tree that was dead but was still standing. The only shade on that barren, shade less road and it was right there where it was needed most, like it was heaven sent for this little guy.

That is where my vision of Toby's epic struggle ended. An incredible story of a turtle's fight for his survival that truly could only be seen as a victory for the moment

.

Chapter 17

The Conditioning

As I sit and ponder on all that has happened here, I am beginning to put my and Toby's connection together. Remember earlier when I spoke about how I felt? How I was feeling trapped in a barren wasteland, far from my home or at least far from where I want to be in this life. And no, I am not in dire straits of a place like Toby, so to speak. I mean let's be totally honest here. Toby was facing imminent death and, I am not in that kind of spot today like Toby. In my reflections, I cannot help but give this turtle some praise for how he did not give up.

So, what about me? Well, I have given up in some ways. Not on life itself, I am not suicidal! I do not show any signs of depression in any way that a person diagnosed with depression would be suffering from, but I have given up on my dreams. I have accepted that I was never going to be successful. I gave up on the life that I used to dream of. I used to believe that everything was possible and that I could achieve it, even though it would not be easy.

So, what happened to me?

If something did happen, how did it happen? When did I start to give up on my dreams? It's not like I made a conscious choice one day saying, that's it, I'm done trying. I give up on my dreams. In my contemplating, I can't help but wonder who is to blame for this. Is there anybody to blame? Is this my ego again, searching for a scapegoat because I want to avoid accountability? Have I conditioned myself through the years to accept a life that I never wanted?

Now I hear her soft soothing voice again, saying.

Voice:

"Bobby dear, you are not all to blame. And yes, you have been conditioned, we call it programming. It's where, at an early age, you have been told lies with the purpose of controlling you. This attempt to control you is to keep you in the state of mind that you are in right now. Where you have given up on the things that you were dreaming of.

In this programming, you were taught that your dreams are just a dream, a simple dream that will never come true. Do you remember being told that you were different? That you were different from the rich, that you could never achieve becoming a wealthy person? Were you told that some people are just poor and that you should be grateful for what you have?"

Me:

"Yes, I do remember my mother comforting me with a talk like that. She told me many stories of her childhood, how she had to live with less than other children. In her stories, it was easy for me to see that my childhood was much better than hers was. She would also tell me stories about my grandmother Alma, who was born in the state of Missouri in a barn with a dirt floor.

Sometime in the 1920s, that's when mom would point out that her upbringing was an improvement from her parents. Mom would also remind me, that my childhood was better than hers and it did remind me that mine was better than both mom's and grandma's. Mom would often use this as a powerful point to encourage me to stay grateful for the life that I have. She always had a way of making me come away with this perspective to always be grateful for what I have. She would enforce this belief by reminding me that so many other people in the world have less than I do. Even pointing out these people with an unfortunate life. A life that is far worse off than anything that I have ever experienced myself.

This reminds me of a time in my mid-twenties. I was complaining to Mom about how I was feeling guilty for not providing better for my children. This is when she told me these stories again, and after hearing them again years later, now as an adult with children, I have begun to compare my children's lives to mine. It was easy for me to see how my children's lives were way better than mine ever was in comparison to what I had received as a child. My children definitely had more than I did, and I made sure of that.

Honestly speaking, I feel like I have given my children more love and more time than I ever received as a child. I had not thought about any of this for at least ten years, and now all of a sudden, I am remembering it like it was yesterday. I can remember that I told these stories to my children.

Oh my lord, I can see it now. That's how it works, isn't it? The passing down from one generation to the next. A programming of the mind, a conditioning that starts at a young age when you are totally unaware of what is going on, and I have begun to do the exact same thing to my children.

"Programming!"

Chapter 18

Stopping the Programming

I feel like my parents were making excuses for their shortcomings. If my parent's lives were that difficult when times were harder and when technology was not as advanced as it was when I was young why didn't they push me to do better than they did?

I don't remember my parents ever talking about their dreams. They never talked about their dreams, or even how they didn't achieve them. They didn't even make excuses blaming someone or something for the reasons why their dreams didn't come true. Nothing of the sort.

In my house, my family didn't ever talk about their dreams. No one talked about their goals or wanted to achieve anything. All I heard growing up was complaints about the rich and how they were keeping us poor. I was taught to be grateful for what I had and how not to expect too much from life. No one asked me what I wanted to be when I was growing up and no one pushed me to be anything or to go off in any direction like towards a career.

Now that I think about it, yeah sure, my parents knew I didn't care for school mainly because I didn't fit in with the other kids. They had nice things like shoes clothes and cool haircuts that's when I was in grade school.

I will confess that this truth is a little upsetting to me today. Why didn't my parents talk to me about trades when I was a teenager or some sort of a career that was other than the ones that involved a lot of schooling? I feel that I am angry at my family and that I am holding them to blame. Blaming them for programming me to be a failure in life without them even knowing that they were making sure that I would never achieve a financially stable life one that would lead me to an abundant and blissful future.

Where does it stop? How do we break this chain? Nothing in this world is easy to come by unless you were born into money. If you come from a family that is well off financially.

In those homes, I'm sure that they were always talking about financial gains, and how to make money, how to invest money. This was the way of life for the wealthy. Their programming was different than mine. I am sure that there were many conversations around the dinner table about their dreams and a future that involved achieving them.

Around my dinner table, we didn't talk about how to make money. Instead, we talked about just the opposite. We talk about how it's not possible for poor people to become wealthy. Actually, we didn't talk much around my dinner table. I come from a dysfunctional family. Where we didn't do wholesome family things. Anyhow when I became old enough to quit school and go to work.

I began to hear things like there are powers to be in the world and that their inside of the governments that run the world. I also heard about the corrupt banking organizations that have a big part in controlling who is prosperous and who is not. We have all heard the saying that the rich get richer and the poor get poorer. And from what I've seen and experienced in my life, this seems to be true.

Honestly, why didn't my parents start talking to me about these things after I was in my 20s? My mom even said something about how they knew about this in the 70s. Well, that's screwed-up parenting if you ask me. I was born in 1975, so I can't help but think that. If I had been taught about these things at an earlier age, then at least I would have understood what it was that I was going to be facing in life.

This is more than unsettling. This is downright upsetting enough to anger somebody. It's not fair, and these things should never happen to any child. Being programmed at a young, defenseless age. At the most important time, when a child should be taught that life is fair. And that we can all achieve our dreams. A child should never be programmed to accept a life of poverty. Being taught that life isn't fair for some people because of who you are and what family you come from. This is not fair, and it needs to stop. Every child on the planet Earth should have an opportunity at a good life.

Voice:

"Yes, dear. Bobby, it's not fair that so many people on Earth are living a life of uncertainty with nothing being made easy for them. Life on Earth is unfair for most human beings. This is why the Earth is shifting its vibration to a higher frequency of 5D. Life for all human beings on the planet Earth will change. Life with equal opportunities for every living being will be the way. Life will be fair and made safer.

Safe from dangerous people who only want to control other human beings. Free from pollutants and poisons that man is making to harm you, keep you sick, to control you.

All of the Earth's inhabitants will experience this shift along with the Earth's transformation. More and more Human Beings will raise their consciousness to a new level of awareness that can no longer be controlled by the matrix. The matrix, along with all the programming, will collapse."

This was a lot to absorb, and while I was trying to take all of this in, I was beginning to feel a personal connection to this Voice. I cannot help but feel her energy. I don't know how she does it, but I can feel her. It's like she is inside of me. I feel her compassion towards me, which makes me feel like she loves me. As strange as it sounds, it's as real as any love that I have ever felt before. It was definitely these intense feelings of emotion that convinced me to believe that all this is real.

Me:

"What do I call you?"

Voice:

"I am one of your Spirit Guides."

Me:

"No name?"

Voice:

"No dear, no name, you will know my voice."

I smiled great big inside, as I thought to myself, that would be enough, and that would be just fine with me.

Me:

"Matrix, programming! What do you mean?"

I had never heard of this Matrix, and from the sounds of it, it didn't sound good.

Me:

"Please tell me more about this Matrix."

And as she began to speak to me telepathically, I couldn't help but to feel more of this unconditional love and with it, a sense of hope for the future.

At this point, my eyes are wide open, and she has my full attention. Even the heat of the day has stopped bothering me as if it couldn't anymore. My thoughts about the heat were interrupted when she began to tell me about the matrix.

Voice:

"It is part of a global system that spreads a programming of fear and control over all of the world. It is embedded in every facet of life that is around you. The matrix is woven into society's belief system. It is specifically designed to manipulate and control people. By using fear to keep mankind so busy being scared, and trying to survive. That you are unaware of what is really happening right before your own eyes and in your ears.

By the use of these war tactics and global economic collapse. The fear tactics are used to scare you into whatever the elite is planning to do with you.

Fear is used with the intention to manipulate you into believing that a war must be at fault when in reality it is only a distraction for things like the control of money and to gain power over everyone. Suppose it is not a war outside of your country, then it is a war inside of it, spreading fear with disease or domestic terrorism threats and the many other things that are used to suppress you. Such as inflation and taxes, which are being used to keep you from experiencing a life with the freedom of your soul.

The political design of your country is an example of the programming of the matrix. Your nation is divided at all times. Your nation is controlled by either the Democratic or the Republican party. These two leaders of your country disagree on almost everything, and there is never a resolution for any of the problems that are hurting the people. The country of the United States of America spends more money on other countries than it does to help its own people.

The United States is part of this global system that is controlled by the elites of the earth, who are only one percent of this planet's population. These human beings live in palaces of bliss while the rest of the people on the planet are suffering. So, as you can see dear, almost everyone has been programmed, and this is why you have not heard of the programming or the matrix. Many of the people who have spoken up about The Matrix have been silenced by these elites and the ones who have been awakening to the programming of the Matrix have been doing it through the raising of their consciousness, becoming conscious of what is happening on Earth.

The ones who have awakened before you have been waiting. Waiting for more to awaken, while they were waiting for the big planetary shift to happen. They have already begun to spread awareness of this programming, sharing with people that the Christ consciousness has arrived."

Chapter 19

Consciousness and The Drive Home

I then asked her what this consciousness is. And how do you become conscious?

She gently laughed and said.

Voice:

"My dear child, you are experiencing it right now."

Me:

"Experiencing what, Consciousness? How am I? "

Voice:

"By speaking with me in your mind, for one. And you have recognized the programming by your parents when you were a child. You already mentioned how it needs to be stopped. And you admitted that you were angry with your family. But you realize that they were programmed as well. This is you experiencing consciousness. "

Me:

"Why now, and not before?"

Voice:

"It wasn't your time yet, sweetheart. You have now started your awakening, you have begun to experience your ascension. "

Me:

"I asked with enthusiasm, How do I become more conscious? "

Voice:

"Do you mean to ask how you become more aware? "

Me:

"Yes, yes, all of that.   And what's this ascension?"

Voice:

"Why don't you go home now, dear, you have much to think about."

I wanted to say no, but I couldn't. Right then, a big diesel truck started its engine up, revving a couple of times before it pulled its boat out of the lake. Right then, I realized that I had lost track of time. How long was I in the parking lot? I looked at the clock in shock when I realized that it had been two hours since my guide and I had begun talking underneath those big oak trees at this boat launch.

At that point, I decided not to go anywhere else. Those errands that I was using as an excuse to kill time with just became the least important. All I wanted to do now was go home and spend some time thinking about what had just happened.

So, I started the car up and being careful like I was. I made sure to look in all three of my mirrors before backing up. The boat launch was quite busy that afternoon. After I safely backed the car up, I then started to slowly pull away. I was no longer in a hurry, and why should I be in a hurry? I only live fifteen minutes away from the lake anyway.

No, I'm not in a hurry because what I mean is that something has changed in me. I was not in a hurry because I noticed that something was different. It's like my mind has slowed down. And not in a bad way, but in a positive way. I felt like my thoughts were more focused. A strange feeling it was, peaceful and sobering at the same time.

On the Way home, I just had to ask.

Me:

"Are you still there? "

She replied ever so gently and comfortingly, saying

Voice:

"Yes, dear."

Me:

"Would you please tell me about the ascension?"

Voice:

"That will be enough for today, Jonathan."

Me:

"Does that mean we will talk again? And Jonathan, when did you start calling me by my middle name?"

Voice:

"Of course, we will Jonathan."

After hearing her say my middle name again, followed by her giggling. I had to ask her,

Me:

"Will you always be around?"

Voice:

"Yes, but not how you think? We always know when, and we are always around when you need us."

She then went on to say that.

Voice:

"You will have a lot of questions in the coming months. So, I will be here to assist you.   Others will also be coming into your life now. "

 I asked

Me:

"Others, what others? "

 Voice:

"Other awakened human beings. They are also like guides to you. Their experiences will help to guide you in your ascension process."

I asked again for reassurance.

Me:

"So, I will definitely be talking to you later?"

Voice:

"Yes, dear, you will definitely hear my voice again."

Right then, I put my turn signal on and pulled into my driveway. As I was parking my car, suddenly I was filled with this reassuring feeling of peace. My worries, the things that I am always uptight about, seem to be gone. I look in my mirror to see a smile on my face. I realize how excited I am about all this new information. I have so many questions now. Not everything I heard was good. Some of it is even quite scary. But at the same time, learning this truth has made me free somehow. I feel empowered now with a strong sense of being on a mission to discover more of these truths.

There was no doubt in my mind that this was the beginning. The beginning of what could only be called my new life. And I just knew that her and I would talk again soon. Right then, it hit me. Oh no, I didn't say goodbye. But that didn't matter because as soon as I thought that. I already knew that we had.

As I was getting out of the car, I was beginning to feel a bit tired, and who wouldn't be tired? My whole world just got turned upside down, and I got a glimpse at this matrix and the programming that I have been subjected to. Let's be honest here: this was a lot of unbelievable, crazy stuff to be hit with just like that on this awfully hot day.

This is way out there in the left field, and I think I might have strained my brain.

"Strained my brain,"

I said it out loud just before I started laughing at myself. I had to laugh, and I think I did so just to make sure that I was still a sane person.

After I was done laughing at myself I took a few deep breaths to assure myself that I was okay. I decided to go inside and lie down in front of the fan. It was still so ungodly hot, and now that I was back home. It seemed to be even hotter here at my house. Hotter than it was at the lake. I have fewer trees than the boat access does, and that breeze was blowing cool air off the lake. It was definitely making a difference.

Chapter 20

Ascension & Purpose

To my surprise, I opened my eyes.

I did not even know that I had dozed off. I must have been more tired than I thought, and the first thing that came to my mind when I awoke I was wondering if all that had happened was just a dream.

No, I said. There is no way that was just a dream! It couldn't have been, it was too real. Then I remembered everything. I know the turtle was real, and now I have these questions about things, things that I have no clue about. And here they are running through my mind. Questions about this programming and the matrix.

I remember driving home, and I remember talking to her, 'The voice'. I was asking her about what the ascension is, and she said, "That will be enough for today". I remember that for sure!

"Wait a minute, what time is it?"

I looked at the clock and I realized that it was only 5:00 pm. I was surprised that I had only been asleep for three and a half hours. I kinda got excited that it was still today. It felt like I was asleep for a much longer time than that. Anyhow, I was glad that I was not. My memory is still fresh, and I know that I could not have had a dream like that in the middle of the afternoon.

Okay, I've made my mind up this is real, and all of that did just happen. And now I'm trying to figure it out. So, I began to think about the things that we talked about, and I remember how she said that I was experiencing consciousness. That in itself is a lot to grasp hold of, and the fact that all of our communication was done telepathically is mind-blowing in itself. I was just telepathically talking with an entity from some other dimension or some other world. I remember feeling her physically when she was speaking to me. It was so real. It was so intense that I could have easily believed that she was God. But she was quick to make it clear that she is not God.

I have always felt like there was more to life than I was being told, and today God sent me proof that there is much more to my life than I presently know. I am not even in shock anymore. It is like all of this is somehow familiar to me. All of a sudden, I felt small, like I was the only one of the stars in the sky, and why would I feel small if I was a star? And why is all of this happening to me? Why did this voice, whoever she is, whoever they are, why did they contact me today?

Right then, I began to feel like I was more important than I had been giving myself credit for. Has God heard my cries? I opened my eyes, turned, looked at the front door, and decided to step outside on the porch for a minute to take a few deep breaths. It is quiet out this evening. I can hear some birds chirping in the pine trees out front.

It was peaceful on the front porch, and believe it or not, I stopped thinking so hard for a minute. Giving me a chance to ponder all of this. "Selah".

Okay, that didn't last long. The moment of silence that I was experiencing was interrupted by thoughts about the programming. Now my focus shifted back to my childhood. And how I was programmed by my parents.

Yes, of course, I remember her explaining the programming to me, and how my unaware parents did exactly what the matrix is designed to have them do. My parents passed that dream-killing negativity on to me, influencing me to accept my life of poverty.

Well, that isn't gonna happen. I'm not accepting any life of poverty, and I'm not even mad at my parents. I mean, how could I be mad at my parents? They were programmed at a young age, just like they were programming me. This is all becoming clear to me. I even have to take accountability for my own actions as a parent, as I was beginning to program my children.

I have got to learn more about this programming and how we can stop it. Now I want to figure out how I can communicate this to my children, how much programming did I put into my children? And as I was beginning to stress myself out with all of this programming stuff, I suddenly stopped myself and began to smile. Because this is what she was talking about.

Awareness is a conscious awareness of things that I previously was not aware of. It's all starting to make some sense now. Instead of being upset because I didn't know about all this, I began to feel gratitude for knowing of it now.

Now that I am aware of this, what do I need to do with it? And this consciousness that she said I am experiencing. What am I supposed to do with this? Questions begin to flood my mind, so many questions that I need answers to. What am I supposed to do? Where do I get the answers? What questions am I supposed to be asking?

Wait a minute, Bob, I tell myself as I take a few deep breaths. After about 10 of them, I tell myself, I can see all better now. I continue saying that all of this has happened for a reason. The answers to the questions that I am seeking will come to me.

I turned and went back into the house. I walked straight over to the table reached down and grabbed my phone. The first thing I did was Google Ascension, and that's a little bizarre in itself because I don't ever Google anything. I don't Google like most people, but I was desiring more of this information. When I googled it, this is what it said? *"To rise to an important position or to a higher level. To rise to a higher level, an important position."* I like the sound of that, and she said that I was experiencing consciousness and that I was beginning to experience my ascension to rise up to a higher level of Consciousness, that's what this ascension means.

All of a sudden, I stood up full of excitement like I just answered a pop quiz question for a prize. Laughing out loud at myself again, I paused while I shook my head, thinking to myself. *"Bob, everything that you think you know is about to change."* I set my phone back down with a smile on my face, as I turned from the kitchen and stepped back outside to look at the sky.

It was about 3 hours before sunset, and the sun was getting into its position to go down. I was looking out of my front door to the west, and I noticed that the sky was clear, not a cloud in sight. It had begun to cool down a little, but not very much. It was still around 80 degrees or more out, and there was only a slight breeze in the air.

After a few minutes out on my front porch, I went back inside and walked straight to my phone. I picked it up and, without even thinking about it like a reflex, I opened it and went straight to Facebook without even giving it any thought. I was still thinking about the ascension process when I did it, and to my surprise, the first post that I saw was someone talking about how they were experiencing their ascension. They said their journey to healing had begun. My first thought was how in the heck could this be? I continued to read on to hear how their life has purpose now, and that they are experiencing self-love.

Chapter 21

Help is coming

After reading the post, I put my phone back down in a hurry. It was still on, and Facebook was still open. I then started backing away from my phone as if I were scared of it. Is my phone possessed? Where did this Facebook post come from? How can the first thing that I see on Facebook be somebody talking about these subjects? Those subjects that I have never heard about until now. I couldn't help but think that this is starting to get freaky again.

How is this even possible?

How can I have spent forty-five years of my life, and never heard about any of this until today? And now, the same information that the Voice was giving me earlier today is somehow now magically in my phone. There is no way that this is only a coincidence, and now I'm getting curious for more information.

I want to know more about this consciousness stuff, and I want to know more about my ascension, and what is my purpose. Do I have a purpose? And if I do, what is it?

Okay, I can't help it. I'm more than curious now. I gotta see what this is about. So, I picked my phone back up to see that it was still on my Facebook page, and I was looking at the post that I was just reading. There wasn't that much information on this particular post. So, I start to scroll through Facebook, through all of the meaningless posts that are only here for our entertainment or to sell you something.

It only took me a second before I saw another one relating to the 'Awakening'. It went on to say that if you have begun to experience your ascension, and you need a coach to help you with it, we are here to help you, then directing you to open the link that's below. I was like, what?

Not only are they talking about the ascension that I have never heard of before, but they are offering help and assistance to guide you along the way. Where did all of this come from? How is it that this information is on my phone now after only just hearing about this today? Suddenly, I feel like I have been given this essential information today about the 'Awakening' and my ascension for a really important reason, and I can't get over this shocking reality that it was delivered to me by a spirit guide, who's from some otherworldly place, who is here to inform me that help would be sent to me? Help for what, I wonder? That doesn't matter much in comparison to everything else. Omg, there is a lot here to digest even for me, who has an imagination that goes deep into rabbit holes looking for mystical creatures and magical things.

You know what's so strange about all of this? It feels so familiar to me, like a dream or something, and I can't help but feel like my life has forever changed. I can feel it in my stomach, like a gut feeling, and it feels safe to me like everything is going to be ok and that all of this is for my best well-being.

When I think about it, the only thing that I can say is wow, wow, wow! And all of this just started five hours ago. Where is it gonna go from here? And now this Facebook thing. This is crazy, too. I have not heard anyone talking about these things until now. These particular subjects, if you will.

While I was standing there thinking about all of this, I lost track of time. I don't know how long I stared off into space, but when I snapped out of it, I looked down at my phone, and even though I wasn't asking for help, I still hit the like button on the post that I was reading. My first thought about getting help was, I don't know what's going on yet. I need more information before I start looking for some help. At this point, I don't even know if I need help, as I do have a Spirit Guide who is helping me.

I continued scrolling along until I saw another post that mentioned something in the vicinity of the awakening. I opened the page up and began to read some of its content. It quickly grabbed my attention because it was about an everyday kind of girl who was talking about normal things like her dog and cats. It was quite obvious that she loves her animals wholeheartedly, and in between her posts about her everyday kind of life, and the things that she loves. In one post, she mentioned that the matrix had no control over her anymore. That caught my attention, so I continued looking at the content of her page. She talked about the journey that she is on. She talked about how she was learning to heal herself. She talked about how she was fixing her own life.

And didn't have time to be concerned about other people right now.

She said she suffered from horrible childhood traumas and that she has a hard time dealing with them. She told how she had been in and out of abusive relationships her whole life. And what she said next sealed the deal for me. She said she has help from her Spirit Guides.

Say what? I'm not the only one that Spirit Guides are talking to. Have other people they have spoken to Spirit Guides, too? After looking at ten, maybe twelve more of her posts. I decided to go back to Facebook and browse around to see what else I could find.

It didn't take long: a couple of swipes with my thumb and there's another one. This one talks about being born again. And how the Awakening has changed their entire life for the better. Ever since they have started their healing journey.

These posts were everywhere now. Post after post, I saw. There was so much talk about this healing journey. I was beginning to feel like I had been taken out of one life and put somewhere else in another. Lots of posts about healing and letting things go. Everything was pointing at it, letting past traumas go, and teaching people to love themselves again.

After reading a few posts on that page. I kept scrolling along until I stopped at another post. This one caught my eye because it was from a beautiful American girl who had a gorgeous smile. She was talking about doing her shadow work and loving herself correctly. She was talking about how her self-love is changing her into the woman that she has always wanted to be. I was captured by what she had to say. I must have liked a hundred of her posts. Before I stopped myself from saying, Bob. You're going to freak this girl out if you don't stop liking all of her posts. There's a lot of weird people out there. And I didn't want to look like one of them. I laughed a couple of times at it. Honestly speaking, though, I had only liked seven or eight of her posts.

Chapter 22

Faith In Question, Answers.

This consciousness stuff and having a purpose, not to mention my ascension, and needing to heal myself, is all so new to me, and now these people popping up out of nowhere. I kept thinking to myself, where have these people been my whole life? And why is this the first time that I have seen them on Facebook?

I found a couple of pages with posts that were specifically designed for sharing this information. They were full of content on these subjects. Without hesitation, I followed some of these Facebook pages as I had noticed that this pretty American girl was following some of them herself. I say American Girl to describe the post I was referring to earlier because I have noticed that these people are from all over the world.

Talking about the same girl still, I noticed on her page that she was in turn sharing some of these other people's posts. More than once, I read how the creator of the page was thanking her for sharing them on her page.

After spending a couple of hours on Facebook searching for more information on ascension and consciousness, it became clear to me that I had the answers to the questions I had, I was going to find them right here on social media, starting with Facebook. I was finding one person after another who was sharing everything about their healing experiences. Lots of posts discussed what you can do to recognize past experiences that you need to heal from. I was amazed to see how many of us have been taught to cover up these traumatizing experiences that have hurt us when we needed to heal from them!

All can say is wow to all of this amazing awareness. There is so much helpful information here, like, for example, there was talk about how to recognize the warning signs that you are in an abusive relationship. And then give you the steps to take to get out of an abusive relationship, and how to protect yourself and your energy from any further abuse from an abusive relationship by teaching you to enforce your boundaries.

There was information on how to relieve stress with meditation and exercise. There are people offering to teach you how to do breathwork or breathing exercises. There were some posts that were just a few positive words that were bright white on a black screen so that the words would jump out at cha. They called these memes or affirmations. I thought those were really cool because I like to tell myself encouraging words to motivate me, or to give myself some praise when I deserve it.

There is so much information here on Facebook, and it is on so many different subjects. The list kept going on and on, and so did the people who were telling their stories. It reminded me of people when they would give their testimonies at church, and the more I heard people talking about how their awakenings started four, five, and six years ago, with some going even further back than that, kept me in total amazement at how all of this is new to me.

Especially when I consider that I am almost fifty years old. And that I was not a sheltered person. I have been all over the United States. I have experienced many things and people through the years. I have learned from and I have been taught by some wise people in my days, and after all of these years, none of them has ever talked about these things. Well, at least not around me.

Not to be conceded, but I do feel like I have a little more than the average guy. When it comes to some things, one of them is common sense, which leads me to believe that there is much more to the stars than what we have been told. In my opinion, it's a no-brainer. I have always believed that there are extraterrestrials out there in the universe, and that is another thing that I am seeing in these posts. Talk about extraterrestrials, even talk about, how we are extraterrestrials, and that some of us have come here on a journey to experience life as a human being with names like indigo children and star seeds who are coming to the Earth for this great awakening.

I saw one post that caught my attention, particularly. It mentioned the name Jesus Christ, calling him an ascended master along with other names such as Buddha, and Saint Germain. Christian and many more like Noah and Ezekiel.

My faith has always been in God, and when I say that, I mean in Jesus Christ. I am baptized in Jesus' Name, and I will tell it to the whole world. I read a post that talked about Jesus being real that he came down from the stars, and that he served his purpose here on Earth while he was going through his process of ascension, and when he finished his task, he left and went back to God-Source in the stars.

When I read that, I just absolutely loved it! Everything inside me felt like it was true, and I had to say to myself that this felt like it was more than a plausible explanation. Anyhow, to be honest, I have always questioned why a loving creator God would send a savior, who would be his only begotten son, who, for a brief moment in time, would be sent here to Earth to teach man how to forgive everything, and how to live life with a loving, charitable heart, only to leave right after being cruelly put to death by crucifixion. Supposedly for the remission of the world's sins, only to have to come back again at an unappointed time in the future to finish saving the people of the Earth who just killed him.

All of this makes a lot of sense to me, and what else is strange is that it feels so right on the inside of me, like I just know it to be true, and now that, I have all of this new information that I want to research. And now, I have these feelings inside of me that are making me want to question my faith.

Omg, I have so many questions now. Questions about things like connecting to your higher self, which, if you ask me, my opinion on that gathering, from what I read in one of the posts, sounds a lot like being born again. I can't help but want to compare all of this new information with my Christian beliefs and what my Bible says about these subjects. But how? And where would I start?

Chapter 23

Ascension or Heatstroke?

Ok, hold up. I gotta stop thinking for a minute, but how am I supposed to do that? My mind is going a hundred miles an hour. I cannot even relate what I have just experienced to anything prior to this day. Here I am digging deep in the memory bank of my mind, trying to remember if I have even seen a movie that resembles this.

All I know is that I can't seem to concentrate. My thoughts are all over the place. Breathe, Bob, I tell myself, then following my own instructions to take a couple of deep breaths. That's evidence right there that I'm not completely myself, and yes, I am aware that I informed you that I do talk to myself sometimes. But it is usually in some sort of comical manner. No joking, this time, I am seriously trying to help myself here.

After I take a few deep breaths, I say to myself. Now let's start from the beginning.   Let's see. I woke up this morning. Feeling perfectly fine. I didn't have anything to do today, and I was perfectly fine with that. Maybe I was a little bit bored, and that's ok too. I didn't really need anything from the store, and still, somehow, I decided to go to the store anyway. On the way to the store, less than five minutes from the house, I find a painted turtle in a bizarre place on the roadway.

Yada, yada, yada in my head I said. "Omg," Did I just say that in my own head? That defeats the purpose of my starting from the beginning and talking myself through this. Oh, bother. Bob, you'd better take a few more deep breaths and start again.

Okay, you find this turtle on the road, and it wasn't even that bizarre because you looked around, and logic said that the turtle's water source dried up on it. Okay, no problem, that's not hard to believe, and for the most part, you can say that's one lucky turtle. Also, going on to say that you are a nice guy, you like to rescue animals when you can, and it's only logical that you would take the turtle to the Simonton Lake boat launch, which you would be passing while on your way to the store.

This is not that strange, not even finding the turtle. It's a hot day, yeah, but it's July and it's always hot in July. Right then, all of a sudden, I stop thinking. It's as if it's because I knew what came next. The voice, the part about voice. That's where everything goes bonkers. After hearing the voice in the car, I came up with every excuse that I could to cover for my hearing it. I even remember trying to ignore it like that would make it go away.

Thinking back on that, I couldn't help but think how that didn't work, as I gave out a couple of chuckles while I'm in the middle of (SMH) shaking my head and laughing out loud at myself. Omg, I'm still shaking my head. At what? What am I trying to do here? Seriously, am I trying to have a self-talk to rationalize my talking to a voice in my head, that I can't believe is anything other than an entity from a faraway place?

This is where I began to question myself. Who did you talk to for 2 hours in your car? Maybe it is the heat? Maybe you are going a little bit crazy? Can that be it? Did you live for almost fifty years, and then one day you wake up and find out that you just slipped off your kilter, without any warning signs, just a hot day in July?

Not hardly, I'm not buying that, not even for a buck, and anyway, what person who just went crazy starts thinking about their childhood and the programming that their parents did to them, while they're sitting in their hot car for two hours talking to a voice in their head. Okay, wait a minute, that does sound crazy, especially if you're not the person who experienced it. I don't care how crazy it sounds, I'm telling you everything that I felt was real. It even had sounds and smells in it. This stuff was as real as real can get.

Even if I was hearing voices in my head, that were telling me that I was experiencing consciousness, that I was beginning my ascension, or that other guides would be coming to help me with all of this, and that all of this happened when it was hot as hell out possibly causing me to fall completely out of my rocker and take a ride on the cuckoo train and even if all of that is so, that still does not explain where all of this newfound information came from on Facebook. Not only is it new to me, but it is as crazy as the voice that I was listening to in my head at the lake, who was telling me all about this crazy ass stuff.

Am I being skeptical here? Of course, I am. Would I believe this if I had not experienced it myself? Probably not. Am I questioning my Faith? I feel like I am about to. My faith in Jesus Christ has never been questioned before, and I don't believe that it is now. It's just that I do not remember any stories in my Bible that relate to this, or any testimonies from the members of the church. Well, at least not in any of the churches that I attended, and in my Bible, whenever someone was visited by the Holy Spirit or a Divine Being of any sort. It would be portrayed by an Angelic figure, like an angel or loud trumpets, rushing waters, earthquakes, or a burning bush. A message from an Angel that was sent by God. You know, that kind of stuff.

My Spirit Guide did not claim to be Angelic, my Spirit Guide didn't claim to be anything other than a guide from a distant place, she didn't say where she was from, and who knows, she may have even been from a different dimension or realm. I don't know for sure, and how would I know that anyway. She could be from the other side of the Milky Way, or some other distant galaxy, or from the local 711 across town, for as far as I know.

I will be sure to ask her these things the next time I talk with her, and a guide for what? I'm gonna ask her that too, but in more detail this time. I'm already anticipating the answer to that question being this journey to healing that everyone is talking about being on, and Jesus, I am definitely gonna ask her about Jesus.

Maybe I should start writing these questions down because I have a feeling I'm gonna be asking her a whole lot of them.

Chapter 24

Grapes, Grace, and the Glimpse of God

Gathering my thoughts before bed, it was getting later now, and I was beginning to feel tired, so I decided to get some sleep. It was still daylight out, so I picked up my phone to check the time, and to my surprise, it was after eight o'clock in the evening, which meant I spent over three hours on my phone doing nothing but going through these Facebook posts.

I suddenly noticed my battery was getting low, so I looked by the bed for my phone cord. Darn, it's not there by the nightstand. I must have left it in the kitchen. No problem, I need something to drink anyway. I will just grab the phone cord and get myself a glass of water while I'm in the kitchen. When I walked into the kitchen, I noticed something. Yeah, my phone cord was right there, but that's not what I noticed, everything feels a little bit different. As soon as I walked into the kitchen, I noticed everything in detail, like the dishes in the sink, and the cup on the counter from earlier.

It was such a weird feeling. It was as if everything slowed down into slow motion. Then I had this feeling of déjà Vu like I had been here before. I felt like I was supposed to reach into the refrigerator to grab the picture of cold water, and while I was in there, I was supposed to grab some grapes to munch on. After I finished pouring my glass of water, I put the pitcher back into the refrigerator and thought about the déjà Vu feeling again when I was grabbing the grapes.

Déjà Vu or not, I thought, those grapes look pretty yummy right now.

After I grabbed a small bowl of grapes and my glass of water, I headed back to the bedroom. I set the glass of water down on the end table and sat down on the edge of my bed. I take a really deep breath and I let it out with a sigh like it's been a long, hard day, and I'm glad that it's over. But it hasn't been a long, hard day, I haven't done anything today. Yes, it's been hot out, but that's about the extent of it. I looked down at my hand to divert my attention away from what I was thinking about, seeing that I still had five big, plump, purple, juicy grapes left.

All of a sudden, I had this strong feeling of gratitude come over me as I was putting a grape into my mouth, and I couldn't help but think. Where did this grape come from? How did it get here? I live in Elkhart, Indiana. There aren't any grape fields within 100 miles of here, and when I was putting the last grape into my mouth. I had become aware. Aware of what, that part was strange?

Strange because it's as if I have become aware of myself not being aware. I have just realized that I have been taking things for granted my whole life, and after everything that happened today, here I am sitting on the edge of my bed feeling grateful for these grapes and this glass of water in a way that I have never ever before. I took a drink of water before I lay back in bed, and as soon as my head hit the pillow, everything that happened today started running through my mind again like it was on repeat or something. I would try to stop at a part and try to focus on it.

And then my thoughts would skip back to somewhere at the beginning of the day or to a non-significant part, like the inner tube that was in the boat. Maybe it was because it was red, white, and blue, and it reminded me of our American flag. My thoughts were sporadic, they were all over the place. I was not in control of them, and I definitely did not like that, as I was thinking of what I could do to gain control of my own thoughts.

Breathing came to mind. Breathe. Bob is what I keep telling myself. You've been doing this all day, and this breathing has been working for you. It has been helping me. So I began to breathe in and out. Deep and slow breaths, in and out, one deep breath after another, focusing on controlling my breathing, even counting to 4 and holding it for a 7 count before exhaling it for 8 more and breathing in for a 4 count again. It was kind of shocking because it felt like I knew how to do this from some other place in time. When I was thinking about where this came from, the name Jesus Christ appeared in my mind, and with it came a sense of comfort and a feeling of peace.

So I continued to picture the Name Jesus in my mind, and as I was speaking His Name with each breath I took, breathing in the Name of Jesus and holding my breath as I pictured His Holy Name. Then, I breathed out the Name Jesus and held my breath again, and, this time, when I was picturing the Name of Jesus, a beautiful white light appeared and began to take the shape of a figure. It was blue and white, and it was the brightest light that I had ever seen. There was a Divine and Holy presence in all of its Glorious Essence. I wanted to tremble and start to weep, but I was instructed not to. There were no words spoken, only the feeling of knowing. I was told that everything was gonna be ok. Then I was told that I must learn patience. I was told that everything that I would need would be provided to me. But I must learn forgiveness. I was told that all of my dreams would come true. But I must learn to love my enemy.

Now all of my thoughts were on one thing and one thing only, and it was my Jesus. I tried to picture Jesus's face in my mind, but it was all blurry. Blurred out with a bright light to tell me not to go there. I was feeling as if Jesus was telling me something. Telling me that there are other things that are far more important to think about than what Jesus looks like.

Chapter 25

WWJD. Where Does Jesus Fit In?

I then looked down at my feet. And notice that my shoes are still on. So, I took them off and set em by the nightstand. I reached over to grab my glass of water, and I started to take a drink. With my thoughts turning to Jesus again, I had to ask myself.

Where does Jesus fit into all of this? As soon as I reached over and turned off the lights. And I lay back on the bed again. Letting out another big sigh of relief with my head snuggling the pillow.

I feel tired, but at the same time, I am not. And as I lay there thinking about the day, and everything that happened in it. I was now trying my hardest to figure out where Jesus fits in all of this. I was thinking about how I went to church for many years, learning about God, and what happened to me today does not align with anything that I have previously learned about God in all of my time in the church.

I was saying to myself, this is not going to change how I feel about Jesus! I love my Jesus. I am baptized in His Holy Name, and I have chosen him as my Savior.

It felt like I was telling myself this as if I was reminding myself of it. So, I began to search my memory. I was looking for stories or testimonials, hoping that there was something in my memory of the Bible that I could compare this crazy ass day to. But I couldn't remember any stories that I may have heard. Nothing resembling anything about this day. I must have laid there in my bed for over an hour.

Before I concluded that I could not find anything. Nothing even close in comparison. Surely something like this would have stood out in my memory. It was here that I started to second-guess myself. I didn't know if my memory was bad, and I had forgotten. Or if I hadn't spent enough time in my Bible. Either way, you look at it, my memory doesn't seem to be helping me with this problem. In fact, it might be making things worse. Am I losing touch with reality here? What is real and what isn't?

What happened to me today when I found the turtle was just too realistic for me to deny, I don't care how strange or bizarre it all seems. I felt these emotions inside of me were incredibly strong feelings of real emotions. These feelings that I felt were nothing less than pure love, so intense that it made my eyes tear up more than once, and when that was happening, I was having whole-body chills, goosebumps everywhere on my body, and on a day so hot, it would have made the devil sigh, and open some windows.

Between my eyes watering up, and then the whole-body chills, I was convinced that something here was real enough to have my full undivided attention.

There it is, I said, the connection I have been looking for, the whole-body chills with goosebumps. This has happened to me before. It happened to me in church on a few special occasions, when church was just right and the word of God was being spoken in its Powerful Truth. I remember experiencing this vividly, and whenever this would happen, it felt like the spirit of God was there, moving over everyone in the church. I remembered one time when this happened to me a long time ago, when I started to weep in church, literally crying tears that were running down my face and dripping to the floor, when this happened, it was because I heard a voice inside of me saying.

"You will do mighty things for the Kingdom of Heaven."

I can remember being scared to talk about that. I was afraid of what people might think or say if I said anything about it. I knew that people would look at me and judge me because people in church seem to judge everything. That's something that we were being taught not to do, but everybody judged everybody. That's how you knew which brother or which sister was close to God, and I was young at the time, having just started going to church. I was just a baby in comparison to the elders of the church that I was attending.

In the years that I was dedicated to attending church, not once did I hear any pastors speaking about anything like this in any of their sermons.

Yeah, sure, I heard testimonials of people saying that they felt the Holy Spirit. I heard people say things like The Lord spoke to me, The Lord told me that this is what I need to do or, The Lord told me that person was no good, I need to stay away from them. I have a thousand examples like these in my memories.

This is one of my favorite ones that I have said many times. The Lord laid it on my heart to do this, but I haven't ever heard anyone say that they heard a voice being spoken to them like I am referring to. This is why I didn't say anything to anyone about it because what I heard was not with my ears. This was a voice inside of me, in my heart, and in my mind. It felt and sounded so real that when it happened. I first thought that it had come from my wife, so I turned towards my wife in the pew that we were sitting in, and I looked into her eyes to see if she had said anything to me. But her eyes were closed because she was praying. After church that night, I spoke to my wife about what happened. She said, "I believe you, Robert, I felt the Holy Spirit too".

After that night, we attended church faithfully for many months without missing any services. My wife and I never really spoke about it again, though looking back on that today, it seems strange that my wife and I never spoke about that again. I kept what happened to me a secret, never speaking about it to anybody in the church.

Through the years, I thought about that night here and there, always wondering if God really spoke to me. I cherished the salt and sometimes imagined what it would be like if I did do great things for the Kingdom of Heaven.

Today, I can see where the lack of confidence in myself left me in doubt, which stole my hopes of being anything great. As time went by, so did the memory of what happened that night in church, only to be dismissed as nothing more than my imagination.

Chapter 26

The Connection

I have finally made a connection between what happened today and my faith in God. Well, kinda, if you count the goosebumps and the whole-body chills. This is definitely the connection that I was looking for, something that goes beyond logic and into the realm of faith because, with everything that I know, it is just not enough knowledge to help me find an explanation. I have to consider this connection to be legitimate.

I believe that the whole-body chills and goosebumps are nothing less than a spiritual visitation from the Holy Spirit.

In my apostolic faith, we are always seeking the truth, and we have a spiritual communication connection with the Holy Spirit of God.

One example of us using our discernment is when we are discussing something of significance. If we get whole-body chills, and goosebumps that are out of the ordinary, we will use our discernment and intuition when it comes to our interpretation of these body chills and goosebumps. I will strongly testify that it is in my opinion that this is to be the Holy Spirit telling you that what you are thinking about, or hearing, is the truth, or, on the other hand, someone can be telling you a whole lot of something. Then they can ask you if you want to be a part of it, and you don't want to be a part of it, but you are not sure if you're making the right decision, and then all of a sudden, you get those goosebumps. Well, I would interpret that to mean a big fat no, a confirmation from the Holy Ghost confirming your gut feeling that was already telling you the answer, which is that you are not supposed to be a part of it. That is why I am not going to dismiss the goosebumps as a mere coincidence.

While I was in my thoughts about this cannot be a coincidence. I decided to say a prayer, so I sat up and turned sideways on the edge of my bed and put my feet on the floor. I clasped my hands together, closed my eyes, and began to pray.

"Lord, did you send me this spirit guide? Am I supposed to be communicating with them? My Lord Jesus, in all the years that I've known you, I haven't ever seen or heard of anything that would even come close to this. My Lord, You already know me, and You know that I do not have anyone in my life that I can talk to about this. and I especially don't have anyone who would believe me let alone someone who would want to try and figure out the meaning of all of this with me. Lord, what am I supposed to do now?"

Right then I stopped praying, and with my eyes still closed I unclasped. My hands. I then placed one hand on each of my knees. I sat there for a few minutes quietly thinking about God, wondering if He sent me a Spirit guide. I have already made up my mind, my discernment tells me that the whole-body chills are not a coincidence. All of my senses and intuition tell me that God has His hands in all of this.

Now I remember back to that night in church when God spoke to my heart, saying, you will do great things for the Kingdom of Heaven.

Honestly, this is quite comforting now when I think about it. At least now I don't feel like my hearing voices is anything crazy. I mean, if you're looking at it from my perspective, I have heard voices before, and when I did, I was going to church, and I was living life the best that I could be. I was sober and kept away from everything that was labeled ungodly.

Even the language I used was kept in order of a Holy nature, and today, I am sober so as not to blame the why I am hearing voices again that are instructing me to do good things. I'm not saying that saving a turtle is doing great things for the Kingdom of Heaven, I'm just saying that I do see a connection here, and as I am trying to piece this together, I'm beginning to believe that I may be in contact with another being from a faraway place, from somewhere out there in the stars. An entity that is here trying to help me. Help me do what? When asking myself this question, I suddenly get a visual, and it is in big, black, and white flashing letters. And they say it plainly,

"Help you to Evolve"

Okay, that was deep, and now that a connection has been made, I am not feeling so much like I'm losing it here. Could it be that this is of a Divine origin? Even though my spirit guide does not claim to be from God.

The message certainly does feel like it is. I keep having this strong feeling that my spirit guide wants what is best for me, even going as far as pointing out that I am holding myself back in life, because of my beliefs in the things that I was taught when I was growing up. She even said that it wasn't all my fault because I was programmed as a child.

This is pretty far out when you think about it. I heard a voice in church twenty years ago, and I was too scared to talk about it to anyone then, afraid of being judged by my peers, and that was over some encouraging words being laid on my heart. From what I believe was the Holy Spirit, and today I'm not just hearing a voice but, having a conversation with one, who sounds just like the one from twenty years ago.

O Lord, comes to mind as I think these things, for whom in the world could I tell this to today? I'm thinking nobody in particular, especially anyone who is of a religious background. Hmm. You know, now that I think about it, I'd better keep this to myself for a while, then say, Lord, what are you trying to tell me? I have prayed to You a thousand times throughout the years. I have asked you for help in almost every prayer and about everything possible. I have always believed that you heard my prayers, and I have been patiently waiting my whole life for the answers to come, never expecting them to come in any other way than something that would seem supernatural, and here I am today, face to face with something that is way out of the ordinary.

I was noticing that my thoughts were more under my control. It was as if my thinking had slowed down to a speed that I could keep up with, and it all started when I began thinking about Jesus. This put a big smile on my face as I lay there and finished up my prayer so that I almost forgot I was praying.

Lord Jesus, I have trusted in your Holy Name for as long as I can remember, and you have always been there for me. I have felt Your love and I have seen Your guiding hand protecting me through the years, always showing me the way back to the Father's light. This time can be no different, Lord. I know that you are involved in this. You have never let me go astray. And I don't believe that You are now, so I am looking for You in this, and I am trusting that I will find You, believing that You will reveal to me in time what it is You're trying to tell me. I trust You, my Lord, I love You, my Lord! And it is in Your Holy name, the Name of Jesus, that I pray, Amen. After I was done praying, I lay there in bed for a few minutes thinking to myself, I think?

Then, I literally spoke these words saying, Jesus will shine a light on this for me, and as soon as I said that, my focus shifted back to the part about ascension. I don't know for sure yet, but I think I might understand, and if I'm right about this ascension stuff, then it is for our way of thinking to go beyond where it presently is, to increase awareness, and to rise to a higher conscious state of mind.

To be more aware of the things that you previously were not. As I was thinking about all of these things that are yet to be known to me, programming came to mind. This is something that I was not previously aware of until now, just like this ascension process stuff that I have not ever heard of until today.

Is humanity moving beyond the physical mind and into conscious awareness with feelings and spirit being one in energy, coming from our thoughts alone? Are we becoming beings in a higher consciousness? I couldn't help but think that this could be endless, infinite like the number of stars in the night sky. I remember reading that we only use a very small portion of our brain and that if we could access the other parts of our brain, we would be like we become superhuman beings.

In all fairness, we would be more equal, and we would not be killing each other with war and man-made poisons. I couldn't help but think that the human being in itself as a civilization would finally be able to be at peace, there would be no need for war because there would be no need for greed, not if everyone were treated more equally. And, if today people knew more about this matrix and its programming, it. It could stop everything bad that's happening on the Earth. People would be helping each other instead of hurting one another. Mostly, everyone that I have ever met in my life despises being tricked or lied to, and if they knew that they were being manipulated by the world leaders and the secret societies and that the only way to stop it was to work together, they would stop with their hatred towards one another and join forces against this unseen enemy.

Okay, wait a minute. Where did all of that just come from? Did I just hear myself right? This is not my kind of language, and these are not my kind of thoughts. I leaned over to look in the mirror to make sure that this was me. Yup, it's me, there's no denying that guy staring back, and I look the same, other than having a bewildered look on my face, hinting at a little disappointment.

Am I disappointed in myself, still looking like me, or am I subconsciously hoping that these new truths will be inspiring changes in me, like this smile that I'm looking at? Can I be happy enough to smile like this all the time? Smiling, I said to myself, I like your smile, Bob. Make sure you keep it!

Chapter 27

Lucid Dreams

I fell asleep, I found myself lost in a strange thought that I was having, and in this thought, I was trying to grasp hold of remembering something about talking to this guy who goes to the same gym that I go to. He knew something about the matrix and this programming stuff that my guide was telling me about. This was double strange because I was like, yeah, I remember that now, but I don't even remember why I am remembering it, or when this conversation started.

How crazy is it that someone had already been trying to tell me about the Matrix, and I wasn't comprehending what was being said to me at the time, and now, all of a sudden, I recall the conversation like it had just happened, and the guy from the gym, he had told me that there was a big convention for all who are seeking the truth. It was coming soon, he said that I should go. He explained to me that it was going to be held downtown, in Elkhart, at the Civic Center.

This is where I must have fallen asleep without even knowing it because what happened next is too bizarre to be real. There's the guy from the gym, and he's in a flashy sports car coming towards me. As we were passing each other, we were looking right into each other's eyes. It was almost like he was asking me, "Are you good?" And I answered back, saying, "Yeah, I'm good."

This mini-conversation felt like it lasted a few seconds, but it happened in a flash, just like his car when buzzed by.

Now, all of a sudden, I am driving down the highway, and I am in some badass convertible sports car. Some foreign job, I don't even know what kind it is, other than it's the coolest car that I have ever imagined driving before and sitting right next to me. She is a wonder woman, the most beautiful woman I have ever seen. She's sitting there with her long, dark hair blowing in the wind. In some places, her hair was almost raven black, it was so dark brown. And when the sun hit it, it was golden brown with blonde highlights. It looked like it changed colors when it captured the light just right.

Her eyes had a strength in them that could not be denied. I could feel it as I began to lose myself in their beauty. There was this light that sparkled so bright in them, like the stars in the darkest of night, commanding your attention, as if in them was the way home.

Her voice was full of powerful energy, like the kind that you feel on a stormy night. Lightning came from her lips as she spoke, thundering deep into my soul. It felt like there was another voice hidden inside the one I was hearing, and it was calling to me like a siren as if it knew that I was lost in her beauty. It gently pulled me closer, saying, "Listen to what I am saying." But these were not the words that she was speaking. Like a lightning strike and the thunder that follows, she says with authority, "The truth is out now!!! The matrix is crumbling into pieces, it is being brought to nothing. They cannot stop what is happening !!!"

She shouts, "We are all conscious, and we see through their lies."

She told me that the Earth is changing its vibration. Changing it to a higher frequency. She said, "Consciousness is here! New Earth is here, we are all going to 5D conscious".

It was a mysteriously enchanting moment that left my mind frozen in time. I was stunned and totally amazed! As I watched her speak with such divine angelic authority, it felt like she was speaking to me about a prophecy being fulfilled.

"You need to raise your vibration", she voiced again. "Raise your vibration, use your love energy, spread your light, spread your light", she yelled. She was talking about the new Earth, saying that heaven is here, heaven is the new Earth. Raise your vibration to match.

"Giai!! The Earth has shifted its frequency !!"

She began to repeat herself, but now with less intensity. Noticing this change in her energy is when I realized that I was dreaming. But this dream was so realistic and so very vivid, with the sounds of the roadway in my ears. Even the smell of her perfume was intoxicating, and now here I am trying to tell myself that I don't own a sports car, and I don't know her.

In my confusion, I say to myself, wait here just a minute, how can I be dreaming this and be looking at myself sleeping, observing that I'm in a dream, and yet I am still dreaming it. I can literally see myself in my dream while I'm still asleep. I remember saying, " Hey Bob, it's time to get up, bud. It's time to rise and shine."

Chapter 28

The Dream

My eyes opened, and when they did, I immediately sat up, thinking Wow, that was by far the most realistic dream I have ever had. I mean, yeah, I've had many dreams that seemed real enough, but I always knew they were dreams, unlike this one.

The emotions that I felt in this dream were as real as the ones you would feel in life. There was even an energy present that felt like love. It wasn't because of the attraction I had for this beautiful woman. The love was not lustful or passionate in that way. In fact, it was somewhat disappointing because that's where it stops.

As quickly as this feeling of me being attracted to her came, it was gone, leaving in its place a wholesome feeling of love that she had for me, like a family member kind of love. The love that I felt towards her was as if I admired her. Her powerful feminine energy. These emotions that I am talking about were like we were friends, and I had that kind of love for her. At the same time, she felt like a stranger to me, and all I knew for sure in this dream was that she was a magnificent woman in all of her beauty.

I was all ears, listening to everything she was telling me. Looking back at my dream today, I can definitely say that she was the kind of woman. That I would choose to dream about. If you know what I mean?

The excitement in the dream was so real, I tell you. It was intense and filled with adrenaline. I seriously believed I was driving this sports car. I remember having to take my eyes away from hers and focus on the road, having to go around these curves that were keeping her. I was feeling impatient while I was waiting for the road to straighten out. All I wanted to do was turn my head and look back into her beautiful eyes which seemed to have an enchanting spell on me.

At the same time, this car was as captivating as she was. In this car was the coolest radio that I have ever seen. It was like a mini laptop computer that pulled out from the dashboard and flipped open. I didn't even know it was there until she reached for it to turn it down when she began to speak.

This car was a deep, dark cherry red, with a clear coat on it. It looked like it was an inch thick. It was shining like it was still wet. It had the darkest tinted windows you've ever seen, which matched the tires perfectly. The deep, dark red paint job, with the black and chrome trimming, everything out, really accentuated this car. Then, to boot, the interior was packed with these seats, which looked to be of fine Italian leather and were soft to the touch. The grey-color interior looked absolutely perfect, being beautifully accented by the black carpet and car council.

The dashboard and radio were lit up with these red lights that put off a glow that looked so cool. I want this car, that's what I was thinking.

When my thoughts were instantly redirected back to the guy from the gym, it was confusing because the guy from the gym was real, and somehow in this dream, I could tell which characters were real and which were not. But nevertheless, he has my attention now. We were by the locker room entrance, that's where the leg press equipment is. I had just finished my last set, I was taking a drink of water from the bottle that I brought with me. I do not drink the city water that comes from the drinking fountain. This is when he approached me and asked me again. "Are you going to the truth convention?"

I don't remember answering him back. but I do remember what the last thing was that I was thinking about before I went to sleep. And it was about Jesus and the Ascension. Fully awake now, and instead of thinking about the ascension. I am wondering what this dream means. I am having this strong feeling here like something is trying to give me a message.

Chapter 29

Memories

Well, I'm awake now, I should probably get up and try to figure some of this out. I looked over at the clock, it was a little after five am. I was surprised that I slept for that long. Let's see if I lied down around nine pm, then that means that I have slept for eight hours. That's plenty of sleep for me, actually, that's about two hours more than I usually get.

Yup, I might as well get up, and let's be honest here, Bob. There isn't any way you're gonna go back to sleep now. Not that I would want to, and now with all of these thoughts bouncing around in my head again. I am seriously wanting to try and figure some of these things out.

I looked out my bedroom window to see that it was still dark out. With daylight beginning to light up the horizon, there was a tiny bit of light shining through the tree tops.

The window in the bathroom faces a different direction from the one in my bedroom, and I just woke up, so that's where I went because I had to use the facilities. When I looked out of the window in the bathroom, I could see these rays of sunlight coming through the trees. They were like golden beams of light shining through the morning mist that was covering the horse pasture. It was a beautiful picture to start my day with. I grabbed my toothbrush with some excitement. I hurried up to put some paste on it and started brushing my teeth. I was thinking that the sun would be up soon. And I wanted to watch it rise this morning, so I went to the kitchen and started to make some coffee. I didn't have anything to do today, so I figured that I could enjoy a cup while I was watching the sunrise to give you a picture to visualize. For you to have an idea of what my surroundings look like, where I was making my coffee, and where I was planning to watch the sunrise that morning. I will describe my home to you.

My kitchen is in the back of my house, facing the east. But I like to think of it more as the front. You know, like a lake house, where the front is always facing the lake, and the road is behind it. It's one of my little jokes because we are always looking out back as if it were a lake view. In the spring, when the snow melts and the fields flood the ground is frozen. It looks like a three-acre lake, a really big pond, to anyone who is unaware that they are horse pasture.

I have a cute little story I'd like to tell you about that I think is still funny today. So, please imagine with me. I would like you to picture this in your mind. I have a company that is visiting for the first time, so she was not familiar with my home and the layout of the land.

I invited her into the dining room where we could sit down and have a few drinks. I said to her Come in here, where we sit down and talk and look out the windows. We were sitting at the small table in the dining room. The table was round in shape, and it only had three chairs. This is because one side of the table had been squared off, and it was against the wall.

We never really had much company over. Maybe one or two people would stop by, and that would only be once in a blue moon. So the fourth chair was kept over in the corner for those special occasions.

On this day, it was just me and her. The way we were sitting there with our chairs slightly angled, and this put her chair close to mine, which was my plan. I could easily smell the perfume that she was wearing, and it smelled like cotton candy. I don't really care for cotton candy, but that day it smelled so yummy on her, and all I wanted to do was eat her all up.

Now that her being this close to me, and looked so sexy in those short shorts and tank tops that she was wearing. I couldn't help but focus all of my attention on her. She was an attractive young white woman in her twenties, around my age at the time, and I had just met her at a party a few days earlier. She had long brown hair with big blonde locks in it. It was a really cool-looking hair doo. She had quite a few tattoos, but the one that caught my attention the most was the one on her thigh. It was a floral scene with bright-colored flowers and lots of green vines and leaves everywhere, and in the center of it was this big beautiful red rose that looked like it was growing out of the center of a much smaller planet Earth. It was absolutely breathtaking artwork.

After she was done telling me where she got the tattoo work done, our focus shifted back to looking out the patio doors at what appeared to be a small lake. Now, while we have been talking back and forth about this and that, and her tattoos, our attention had been elsewhere, away from the view of the window. It was only for a few minutes, but that's all it took because when we looked back out the window at the lake, we saw a horse standing in the middle of it.

Of course, I knew that it was just a puddle of water, not a lake, but she didn't, and nevertheless, there was the horse standing there ankle deep in the water, and from the distance that we were away from it made it appear like the horse was standing on top of the water, especially from the angle that we were looking at it from.

The scene appeared to be magical for a brief moment, and I am not exactly sure what it is that she was thinking when she gave me that look. But the look she gave me was as if she had just seen Jesus's horse. Lol…

Of course, I had to play it for all that it was worth. I got all excited and made a big deal out of it, like it was for real, a horse walking on water. I even said, "Oh my God, where's Jesus?" For about thirty seconds, she was fooled, until her common sense kicked in, and she saw that I was playing a joke on her. We both laughed at it for a few minutes before we went on to talk about something else. It is still funny as hell to me today as I write about it here.

Maybe it's one of those jokes, where you had to be there to get in on the funny feeling part, or possibly it was our refreshments that day that made it all so humorous. I'm not too sure, but anyway I look at it, it was a lot of fun and a wonderful memory to have and share. I wonder what ever happened with her? I only saw her a couple of times after that day. I think her name was Elizabeth, yeah, that's it, and everyone called her Beth.

Chapter 30

The house

In my opinion, it is a beautiful view looking out of the kitchen window or the patio doors, and the way that the house is angled, puts our largest wall facing the east. That's where the windows are, with the blinds being open most of the time. It looks like they are always inviting in the glorious rays of the sun. When you are looking out the windows, all that you see is the horse pasture and the woodline in the back of it. There are no houses in sight, and the only structures that are visible are ours and the neighbor's horse barn.

With nothing else in sight, it has a real rustic feeling too, giving you the impression that you're further out in the country than you actually are, and with the smells of the farm fresh air that the animals are providing. You get the feeling of being on a bigger farm than you actually are. And that is why we spend a lot of time in this part of the house.

Back to the kitchen where this all took place. Let me give you more of an idea of what the layout of this part of the house looked like. The dining room is attached to the kitchen, making it one big rectangular room that has been divided in half by the countertop, putting the kitchen on the left side of the rectangle. It kinda looks like the Florida Peninsula, with the sink being in Tallahassee, and on the right side of the countertop is the dining room. On that side, we had a couple of bar stools to sit at, a small but quaint kitchen, and a dining room.

Ok, I think you're beginning to get a better idea of what the kitchen and dining room space looked like. Now, for the size of the two, they only measured out to be about four hundred and fifty square feet, and that was between the two rooms combined.

The kitchen was really small, and it had an abnormally big sink in it, which was all custom-built and handcrafted to fit the countertop. I can remember Dad building the countertop to match the size of the strangely shaped sink. I remember him installing the only window that we had in the kitchen area, directly over top of the sink, centering it with the window like they normally go.

The window was much smaller than the sink. And I used to joke with the old man about the window being only half the size of the sink. We talked about changing the window over the years, but we never got around to it. Dad always said that the reason he put the smaller window in was that there would be more cabinet space. And I always said that we only use half of the cabinets anyway, Pops.

Now, right next to the countertop where the patio doors were, and right next to the door in the corner of the room was a small antique hutch. It was four feet in height, and it had the cutest little glass door on the front of it. You could view Dad's miniature Harley-Davidson collection.

And about a foot and a half to the right side of the hutch is where the other small window is. Underneath the window is where the small dining room table was always kept. It was a small home with small rooms that provided small living spaces in it to match. Really small in comparison to the houses that I have built in my life. On average, the majority of your kitchens and dining rooms are about 350 square feet each. With each room having multiple windows.

Here we have a kitchen and dining room that are the same size as just one, which you would find in your average modern-day home. We had only two windows and one glass patio door between the two of them. It was not a fancy home at all, actually, it wasn't much of anything to most people, but it was our cute little home, and we loved it.

Outside of those patio doors is where we spent a lot of our time in the summer months. It's where we would relax and have a few drinks while we sat and talked. On occasions, we would have company over and grill out in the evening. It was nice to have the deck on the east side of the house. It would conveniently provide shade for our company in the late afternoon. Whenever we did have company over, we would always be entertaining them out on the deck.

The deck was sweet, it was around 550 square feet. It's easy to see that there is a lot more room on the deck than in the dining room, and out there was a big table and five chairs with a couple of small end tables. I always enjoyed having company over, especially when we would be sitting around the table, talking about life and looking out back. That is where the main focus of our home is. Except for the living room and one of the bedrooms, the rest of the house is facing the east. Dad angled the house that way in order to be able to see the horses when they were in the pasture. Pop's said that it's not much to look at, but it sure beats the hell out of looking at the neighbors.

And I agreed!

Chapter 31

Memories of Dad

In the very back of my property is a small wooded area where the deer would come from when they visited. Sometimes we were blessed with an enchanting scene where the horses and the wild deer would be nose to nose. Remembering back to one of those times years ago, when my dad was still alive. It was on a beautiful summer's evening, and the two of us were sitting on the deck having a few drinks and talking like a father and son do.

When we saw three deer come out of the wooded area, they all stood there for 10 or 15 minutes, and then the deer approached Dolly and Shelter, our two horses. One of them said a quick hello to Dolly, our other paint pony, and then to one of the deer, which was the biggest of them. Probably the oldest one we figured went straight up to Shelter, that was the name of our appaloosa horse, the one my dad adopted from the Shelter, that's what we call the local humane society, animal shelter. Now the biggest of the deer was nose to nose with Shelter for about five minutes. It really looked like the two of them knew each other. My pops and I were smiling great big when we looked at each other, and that's when Pop said, "Well, it looks like they stopped to say hello.

My dad was the coolest dad ever. He was definitely my best friend in the whole wide world. We would talk about everything, and with that being said, we could talk about anything. It will have been fifteen years now since his passing, come May 10th, 2025.

With Dad being my best friend and still being my pop, it should be easy to see that he meant the world to me. Of course, I miss him dearly.

None of it has been easy, but the first five years were definitely the toughest. There were a couple of times when it was almost too much for me to bear. My drinking and my drug use became a problem, and quickly got way out of control after his death.

Bringing up the question was my losing the old man to blame? This we will never know. But what I do know is that my life was getting too difficult for me to handle without my best friend, and because of it, I came really close to unintentionally killing myself a few times.

It was only by the grace of God that I made it through this hell that I was experiencing. I can't tell you how many times I prayed to Jesus, or how many buckets of tears I shed. Today, I am extremely grateful to be sober and to be here as a witness. A person who has survived a loss that they did not think they could. Now I'm in a place where I am able to relive these memories. Bringing them back to life in such a way that I can share my dear old pops with the rest of the world now. Along with all of my other experiences.

Dad was born on July 19th, 1948. Making him a Cancer, which is a water sign, of course. I was born March 19th, 1975, making me a Pisces, which is another water sign like my dad. I always cherished sharing these two things with

Pops. Both of us are water signs who were also born on the nineteenth. This always made me feel like we were specially connected in ways that go beyond us just being a father and son in this space that we call a lifetime.

I always thought Dad was kinda psychic. He seemed to know things that he shouldn't have, but somehow, he always did. I wondered if it was because Dad was always paying attention to the moon, like he was waiting for it to become full, always making sure to remind me of it being full whenever it was. He would tell me to be careful, saying, "Son, the moon is powerful". Also, going on to say that there are people who cannot handle the moon's energy. I've heard him say more than once that some people make really bad decisions on a full moon.

He would tell me, "Son, be extra careful these next few days. "And whenever Dad said this, he would remind me not to become a part of their mistakes. Then saying something like.

"Son, a wise man will learn from another man's mistakes without being a part of them."

My dad was always looking out for me. He would start our conversations off with "How are you doing, son? Is there anything troubling you today?". And there usually was. So, he would then ask me, "Do you want to talk about it?", and I always did. This is one of the reasons why I miss him so much. Looking back, I can see that he was the only one in my life who ever cared for me so deeply in this way. Ever since I was a little boy, my dad would tell me, "Son, you are a better man than I am". He would then say, "Son, you are just like me, accept that you are the improved version. You will go on to do great things in your life. Things that I cannot do".

He always told me that he loved me and that he was proud of me. Even when I wasn't doing my best and I was getting into trouble. My dad always gave me love and treated me with respect, always telling me that he was proud of me. Saying "Son, you will do better next time". Then he would say one of his famous quotes. This one is my favorite!

"Who do they think they're messing with!"

I would tell him back, "Yeah! Who do they think they're messing with?"

Chapter 32

The Morning

After I finished setting up the coffee pot. I figured I would sit on the deck while it was brewing. So, I opened the patio doors up and I went out to meet the day. It was beautiful outside that morning, and it was much cooler than the day before. The temperature had dropped 20° overnight, and it was now in the mid-70s, which, in my opinion, is absolutely perfect.

That morning, the air was moist, and it was heavy from the dew the night before. Everything on the deck was wet. I had to flip a cushion over before I could sit down. You could feel the moisture in your lungs as you were breathing it in. It left me feeling clean and refreshed after each and every breath that I took.

It felt like I was literally breathing in this new day. This is when I noticed how quiet it was. It was calm that morning with no breeze to be felt. Only the cool, moist air was caressing my skin, leaving it feeling rejuvenated and refreshed. There was a peaceful feeling that morning that only the stillness of a quiet summer's morning like this can provide.

As I was sitting there in this newfound awareness of mine, I was observing everything that I could, taking it all in with every breath that I took. I heard a rooster crow off in the distance, and I knew it was my neighbors who lived to the north of me. He has three chickens that I personally know. I know his chickens better than I know him. I call the rooster Rick, and his hens Thelma and Louise. Right then, I heard another rooster crow. This one I do not personally know.

I have never met the neighbor who lives four houses up my road to the north. But, I do know that he has a few chickens himself. I would guess it to be around ten or so, and he has two emus in a pen next to the chickens. He keeps them locked up in their enclosure, while he lets his chickens run around. I hear his rooster crowing all the time, and he crows a hell of a lot more than Rick does. In fact, Rick thinks he crows too much. I know he does it just to mess with Rick! And it definitely does, because he's always getting on my and Rick's nerves.

I have spent a lot of time with Rick and the woman these last few years. I've gotten to know them pretty well. I'm home alone a lot these days, it seems, and when they come over for a bite to eat. I like to talk to the chickens, and my cats, I talk to them like they are people. I will tell the cats to never mind them chickens, let them have some of your Friskies. I will fill your bowl back up when they leave.

One of my cats, Samson, he such a funny cat. He will never mind their chickens, but not without looking at me first with much content in his eyes. While we both watch the girls eat some of their food, Rick is such a good guy to his girls, he always eats last. He will grab a few bites when the girls are heading back home. When the girls are eating, me and Rick are usually staring at each other, listening for that damn rooster down the street to crow. I get a kick out of Rick when he is looking at me, and then that other rooster crows. Rick will turn his head sideways, looking at me with only one of his eyes. Then he will straighten it back up and look at me. He will give a couple of clucks, and then his eyes get really big, as he starts to straighten out his neck. It looks like he's summoning some superpowers from the earth up through his legs into his body so that he can let out a crow like the biggest dagone rooster you ever did see. Every time that this happens, I can't help but laugh at it.

What a silly experience to get to enjoy. At least during the summer months.

Thinking back on all the different times that Rick and I had this fun together. It reminds me that these are my memories. I get to keep them, and they are always with me. I don't have to live the experience all over again to enjoy them. Like now, hearing the roosters crow. It reminds me of the times when Rick and the women came over.

Chapter 33

The Sunrise

While I was reminiscing some of these memories of mine. I noticed, that the day had begun to awaken. The birds were waking up too now, and they were beginning to sing their songs, I could hear their cute little chirps and their whistles. But I couldn't see any of the birds yet, for it was still too early. The day was still in its twilight of becoming its new self, and I could hear where they were coming from.

The whistles and the singing were coming from the three big white pines, that are in Rick's yard near his chicken's coop. These sixty-foot-tall beautiful pine trees are as thick and bushy as they are tall. Many birds call these trees their home. These trees also are a refuge for so many more during thunderstorms and really hot days. These beautiful trees even act as a motel for the birds who are just flying through.

Even though you can't see em you can definitely hear them. Their beautiful singing seemed to be coming from everywhere. The morning was alive with the beautiful sounds of summer. I heard one of the neighbor's horses off in the distance. It sounded as if it was saying good morning to the day.

I can smell the coffee now, and I hear it percolating. This particular coffee pot doesn't make any noise until it is almost done. It gives off the smell of freshly brewed coffee and the all too familiar iconic sound of the coffee percolating when it is done. So, I went back inside to fix myself a cup, grabbing my favorite mug that morning. I poured some coffee into it. When I reached for the honey, I noticed that we were close to being out.

I'm not very good at remembering things like this when I'm in the store. I don't know how many times I tried the mental note thing with no success in doing it, since I know that it doesn't always work for me. I looked for something to write it down and on. How convenient right there is the electric bill sitting on the counter. I grabbed the envelope and flipped it over to the backside and I wrote honey on it, noticing that the envelope had not been opened yet. I decided to open it later. I didn't want to change the mood that I was in right now. I just want to finish making my coffee and watch the sunrise.

I reached into the refrigerator to grab some coffee creamer. I poured a little creamer into my coffee stirring it a few times. When I finished I turned to go back outside again, and as soon as I rounded the countertop and looked through the patio doors, I saw that the sun was beginning to peak over the top of the trees.

As I opened the doors and stepped through them I noticed that the sun seemed extra big to me that morning, and what immediately caught my attention was how the sun was making the trunks of the trees stand out like these huge dark pillars that were off in the distance. These are the trees that make up the treeline that borders the edge of the horse's pasture. And now, with the sun rising up from behind the canopies of these trees, it was absolutely magical looking with the sunlight beautifully illuminating them like Christmas ornament commanding the day in its majestic way while looking brighter and even bigger than it usually does, with its golden rays of light now gleaming through the morning fog.

And wherever these golden rays of light reached the ground. It revealed all of the water droplets that were on the plants. The morning dew that was left from last night was heavy, leaving millions on top of millions of water droplets that were everywhere. These tiny drops of water were catching the sun's light from every angle possible making them sparkle like jewels illuminating all the colors of the rainbow in a glimmering pearl essence.

It was the most beautiful thing that I had seen in a very long time. I couldn't help but think to myself here it is mid-July, and I am just now taking the time to enjoy a beautiful summer morning sunrise. Right then I made a promise to myself that I would be getting my butt up in the mornings. Well, at least for the rest of this summer I figure.

I took a seat in one of the patio chairs being extra careful not to spill any of my coffee. I had filled the cup up to the brim, a little bit too much for the walk outside. So before leaning back, I had a few sips of it. After I was done I set the cup on the table and then sat back to relish the moment. As soon as I did the back of my shirt got wet. Yup, I said. I was in a hurry and I forgot to wipe off that portion of the chair. I just smiled at it as I sat there.

I sipped on my coffee and watched how fast the sun was rising above the trees. Using the trees as a reference for measuring how quickly the sun was climbing, and when it had cleared the top of trees. All of a sudden, the sun's light hit the patches of fog, making the fog appear to be steaming as they began to dissipate.

The sun rose the light began shining on other parts of the field causing them to sparkle. Now both horse pastures, ours and the neighbors, are glistening in the morning sun like fields full of treasures.

Everything was just so perfect out that morning. The sky was absolutely gorgeous in its different shades of blues and purples. The stars that were left were still very bright as they shone their light, beautifully decorating what was still left of the night sky which was now quickly fading away. From the twilight it seems, that is now taking over what we call a new day. And if that's not amazing enough topping off this picture-perfect morning. There, off in the eastern sky just south of the sunrise, is a crescent moon with a lone star, and they are sitting there in the night sky positioned so perfectly to watch the sunrise. I thought it was just the coolest thing ever, and I will never forget any of it.

As I was watching the sky I started to feel this enchanting presence of love leaving me in the most peaceful state of mind imaginable. All of this felt so new to me I thought. As strange as this may sound I believe that I am becoming more aware, aware of being an extremely stressed-out individual, who is overly uptight and doesn't even realize it. When did this happen to me?

Why am I living a life where I am always making my outside look like everything is good when on the inside everything is not ok? Have I succumbed to a life of misery, by turning around and acting like I am happy? I feel like I have unknowingly become numb to this life of mine. Even accepting it as if it is just a normal way to be living life, just a part of the life that I was dealt. It's like I am in a cosmic card game with a Joker or something. A game that nobody offered me a cut in. One where there are no re- deals, and no five-card draws.

Now that I have experienced this kind of peace while holding a dead hand, it's got me thinking that I might be holding some wild cards here. I mean if I can experience this kind of peace today, then why aren't I feeling like this every day? Why don't I feel this way more often!? If I had a choice in this, I would prefer to feel the way I am feeling right now all of the time! And I deserve to feel this way! I deserve to experience this kind of peaceful bliss on a regular basis in my life.

Look, I'm aware of my astrological sign being Pisces, and I know that I am prone to over-thinking. I'm also aware of my stressing too much, over stuff that I can't control, and how it can lead to me overly analyzing everything. This mind of mine has been beyond busy my entire life I tell you! It will run over a hundred mph if I let it. Ever since I can remember I've had to focus on focusing, always have to deal with trying not to interpret my thinking with every random thought that I have. Random thoughts come and go whenever they want always interrupting my train of thought causing me confusion when I need clarity the most, always seeming to be just out of my control. A 24/7 - 365-day problem.

For me to say that I am in a peaceful state of mind, one where the things in my head have slowed down enough that I have to acknowledge it because it is more than a mere whisper of peaceful bliss. There is an ever-loving essence in the way that I am feeling. It's as if I already know in my soul that this is true and that we can feel good about everything in our lives without needing anything to achieve it.

That would be the most beautiful gift ever. For me to receive a peaceful state of mind, preferably all of the time. My body, my emotions, and my soul. Would be in balance and more in my control. This is really starting to make sense to me. Even though I have only now experienced something like this in my life.

Strange this is, I thought. I just know this to be true, it's like there's someone inside of me, who feels separate from me, but who is still me, and who is telling me that I am safe.

It's gotta be my higher self, the one everyone is talking about on social media/Facebook, the part of us that every human being needs to be getting in touch with. That is, who is telling me that this is true, giving me the confidence to trust these feelings like they are a confirmation from my soul.

'My Intuition', I totally get it now! - I thinks. I am Just kidding about the totally get-it part but, I am beginning to put some of these pieces of this puzzle together and, it's already making forever changes in the way I think. Like now, whenever I hear someone say I can feel it in my soul, it's gonna bring me back to this place in time.

When I discovered how much more in-depth the phrase really does go by my soul's own experience where it was touched in a way that I will never forget. One that is leaving me to remember this day in its special way because of this Divine discovery. For in it, I was given every reason to believe in the supernatural.

It's like everything is illuminated in my mind. I can see my problems plain as day. But instead of them being in these giant flashing neon lights with letters spelling out my problems. Like they always are. They are up and out of my way now so I can relax for a few minutes. It's like I have this knowing inside telling me so, even illuminating my problems with a bright white golden light, which feels like hope.

There are no distinct words spelling out any solutions. Or, any voices explaining which way to go. None of that this time only a strong feeling of hope that feels like it is relighting my lamp and bringing my faith back to life. Let me know that help is here.

But why am I only now becoming aware of all of this? I want to know when this happened and what caused it. Most of my problems are related to my financial situation. The bills that I have trouble paying are always on my mind stressing me the heck out and, that's why I know for a fact that yesterday morning they did not appear to me in this way.

So what happened to me last night when I was asleep? Did something magical happen in my sleep that would enable me to perceive my problems so differently today? And how is it that just now when I was looking back to see if my problems were still there? I am instantaneously filled with hope that feels like an energy to my soul.

If I have a choice in this matter, then I choose to live a life where I can feel like this every day, especially after experiencing this kind of peace right now. And, why is it exactly that I am feeling so on top of the world today? Nothing in my circumstances has changed. I am still the same person in the exact same place in life. The work that I do for a living is less than desirable. I still have bills that need to be paid with the money that I do not have and, still here I am at peace this morning, sitting here in my newfound awareness, asking myself how is this possible. What could cause this kind of peace that I am experiencing right now?

I wanted to know exactly what was causing this peaceful state of being that I was in, and if there was a recipe that I could make part of my life to ensure that I can feel this way on command. Or better yet, to live life like this, always in a peaceful Zen state of mind.

I have seen many other sunrises throughout my years, and they did not give me this kind of a peaceful feeling. I believe that something new is happening inside of me, and it started yesterday continuing through the night bringing me here to this place where I am right now, asking myself these questions. How is this possible? And why is this happening to me now, and not sooner in my life? I am definitely gonna ask my guide about this when I speak to her or them.

Right then, my phone rang, I looked and saw that it was a message from someone on Facebook. It's a reply to last night's comment that I left on their page. In their reply, they are thanking me for the comment that I left. Then, saying we are happy that you resonate with our message and that it was helpful to you too, going on to say that we are here to help each other, and we would like to help you. A community of supportive individuals who are sharing their experiences while on a journey to healing with a beautiful invitation to join their group @ such and such address, click here.

After reading it, I smiled great big, thinking, wow! Then I replied back saying you are very welcome, wishing them a blessed day, and thanking them again for the invite to join their group. After I finished sending the message, I set my phone back down on the table and picked up my coffee. I figured I would have a drink or two while I took a minute to think about all the things that had just happened.

I am in absolute amazement when I add up the number of things that have happened. And then the degree of the things being discussed, with all of them being a bit more than your average topic, and then when I look at the time frame that all of this has happened in, with all of it being in less than a 24-hour period, that's including being invited to join a group that is about healing and healthy living talks.

In my opinion, here, there are too many coincidences, and there's no such thing as coincidence in my book. Especially ones like these. I can't help but feel like someone is trying to give me a message here. Although I'm not quite sure what it is, they have definitely gotten hold of my attention.

I mean, here it is less than 24 hours since I found that blessed turtle, Toby, and I am already talking with people on a social media platform about this kind of stuff. What are the odds of that? And look at me now doing something that I have not done in a very long time. Here I am watching this beautiful sunrise, feeling like a born-again man, who is sitting on top of his mountain of peace, within this incredibly powerful Zen-full state of being.

What do I do now? I thought while I stood there, letting the sun's rays caress my face, as I was enjoying the warmth of the sun touching my skin. I felt this urge to take a deep breath, and to my surprise, I instinctively exhaled almost completely and paused for a few seconds. Then I started to take this really long, slow, deep breath in with my eyes closed. I held my breath for a few seconds before exhaling it slower than when I had inhaled it. When I was doing this, I began to feel these strong emotions of gratitude come over me, and I instantly began questioning these emotions, asking if they were all mine or not. I know this sounds strange, but I felt like part of this gratitude that I was feeling was someone else's, too. I don't know if it is my higher self or one of my spirit guides, but it was definitely not all mine.

And while I was experiencing this emotional state of gratitude, I also felt like everything was gonna be different now. I could tell that my appreciation for everything in life had just changed, leaving me feeling grateful for my life in a way like I haven't ever before. That's when I said, "I am doing pretty good, and everything is gonna be okay, too!"

"And, I think I am doing a pretty good job of handling all of this."

I was speaking powerful mantras to myself with the energy of it being an absolute thing.

As I sat there thinking about what I had just said, I cracked a smile and began to laugh a little at the whole thing, finishing it up by bringing my lips into a little smirk like I just had an ah-ha moment, leaving me with this feeling like I am that guy!

I am worthy of great things, and I am capable of making my dreams come true. Now relishing in this newly found confidence along with this state of peace that I am in, still feeling smothered in gratitude, especially now after becoming aware of how powerful this spiritual enlightenment really is.

I had to stop right there and just pause for a minute. Breathing normally, I closed my eyes and remained still for some time.

After several minutes went by I opened my eyes, and it was as though everything had become even clearer to me. It was undeniable that something had just changed in me. This change wasn't something minor, it was something huge! And it was an absolute, and there wasn't any going back. I felt more confident than ever before, especially in my intuition when it comes to feeling out the truth in a matter.

Now with this new clarity and my heightened intuition, I am beginning to ask these difficult questions, feeling foolishly eager to dive back into this rabbit hole that I have been forced into experiencing these last 24 hours. Which, in my opinion, has been filled with enough strange things happening to be called a wonderland of my own unbelievable experiences with a turtle being the spirit animal that led me to this magical discovery of consciousness. I wonder how it is that I get a turtle instead of a rabbit-like Alice did in her adventures.

I have already been meticulously examining everything that has happened in the past 24 hours, and as I was observing everything that happened, I was becoming aware that I was not getting drawn into the emotional side of what happened. It felt really cool to be the observer of my thoughts without any of my ego giving its biased opinion on the subjects at hand. I could distinctly see that my ego and my conscious self were in separation.

I had only just thought those words when my eyebrows sequenced together with my right one cocking up a little to give the impression that a bright idea had just been comprehended.

After acknowledging the bright idea with a theatrical display of my talented eyebrows, I then took a sip of my coffee, swallowing it with a bigger-sounding gulp than I normally would have. Immediately after making the dramatic swallowing noise, I let out a big sigh when I set my cup down, shaking my head at everything thing that just happened. Not even knowing why, I just sighed. I had to laugh at it. Why did I just sigh? Here I am, the one doing the sighing. And I do not know why.

Is it because I am feeling relieved to find out that there is more to this life than what they have been telling us? Or maybe perhaps, it is because now I know that I am not the only crazy person on the planet.

I am finding other people all over social media, on pretty much every platform that I use. Facebook, Threads, TikTok, Instagram, so many people that it reminds me of my Bible, where it references the terminology of a large number of people, being a multitude!

What a relief it is to find out that I am not the only one who's having these strange thoughts and experiences.

I am beginning to see that there are thousands of other people who are experiencing things like I am. I see them in England, Scotland, and France. Here in the United States and Canada, too. Australia, New Zealand, Africa, China, and Japan. Russia, Saudi Arabia, and the list goes on.

Starting today, I can see that the EARTH and all of her inhabitants are AWAKENING!

I have never felt so alive as I do today.

I AM READY TO LIVE MY LIFE IN A NEW WAY ON THE NEW EARTH 🌑

Behind the Pages
A Note from the Author

Here are some fun facts about the writer that might help answer any unasked questions you might have. Starting with the one you're probably asking right now: What am I going to say in this portion of my book? And I hope you are wondering, because in this section, I'm writing a little bit more to you.

This is where I'll describe the living situation I was in when I wrote this book. There are a couple of reasons why I'm telling you more about myself. One of them is because I feel that we've now become somewhat acquainted. And I'd like to think that, with you being a reader of my writing now, a door has been opened through our literary connection, linking the two of us in this unique way.

I also want you to know that I love you. Truly. I love you in a reader-and-writer sort of way, yes, but more importantly, I love you in the Unity of our Creation. ♡ I understand that you and I are both co-creators on this Earth.

I felt this story, and you deserved a little more insight into me for it to achieve its purpose. Especially regarding how it came to be that I wrote this story and what I was going through at the time.

So, I see it only fitting to share some things from behind the scenes.

The story within the story.

My future writings will include many "inner story" moments, as I hope you begin to see here. Much like life, there's more depth to a story than what meets the eye. Or in this case, what's written on the page. Like, for instance, what was the writer, me, of course, going through when I wrote my first book using only my cellphone?

Let me begin by saying, I truly hope you enjoyed reading this story.

And I thank you sincerely for your interest in my writings and in the story behind the man writing them.

I'm also very grateful to you for purchasing my book. Your financial support has truly been a blessing.

So, thank you.

I've prayed over my readers, yes, asking that you receive blessings in return for your kind hearts. I've prayed that all who read my writings be blessed with truth, love, and peace that leads to prosperity. I've asked God to keep His watchful eyes on you. That you are kept safe. That you are blessed with the knowing. That you will have everything you need on your journey to healing.

I've also prayed that we can become a family. A literary family. A soul tribe, maybe. A spiritual family.

Soul family, so to speak.

And I hope you've enjoyed this book enough to want to follow my journey and remain interested in my future writings. I invite you to follow me on social media, where we can continue to grow our connection. There, I'll share stories from my past healing experiences along with the new ones I may be having in the present. I believe there is so much to learn by sharing our experiences with one another. That's why I'm sharing mine with you and the world. Sharing healing is therapeutic. A powerful way to release old, heavy energy.

It's been a pleasure getting to know you in this way. I want you to know that everything I've shared is in the hope that you will benefit in some way. Maybe by hearing about my mistakes, you'll avoid making the same ones. And that, in itself, would be a victory in my book.

I've shared an intimate side of myself—one that even people in my life haven't taken the time to discover. That's another reason I wrote this book, so they too can get to know the real me. The new me.

All my writings have a purpose woven into them. I'm trying to reach you on a deeper level, beyond the obvious. And that's partly why I'm sharing my experiences. With the hope that you'll walk away with a new perspective on some things in your life.

I hope you're empowered to finally do the things you've always wanted to do but haven't yet. Whatever the reason, you can. I hope I can help you discover what's been holding you back from living your dreams.

Did I say that?

Yes, I did!

I want you to dream again.

I want you to believe in yourself in a new way.

I want you to know that you are enough and more than capable of fulfilling your dreams.

You are worthy of blessings.

You deserve joy.

And yes, I want a lot for you.

I want you to want for yourself. Want healing. Want change. Want love.

That's one of the key points I'm trying to make here.

I hope you begin asking yourself again: What do I want out of life?

In my story, I've shown you it's absolutely possible for an ordinary person, facing extraordinary hardship, to change their reality and bring their dreams to life.

I've written this story so that maybe, just maybe, you can get a glimpse of what a spiritual encounter might look like. It might not happen the same way, but maybe someone you know will experience something similar.

In my story, I think anyone can see how crazy it might seem, especially to someone who hasn't experienced it firsthand.

It's definitely out-of-this-world crazy by most 3D-programmed standards.

And yes, of course, I questioned my sanity after this encounter, and many others down the rabbit hole.

That's part of why I'm telling you about it. I hope that by sharing it, I can lessen the shock if and when something like this happens to you.

(Not to you… But with you.)

Because I never once felt like I was alone. Or that this was happening to me from some separate source of love.

Now that you know where I stand, let me tell you a bit about what I was experiencing while writing this story.

For example, how did an average guy with a basic education, earned while incarcerated in Elkhart County Jail, write a whole book?

Six months off, well, technically 5 months and 3 weeks. The state shorted me on time due to slow paperwork.

Time-cut. Jail-house GED.

So, how did I do it? Using nothing but my Android phone and Google Docs.

This very letter, for instance, is being written on June 25, 2025, on my Cricket phone. I'm sitting in a little room attached to the back of the barn on my property. Just me and my cat, Samson, lying beside me. I don't know where the other cats are; they come and go as they please. They aren't mine. They're my friends. I treat them with love and respect. I don't own them.

The only thing I ask? Please don't kill the songbirds. Actually, that goes for all birds.

Yes, it'll be said that I wrote this book while living in a barn. Writing little by little. Some of these pages were written at the gym on an exercise bike. Or while waiting for a doctor's appointment.

My creative energy is sacred. Sometimes, if I couldn't get the energy right, even five words wouldn't come. I'd try meditating, begging creativity to show up. But often, I had no choice but to wait. So I sought out peace and quiet next to a river, in a park, breathing in fresh air under old trees.

I watched people sometimes. Politely. Just people walking, laughing, living their lives. And I'd think to myself: I want that. I want to be happy.

That very thought came to me one day in Island Park, while I was working on this book.

I hope you're seeing my point: If we set our minds to something within reason, we can achieve it.

Part of my life's purpose is to show you that this is true. I've even told you that I've been blessed to be guided by Spirit. To learn how to recognize and remove the blocks to my growth.

What kinds of things stop you before you even begin?

Ask yourself: Where would I be right now if I had waited for a better place to live?

What if I said I can't write this without a laptop, a laptop I didn't own and didn't know how to use anyway? Or waited for someone to come help me?

Truth is, I waited over two years for someone to save me. Until I realized… no one's coming. And I had the power to help myself all along.

Back to the point, today is April 20, 2025. And I'm adding this just before publishing. That's a big part of the story.

I stopped waiting, and I started. I told myself, "I'm going to learn how to tell my story." And I did right here in this first book of my own creation.

From the November entry until now, I've gone through so much. I even rewrote a lot during the editing phase. Especially after Chapter 10, the whole book transformed. I rewrote, revised, and replaced repetitive sentences with more descriptive ones. My publisher has been patient. And I'm thankful.

And now, I definitely want to write another book just about what it took to create this one.

One of the most important things I want you to understand is this: I had to learn how to identify what was holding me back from my dreams.

I went through a major transformation. I did it during the most chaotic time in my 47 years of life. Suffering from man-made depression that nearly killed me. I lost my parents. My 9-year relationship ended. My children grew distant. My house and animals burned. No insurance. I became homeless. I lived on SSI. Dreading every winter as though it could mean death.

But here I am telling you my story. Sharing how I began to heal. Just like you, I've had to endure. I've been through damage, pain, and programming that almost broke me. But I transmuted it into healing.

If you're reading this, I want you to know:

I believe in you.

It's no coincidence that you're holding this book. If you've started your healing journey, you're going to be just fine. If you haven't yet, then what a blessing it is to have you here. Either way, I pray that something in my story has inspired you. I hope you walk away with a new mindset. A new perspective.

A Yes, I can kind of attitude, because

"I AM" is who you are.

You are a powerful, sovereign being.

You are an I AM

And yes, You Can

So, look at me, and ask yourself: Can I do something like this?

Can I learn to heal while I'm still hurting?

Like Robert, who learned to heal from a lifetime of hell, even while still walking through the fire, because if I can write this book on my phone, while in deep depression, living on a disability check…

Then, my friend, you can too.

Sincerely, with love

Robert Jon Tengelitsch

Robert Tengelitsch

Robert Tengelitsch